SHEA FONTANA   CELIA MOSCOTE
GLORIA MARTINELLI

GETTING DIZZY ™

Published by
BOOM! BOX ™

COLLECTION DESIGNER
MARIE KRUPINA

SERIES DESIGNER
GRACE PARK

ASSISTANT EDITOR
KENZIE RZONCA

EDITOR
SOPHIE PHILIPS-ROBERTS

SENIOR EDITOR
SHANNON WATTERS

GETTING DIZZY, July 2022. Published by BOOM! Box, a division of Boom Entertainment, Inc. Getting Dizzy is ™ & © 2022 Shea Fontana Productions, Inc. Originally published in single magazine form as GETTING DIZZY No. 1-4 ™ & © 2021-2022 Shea Fontana Productions, Inc. All rights reserved. BOOM! Box™ and the BOOM! Box logo are trademarks of Boom Entertainment, Inc., registered in various countries and categories. All characters, events, and institutions depicted herein are fictional. Any similarity between any of the names, characters, persons, events, and/or institutions in this publication to actual names, characters, and persons, whether living or dead, events, and/or institutions is unintended and purely coincidental. BOOM! Studios does not read or accept unsolicited submissions of ideas, stories, or artwork.

BOOM! Studios, 5670 Wilshire Boulevard, Suite 400, Los Angeles, CA, 90036-5679. Printed in China. First Printing.

ISBN: 978-1-68415-838-6, eISBN: 978-1-64668-737-4

GETTING DIZZY

WRITTEN BY
SHEA FONTANA

ILLUSTRATED BY
CELIA MOSCOTE

COLORED BY
NATALIA NESTERENKO (CHAPTER 1)
GLORIA MARTINELLI (CHAPTERS 2-4)

LETTERED BY
JIM CAMPBELL

COVER AND CHAPTER HEADER ART BY
CELIA MOSCOTE
WITH COLORS BY NATALIA NESTERENKO

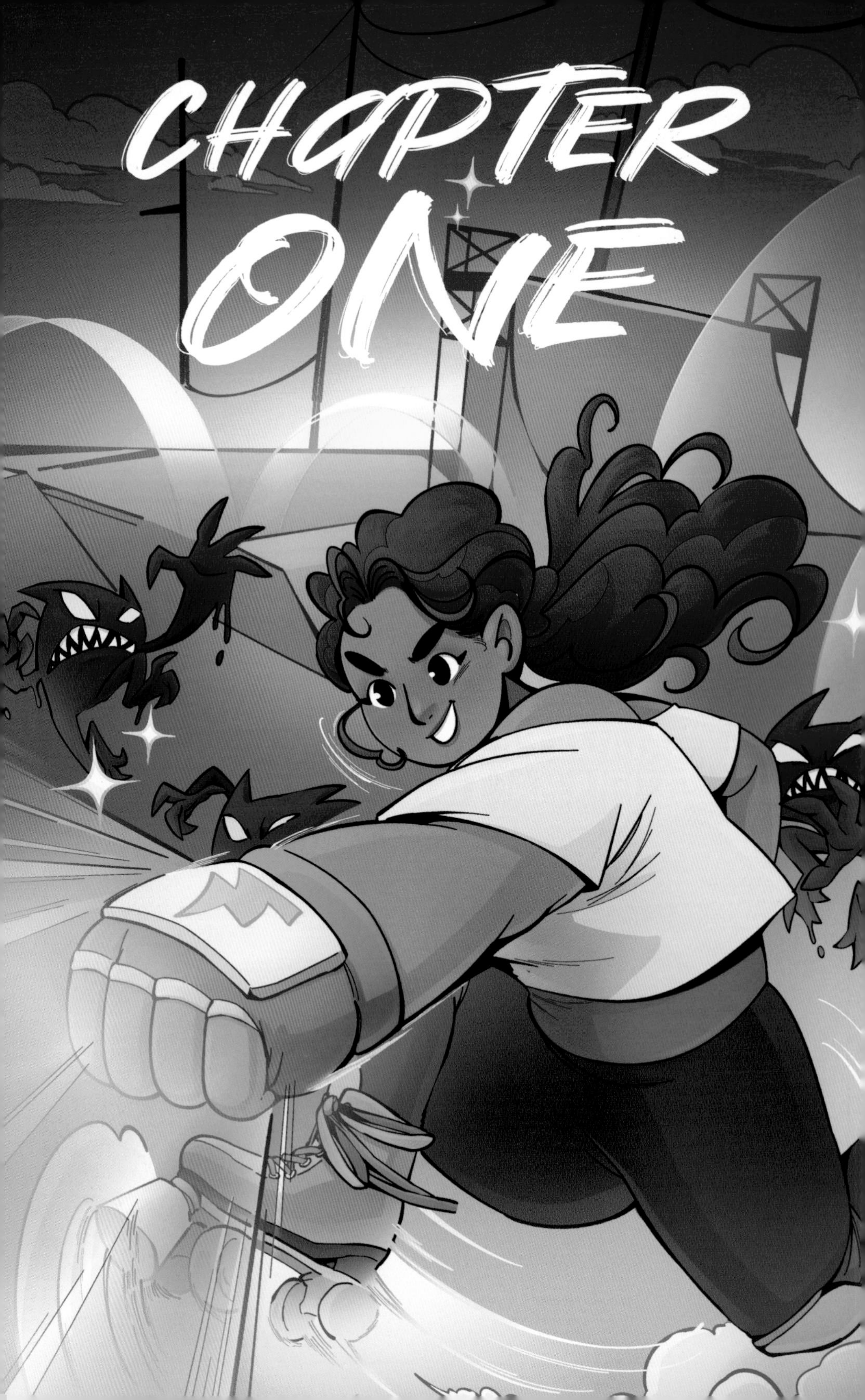
CHAPTER
ONE

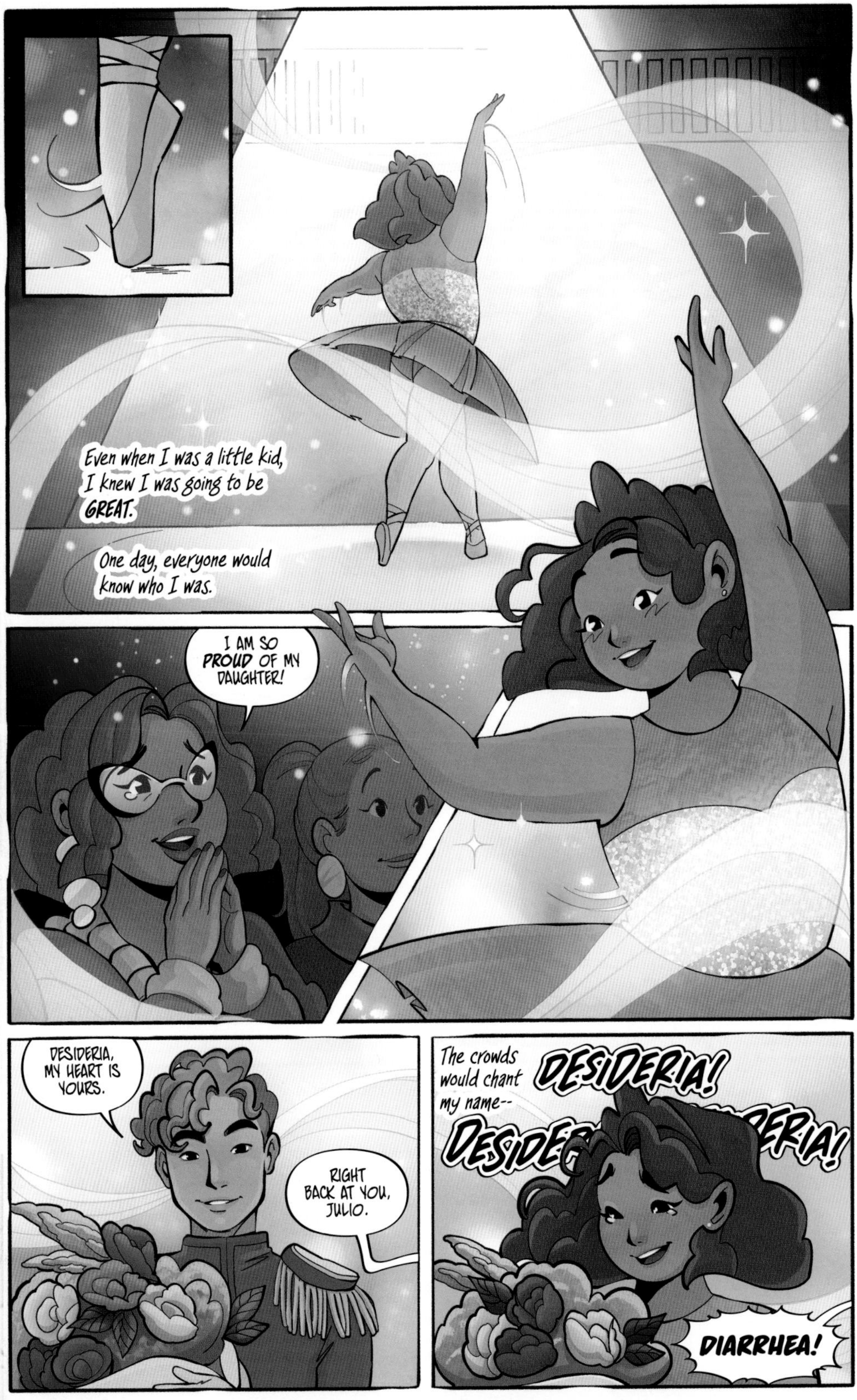

Even when I was a little kid, I knew I was going to be GREAT.
One day, everyone would know who I was.
I AM SO PROUD OF MY DAUGHTER!
DESIDERIA, MY HEART IS YOURS.
RIGHT BACK AT YOU, JULIO.
The crowds would chant my name--
DESIDERIA!
DIARRHEA!

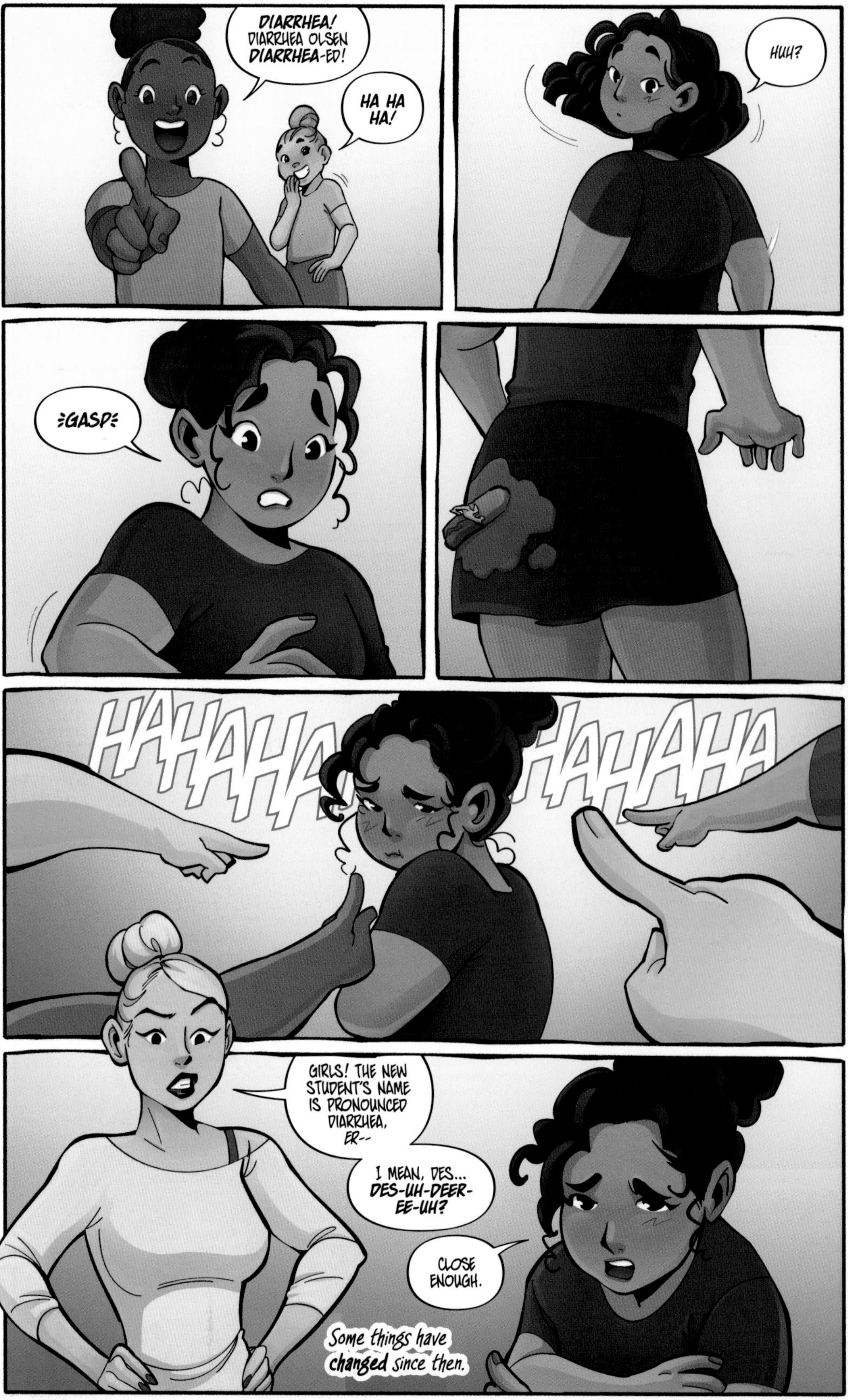
DIARRHEA! DIARRHEA OLSEN DIARRHEA-ED!
HA HA HA!
HUH?
GASP
HAHAHAHAHAHAHA
GIRLS! THE NEW STUDENT'S NAME IS PRONOUNCED DIARRHEA, ER--
I MEAN, DES... DES-UH-DEER-EE-UH?
CLOSE ENOUGH.
Some things have changed since then.

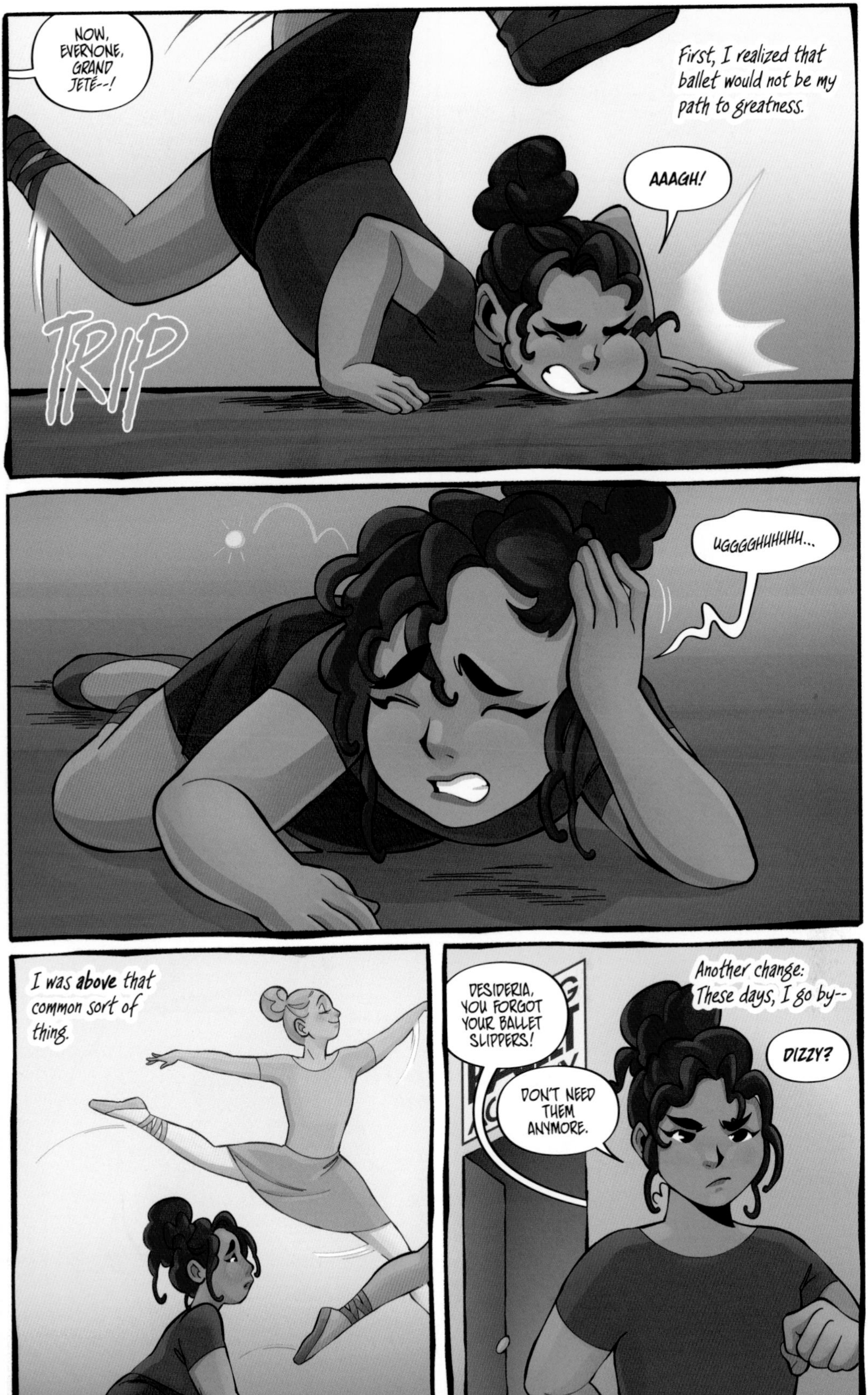

NOW, EVERYONE, GRAND JETÉ--!
First, I realized that ballet would not be my path to greatness.
AAAGH!
TRIP
UGGGGHHHHH...
I was **above** that common sort of thing.
Another change: These days, I go by--
DESIDERIA, YOU FORGOT YOUR BALLET SLIPPERS!
DIZZY?
DON'T NEED THEM ANYMORE.

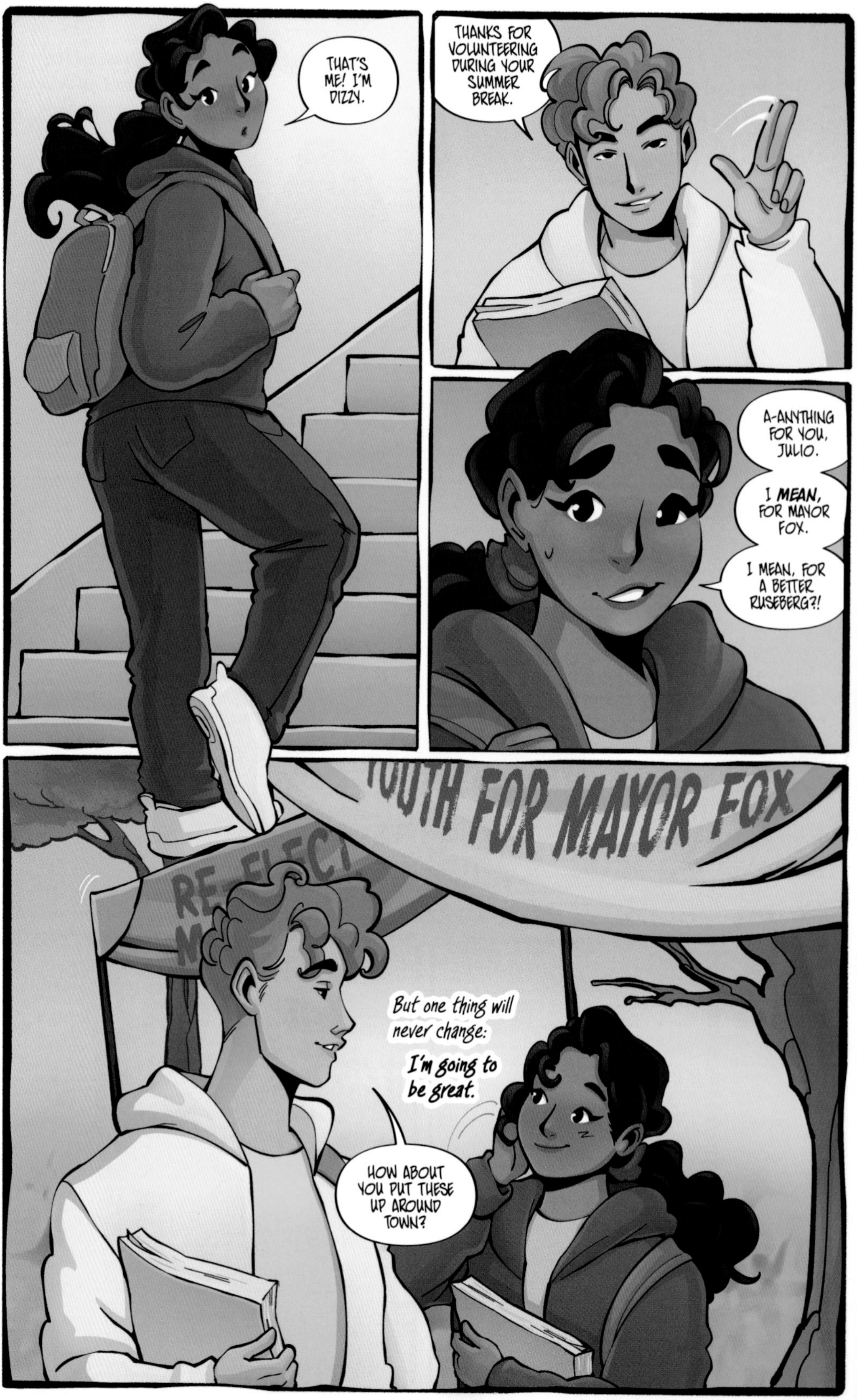

THAT'S ME! I'M DIZZY.
THANKS FOR VOLUNTEERING DURING YOUR SUMMER BREAK.
A-ANYTHING FOR YOU, JULIO.
I **MEAN**, FOR MAYOR FOX.
I MEAN, FOR A BETTER RUSEBERG?!
YOUTH FOR MAYOR FOX
RE-ELECT
But one thing will never change:
I'm going to be great.
HOW ABOUT YOU PUT THESE UP AROUND TOWN?

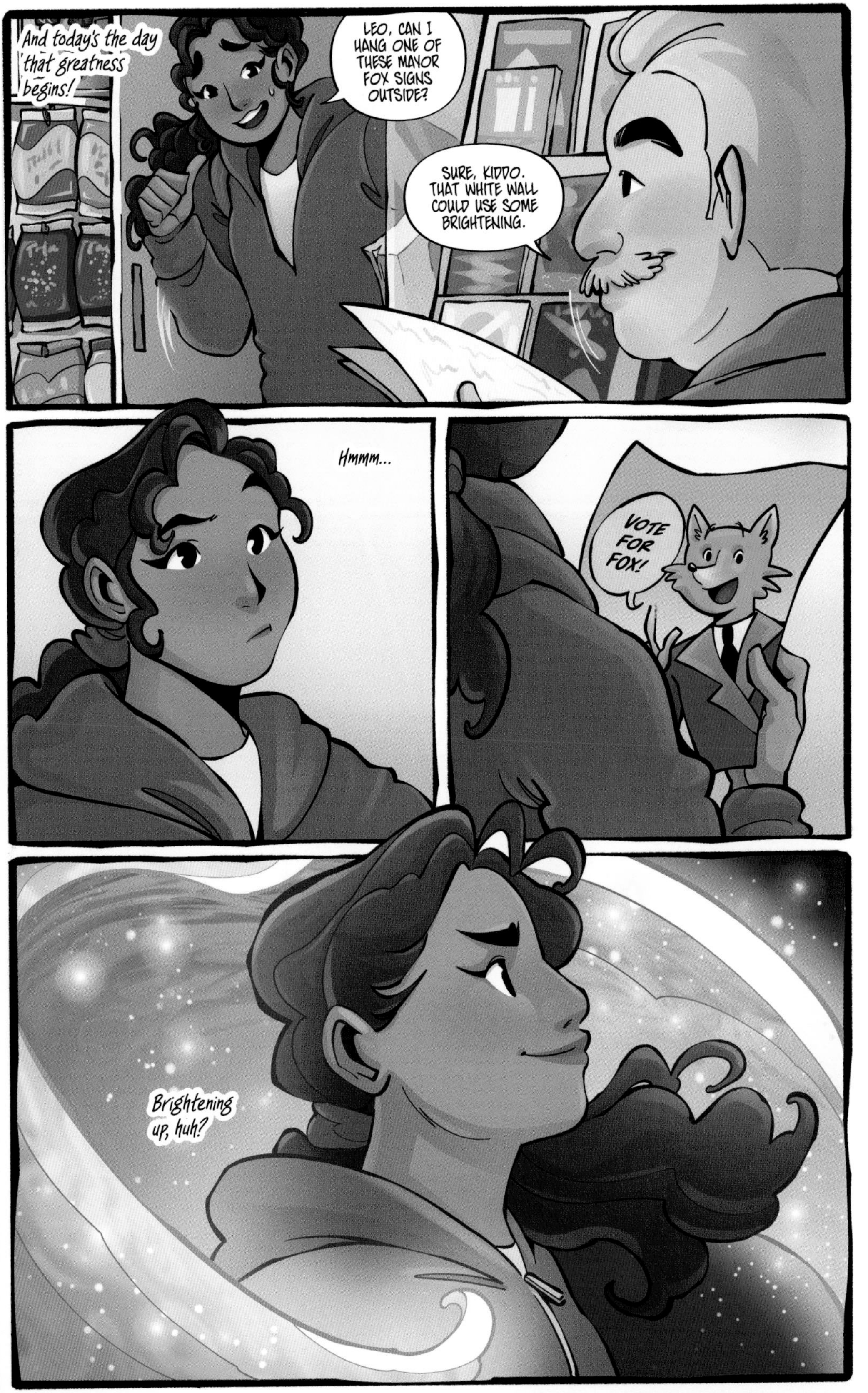
And today's the day that greatness begins!
LEO, CAN I HANG ONE OF THESE MAYOR FOX SIGNS OUTSIDE?
SURE, KIDDO. THAT WHITE WALL COULD USE SOME BRIGHTENING.
Hmmm...
VOTE FOR FOX!
Brightening up, huh?

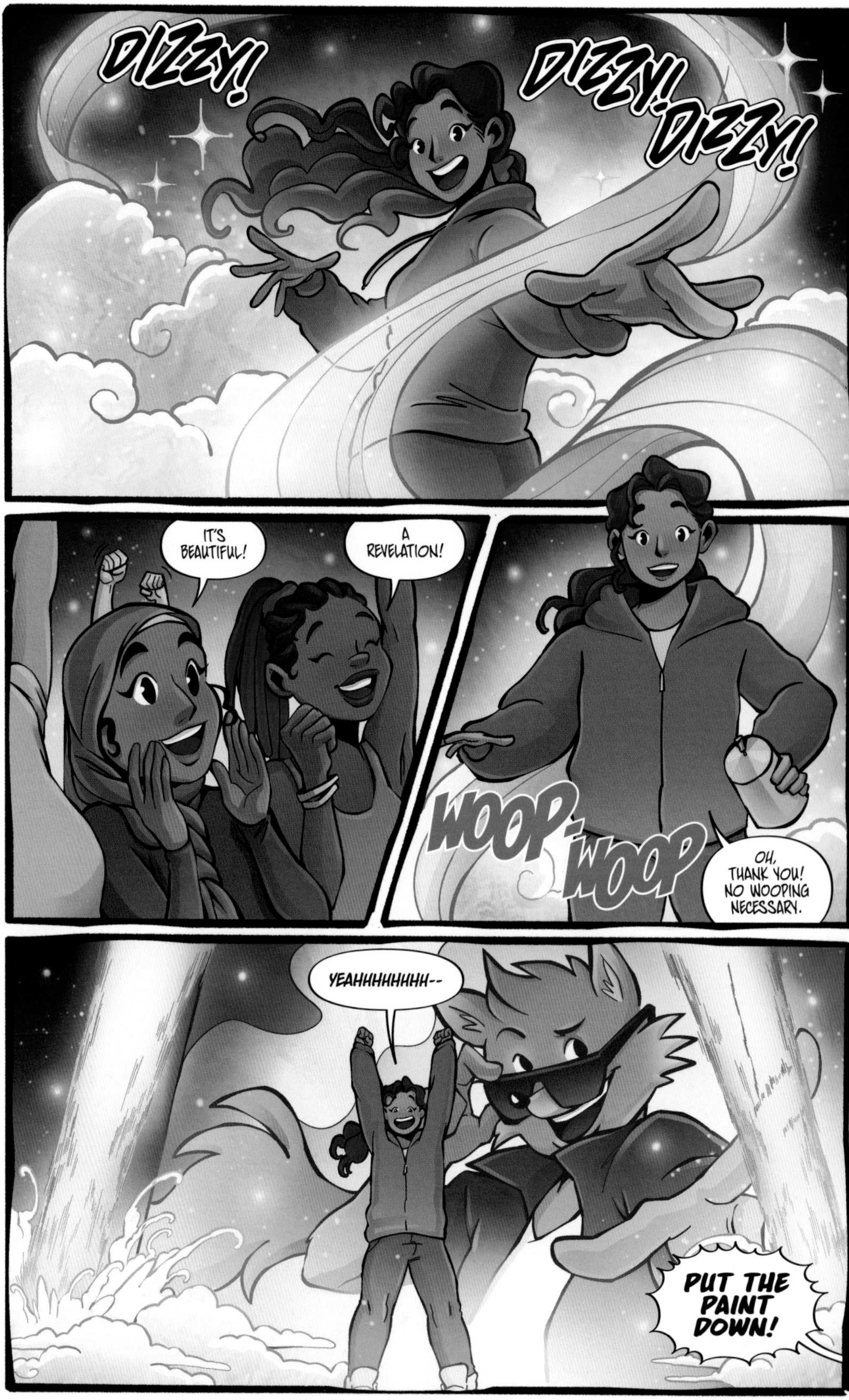
DIZZY!
DIZZY! DIZZY!
IT'S BEAUTIFUL!
A REVELATION!
WOOP-WOOP
OH, THANK YOU! NO WOOPING NECESSARY.
YEAHHHHHHHH--
PUT THE PAINT DOWN!

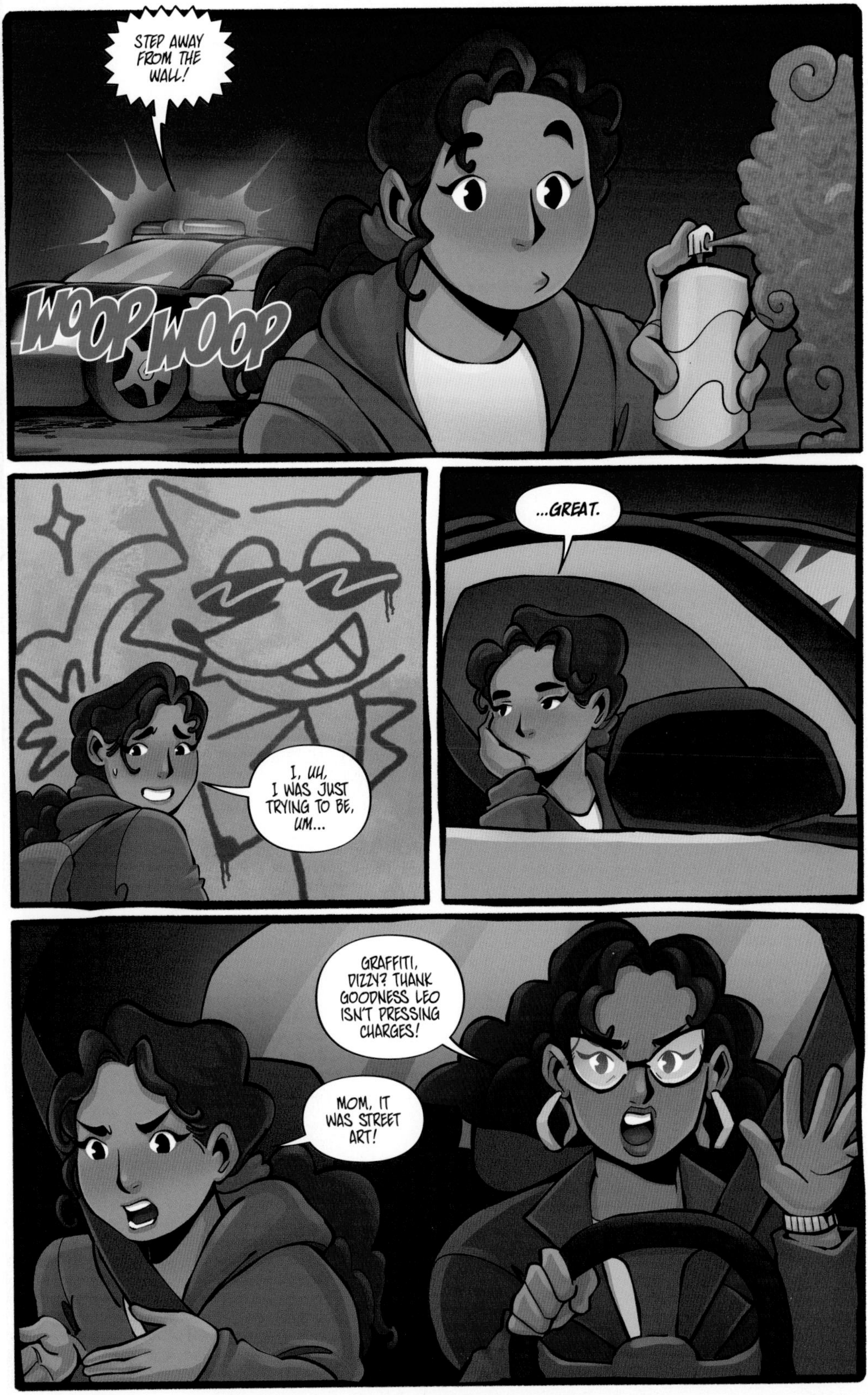
STEP AWAY FROM THE WALL!
WOOP WOOP
I, UH, I WAS JUST TRYING TO BE, UM...
...GREAT.
GRAFFITI, DIZZY? THANK GOODNESS LEO ISN'T PRESSING CHARGES!
MOM, IT WAS STREET ART!

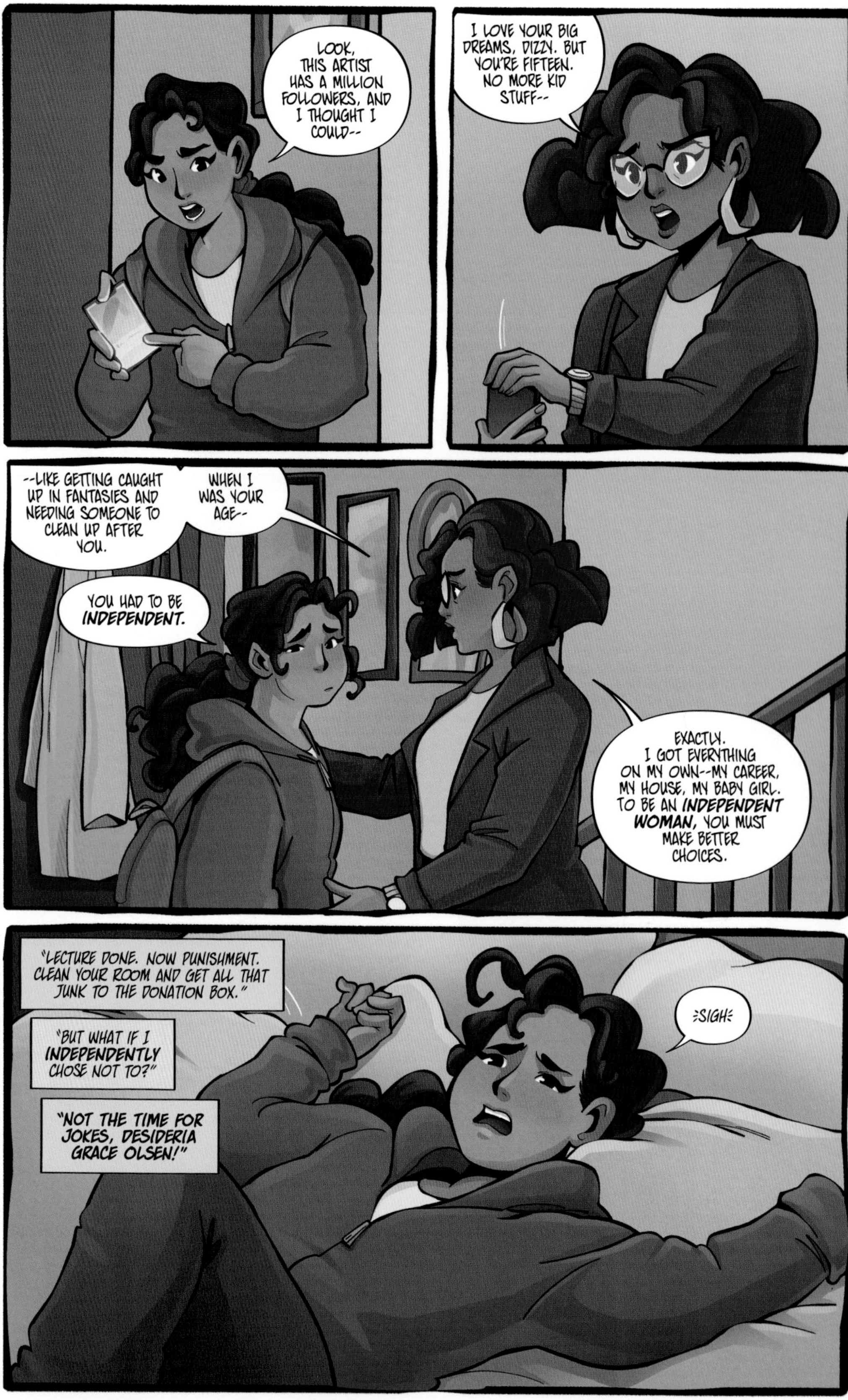
LOOK, THIS ARTIST HAS A MILLION FOLLOWERS, AND I THOUGHT I COULD--
I LOVE YOUR BIG DREAMS, DIZZY. BUT YOU'RE FIFTEEN. NO MORE KID STUFF--
--LIKE GETTING CAUGHT UP IN FANTASIES AND NEEDING SOMEONE TO CLEAN UP AFTER YOU.
WHEN I WAS YOUR AGE--
YOU HAD TO BE **INDEPENDENT.**
EXACTLY. I GOT EVERYTHING ON MY OWN--MY CAREER, MY HOUSE, MY BABY GIRL. TO BE AN ***INDEPENDENT WOMAN,*** YOU MUST MAKE BETTER CHOICES.
"LECTURE DONE. NOW PUNISHMENT. CLEAN YOUR ROOM AND GET ALL THAT JUNK TO THE DONATION BOX."
"BUT WHAT IF I **INDEPENDENTLY** CHOSE NOT TO?"
"NOT THE TIME FOR JOKES, DESIDERIA GRACE OLSEN!"
SIGH

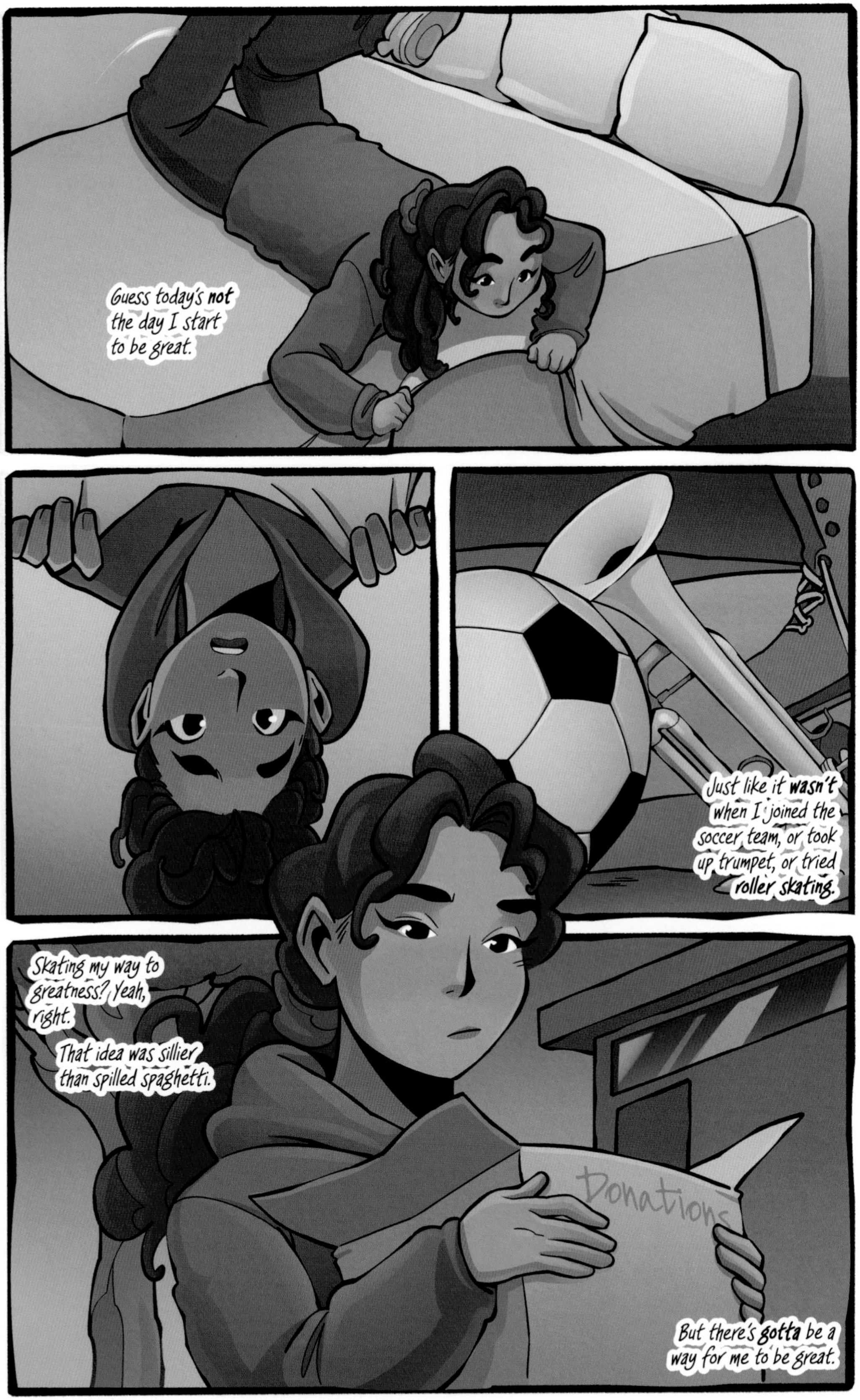
Guess today's **not** the day I start to be great.
Just like it **wasn't** when I joined the soccer team, or took up trumpet, or tried **roller skating.**
Skating my way to greatness? Yeah, right.
That idea was sillier than spilled spaghetti.
Donations
But there's **gotta** be a way for me to be great.

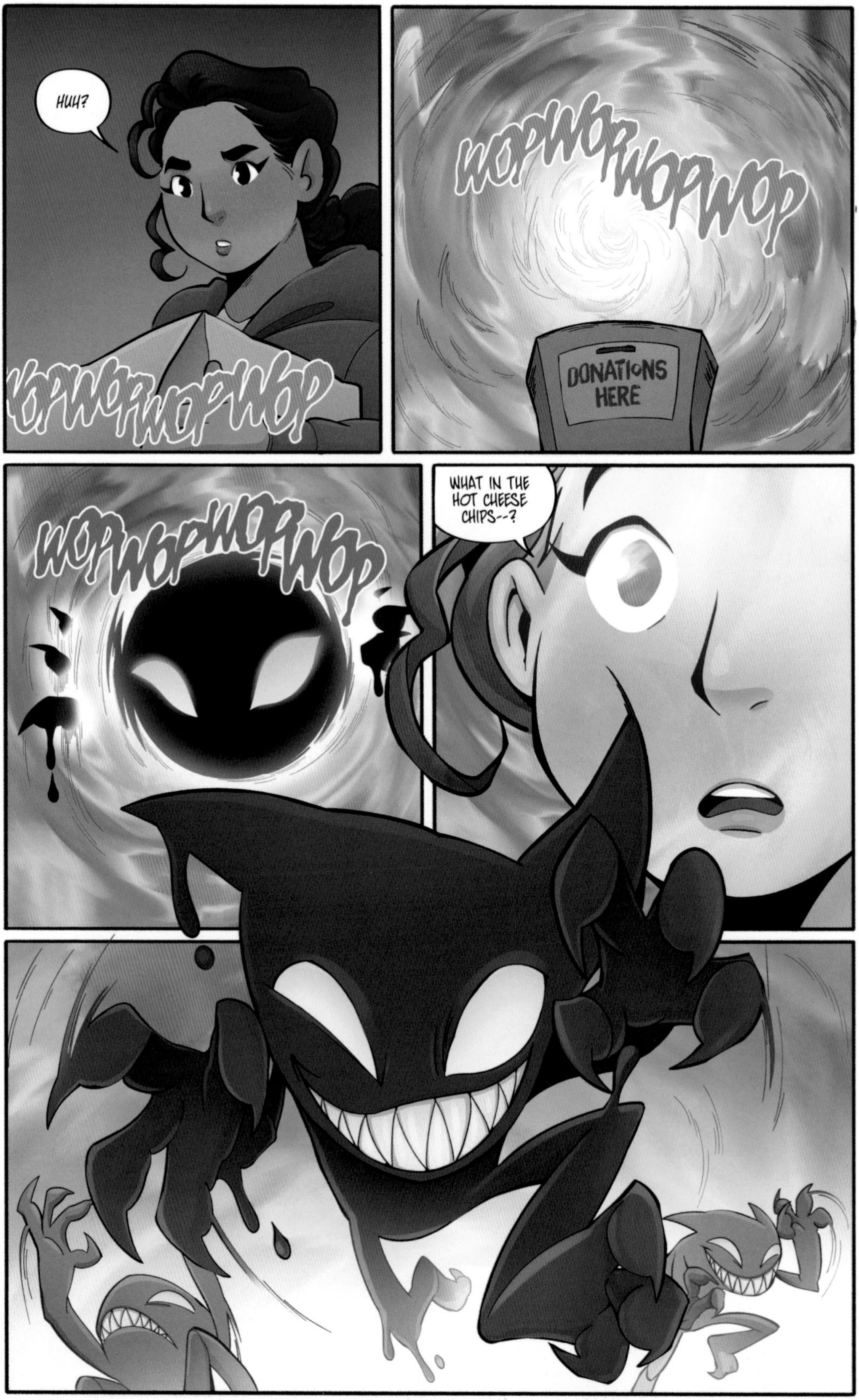
HUH?
WOPWOPWOPWOP
WOPWOPWOPWOP
DONATIONS HERE
WOPWOPWOPWOP
WHAT IN THE HOT CHEESE CHIPS--?

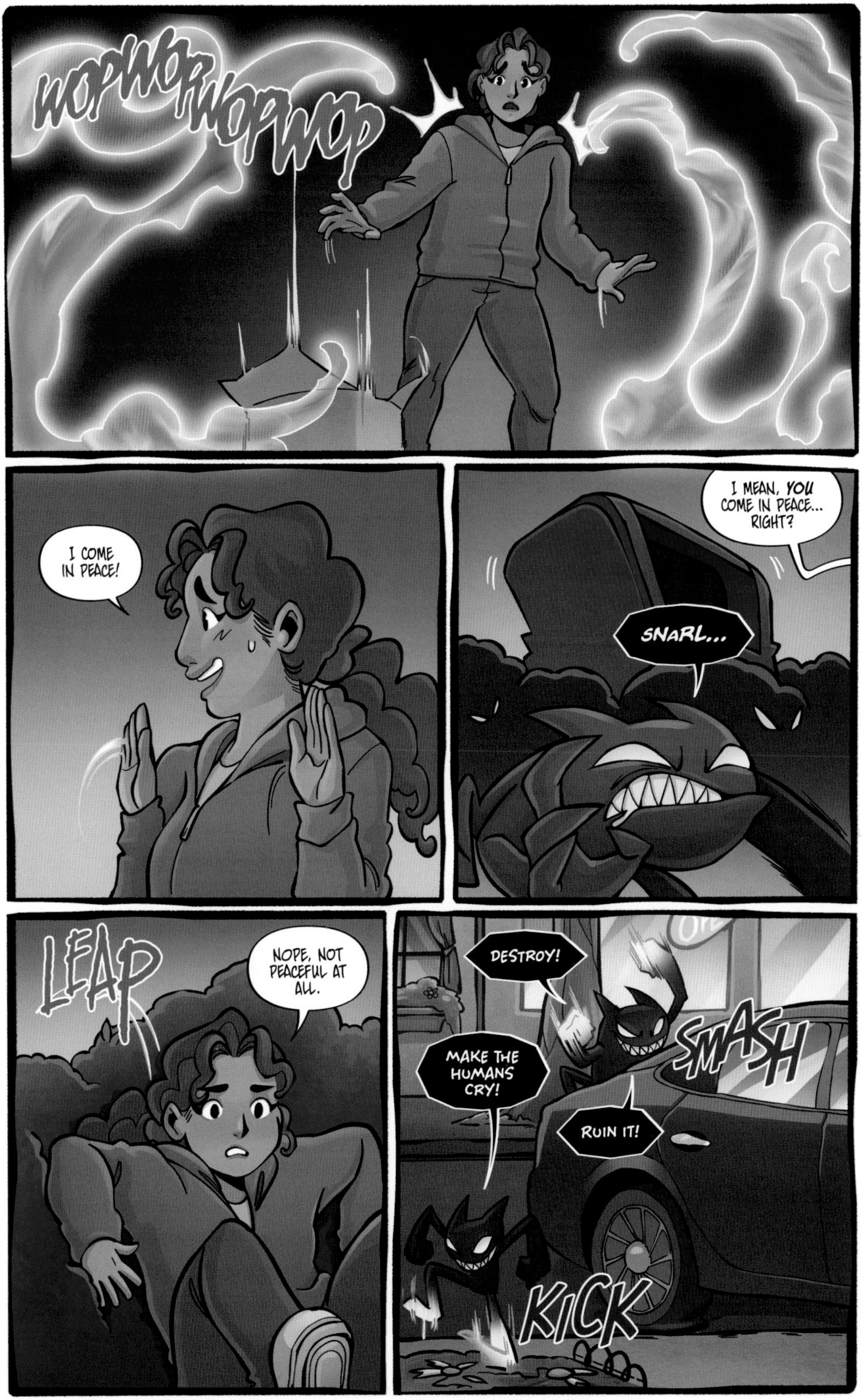
WOPWOPWOPWOP
I COME IN PEACE!
I MEAN, YOU COME IN PEACE... RIGHT?
SNARL...
LEAP
NOPE, NOT PEACEFUL AT ALL.
DESTROY!
SMASH
MAKE THE HUMANS CRY!
RUIN IT!
KICK

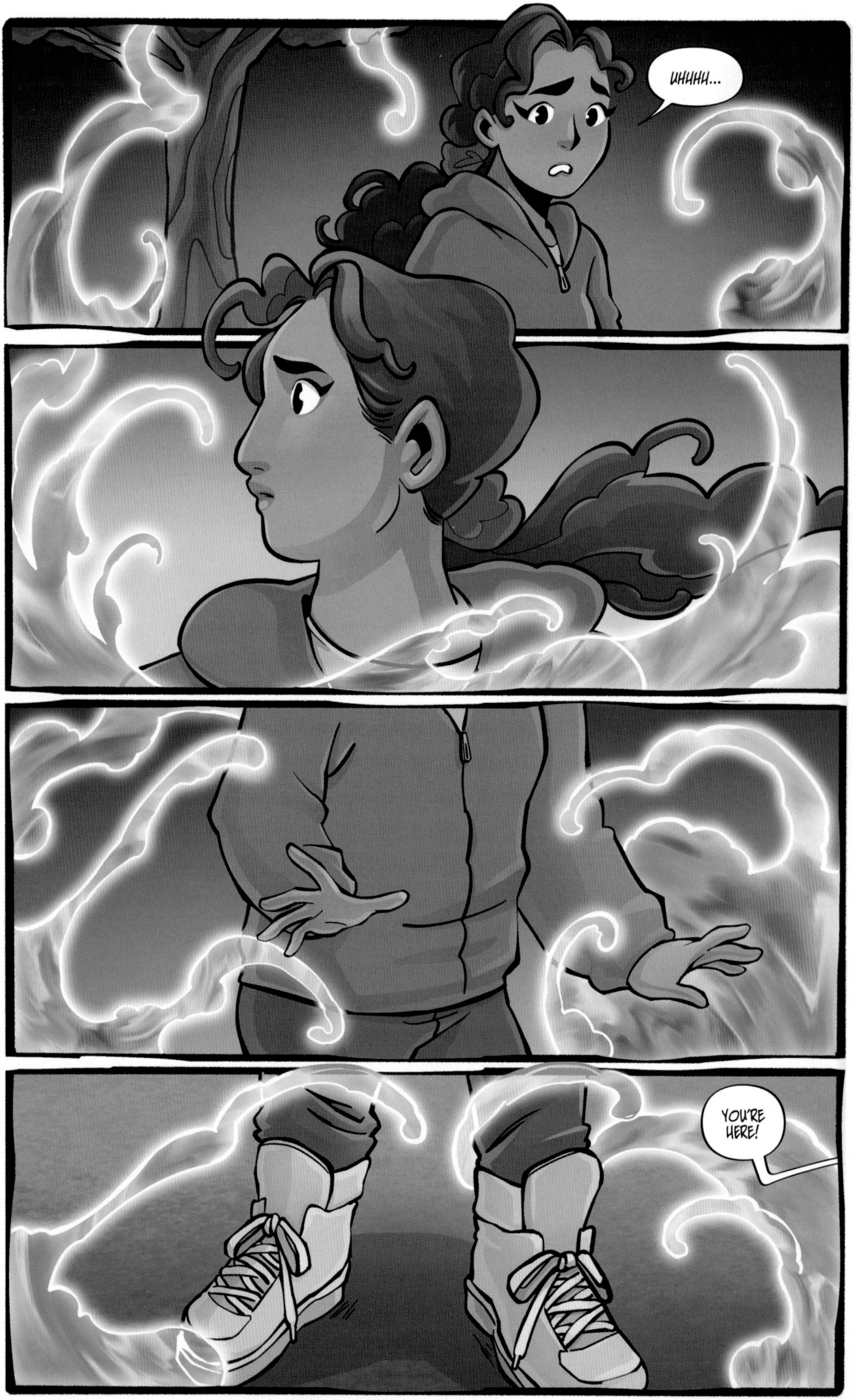
UHHHH...
YOU'RE HERE!

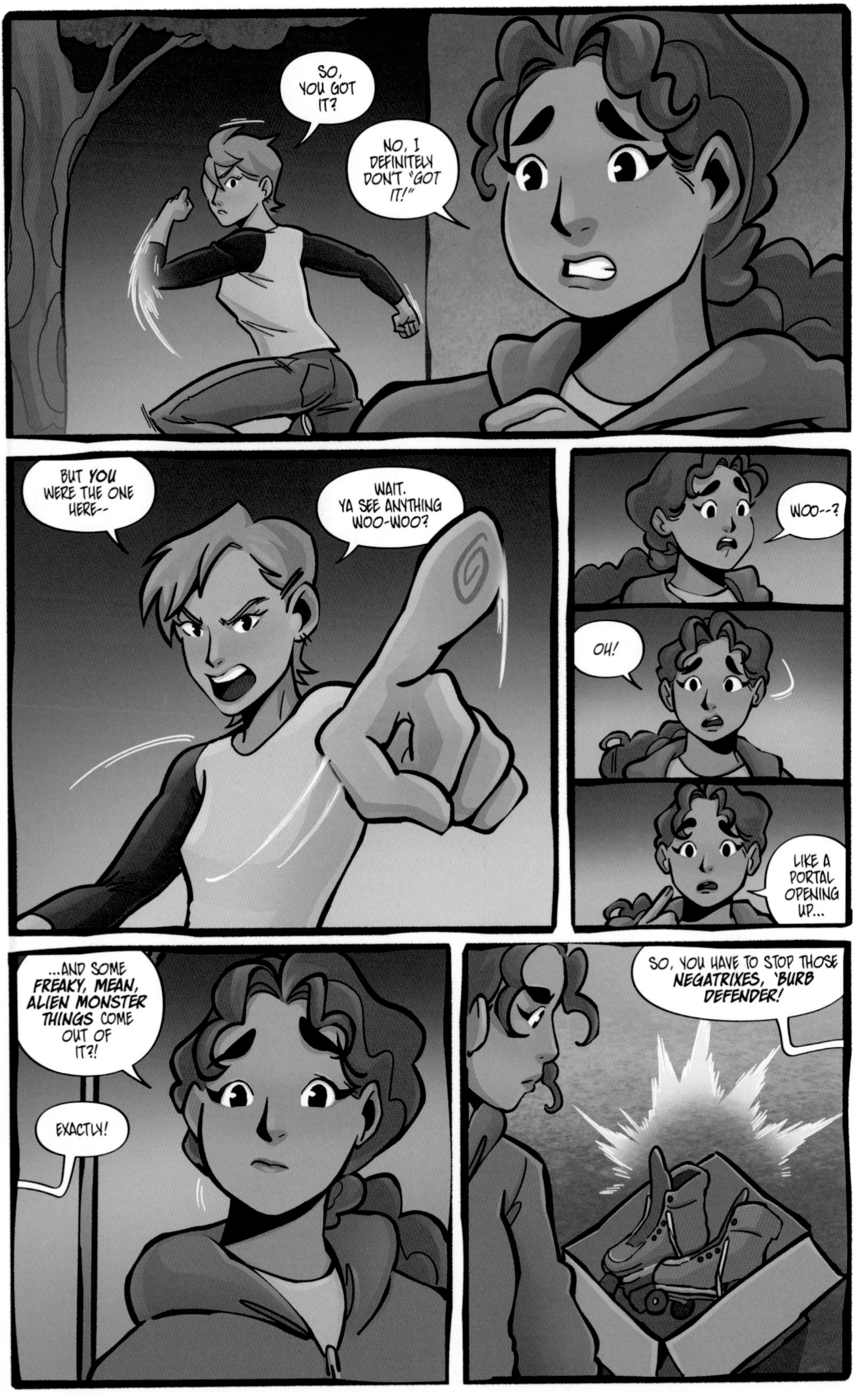
SO, YOU GOT IT?
NO, I DEFINITELY DON'T "GOT IT!"
BUT *YOU* WERE THE ONE HERE--
WAIT. YA SEE ANYTHING WOO-WOO?
WOO--?
OH!
LIKE A PORTAL OPENING UP...
...AND SOME ***FREAKY, MEAN, ALIEN MONSTER THINGS*** COME OUT OF IT?!
EXACTLY!
SO, YOU HAVE TO STOP THOSE **NEGATRIXES, 'BURB DEFENDER!**

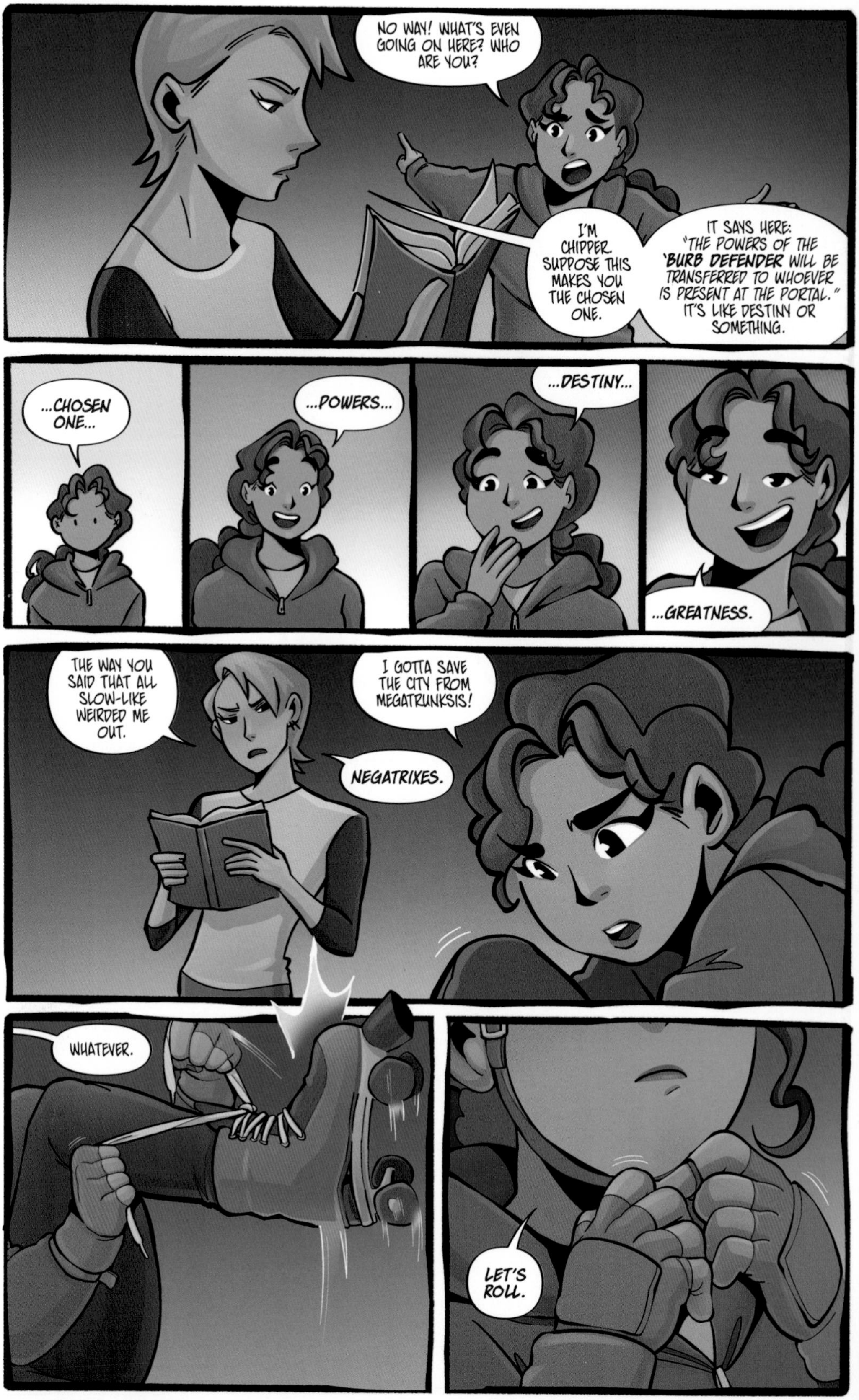
NO WAY! WHAT'S EVEN GOING ON HERE? WHO ARE YOU?
I'M CHIPPER. SUPPOSE THIS MAKES YOU THE CHOSEN ONE.
IT SAYS HERE: "THE POWERS OF THE 'BURB DEFENDER WILL BE TRANSFERRED TO WHOEVER IS PRESENT AT THE PORTAL." IT'S LIKE DESTINY OR SOMETHING.
...CHOSEN ONE...
...POWERS...
...DESTINY...
...GREATNESS.
THE WAY YOU SAID THAT ALL SLOW-LIKE WEIRDED ME OUT.
I GOTTA SAVE THE CITY FROM MEGATRUNKSIS!
NEGATRIXES.
WHATEVER.
LET'S ROLL.

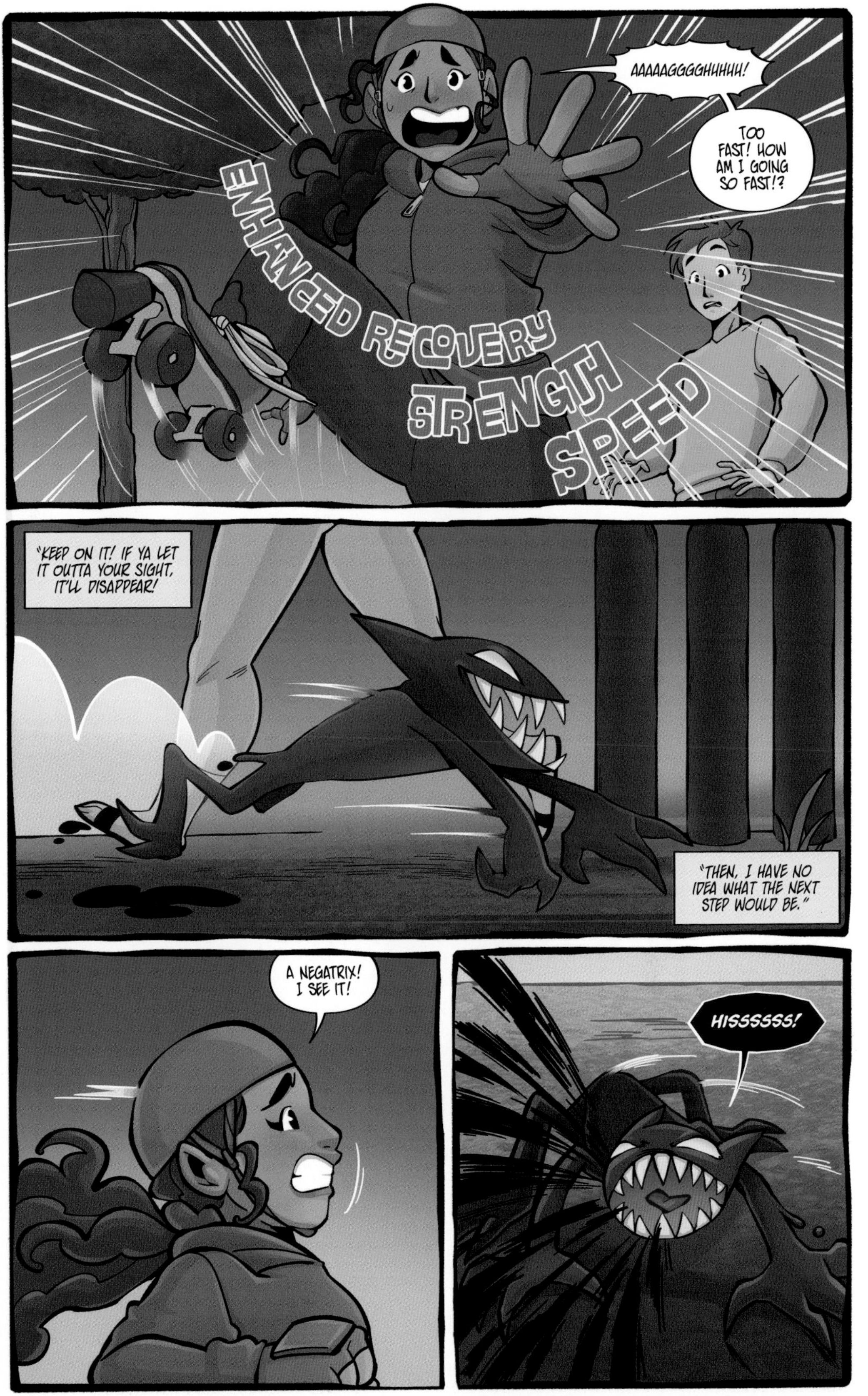
AAAAAGGGGHHHHH!
TOO FAST! HOW AM I GOING SO FAST!?
ENHANCED RECOVERY
STRENGTH
SPEED
"KEEP ON IT! IF YA LET IT OUTTA YOUR SIGHT, IT'LL DISAPPEAR!
"THEN, I HAVE NO IDEA WHAT THE NEXT STEP WOULD BE."
A NEGATRIX! I SEE IT!
HISSSSSS!

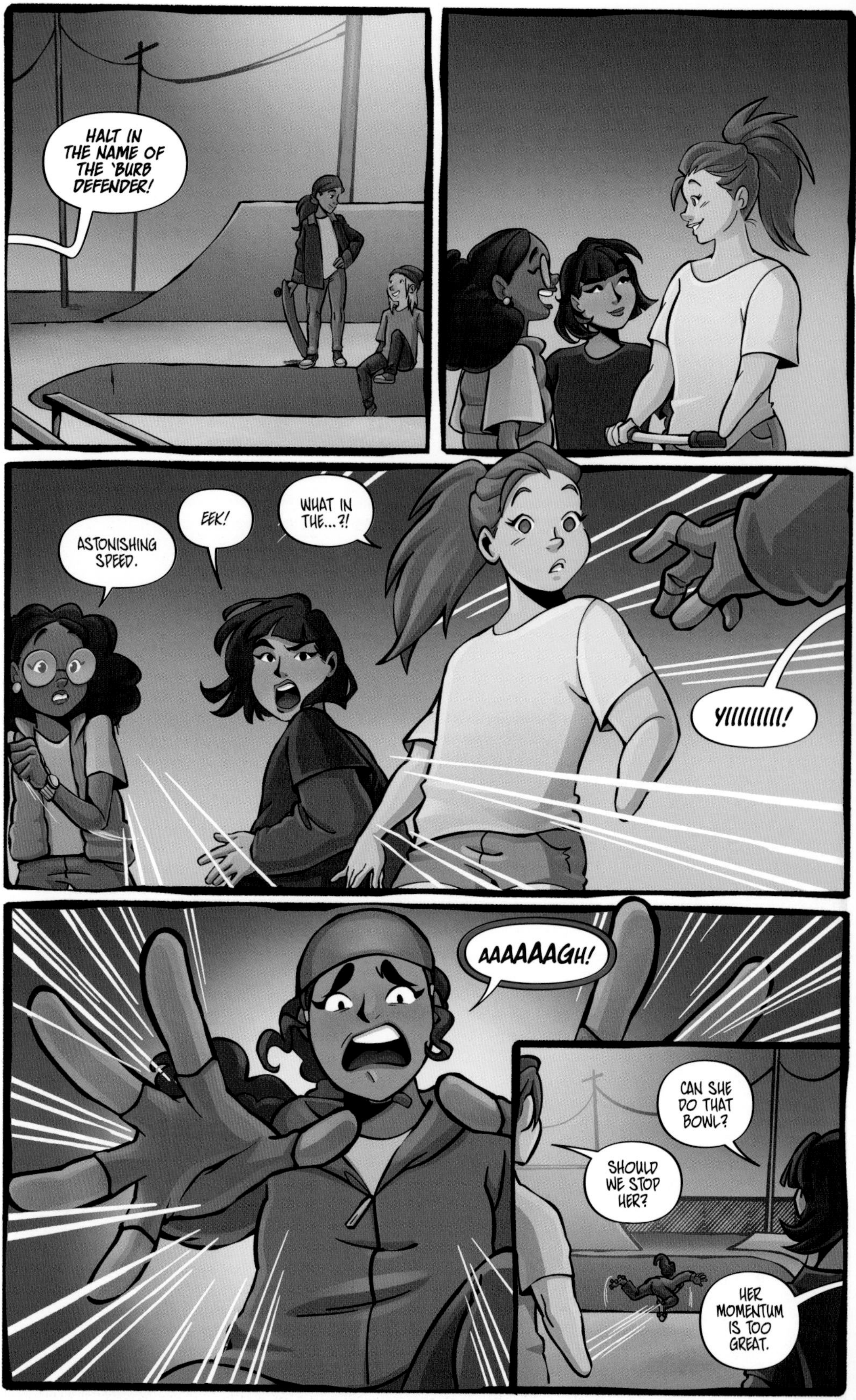
HALT IN THE NAME OF THE 'BURB DEFENDER!
ASTONISHING SPEED.
EEK!
WHAT IN THE...?!
YIIIIIIIII!
AAAAAAGH!
CAN SHE DO THAT BOWL?
SHOULD WE STOP HER?
HER MOMENTUM IS TOO GREAT.

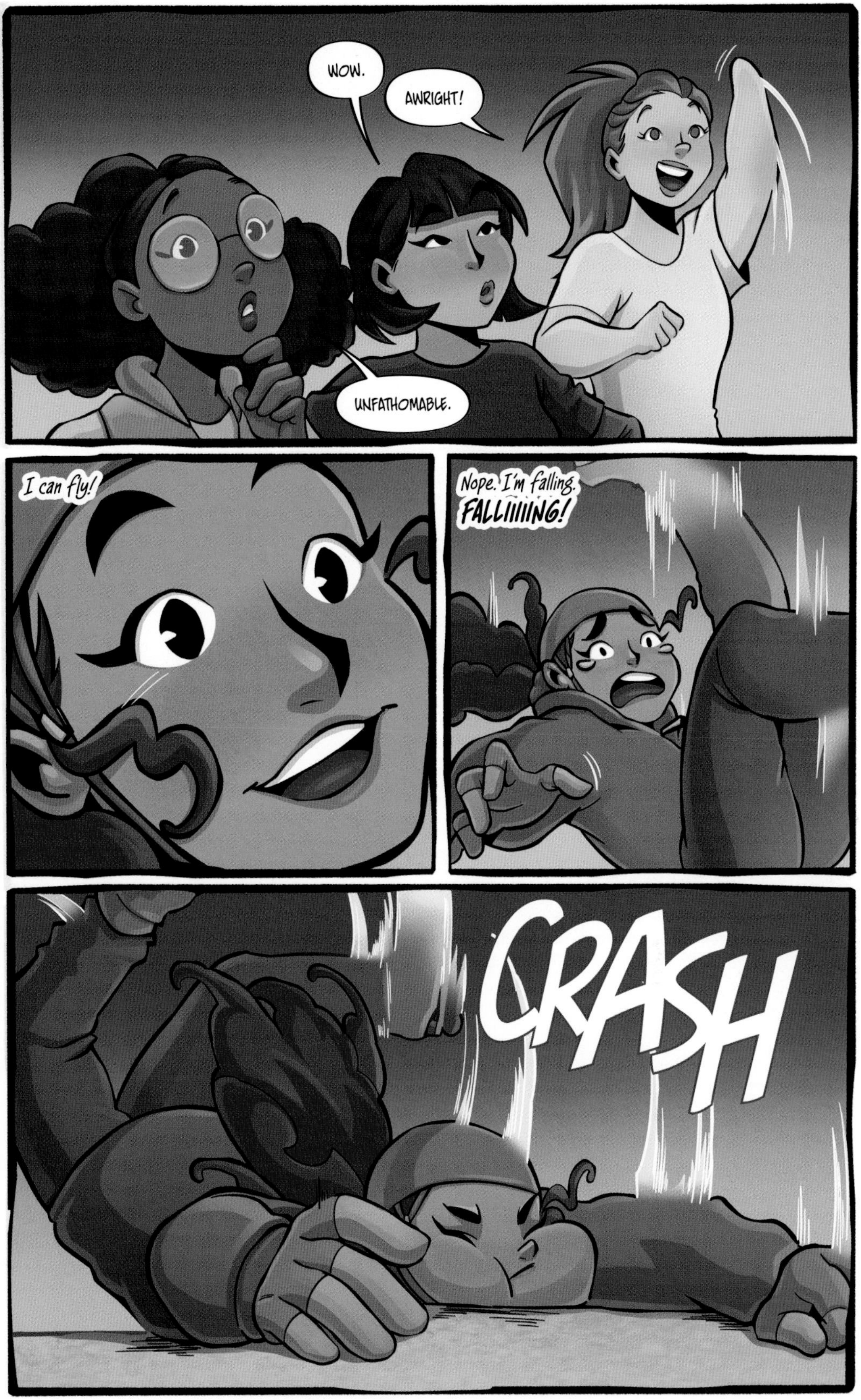
WOW.
AWRIGHT!
UNFATHOMABLE.
I can fly!
Nope. I'm falling.
FALLIIIIING!
CRASH

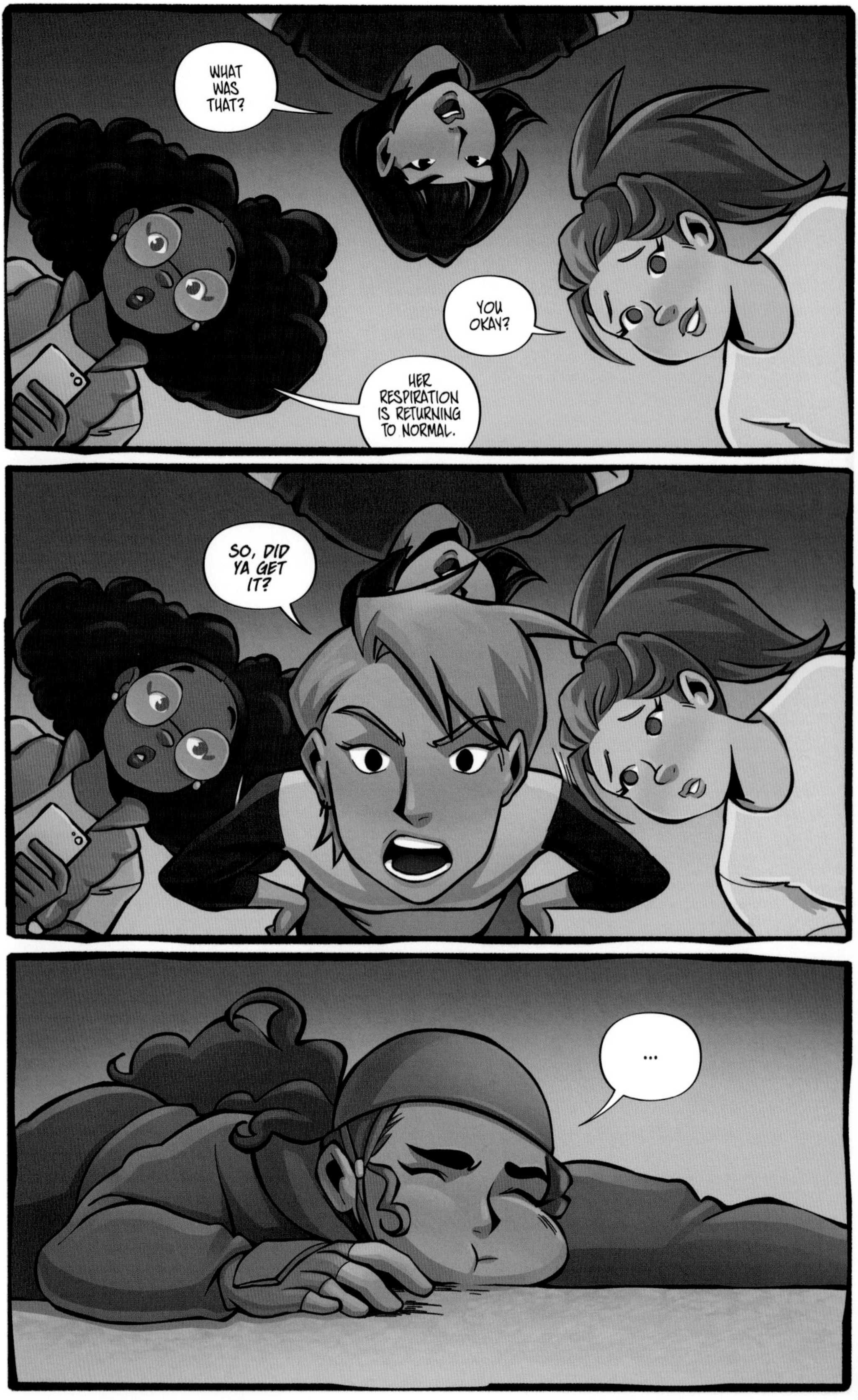
WHAT WAS THAT?
YOU OKAY?
HER RESPIRATION IS RETURNING TO NORMAL.
SO, DID YA GET IT?
...

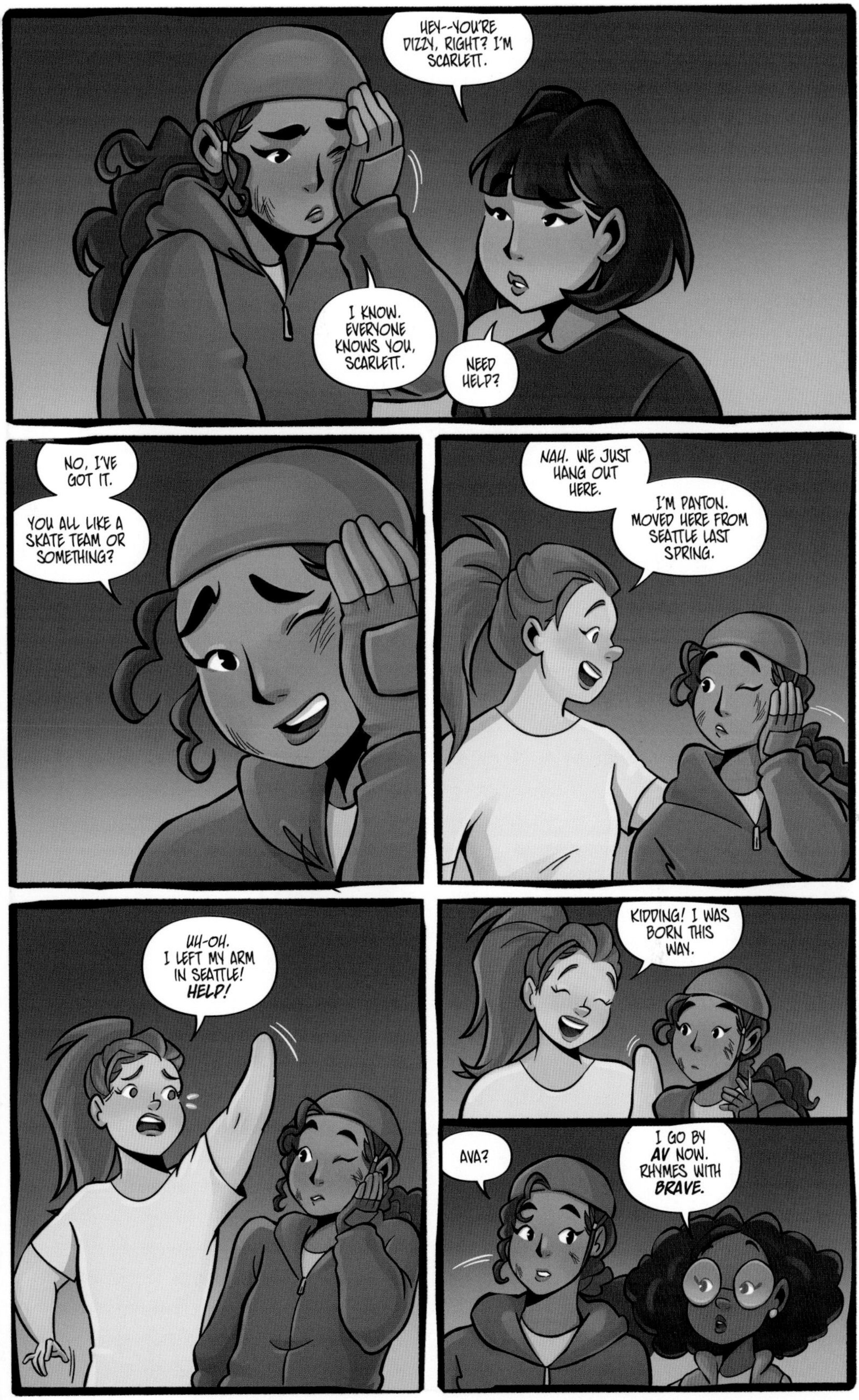
HEY--YOU'RE DIZZY, RIGHT? I'M SCARLETT.
I KNOW. EVERYONE KNOWS YOU, SCARLETT.
NEED HELP?
NO, I'VE GOT IT.
YOU ALL LIKE A SKATE TEAM OR SOMETHING?
NAH. WE JUST HANG OUT HERE.
I'M PAYTON. MOVED HERE FROM SEATTLE LAST SPRING.
UH-OH. I LEFT MY ARM IN SEATTLE! **HELP!**
KIDDING! I WAS BORN THIS WAY.
AVA?
I GO BY **AV** NOW. RHYMES WITH **BRAVE.**

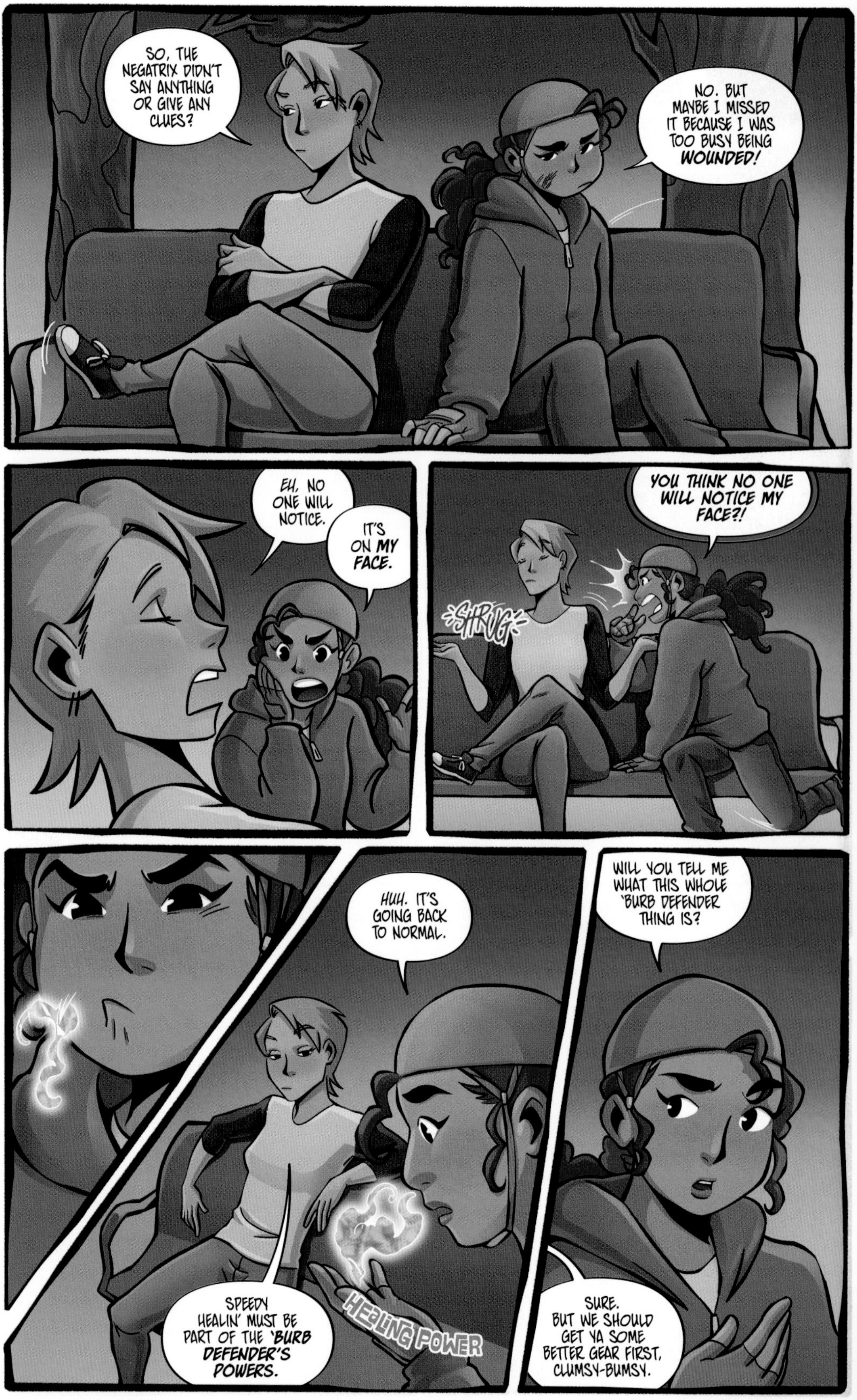
SO, THE NEGATRIX DIDN'T SAY ANYTHING OR GIVE ANY CLUES?
NO. BUT MAYBE I MISSED IT BECAUSE I WAS TOO BUSY BEING WOUNDED!
EH, NO ONE WILL NOTICE.
IT'S ON MY FACE.
YOU THINK NO ONE WILL NOTICE MY FACE?!
SHRUG
HUH. IT'S GOING BACK TO NORMAL.
SPEEDY HEALIN' MUST BE PART OF THE 'BURB DEFENDER'S POWERS.
HEALING POWER
WILL YOU TELL ME WHAT THIS WHOLE 'BURB DEFENDER THING IS?
SURE. BUT WE SHOULD GET YA SOME BETTER GEAR FIRST, CLUMSY-BUMSY.

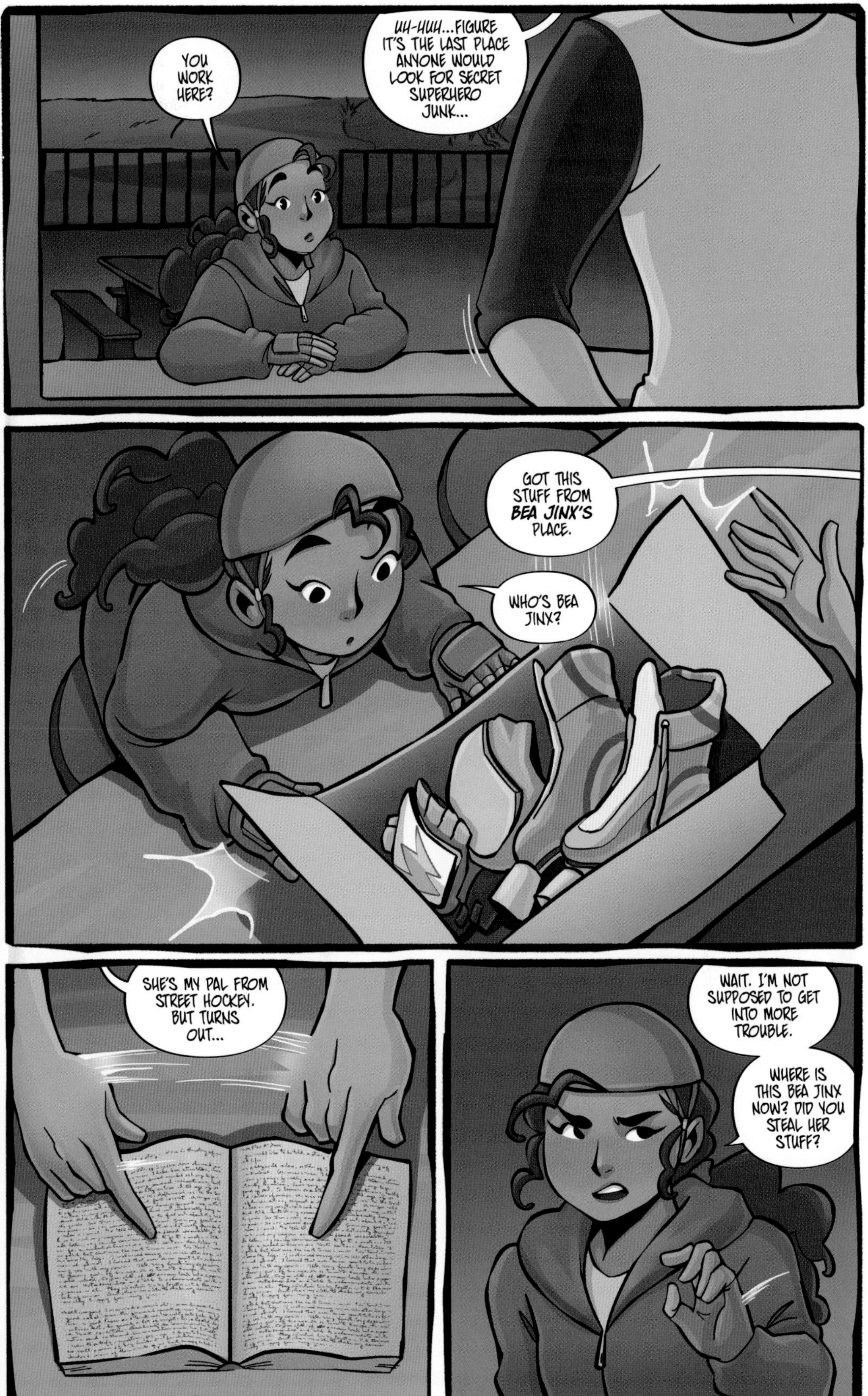
YOU WORK HERE?
UH-HUH...FIGURE IT'S THE LAST PLACE ANYONE WOULD LOOK FOR SECRET SUPERHERO JUNK...
GOT THIS STUFF FROM **BEA JINX'S** PLACE.
WHO'S BEA JINX?
SHE'S MY PAL FROM STREET HOCKEY. BUT TURNS OUT...
WAIT. I'M NOT SUPPOSED TO GET INTO MORE TROUBLE.
WHERE IS THIS BEA JINX NOW? DID YOU STEAL HER STUFF?

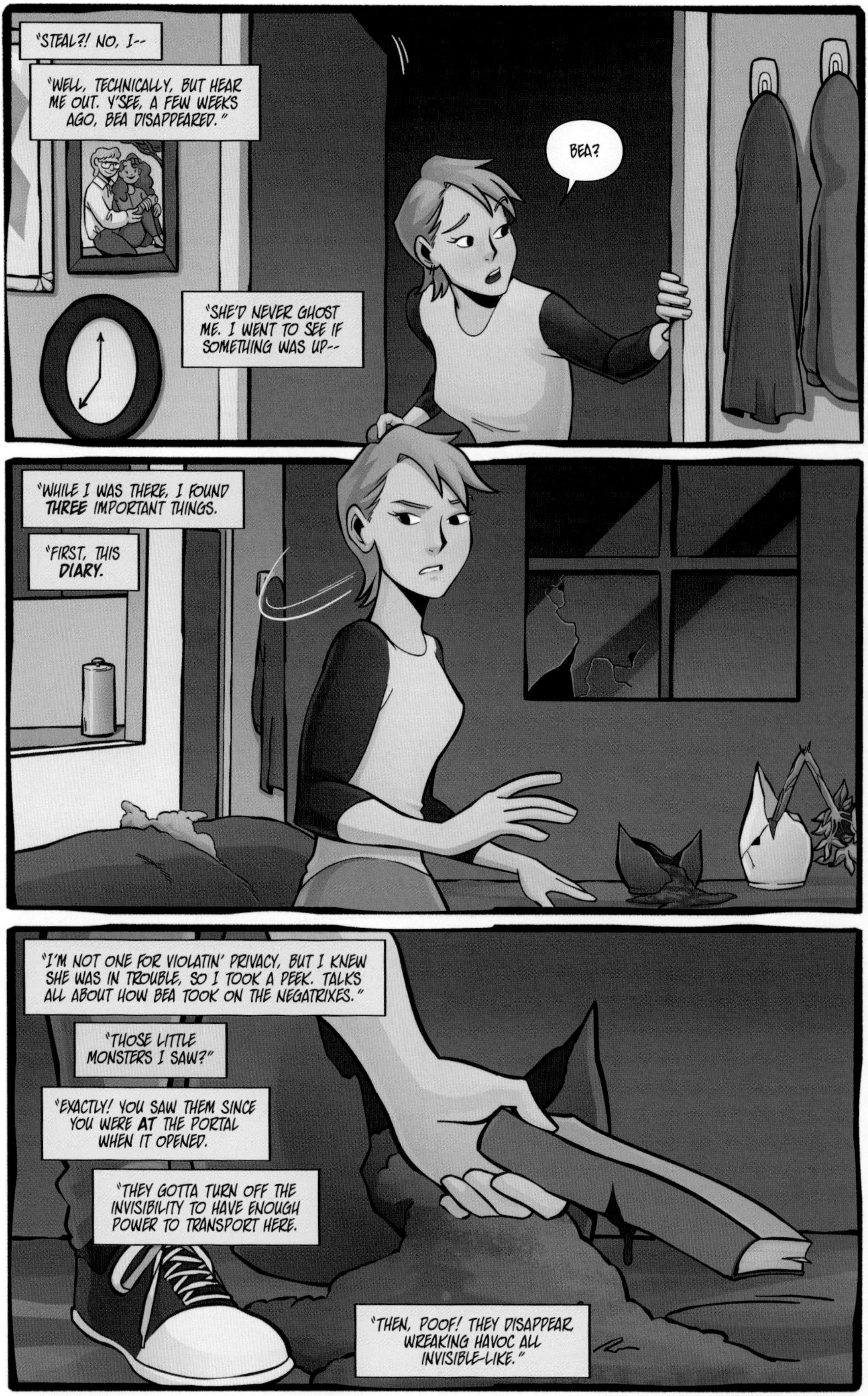
"STEAL?! NO, I--
"WELL, TECHNICALLY, BUT HEAR ME OUT. Y'SEE, A FEW WEEKS AGO, BEA DISAPPEARED."
BEA?
"SHE'D NEVER GHOST ME. I WENT TO SEE IF SOMETHING WAS UP--
"WHILE I WAS THERE, I FOUND THREE IMPORTANT THINGS.
"FIRST, THIS DIARY.
"I'M NOT ONE FOR VIOLATIN' PRIVACY, BUT I KNEW SHE WAS IN TROUBLE, SO I TOOK A PEEK. TALKS ALL ABOUT HOW BEA TOOK ON THE NEGATRIXES."
"THOSE LITTLE MONSTERS I SAW?"
"EXACTLY! YOU SAW THEM SINCE YOU WERE AT THE PORTAL WHEN IT OPENED.
"THEY GOTTA TURN OFF THE INVISIBILITY TO HAVE ENOUGH POWER TO TRANSPORT HERE.
"THEN, POOF! THEY DISAPPEAR, WREAKING HAVOC ALL INVISIBLE-LIKE."

"NEGATRIXES FEED OFF 'NEGATIVE VIBES.'"

"THEY ENCOURAGE PEOPLE TO BE JERKS SO THEY CAN EAT THOSE NEGATIVE VIBES."

WHATEVER HAPPENED, I'M GONNA FIND YOU, BEA.

"THE 'BURB DEFENDER IS THE ONLY ONE WHO CAN STOP THOSE MONSTERS BEFORE THEY INFECT THE WHOLE TOWN."

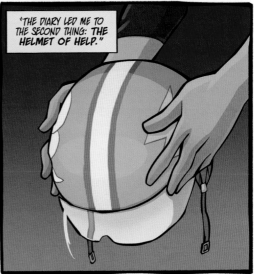

"THE DIARY LED ME TO THE SECOND THING: THE HELMET OF HELP."

HOPPING HAIRY JALAPEÑOS.

EW. WE CAN DISCUSS YOUR OFF-PUTTIN' EXCLAMATIONS LATER.

NOW, WHAT DO YA SEE?

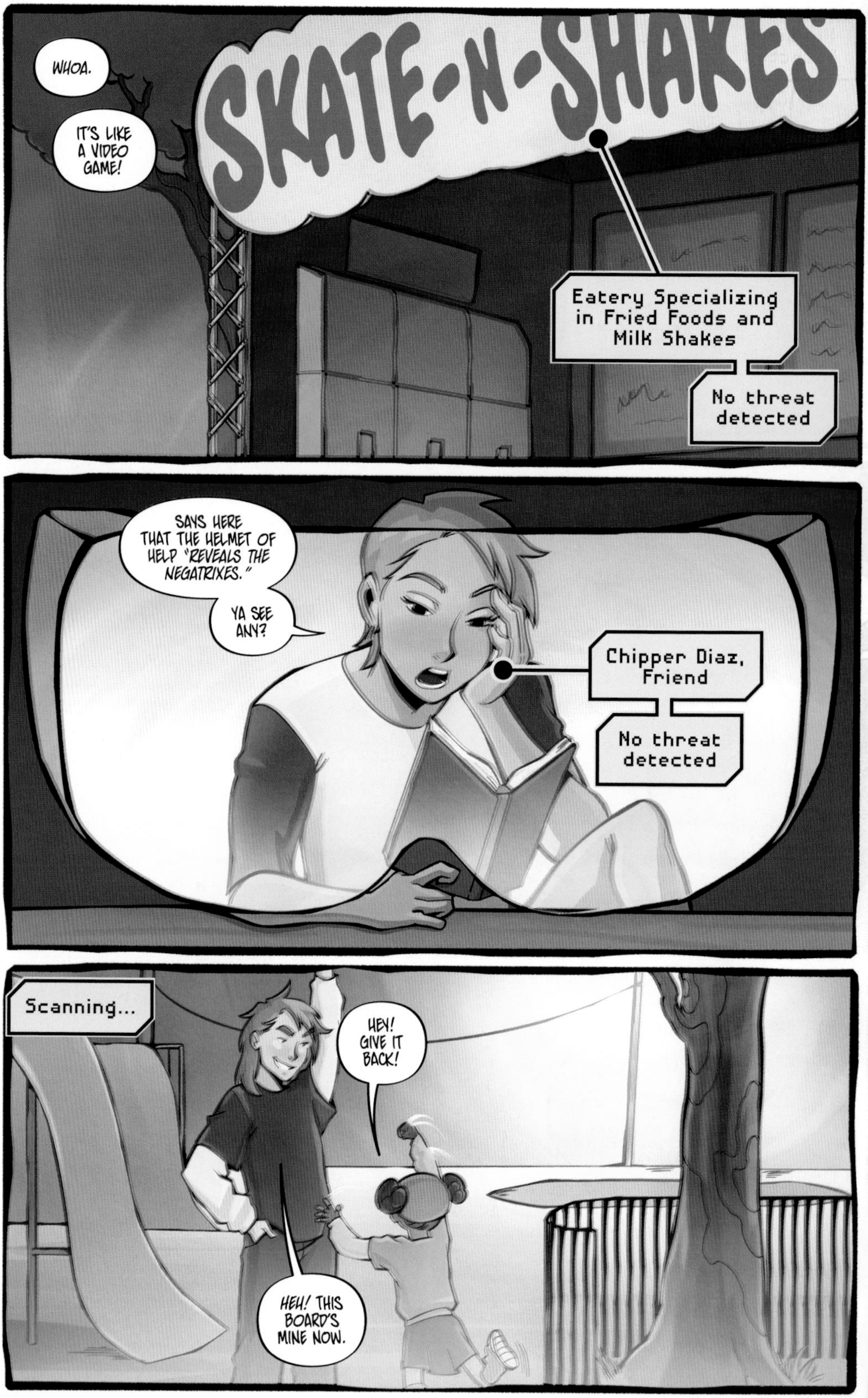

WHOA.
IT'S LIKE A VIDEO GAME!
SKATE-N-SHAKES
Eatery Specializing in Fried Foods and Milk Shakes
No threat detected
SAYS HERE THAT THE HELMET OF HELP "REVEALS THE NEGATRIXES."
YA SEE ANY?
Chipper Diaz, Friend
No threat detected
Scanning...
HEY! GIVE IT BACK!
HEH! THIS BOARD'S MINE NOW.

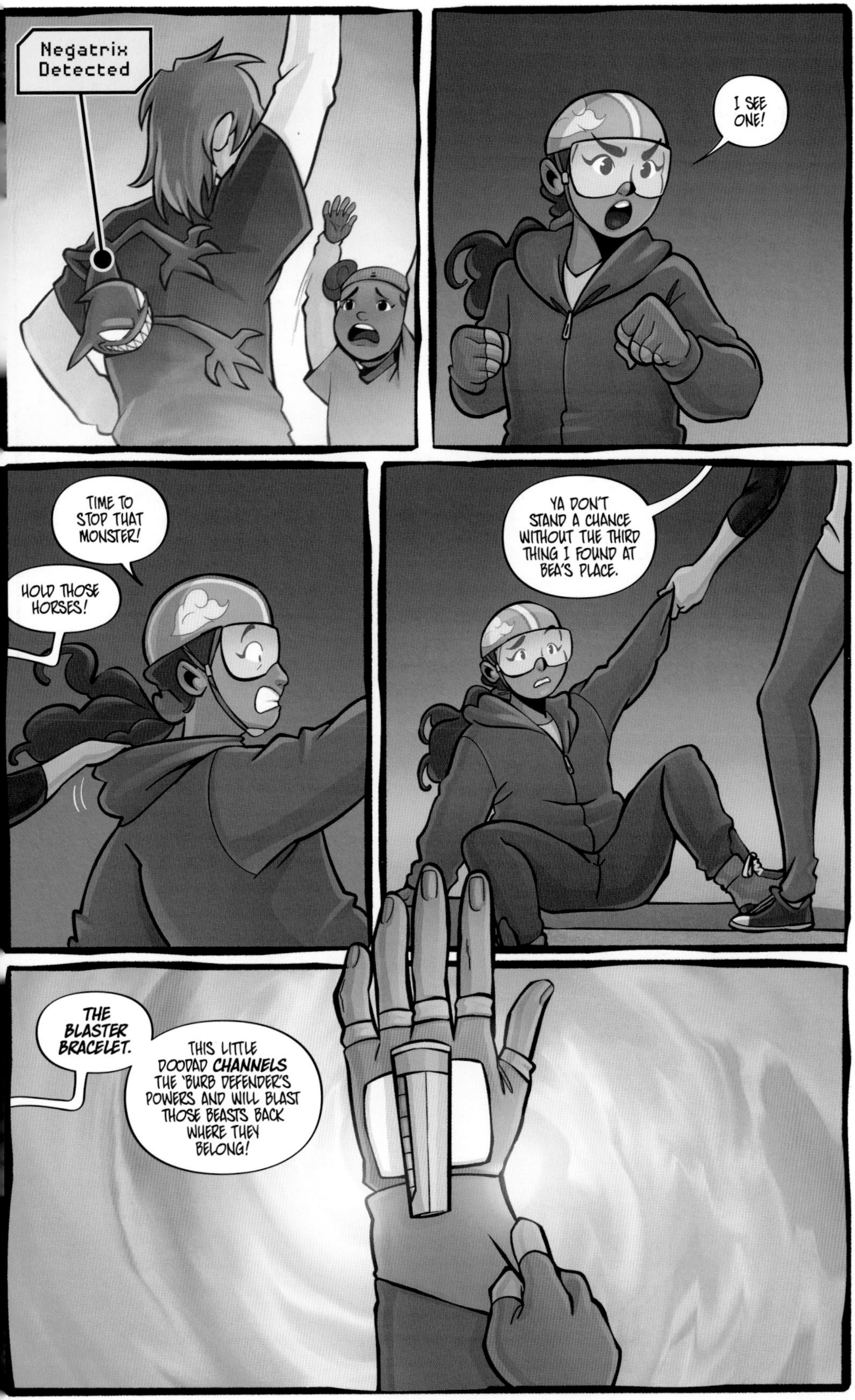
Negatrix Detected
I SEE ONE!
TIME TO STOP THAT MONSTER!
HOLD THOSE HORSES!
YA DON'T STAND A CHANCE WITHOUT THE THIRD THING I FOUND AT BEA'S PLACE.
THE BLASTER BRACELET.
THIS LITTLE DOODAD CHANNELS THE 'BURB DEFENDER'S POWERS AND WILL BLAST THOSE BEASTS BACK WHERE THEY BELONG!

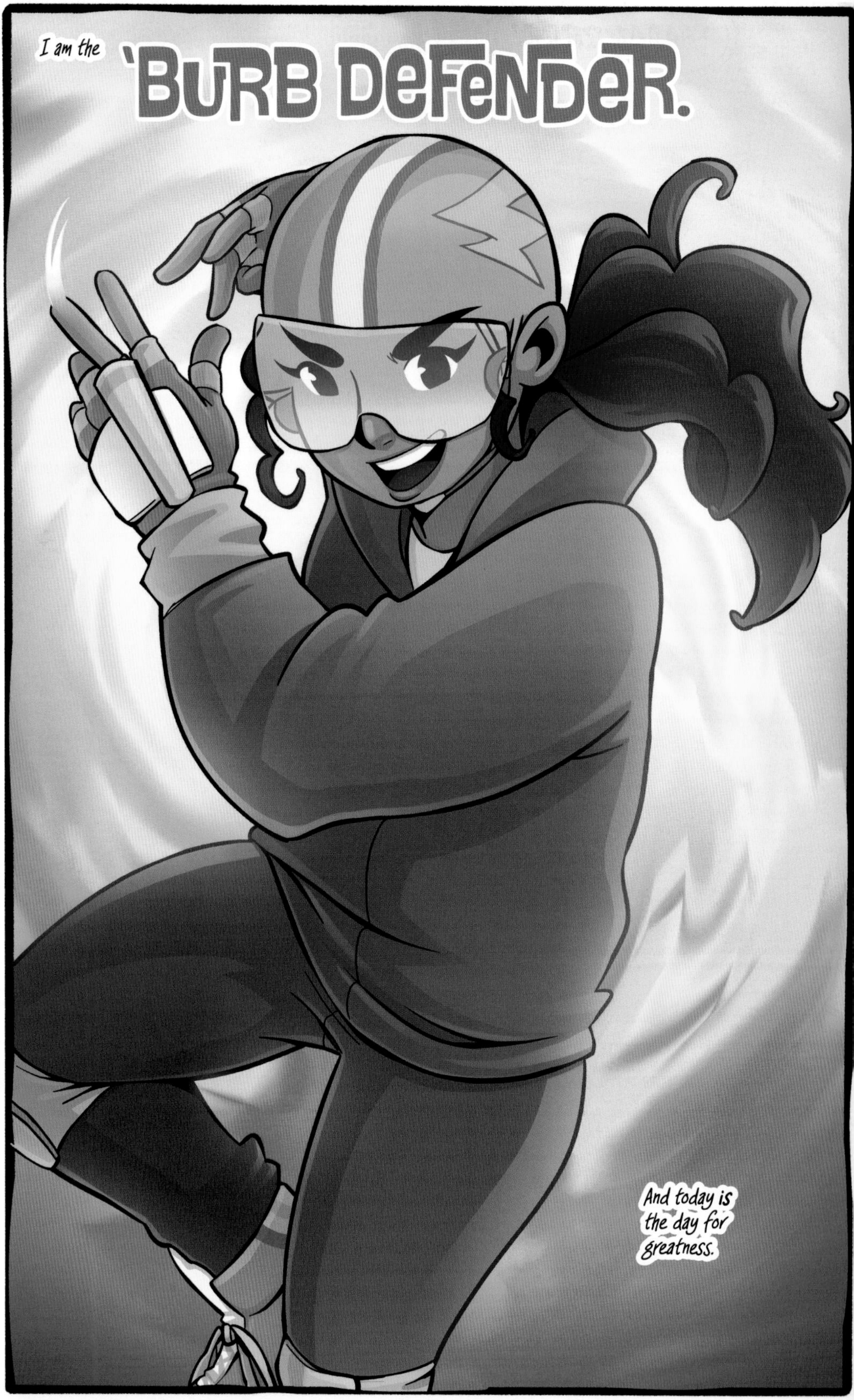
I am the 'BURB DEFENDER.
And today is the day for greatness.

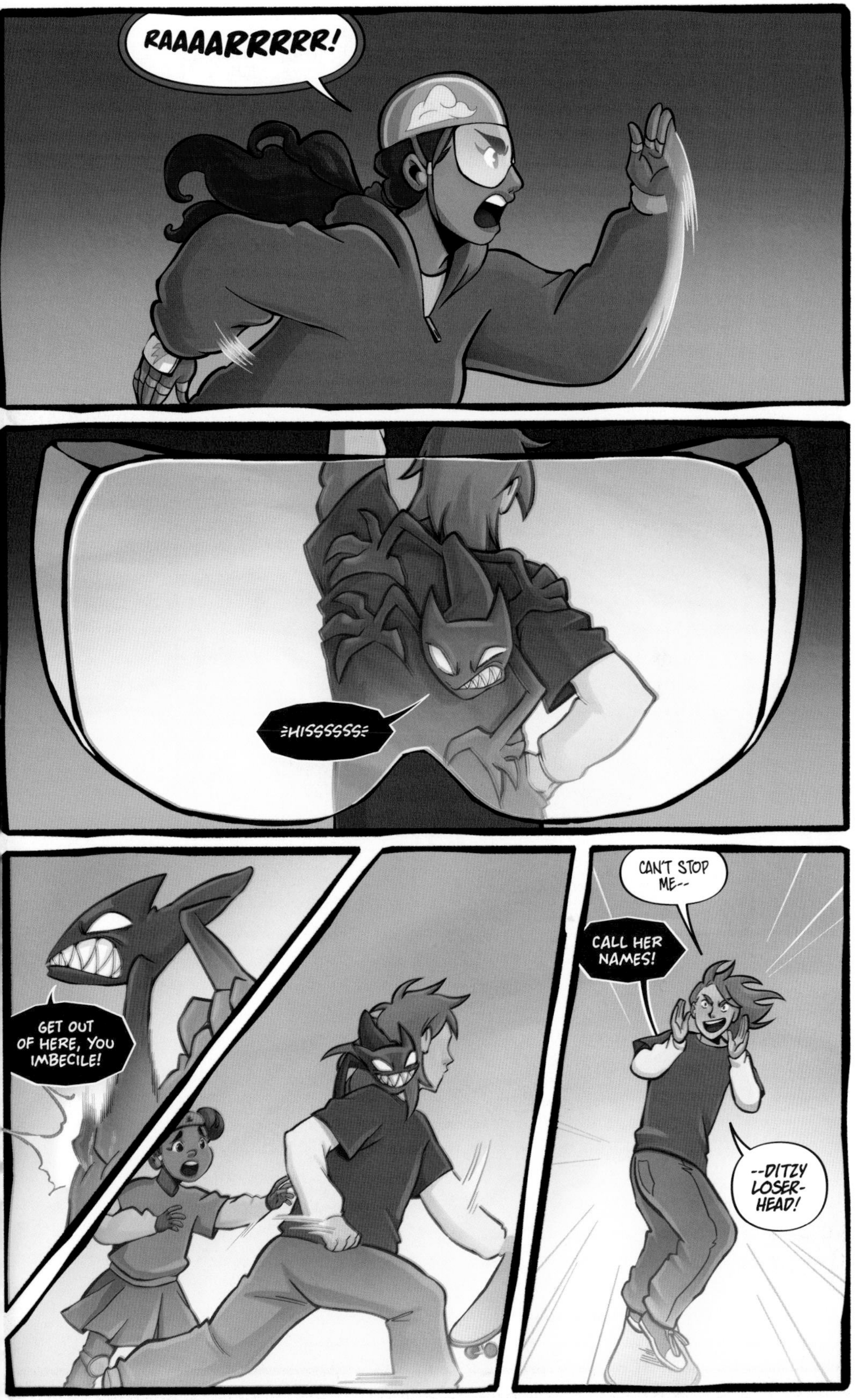
RAAAARRRRR!
HISSSSSS
GET OUT OF HERE, YOU IMBECILE!
CAN'T STOP ME--
CALL HER NAMES!
--DITZY LOSER-HEAD!

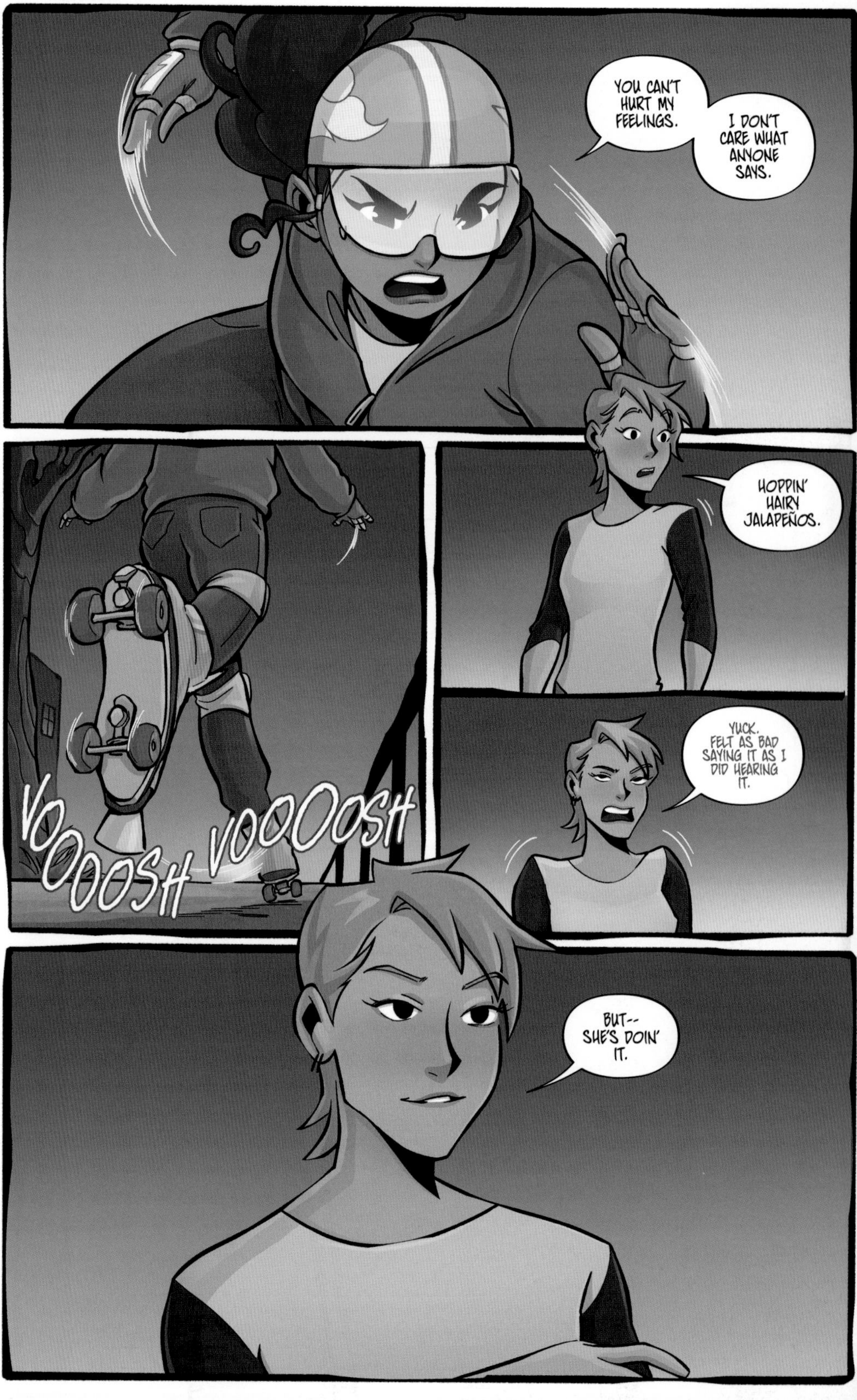
YOU CAN'T HURT MY FEELINGS.
I DON'T CARE WHAT ANYONE SAYS.
HOPPIN' HAIRY JALAPEÑOS.
VOOOOOSH VOOOOOSH
YUCK. FELT AS BAD SAYING IT AS I DID HEARING IT.
BUT-- SHE'S DOIN' IT.

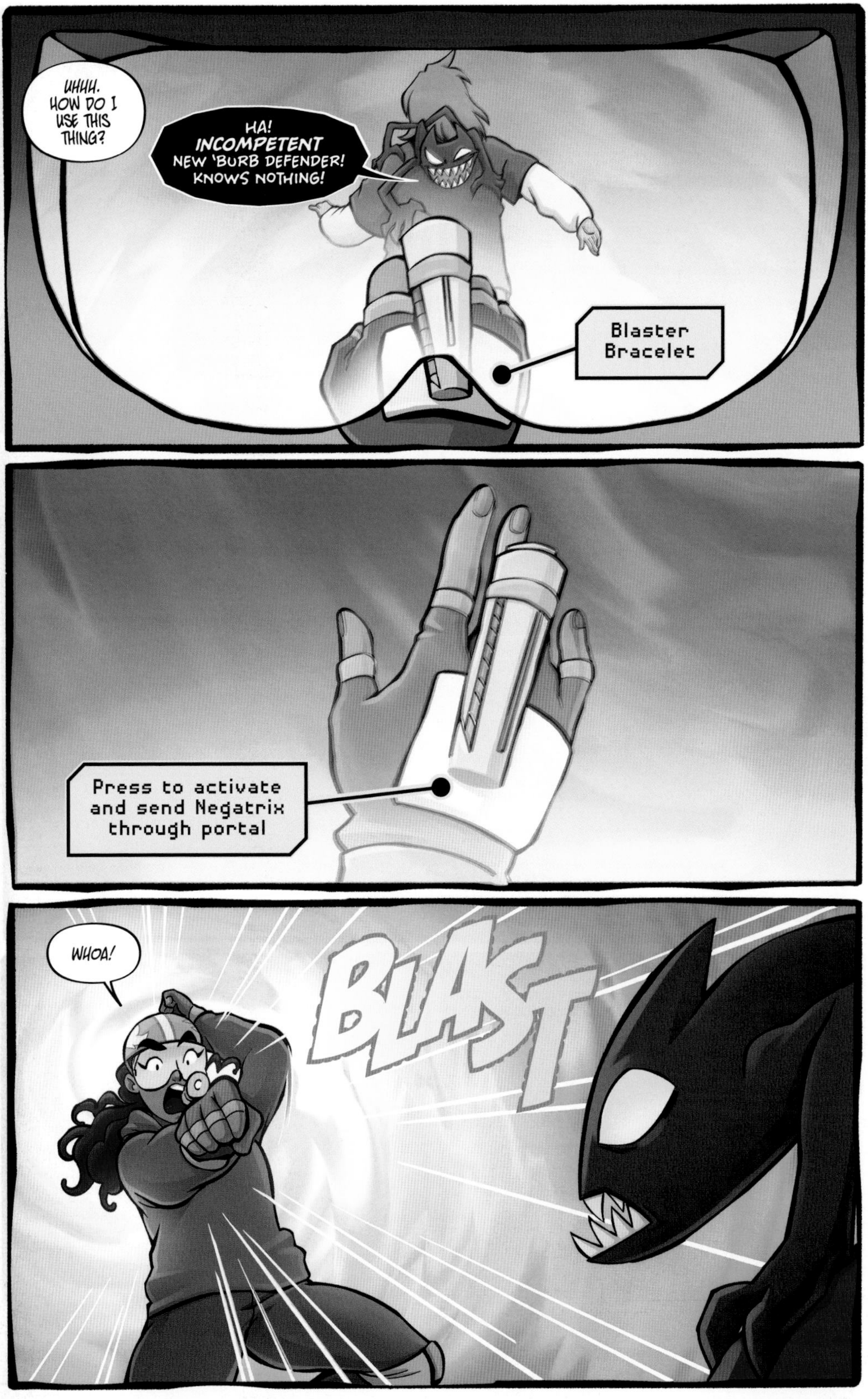
UHHH. HOW DO I USE THIS THING?
HA! INCOMPETENT NEW 'BURB DEFENDER! KNOWS NOTHING!
Blaster Bracelet
Press to activate and send Negatrix through portal
WHOA!
BLAST

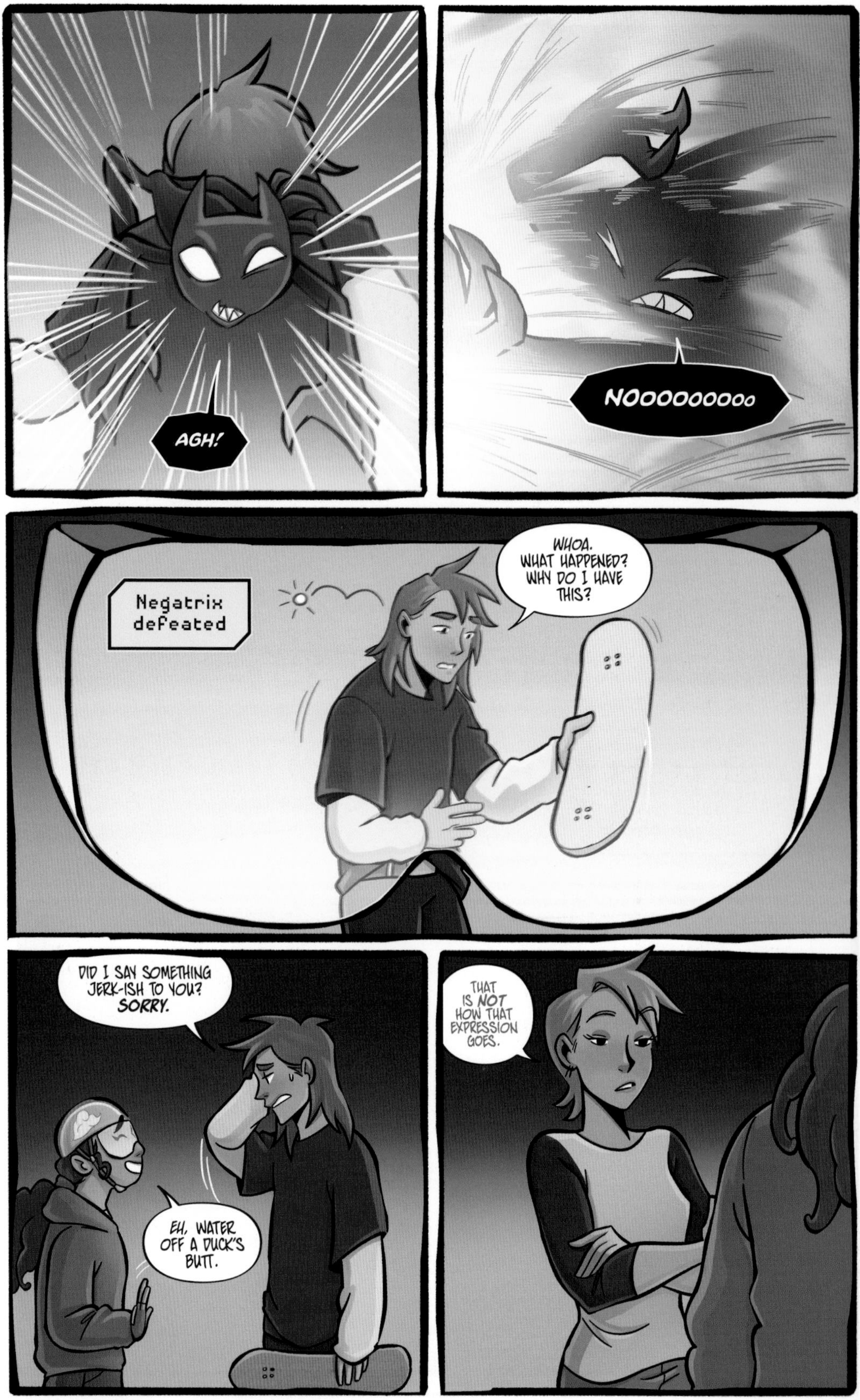
AGH!
NOOOOOOOOo
Negatrix defeated
WHOA. WHAT HAPPENED? WHY DO I HAVE THIS?
DID I SAY SOMETHING JERK-ISH TO YOU? SORRY.
EH, WATER OFF A DUCK'S BUTT.
THAT IS NOT HOW THAT EXPRESSION GOES.

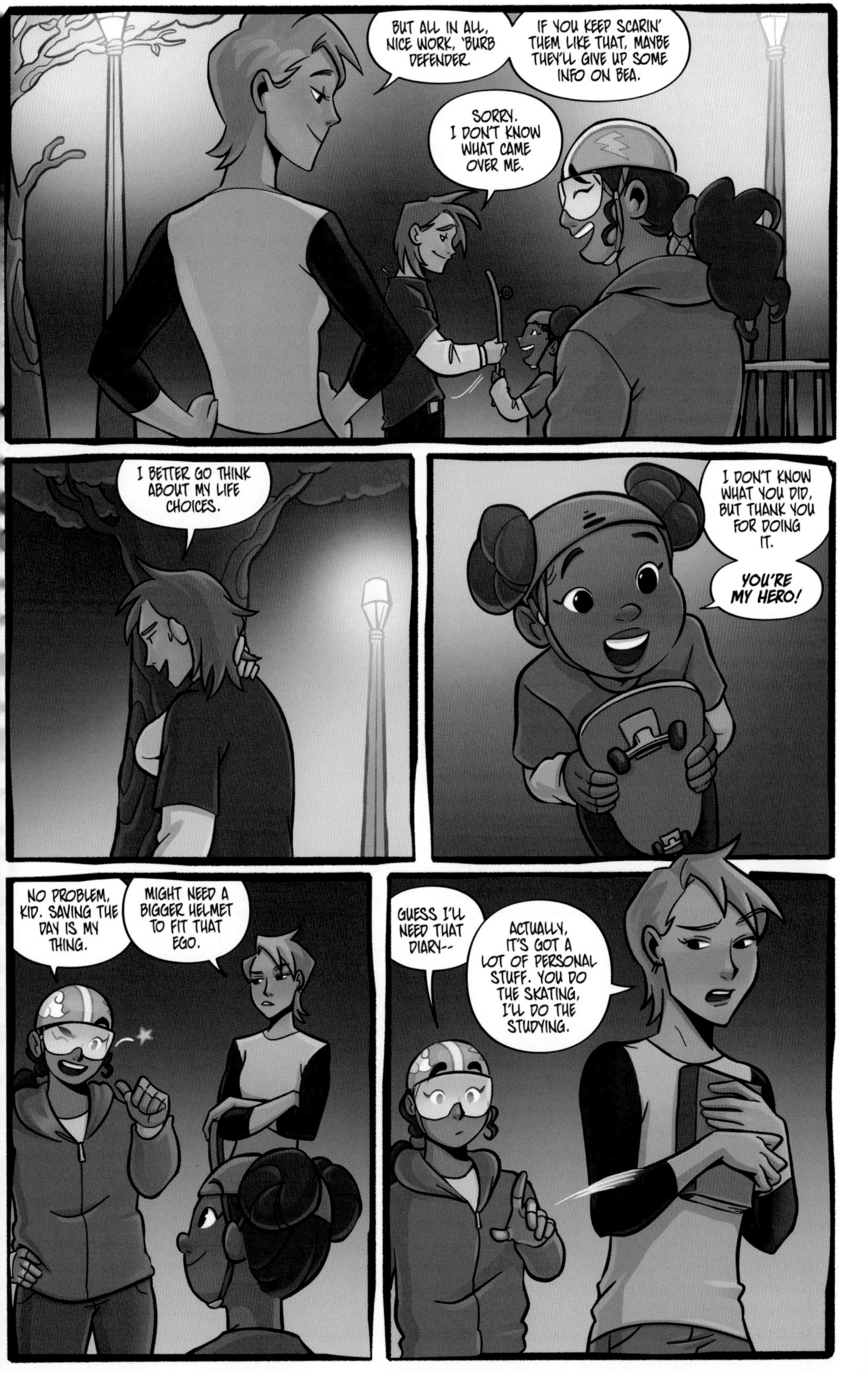

BUT ALL IN ALL, NICE WORK, 'BURB DEFENDER.
IF YOU KEEP SCARIN' THEM LIKE THAT, MAYBE THEY'LL GIVE UP SOME INFO ON BEA.
SORRY. I DON'T KNOW WHAT CAME OVER ME.
I BETTER GO THINK ABOUT MY LIFE CHOICES.
I DON'T KNOW WHAT YOU DID, BUT THANK YOU FOR DOING IT.
YOU'RE MY HERO!
NO PROBLEM, KID. SAVING THE DAY IS MY THING.
MIGHT NEED A BIGGER HELMET TO FIT THAT EGO.
GUESS I'LL NEED THAT DIARY--
ACTUALLY, IT'S GOT A LOT OF PERSONAL STUFF. YOU DO THE SKATING, I'LL DO THE STUDYING.

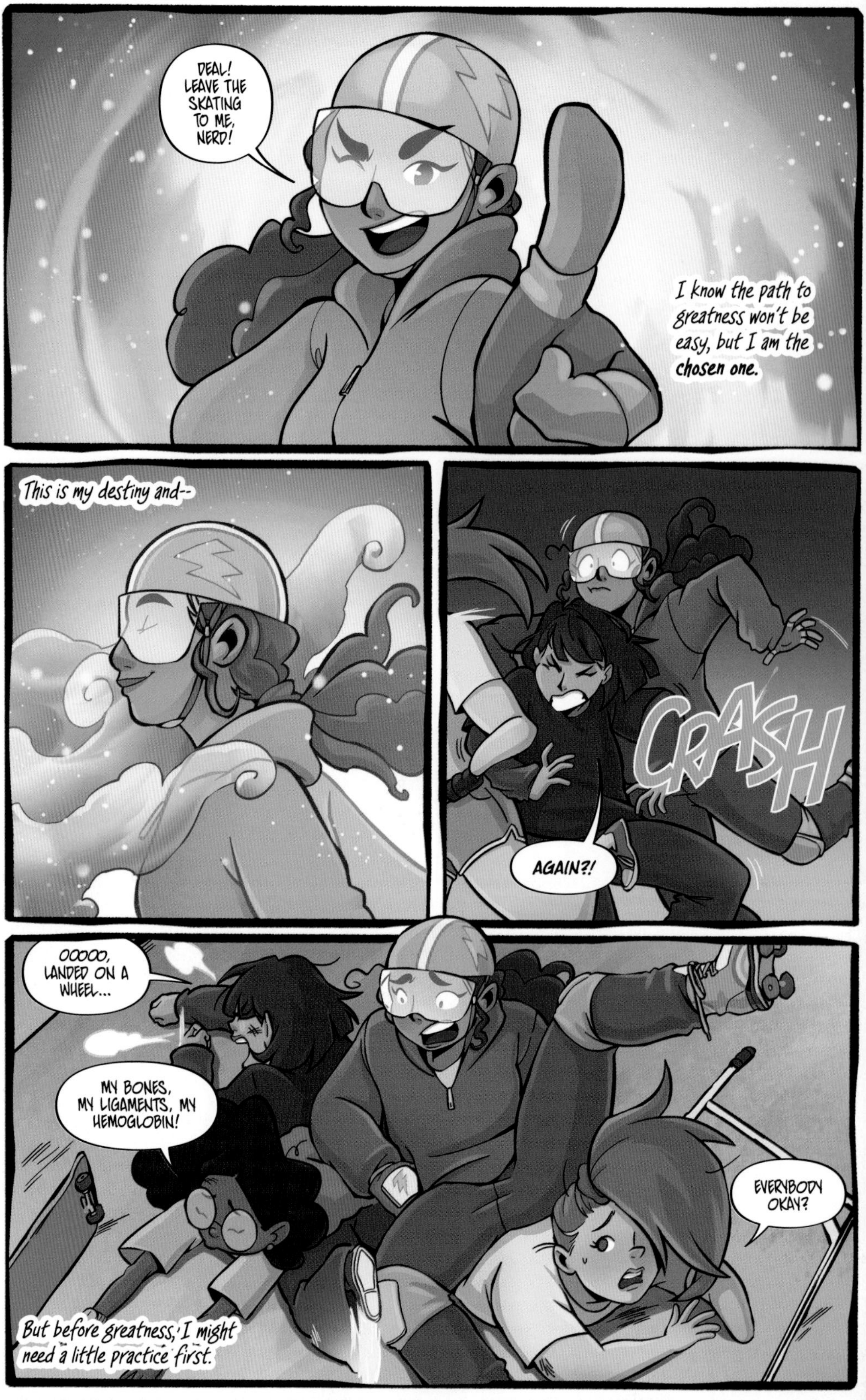
DEAL! LEAVE THE SKATING TO ME, NERD!
I know the path to greatness won't be easy, but I am the **chosen one.**
This is my destiny and--
CRASH
AGAIN?!
OOOOO, LANDED ON A WHEEL...
MY BONES, MY LIGAMENTS, MY HEMOGLOBIN!
EVERYBODY OKAY?
But before greatness, I might need a little practice first.

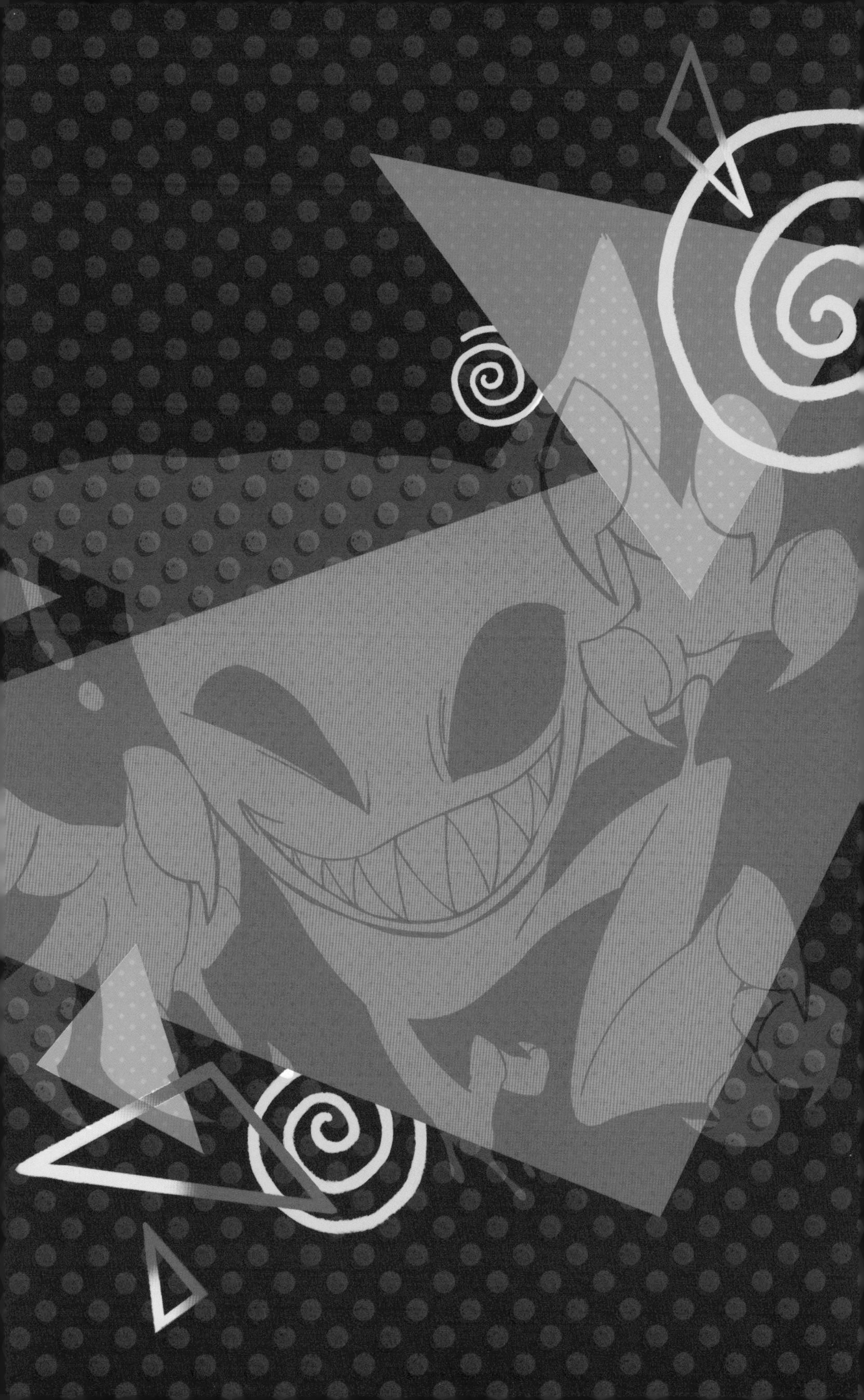

CHAPTER TWO

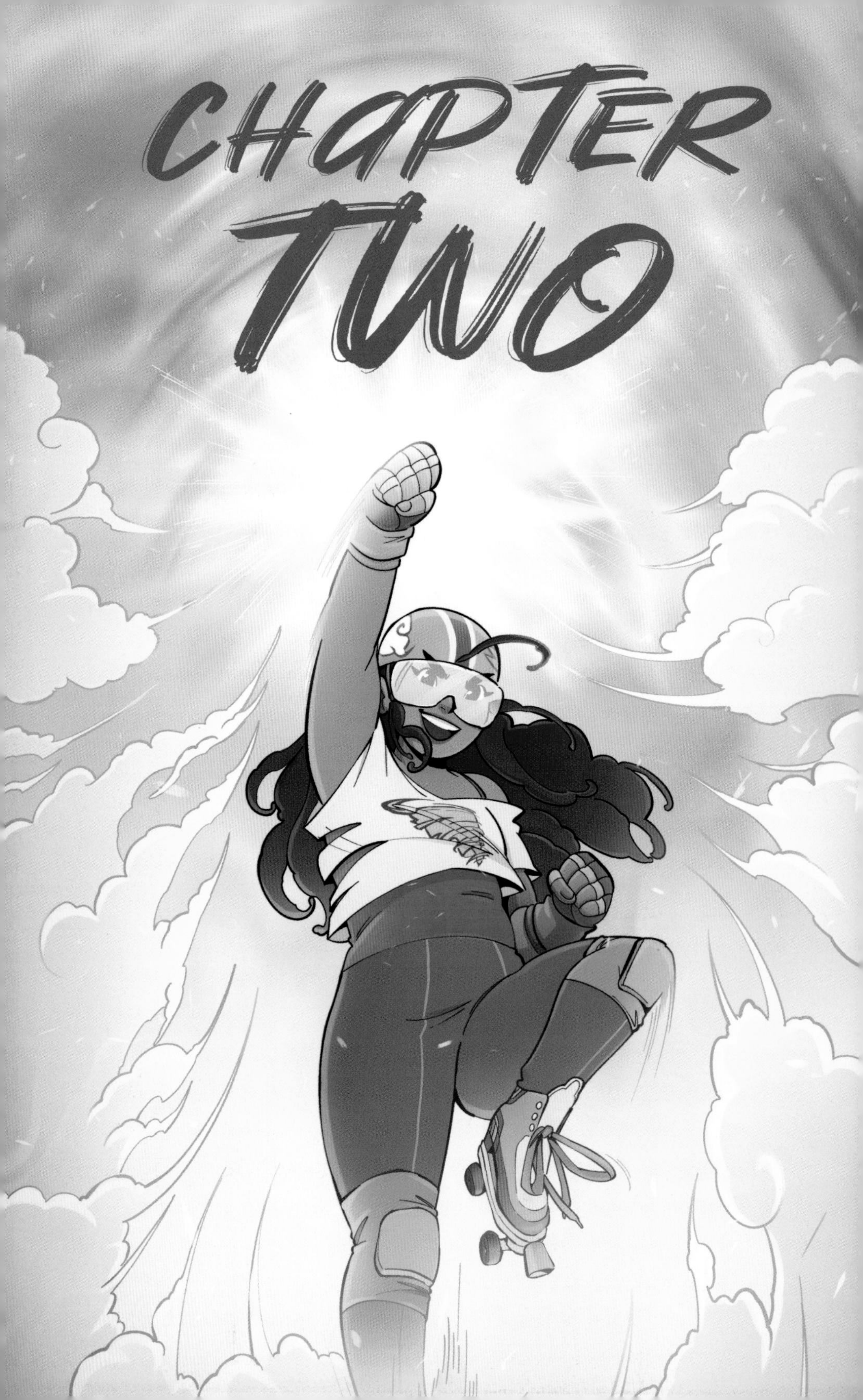

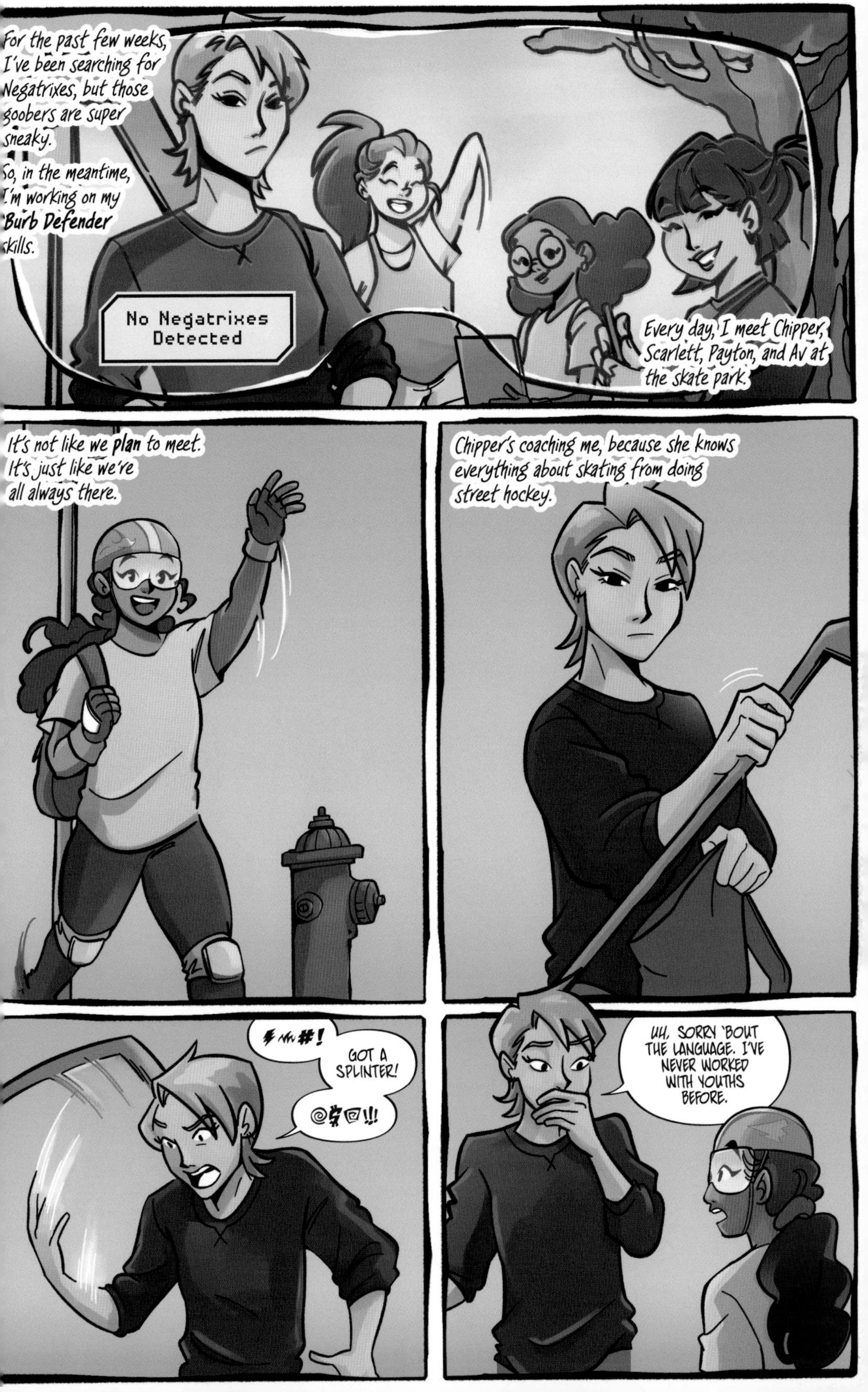
For the past few weeks, I've been searching for Negatrixes, but those goobers are super sneaky.
So, in the meantime, I'm working on my **Burb Defender** skills.
No Negatrixes Detected
Every day, I meet Chipper, Scarlett, Payton, and Av at the skate park.
It's not like we **plan** to meet. It's just like we're all always there.
Chipper's coaching me, because she knows everything about skating from doing street hockey.
GOT A SPLINTER!
UH, SORRY 'BOUT THE LANGUAGE. I'VE NEVER WORKED WITH YOUTHS BEFORE.

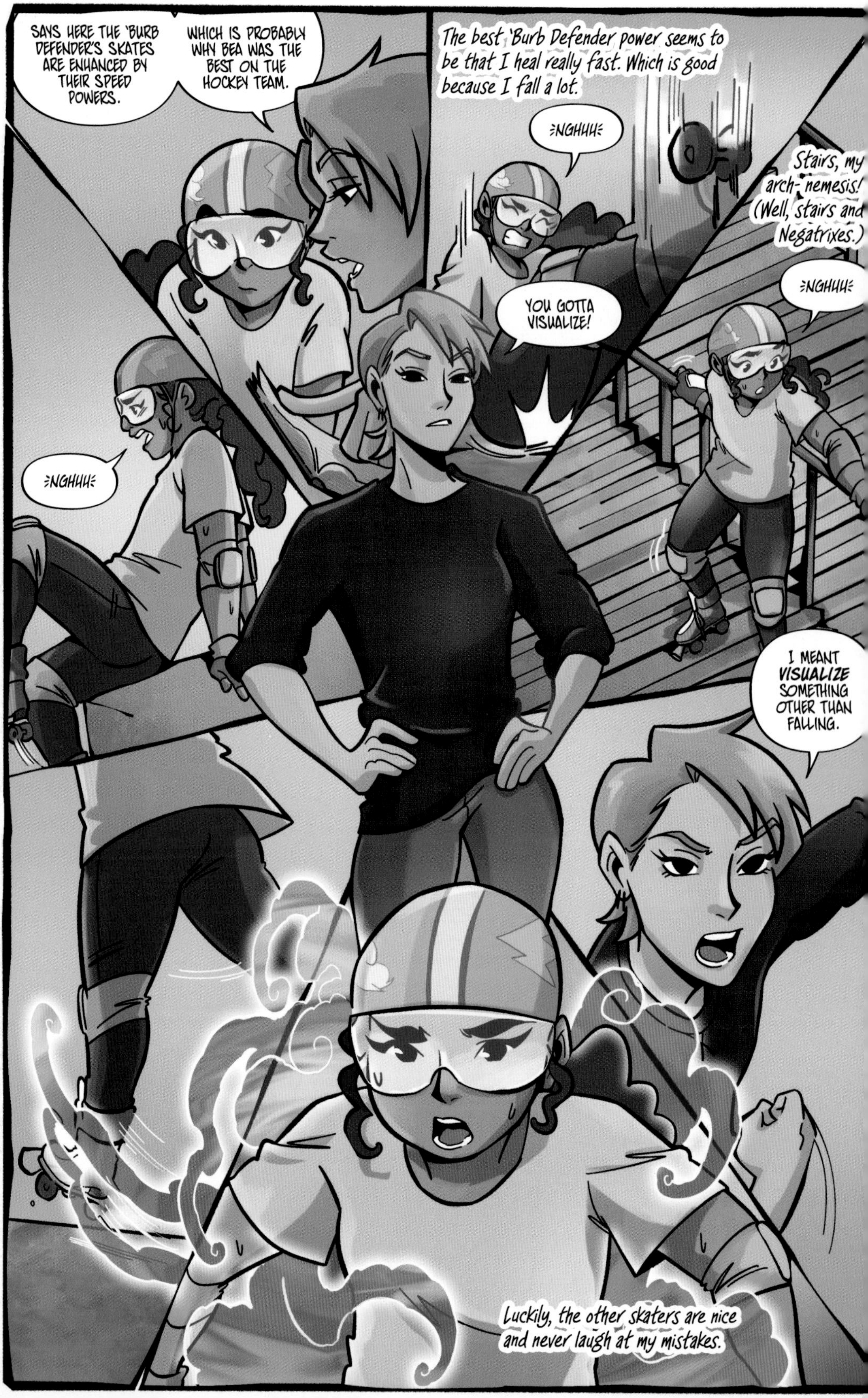

SAYS HERE THE 'BURB DEFENDER'S SKATES ARE ENHANCED BY THEIR SPEED POWERS.
WHICH IS PROBABLY WHY BEA WAS THE BEST ON THE HOCKEY TEAM.
The best 'Burb Defender power seems to be that I heal really fast. Which is good because I fall a lot.
NGHHH
Stairs, my arch-nemesis! (Well, stairs and Negatrixes.)
YOU GOTTA VISUALIZE!
NGHHH
NGHHH
I MEANT VISUALIZE SOMETHING OTHER THAN FALLING.
Luckily, the other skaters are nice and never laugh at my mistakes.

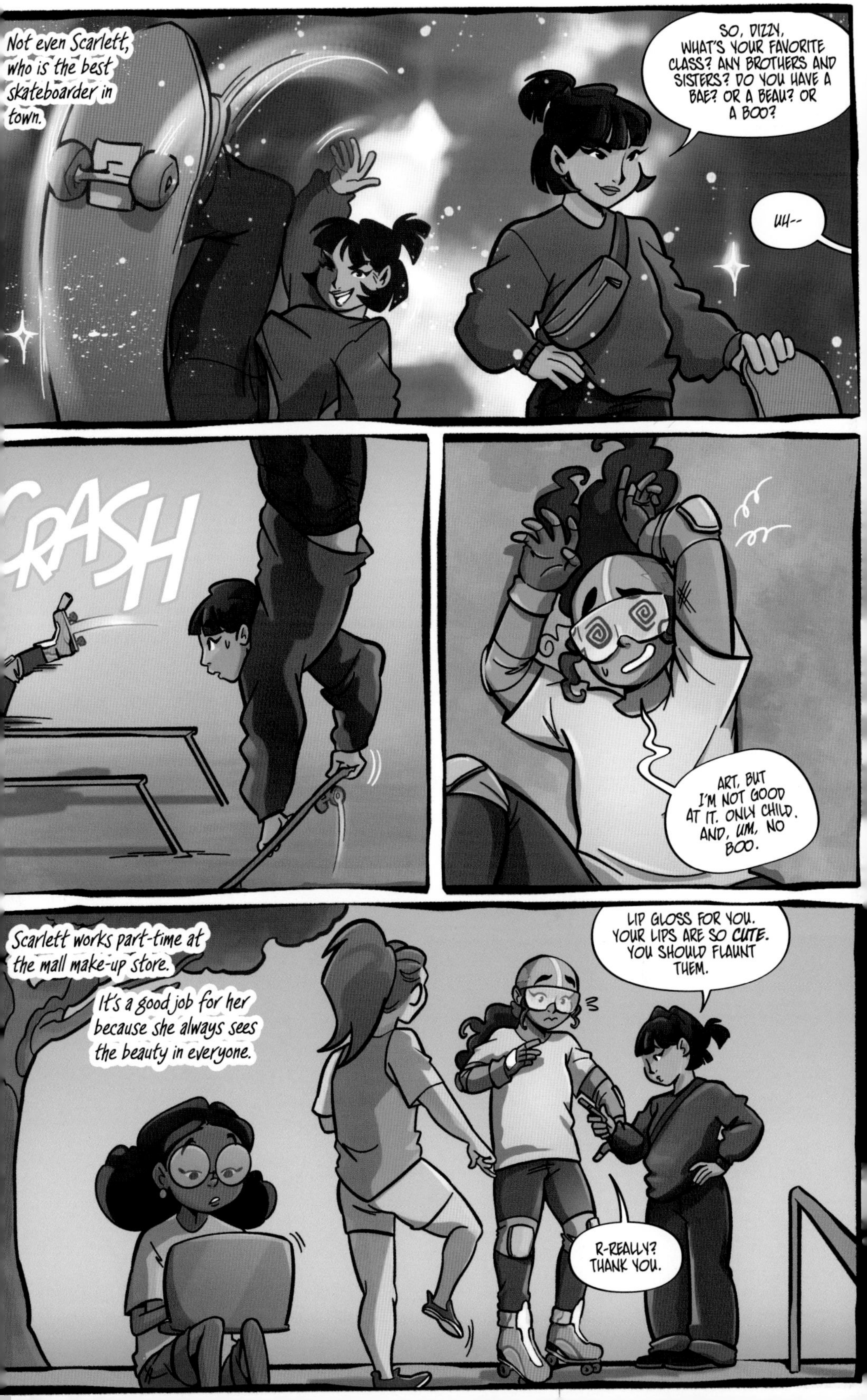
Not even Scarlett, who is the best skateboarder in town.
SO, DIZZY, WHAT'S YOUR FAVORITE CLASS? ANY BROTHERS AND SISTERS? DO YOU HAVE A BAE? OR A BEAU? OR A BOO?
UH--
CRASH
ART, BUT I'M NOT GOOD AT IT. ONLY CHILD. AND, UM, NO BOO.
Scarlett works part-time at the mall make-up store.
It's a good job for her because she always sees the beauty in everyone.
LIP GLOSS FOR YOU. YOUR LIPS ARE SO CUTE. YOU SHOULD FLAUNT THEM.
R-REALLY? THANK YOU.

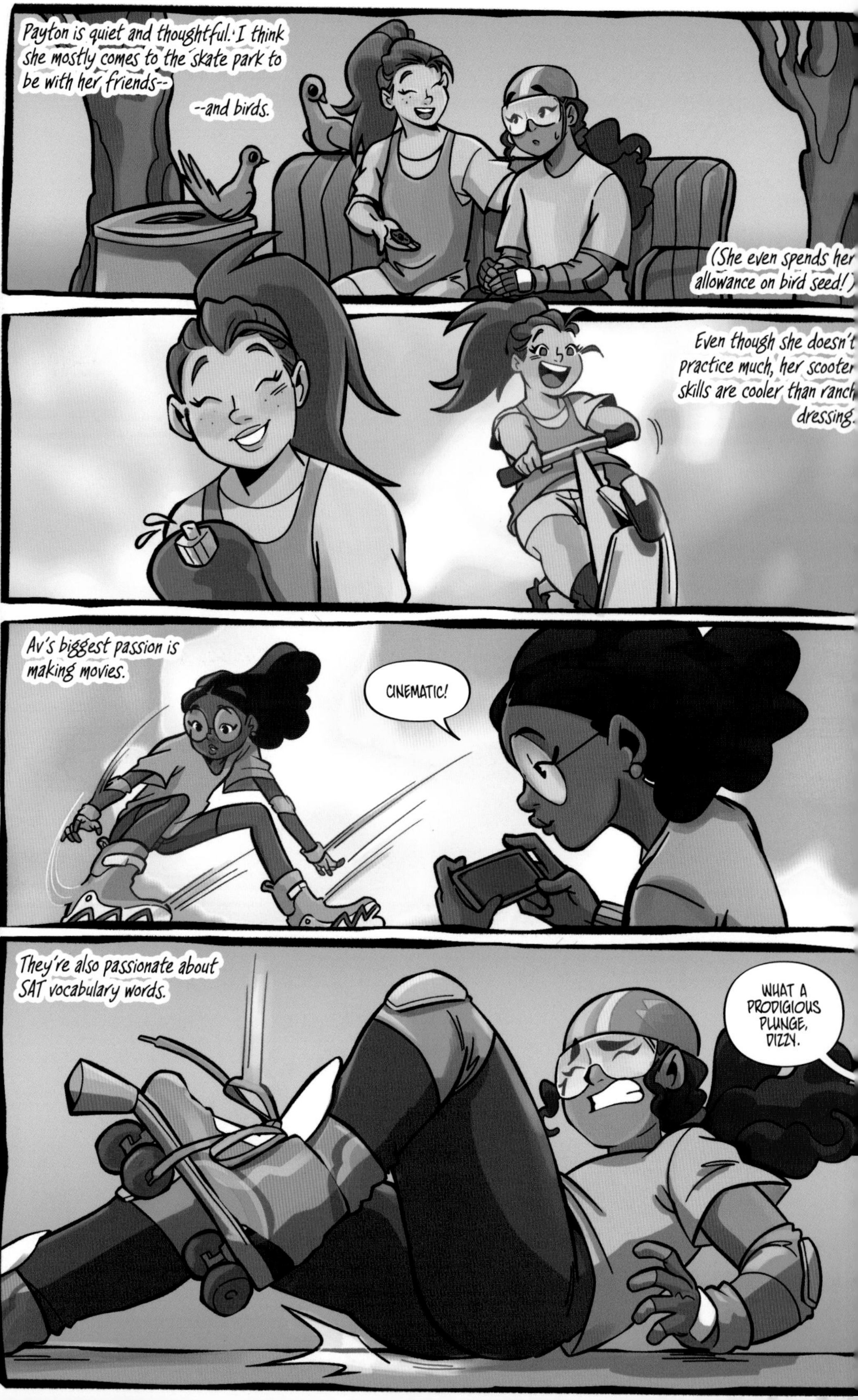

Payton is quiet and thoughtful. I think she mostly comes to the skate park to be with her friends--
--and birds.
(She even spends her allowance on bird seed!)
Even though she doesn't practice much, her scooter skills are cooler than ranch dressing.
Av's biggest passion is making movies.
CINEMATIC!
They're also passionate about SAT vocabulary words.
WHAT A PRODIGIOUS PLUNGE, DIZZY.

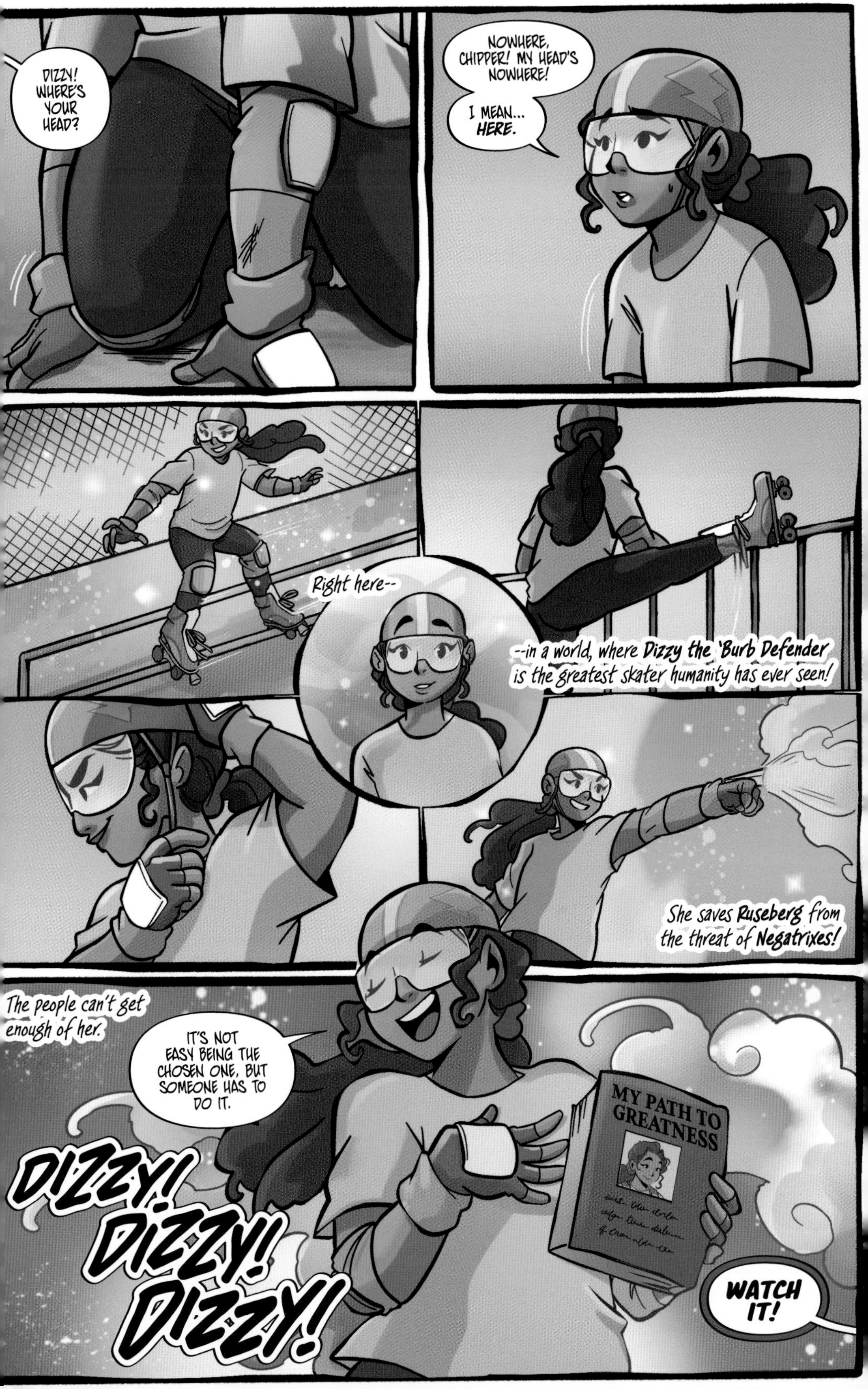

DIZZY! WHERE'S YOUR HEAD?
NOWHERE, CHIPPER! MY HEAD'S NOWHERE!
I MEAN... HERE.
Right here--
--in a world, where Dizzy the 'Burb Defender is the greatest skater humanity has ever seen!
She saves Ruseberg from the threat of Negatrixes!
The people can't get enough of her.
IT'S NOT EASY BEING THE CHOSEN ONE, BUT SOMEONE HAS TO DO IT.
MY PATH TO GREATNESS
DIZZY! DIZZY! DIZZY!
WATCH IT!

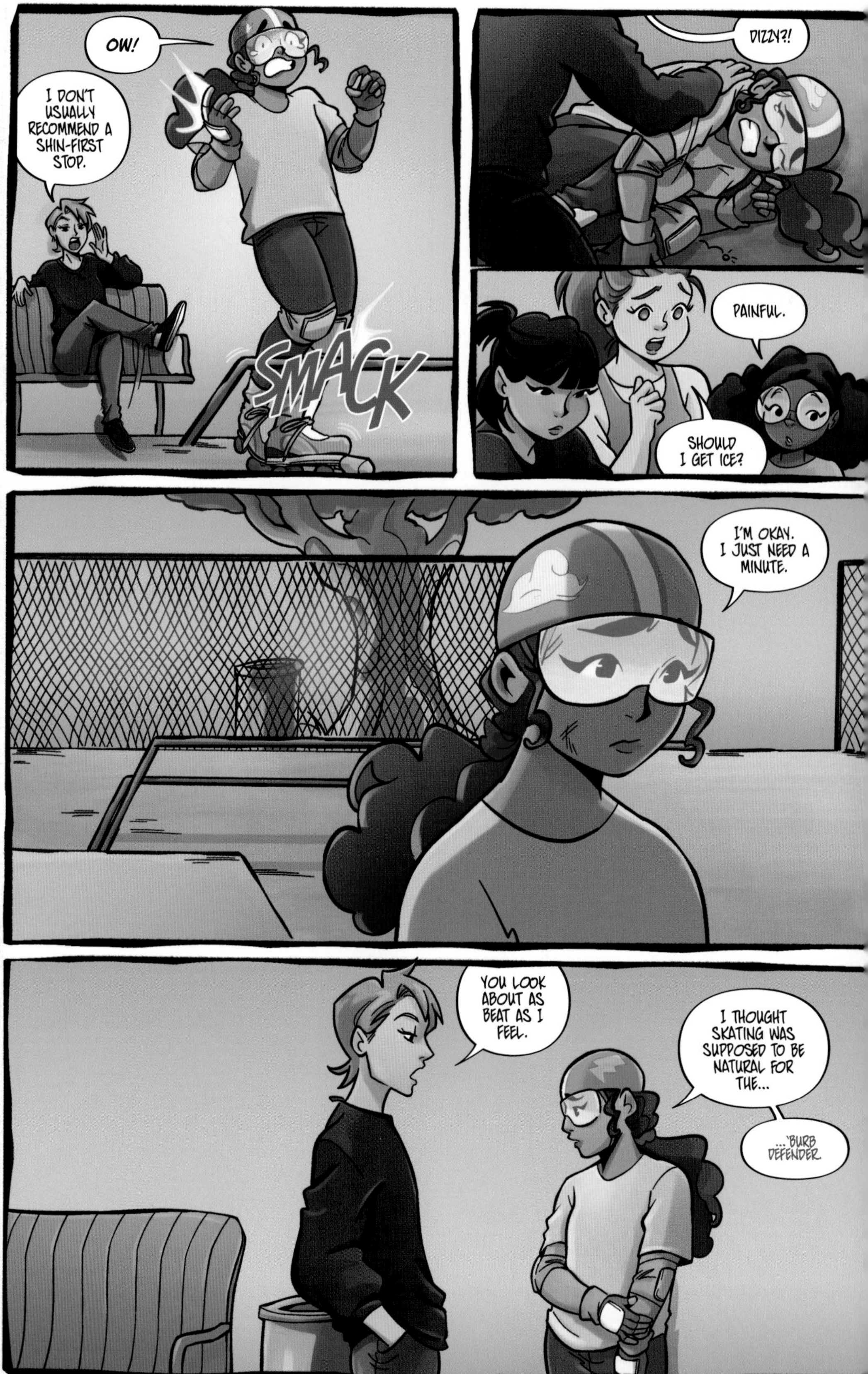
OW!
I DON'T USUALLY RECOMMEND A SHIN-FIRST STOP.
SMACK
DIZZY?!
PAINFUL.
SHOULD I GET ICE?
I'M OKAY. I JUST NEED A MINUTE.
YOU LOOK ABOUT AS BEAT AS I FEEL.
I THOUGHT SKATING WAS SUPPOSED TO BE NATURAL FOR THE...
...'BURB DEFENDER.

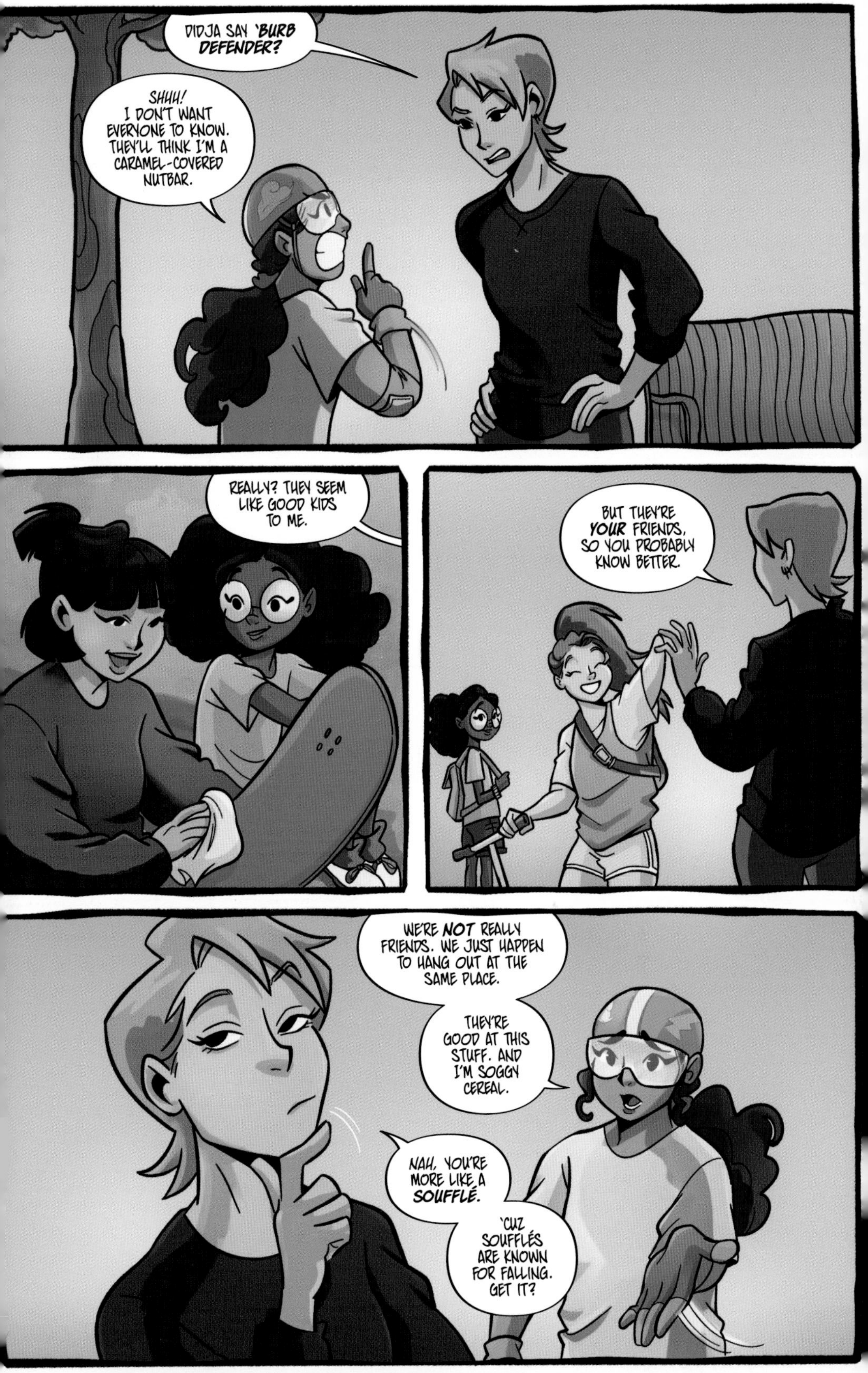
DIDJA SAY 'BURB DEFENDER?
SHUU! I DON'T WANT EVERYONE TO KNOW. THEY'LL THINK I'M A CARAMEL-COVERED NUTBAR.
REALLY? THEY SEEM LIKE GOOD KIDS TO ME.
BUT THEY'RE YOUR FRIENDS, SO YOU PROBABLY KNOW BETTER.
WE'RE NOT REALLY FRIENDS. WE JUST HAPPEN TO HANG OUT AT THE SAME PLACE.
THEY'RE GOOD AT THIS STUFF. AND I'M SOGGY CEREAL.
NAH, YOU'RE MORE LIKE A SOUFFLÉ.
'CUZ SOUFFLÉS ARE KNOWN FOR FALLING. GET IT?

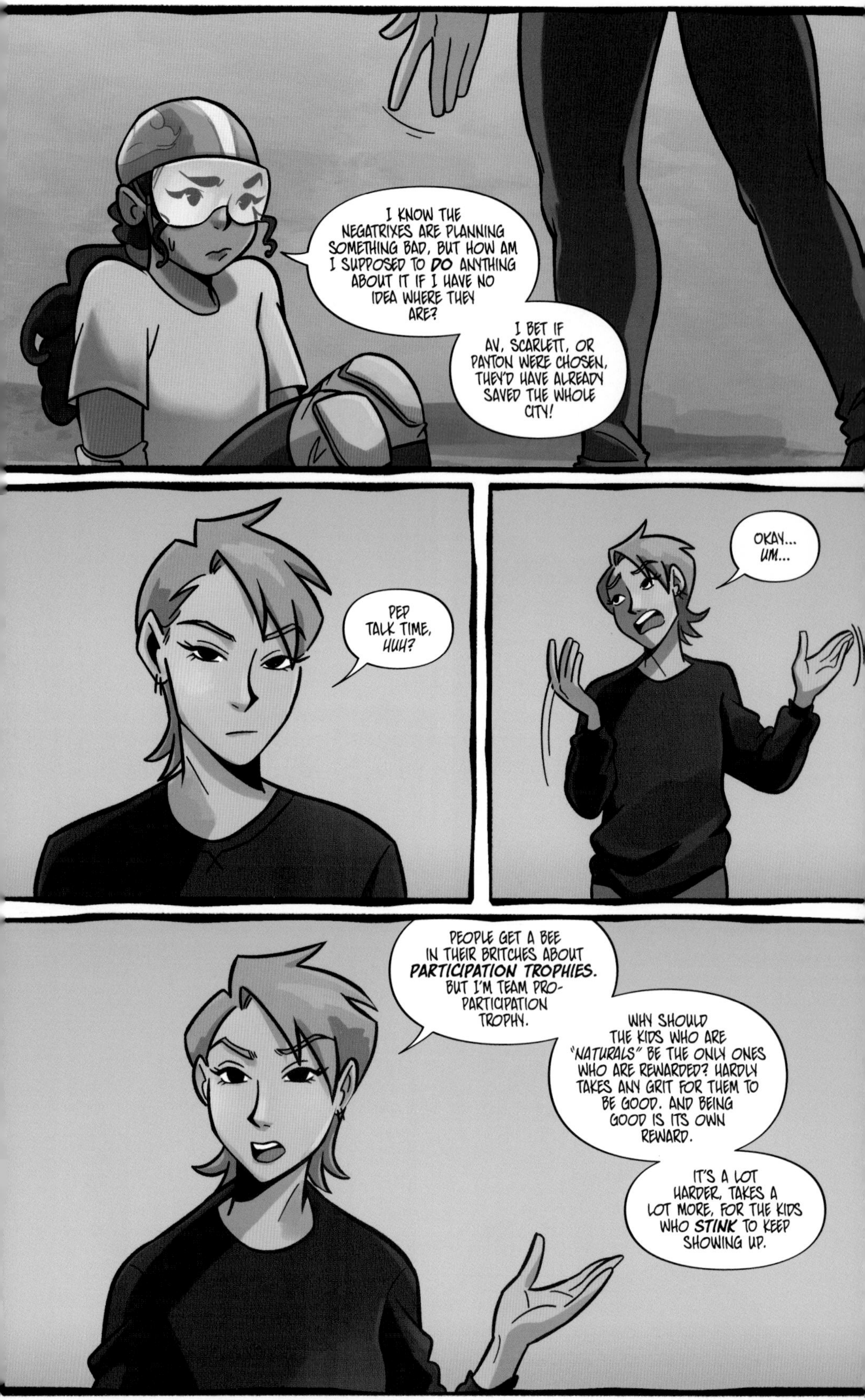
I KNOW THE NEGATRIXES ARE PLANNING SOMETHING BAD, BUT HOW AM I SUPPOSED TO **DO** ANYTHING ABOUT IT IF I HAVE NO IDEA WHERE THEY ARE?
I BET IF AV, SCARLETT, OR PAYTON WERE CHOSEN, THEY'D HAVE ALREADY SAVED THE WHOLE CITY!
PEP TALK TIME, *HUH?*
OKAY... UM...
PEOPLE GET A BEE IN THEIR BRITCHES ABOUT **PARTICIPATION TROPHIES.** BUT I'M TEAM PRO-PARTICIPATION TROPHY.
WHY SHOULD THE KIDS WHO ARE "*NATURALS*" BE THE ONLY ONES WHO ARE REWARDED? HARDLY TAKES ANY GRIT FOR THEM TO BE GOOD. AND BEING GOOD IS ITS OWN REWARD.
IT'S A LOT HARDER, TAKES A LOT MORE, FOR THE KIDS WHO **STINK** TO KEEP SHOWING UP.

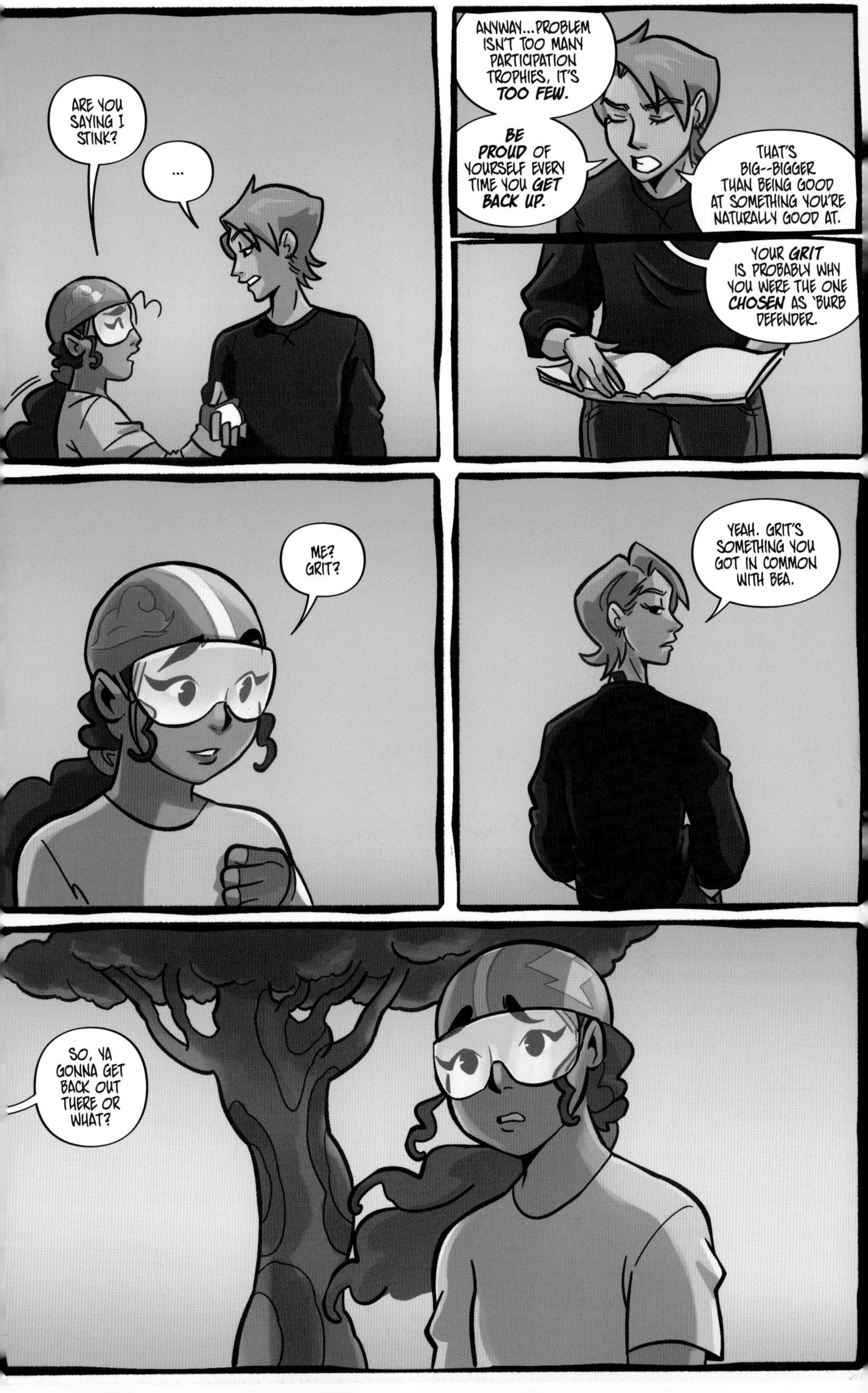
ARE YOU SAYING I STINK?
...
ANYWAY...PROBLEM ISN'T TOO MANY PARTICIPATION TROPHIES, IT'S **TOO FEW.**
BE PROUD OF YOURSELF EVERY TIME YOU **GET BACK UP.**
THAT'S BIG--BIGGER THAN BEING GOOD AT SOMETHING YOU'RE NATURALLY GOOD AT.
YOUR **GRIT** IS PROBABLY WHY YOU WERE THE ONE **CHOSEN** AS 'BURB DEFENDER.
ME? GRIT?
YEAH. GRIT'S SOMETHING YOU GOT IN COMMON WITH BEA.
SO, YA GONNA GET BACK OUT THERE OR WHAT?

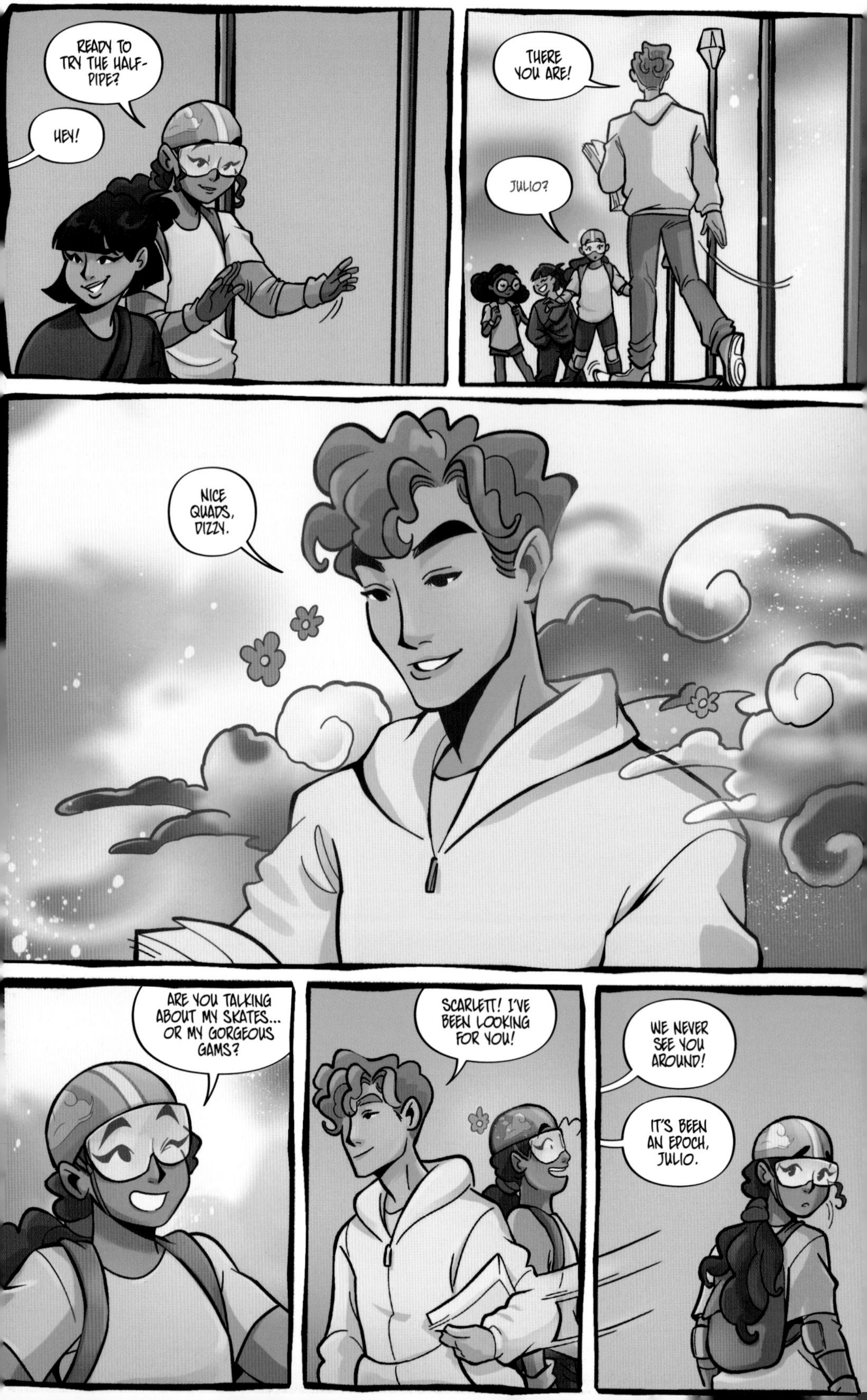
READY TO TRY THE HALF-PIPE?
HEY!
THERE YOU ARE!
JULIO?
NICE QUADS, DIZZY.
ARE YOU TALKING ABOUT MY SKATES... OR MY GORGEOUS GAMS?
SCARLETT! I'VE BEEN LOOKING FOR YOU!
WE NEVER SEE YOU AROUND!
IT'S BEEN AN EPOCH, JULIO.

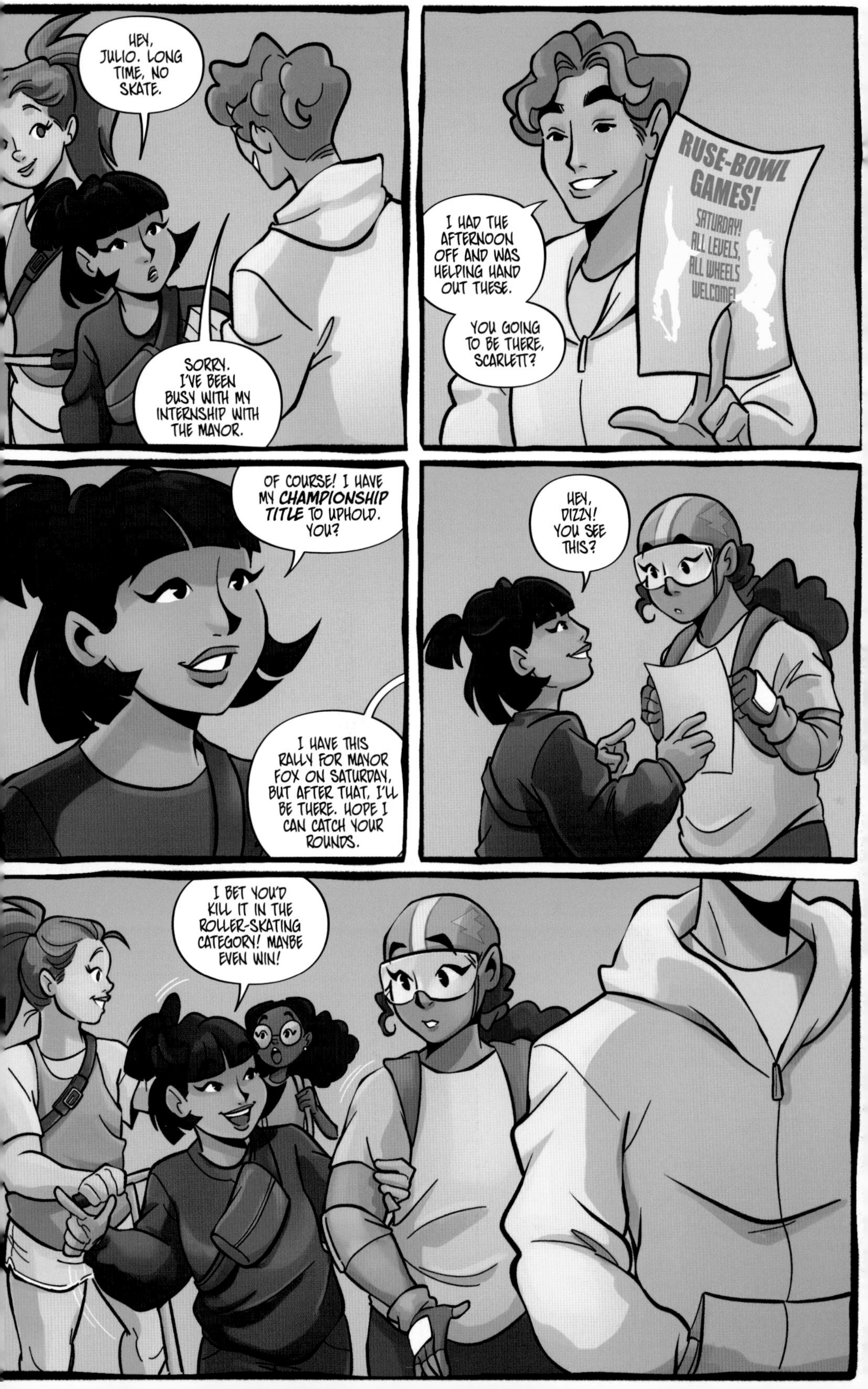
HEY, JULIO. LONG TIME, NO SKATE.
SORRY. I'VE BEEN BUSY WITH MY INTERNSHIP WITH THE MAYOR.
I HAD THE AFTERNOON OFF AND WAS HELPING HAND OUT THESE.
YOU GOING TO BE THERE, SCARLETT?
RUSE-BOWL GAMES!
SATURDAY! ALL LEVELS, ALL WHEELS WELCOME!
OF COURSE! I HAVE MY CHAMPIONSHIP TITLE TO UPHOLD. YOU?
I HAVE THIS RALLY FOR MAYOR FOX ON SATURDAY, BUT AFTER THAT, I'LL BE THERE. HOPE I CAN CATCH YOUR ROUNDS.
HEY, DIZZY! YOU SEE THIS?
I BET YOU'D KILL IT IN THE ROLLER-SKATING CATEGORY! MAYBE EVEN WIN!

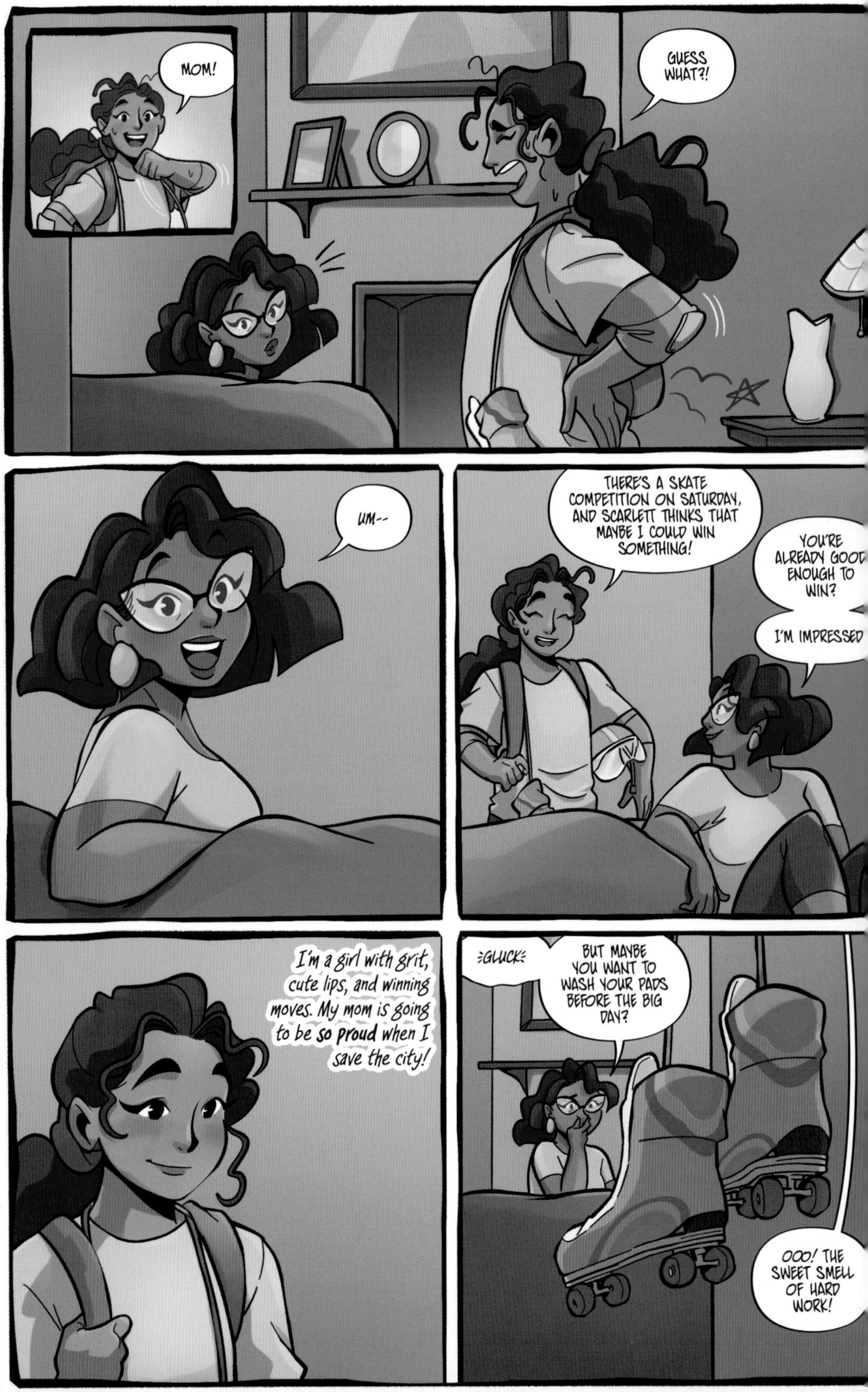
MOM!
GUESS WHAT?!
UM--
THERE'S A SKATE COMPETITION ON SATURDAY, AND SCARLETT THINKS THAT MAYBE I COULD WIN SOMETHING!
YOU'RE ALREADY GOOD ENOUGH TO WIN?
I'M IMPRESSED
I'm a girl with grit, cute lips, and winning moves. My mom is going to be so proud when I save the city!
GLUCK
BUT MAYBE YOU WANT TO WASH YOUR PADS BEFORE THE BIG DAY?
OOO! THE SWEET SMELL OF HARD WORK!

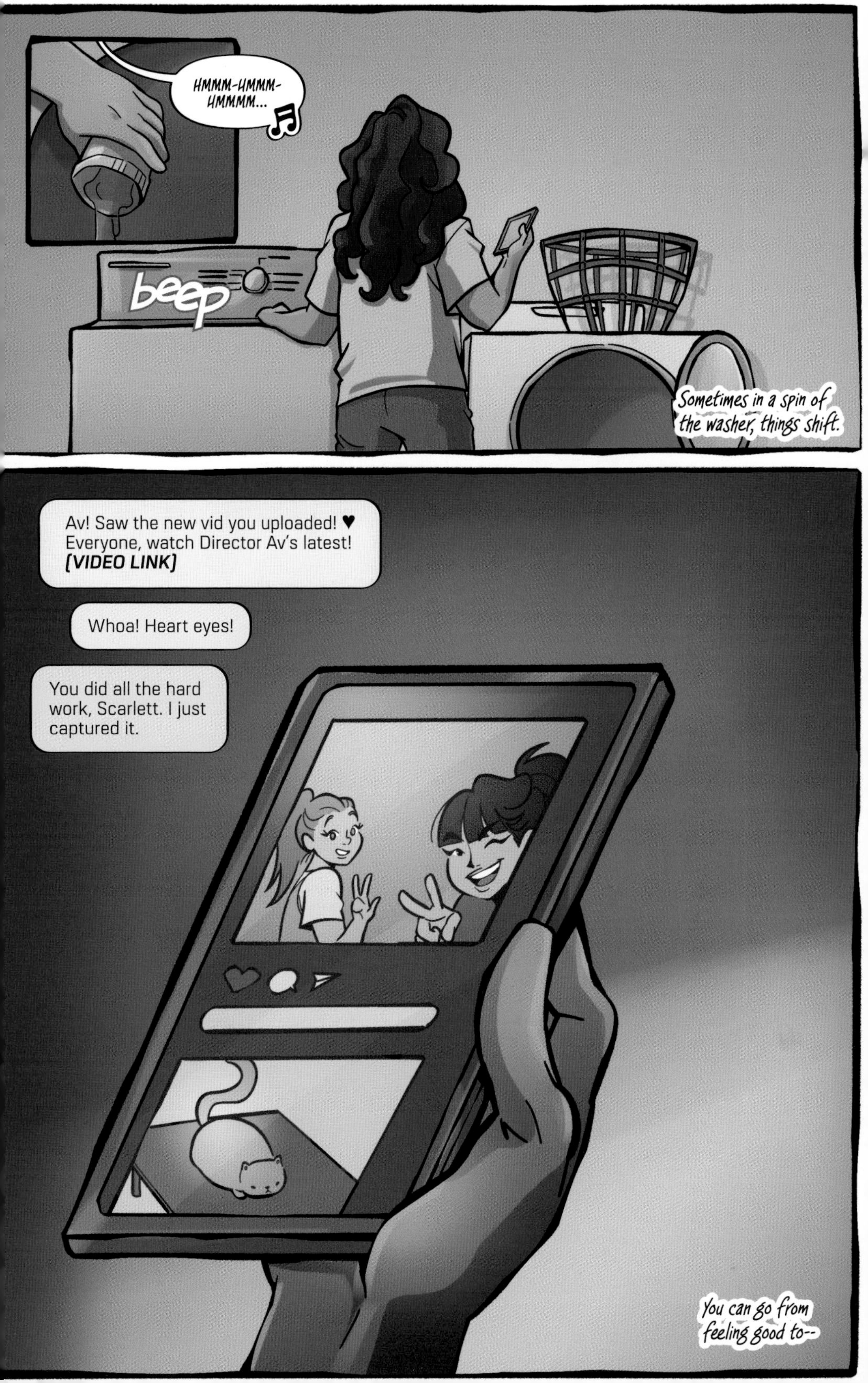
HMMM-HMMM-HMMMM...
beep
Sometimes in a spin of the washer, things shift.
Av! Saw the new vid you uploaded! ♥ Everyone, watch Director Av's latest! (VIDEO LINK)
Whoa! Heart eyes!
You did all the hard work, Scarlett. I just captured it.
You can go from feeling good to--

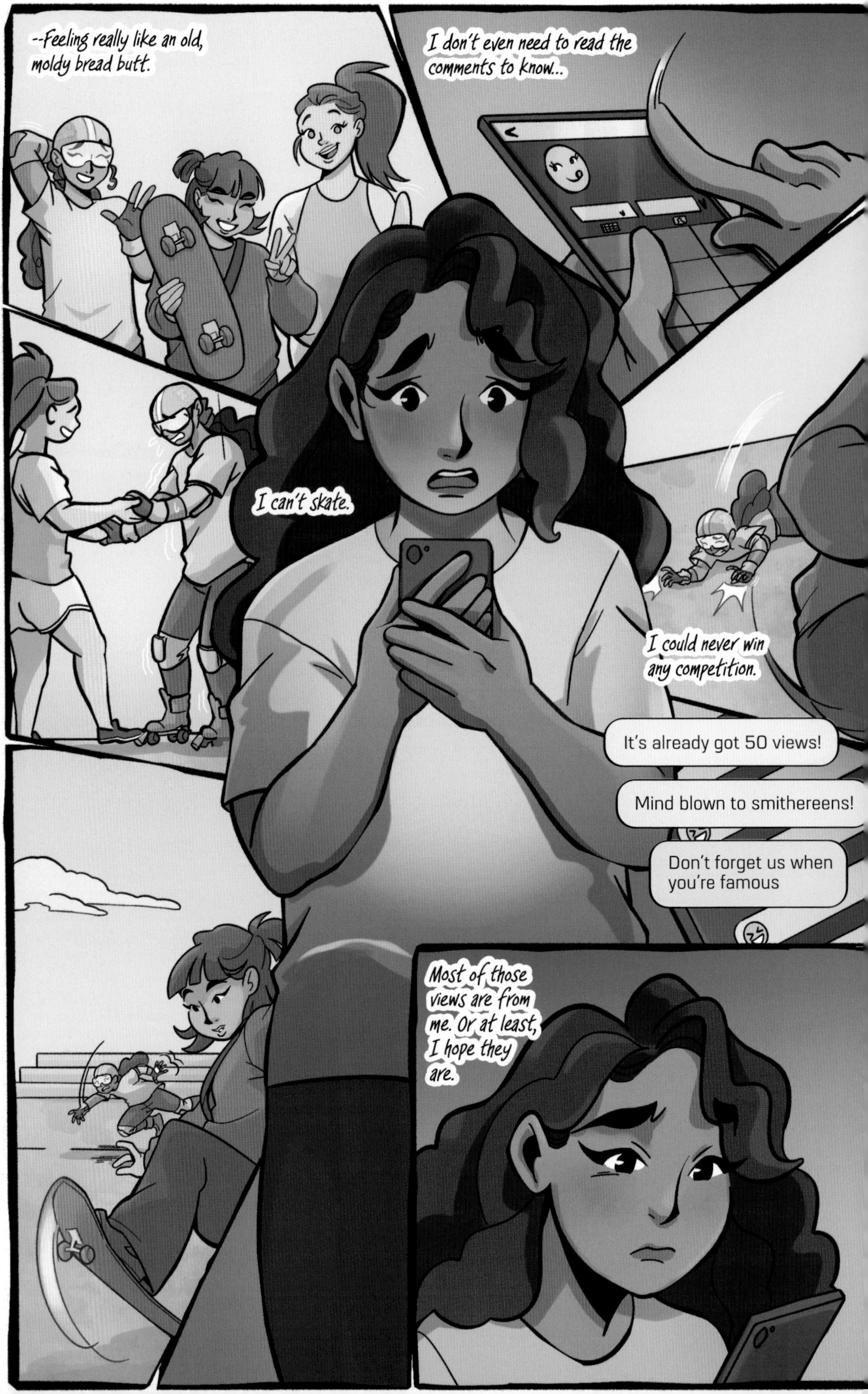
--Feeling really like an old, moldy bread butt.
I don't even need to read the comments to know...
I can't skate.
I could never win any competition.
It's already got 50 views!
Mind blown to smithereens!
Don't forget us when you're famous
Most of those views are from me. Or at least, I hope they are.

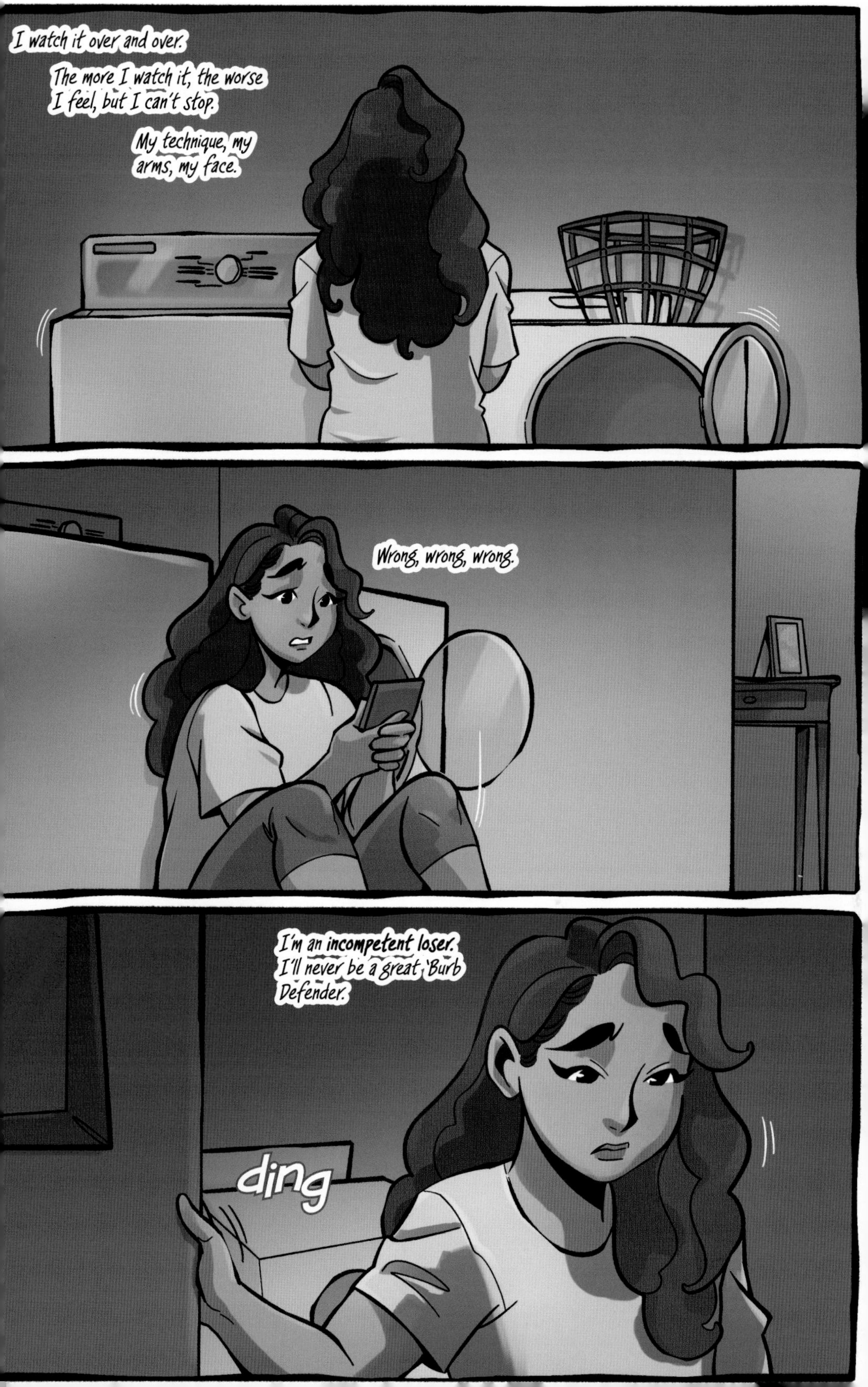
I watch it over and over.
The more I watch it, the worse I feel, but I can't stop.
My technique, my arms, my face.
Wrong, wrong, wrong.
I'm an incompetent loser. I'll never be a great 'Burb Defender.
ding

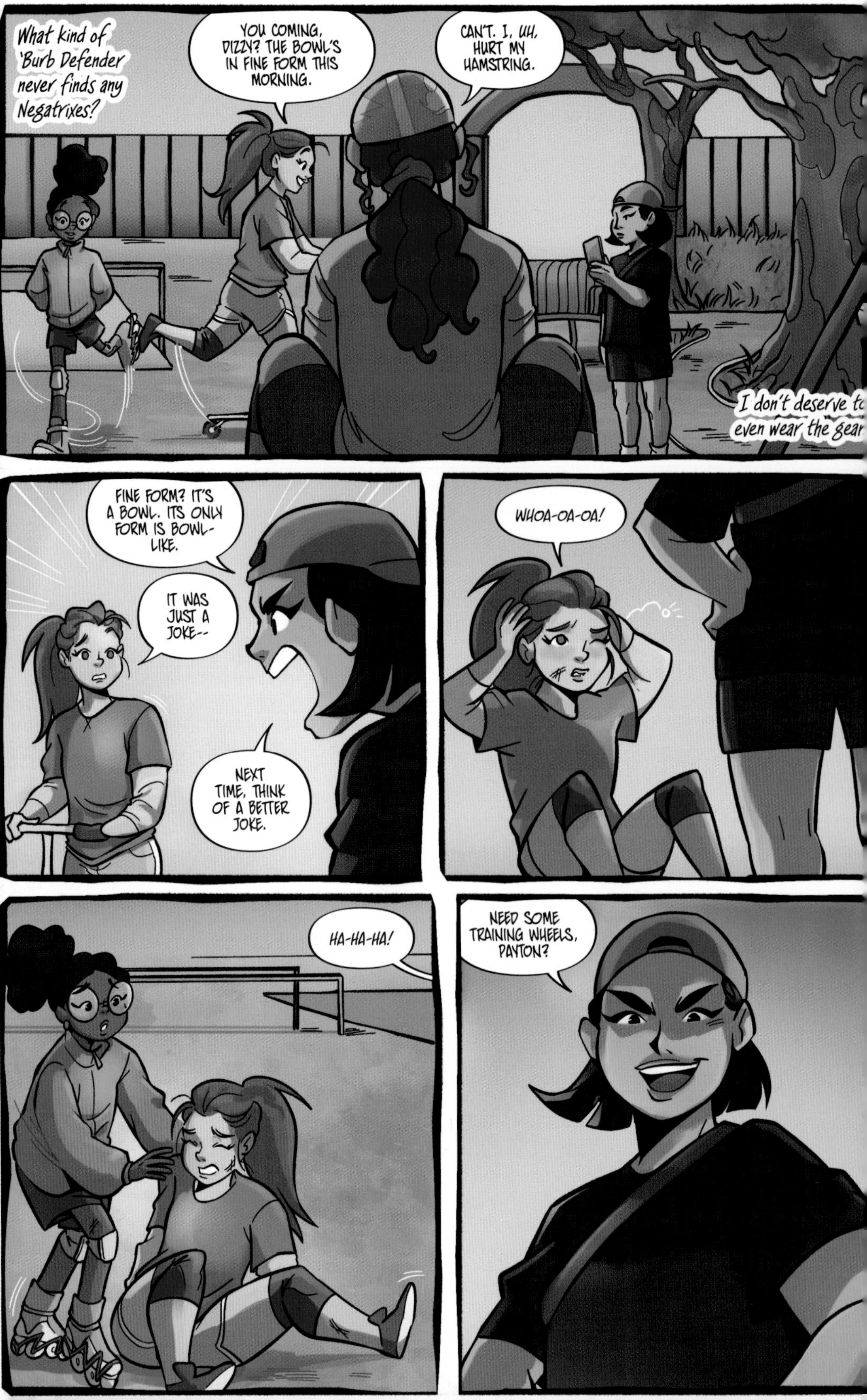
What kind of 'Burb Defender never finds any Negatrixes?
YOU COMING, DIZZY? THE BOWL'S IN FINE FORM THIS MORNING.
CAN'T. I, UH, HURT MY HAMSTRING.
I don't deserve to even wear the gear
FINE FORM? IT'S A BOWL. ITS ONLY FORM IS BOWL-LIKE.
IT WAS JUST A JOKE--
NEXT TIME, THINK OF A BETTER JOKE.
WHOA-OA-OA!
HA-HA-HA!
NEED SOME TRAINING WHEELS, PAYTON?

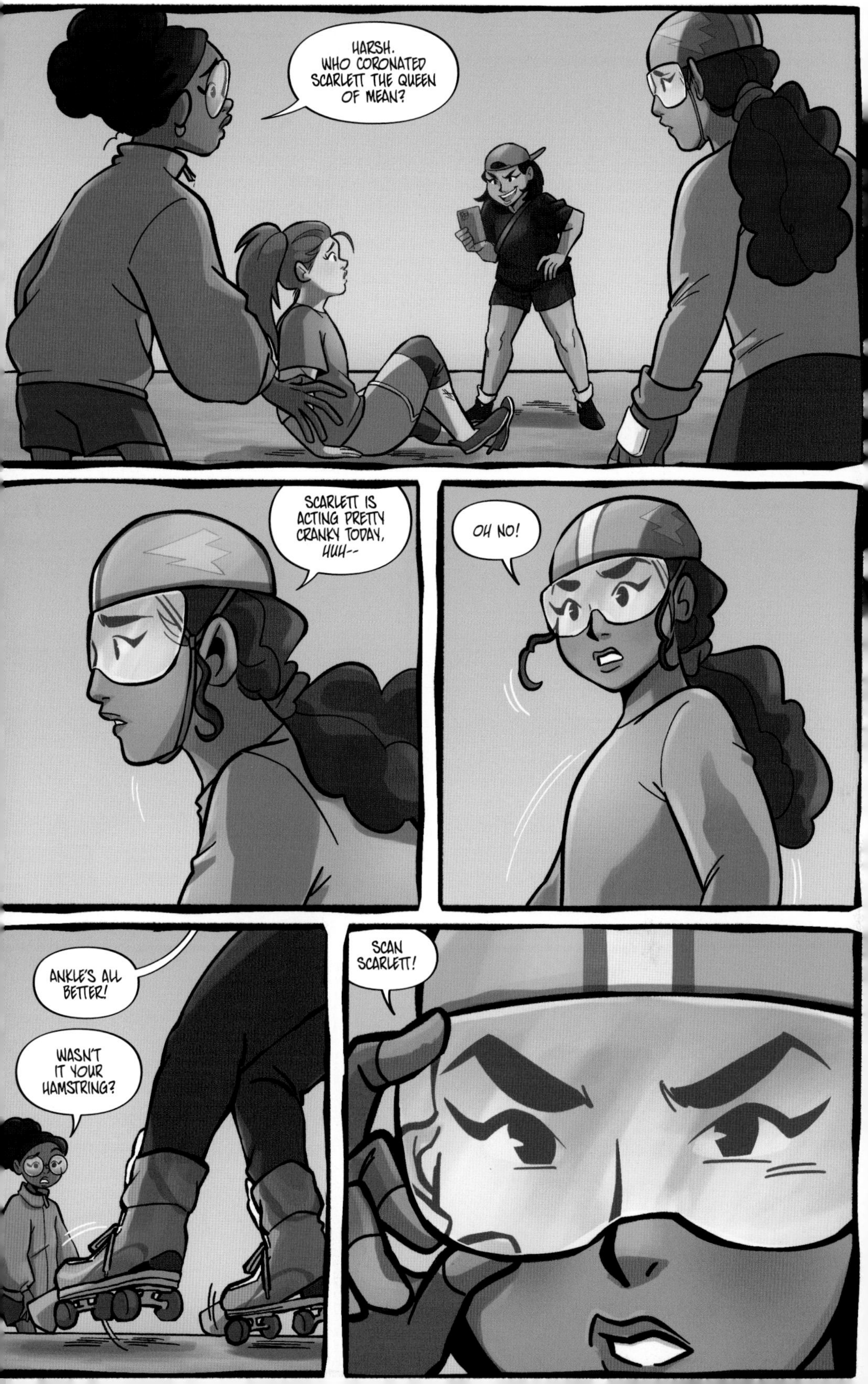
HARSH. WHO CORONATED SCARLETT THE QUEEN OF MEAN?
SCARLETT IS ACTING PRETTY CRANKY TODAY, HUH--
OH NO!
ANKLE'S ALL BETTER!
WASN'T IT YOUR HAMSTRING?
SCAN SCARLETT!

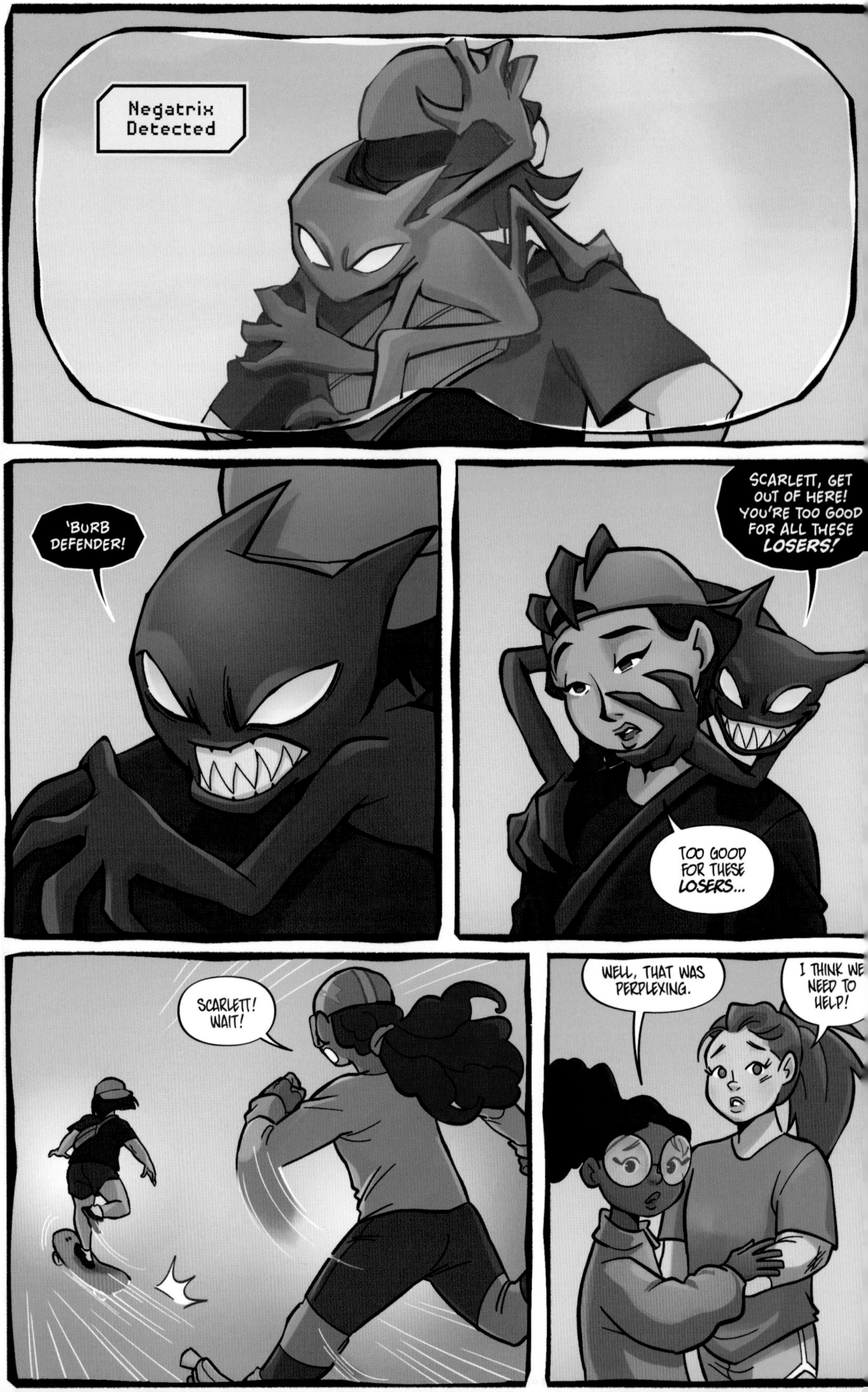
Negatrix
Detected
'BURB DEFENDER!
SCARLETT, GET OUT OF HERE! YOU'RE TOO GOOD FOR ALL THESE LOSERS!
TOO GOOD FOR THESE LOSERS...
SCARLETT! WAIT!
WELL, THAT WAS PERPLEXING.
I THINK WE NEED TO HELP!

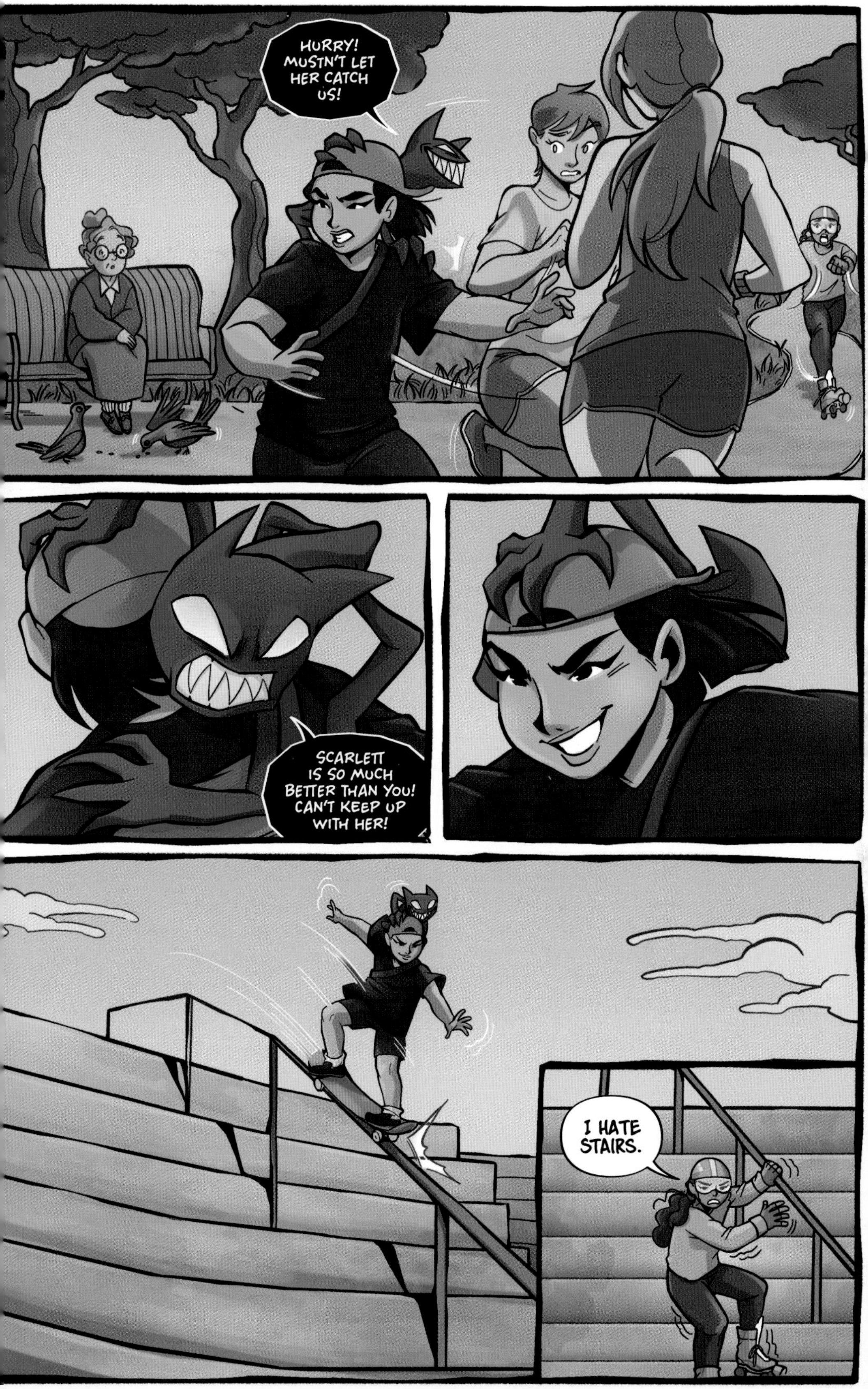
HURRY! MUSTN'T LET HER CATCH US!
SCARLETT IS SO MUCH BETTER THAN YOU! CAN'T KEEP UP WITH HER!
I HATE STAIRS.

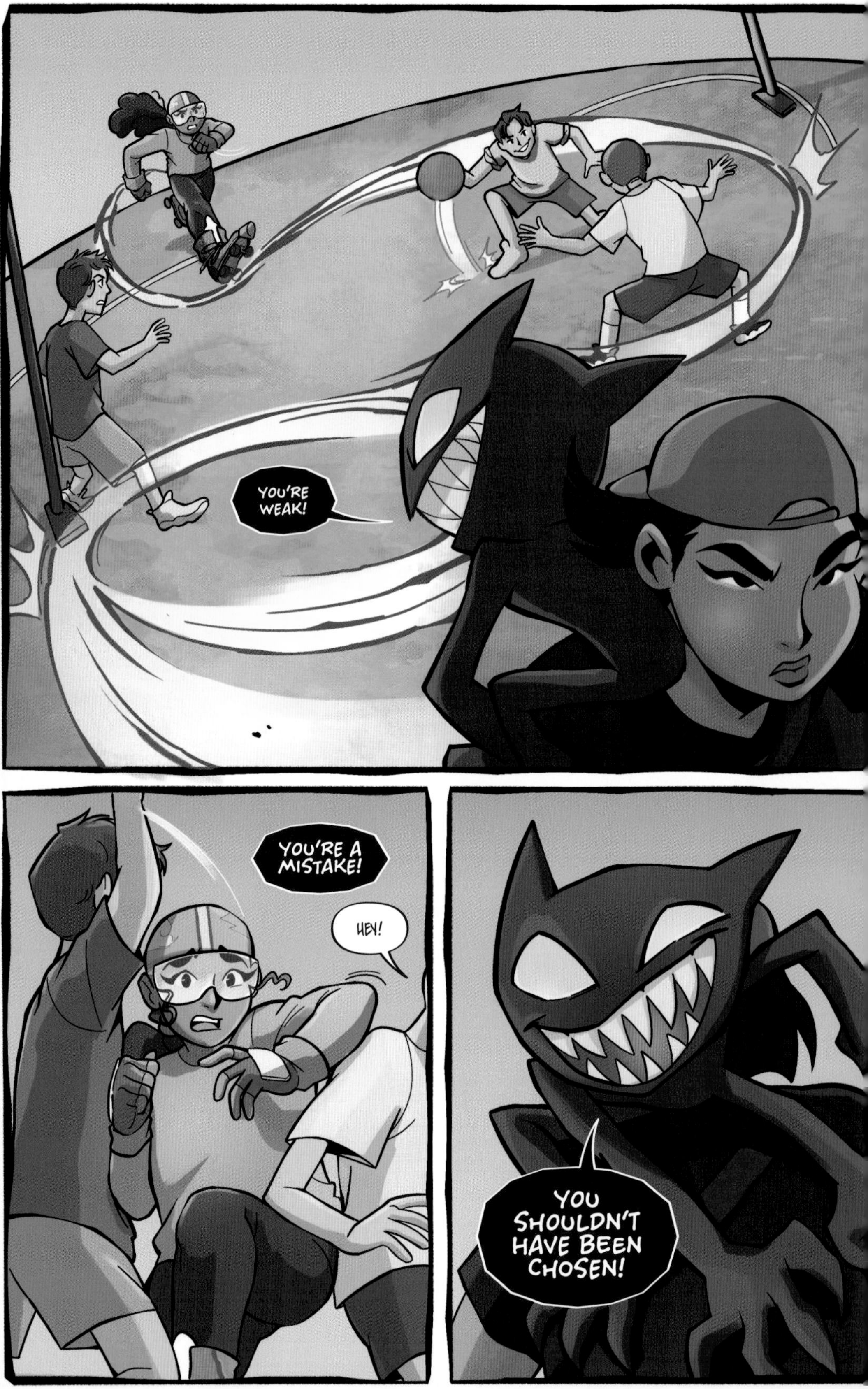
YOU'RE WEAK!
YOU'RE A MISTAKE!
HEY!
YOU SHOULDN'T HAVE BEEN CHOSEN!

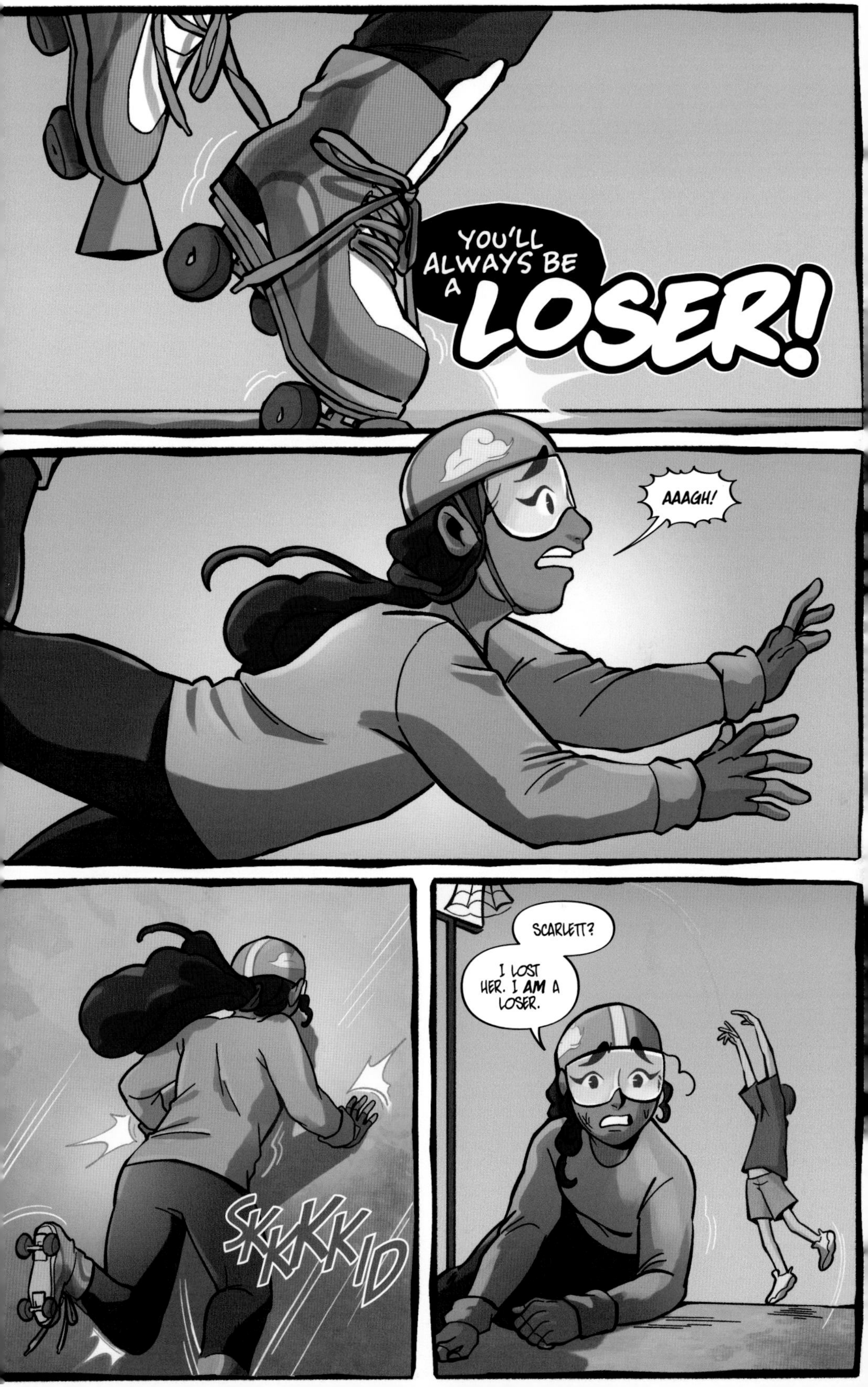
YOU'LL ALWAYS BE A LOSER!
AAAGH!
SKKKKID
SCARLETT?
I LOST HER. I AM A LOSER.

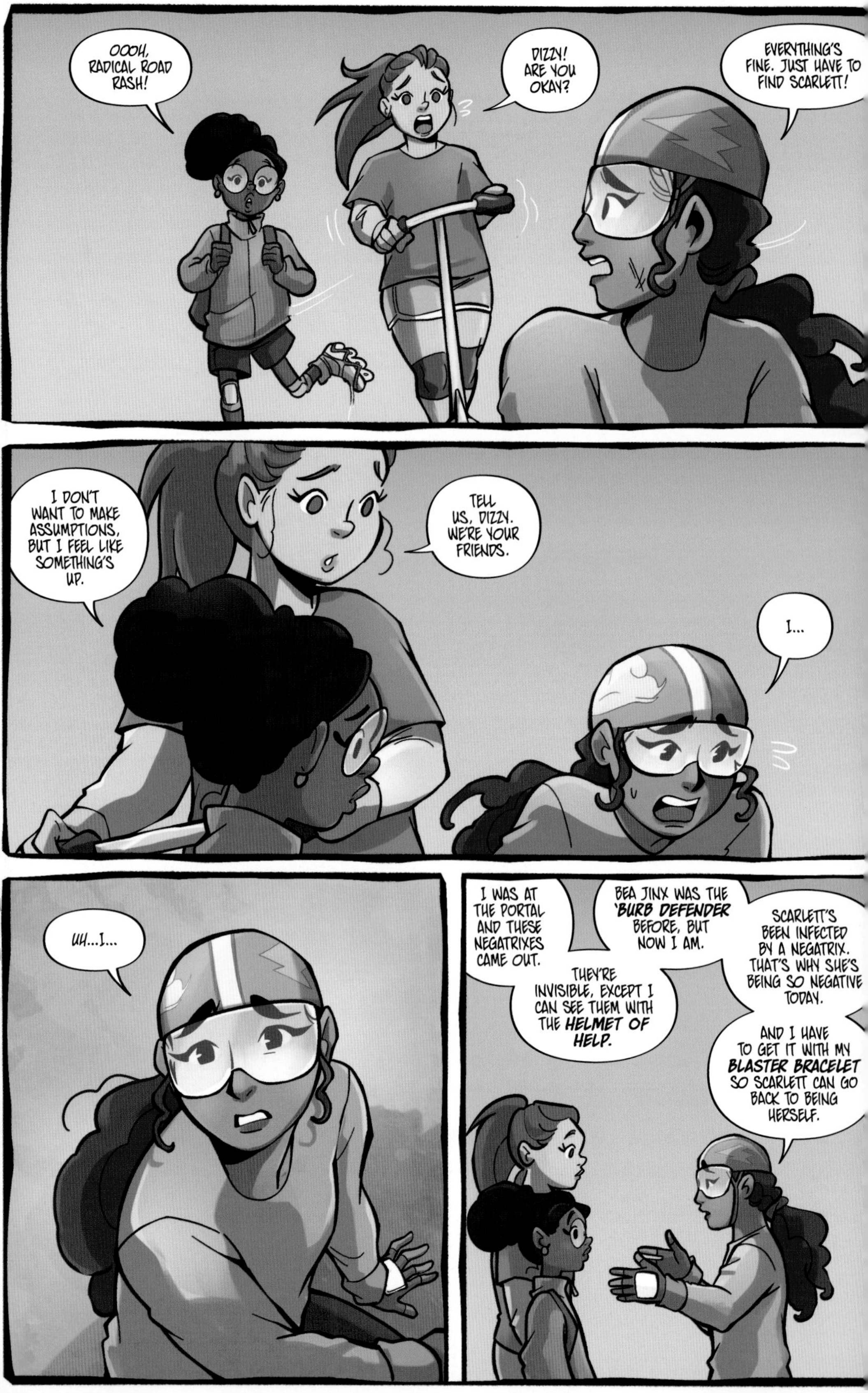
OOOH, RADICAL ROAD RASH!
DIZZY! ARE YOU OKAY?
EVERYTHING'S FINE. JUST HAVE TO FIND SCARLETT!
I DON'T WANT TO MAKE ASSUMPTIONS, BUT I FEEL LIKE SOMETHING'S UP.
TELL US, DIZZY. WE'RE YOUR FRIENDS.
I...
UH...I...
I WAS AT THE PORTAL AND THESE NEGATRIXES CAME OUT.
BEA JINX WAS THE 'BURB DEFENDER BEFORE, BUT NOW I AM.
THEY'RE INVISIBLE, EXCEPT I CAN SEE THEM WITH THE HELMET OF HELP.
SCARLETT'S BEEN INFECTED BY A NEGATRIX. THAT'S WHY SHE'S BEING SO NEGATIVE TODAY.
AND I HAVE TO GET IT WITH MY BLASTER BRACELET SO SCARLETT CAN GO BACK TO BEING HERSELF.

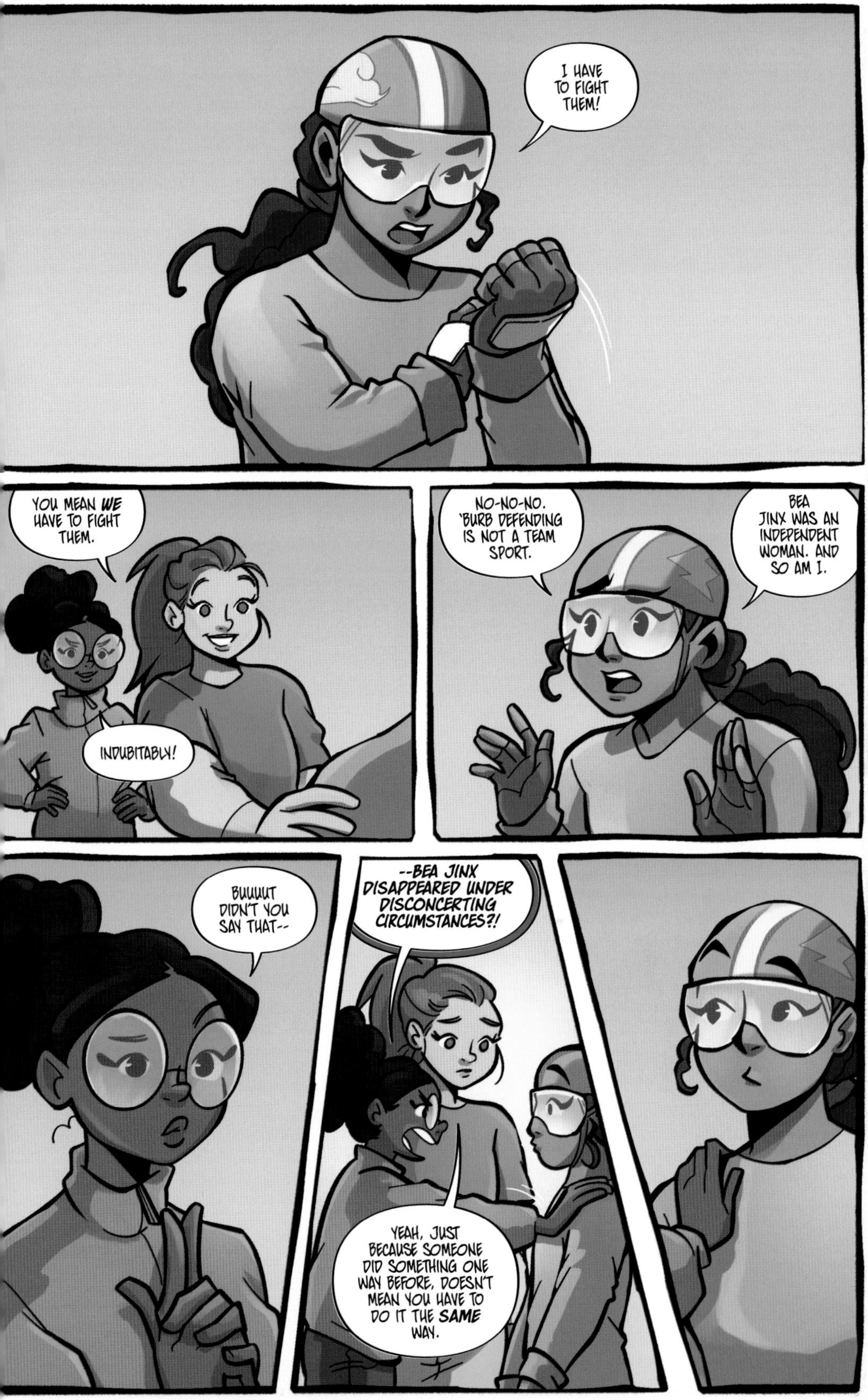
I HAVE TO FIGHT THEM!
YOU MEAN WE HAVE TO FIGHT THEM.
INDUBITABLY!
NO-NO-NO. 'BURB DEFENDING IS NOT A TEAM SPORT.
BEA JINX WAS AN INDEPENDENT WOMAN. AND SO AM I.
BUUUUT DIDN'T YOU SAY THAT--
--BEA JINX DISAPPEARED UNDER DISCONCERTING CIRCUMSTANCES?!
YEAH, JUST BECAUSE SOMEONE DID SOMETHING ONE WAY BEFORE, DOESN'T MEAN YOU HAVE TO DO IT THE SAME WAY.

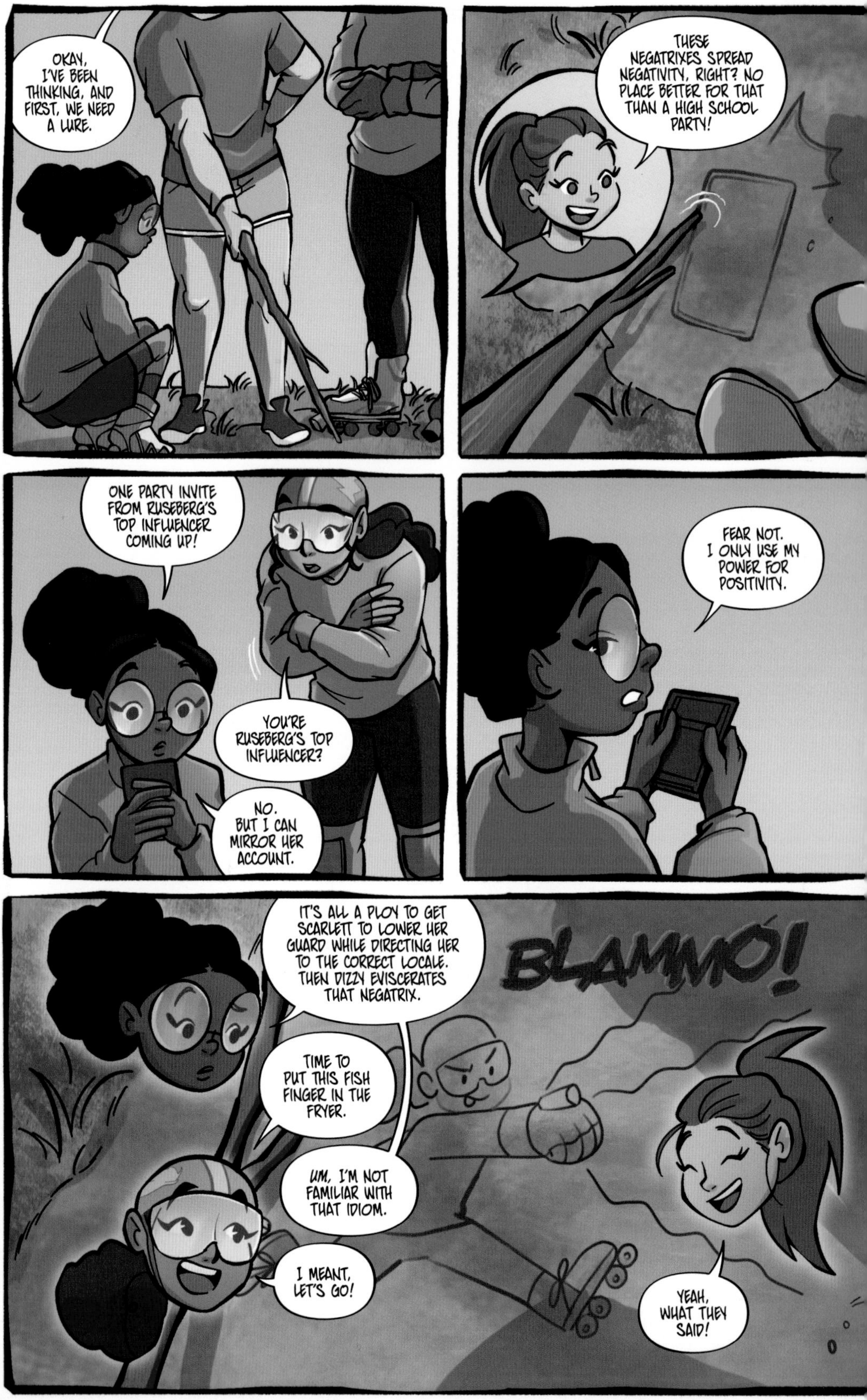
OKAY, I'VE BEEN THINKING, AND FIRST, WE NEED A LURE.
THESE NEGATRIXES SPREAD NEGATIVITY, RIGHT? NO PLACE BETTER FOR THAT THAN A HIGH SCHOOL PARTY!
ONE PARTY INVITE FROM RUSEBERG'S TOP INFLUENCER COMING UP!
YOU'RE RUSEBERG'S TOP INFLUENCER?
NO. BUT I CAN MIRROR HER ACCOUNT.
FEAR NOT. I ONLY USE MY POWER FOR POSITIVITY.
IT'S ALL A PLOY TO GET SCARLETT TO LOWER HER GUARD WHILE DIRECTING HER TO THE CORRECT LOCALE. THEN DIZZY EVISCERATES THAT NEGATRIX.
BLAMMO!
TIME TO PUT THIS FISH FINGER IN THE FRYER.
UM, I'M NOT FAMILIAR WITH THAT IDIOM.
I MEANT, LET'S GO!
YEAH, WHAT THEY SAID!

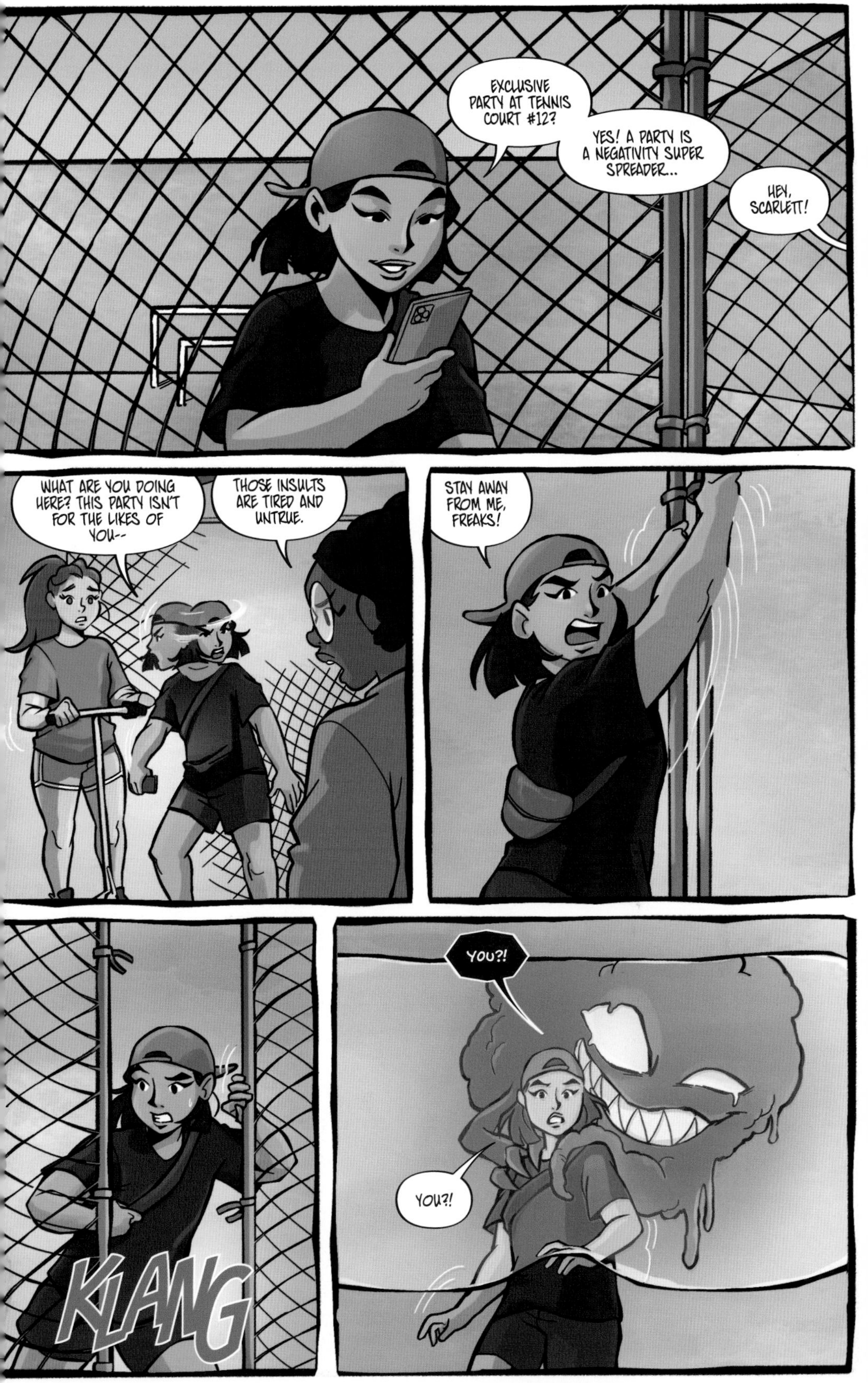
EXCLUSIVE PARTY AT TENNIS COURT #12?
YES! A PARTY IS A NEGATIVITY SUPER SPREADER...
HEY, SCARLETT!
WHAT ARE YOU DOING HERE? THIS PARTY ISN'T FOR THE LIKES OF YOU--
THOSE INSULTS ARE TIRED AND UNTRUE.
STAY AWAY FROM ME, FREAKS!
KLANG
YOU?!
YOU?!

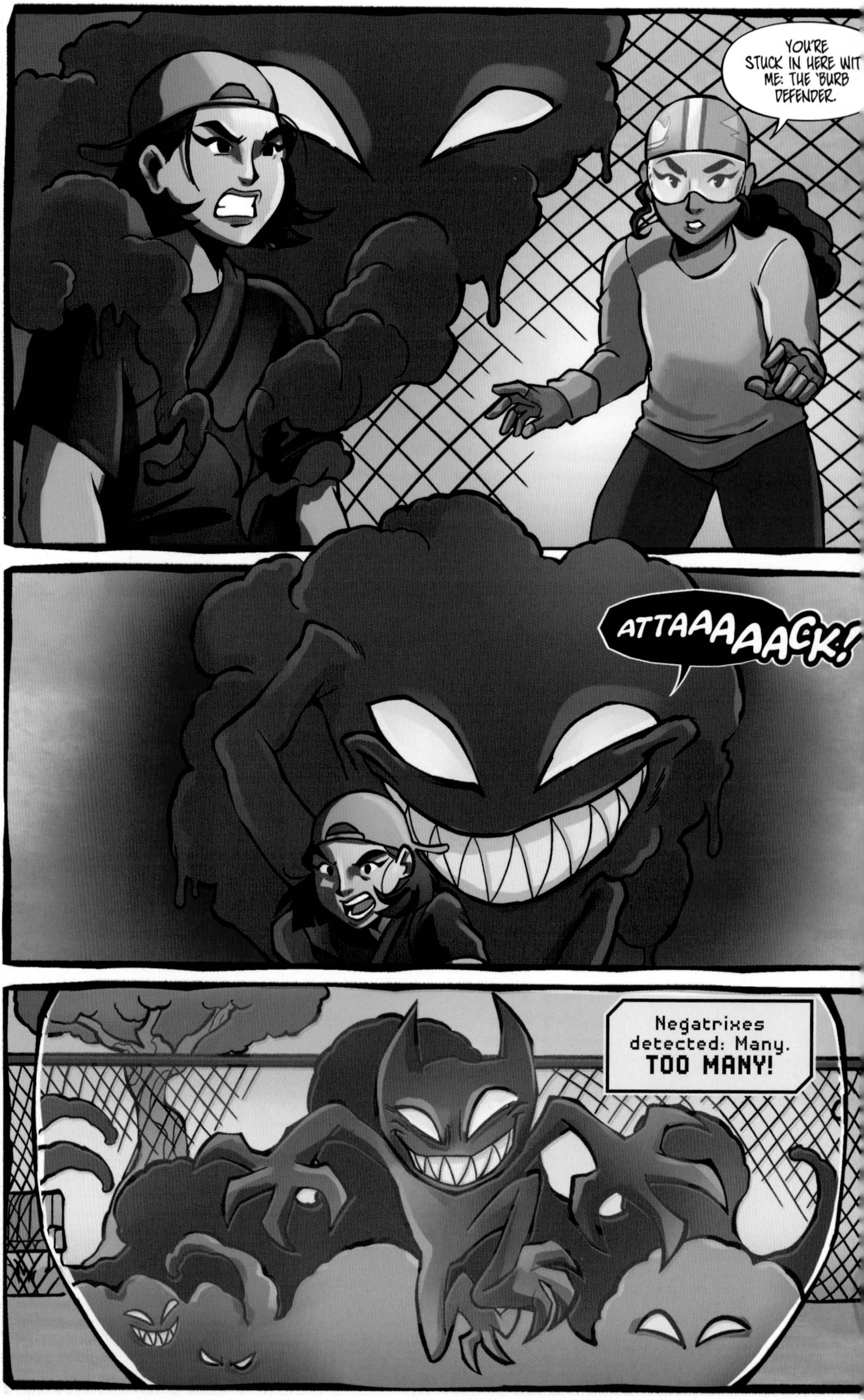
YOU'RE STUCK IN HERE WIT ME: THE 'BURB DEFENDER.
ATTAAAAAACK!
Negatrixes detected: Many. TOO MANY!

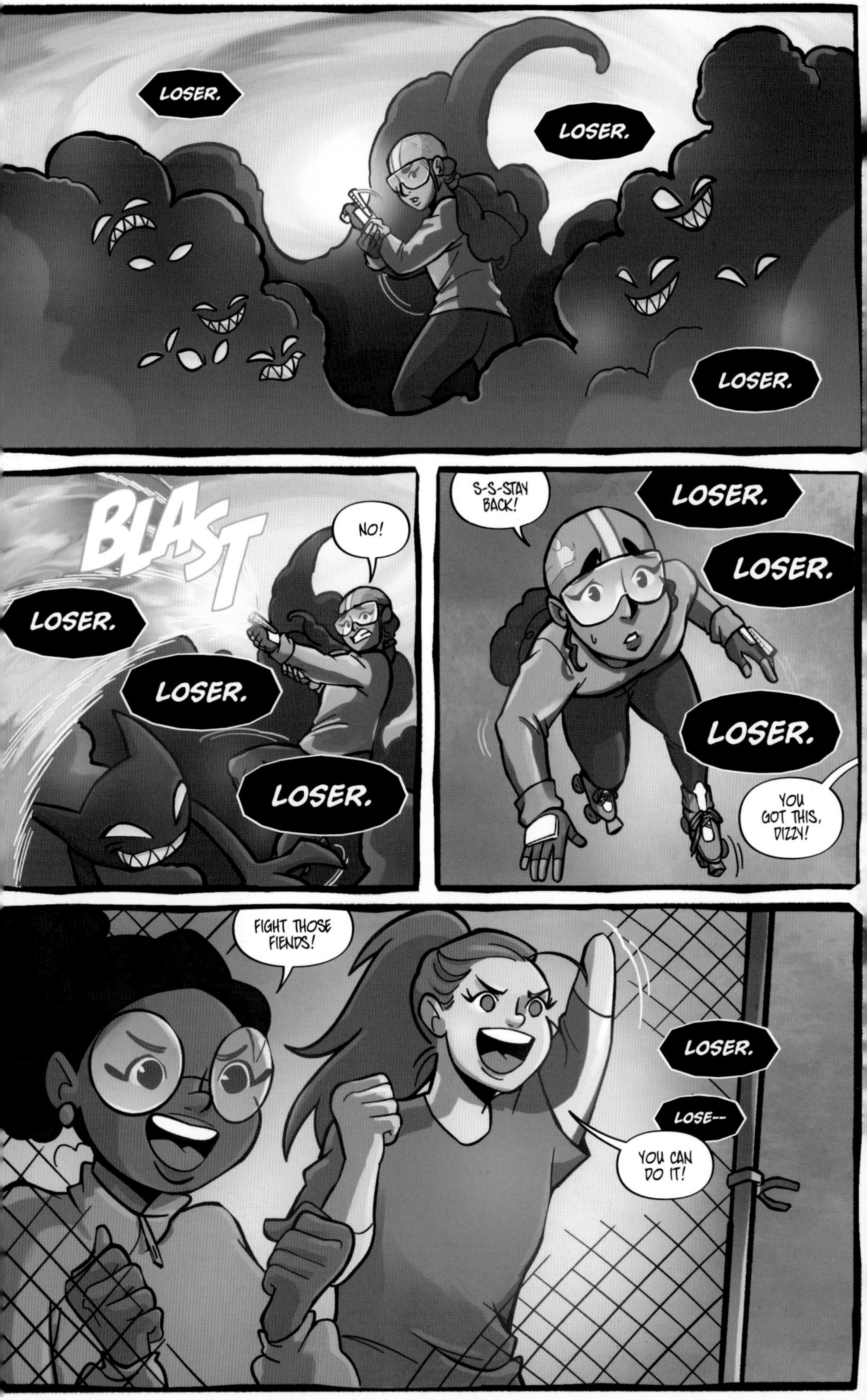
LOSER.
LOSER.
LOSER.
BLAST
NO!
LOSER.
LOSER.
LOSER.
S-S-STAY BACK!
LOSER.
LOSER.
LOSER.
YOU GOT THIS, DIZZY!
FIGHT THOSE FIENDS!
LOSER.
LOSE--
YOU CAN DO IT!

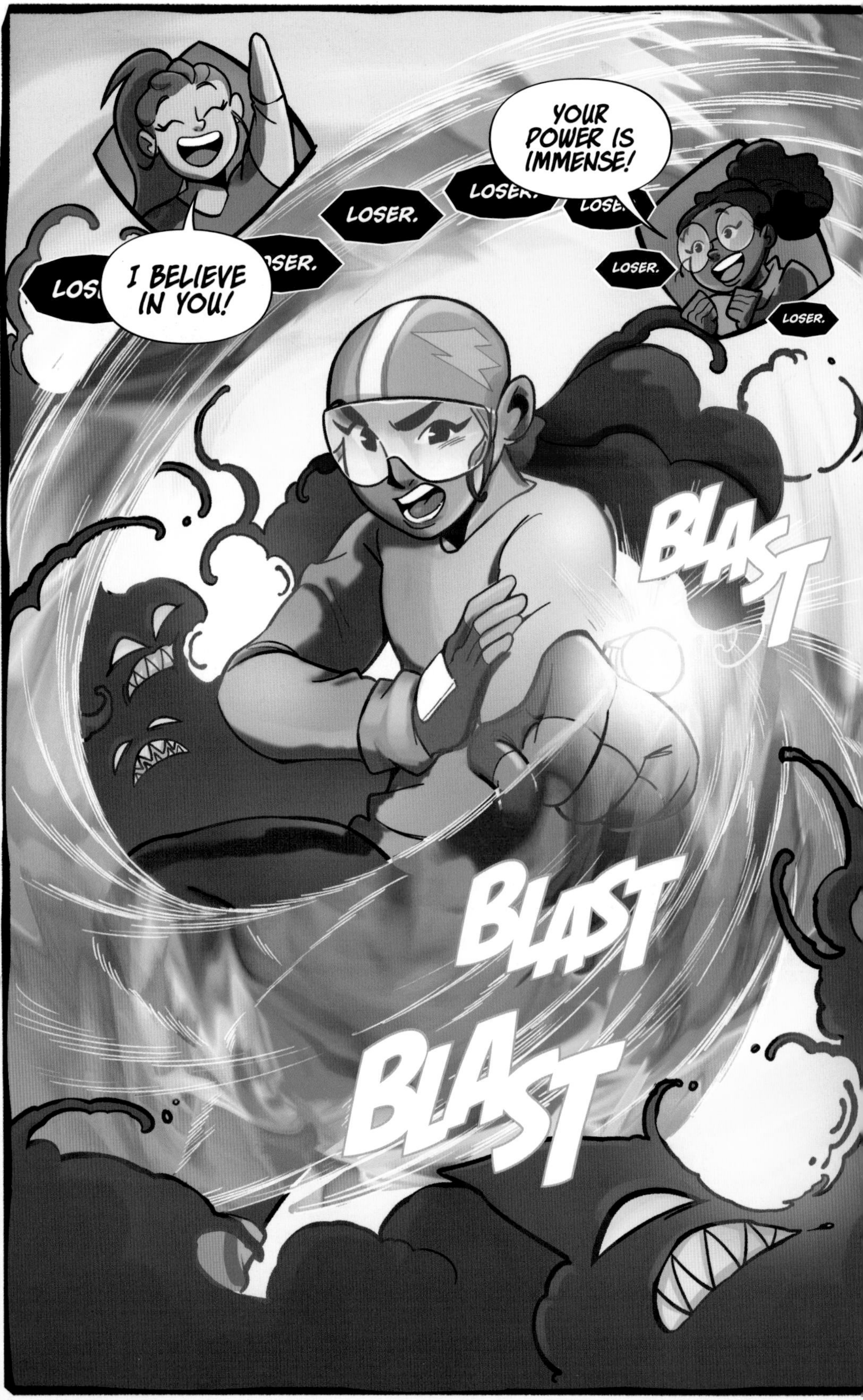

I BELIEVE IN YOU!
YOUR POWER IS IMMENSE!
LOSER.
LOSER.
LOSER.
LOSER.
BLAST
BLAST
BLAST

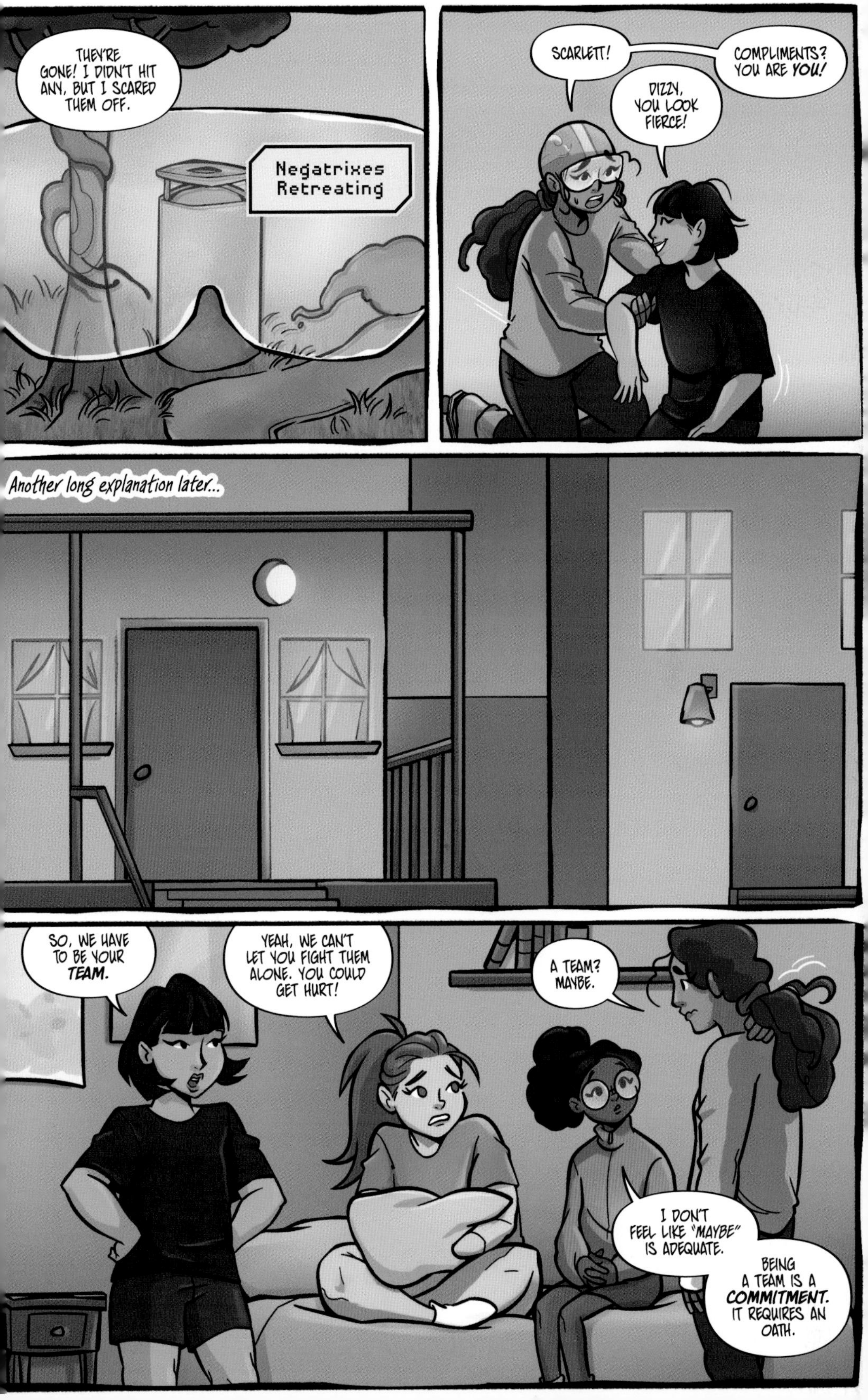
THEY'RE GONE! I DIDN'T HIT ANY, BUT I SCARED THEM OFF.
Negatrixes Retreating
SCARLETT!
COMPLIMENTS? YOU ARE YOU!
DIZZY, YOU LOOK FIERCE!
Another long explanation later...
SO, WE HAVE TO BE YOUR TEAM.
YEAH, WE CAN'T LET YOU FIGHT THEM ALONE. YOU COULD GET HURT!
A TEAM? MAYBE.
I DON'T FEEL LIKE "MAYBE" IS ADEQUATE.
BEING A TEAM IS A COMMITMENT. IT REQUIRES AN OATH.

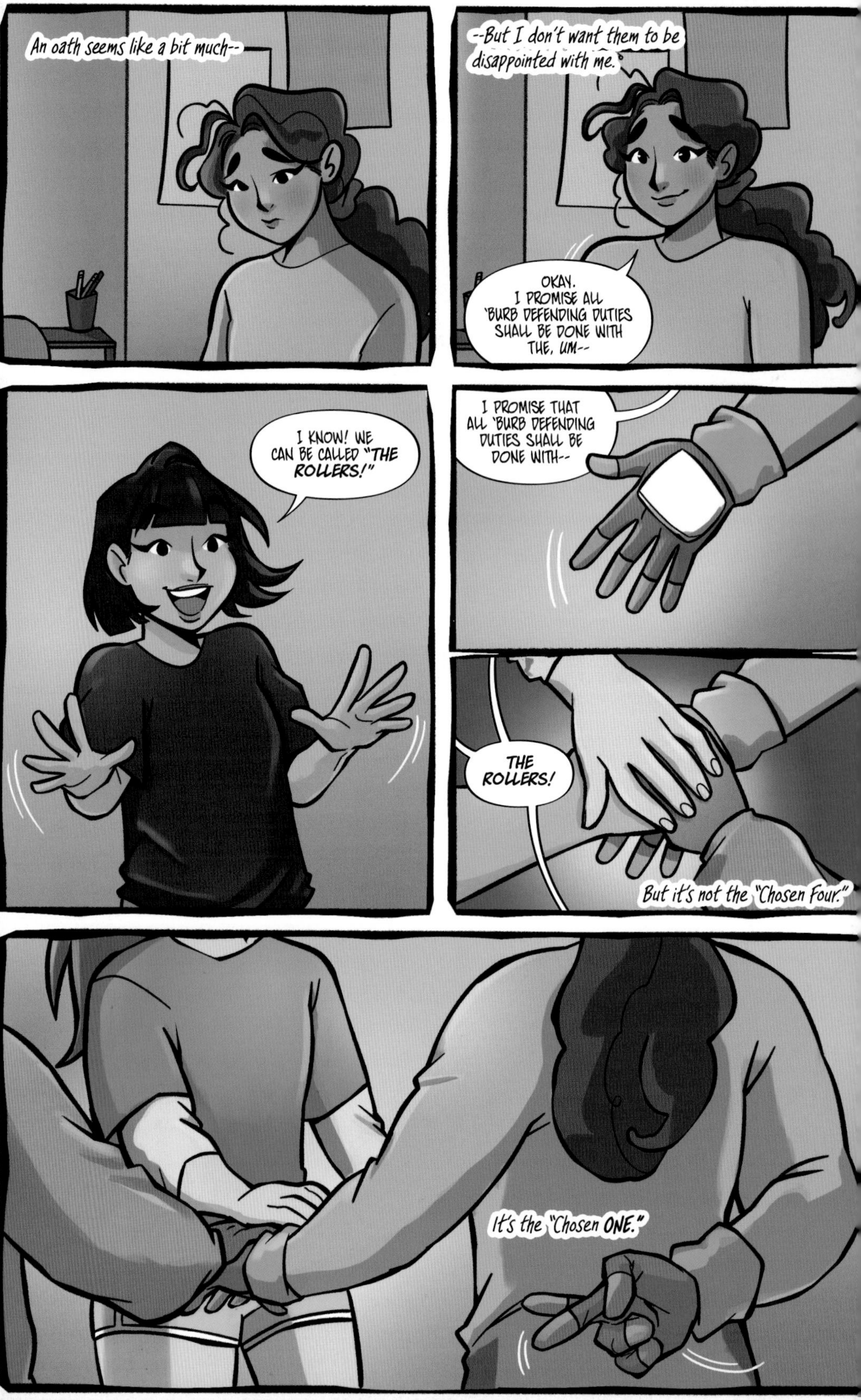
An oath seems like a bit much--
--But I don't want them to be disappointed with me.
OKAY. I PROMISE ALL 'BURB DEFENDING DUTIES SHALL BE DONE WITH THE, UM--
I KNOW! WE CAN BE CALLED "THE ROLLERS!"
I PROMISE THAT ALL 'BURB DEFENDING DUTIES SHALL BE DONE WITH--
THE ROLLERS!
But it's not the "Chosen Four."
It's the "Chosen ONE."

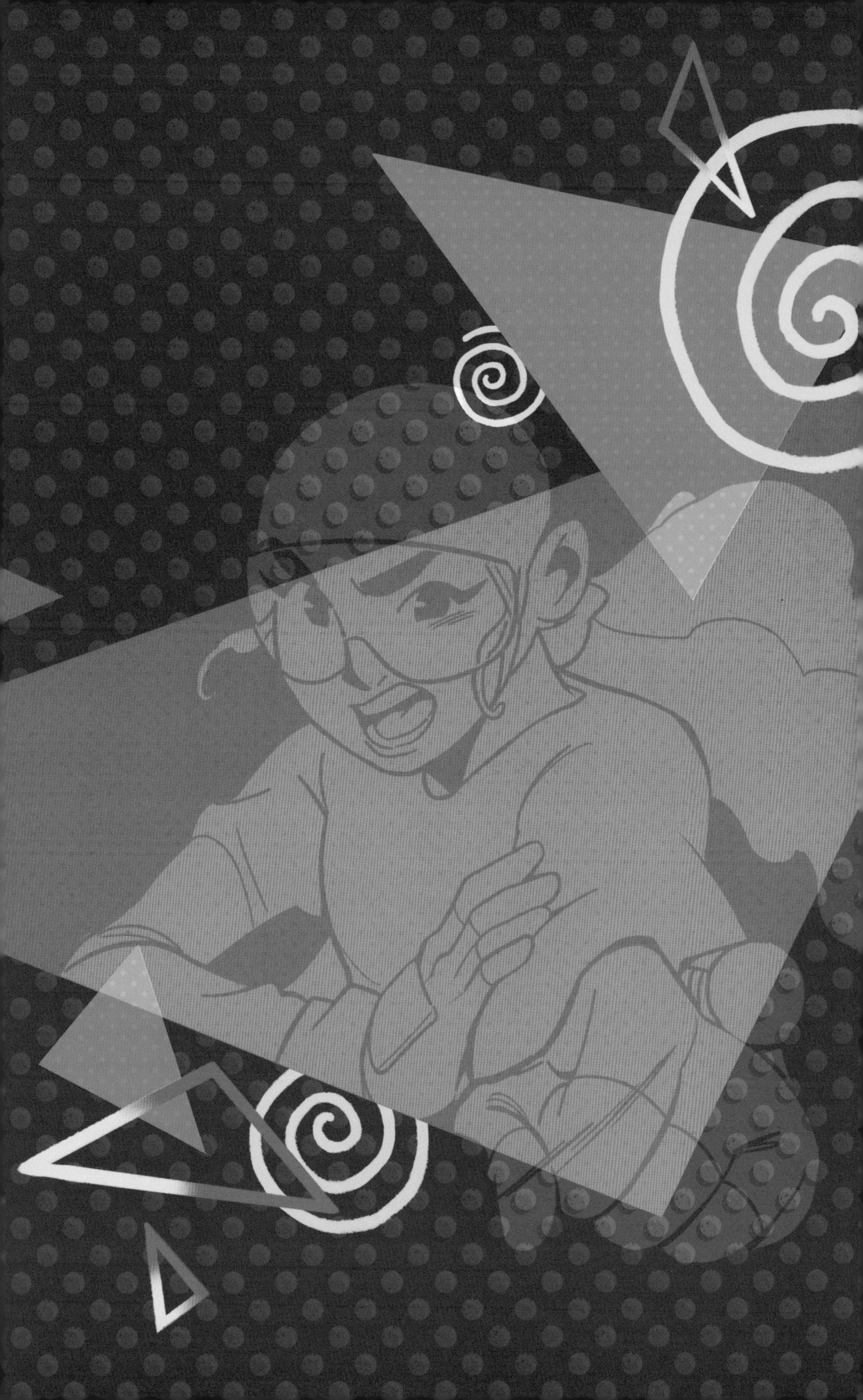

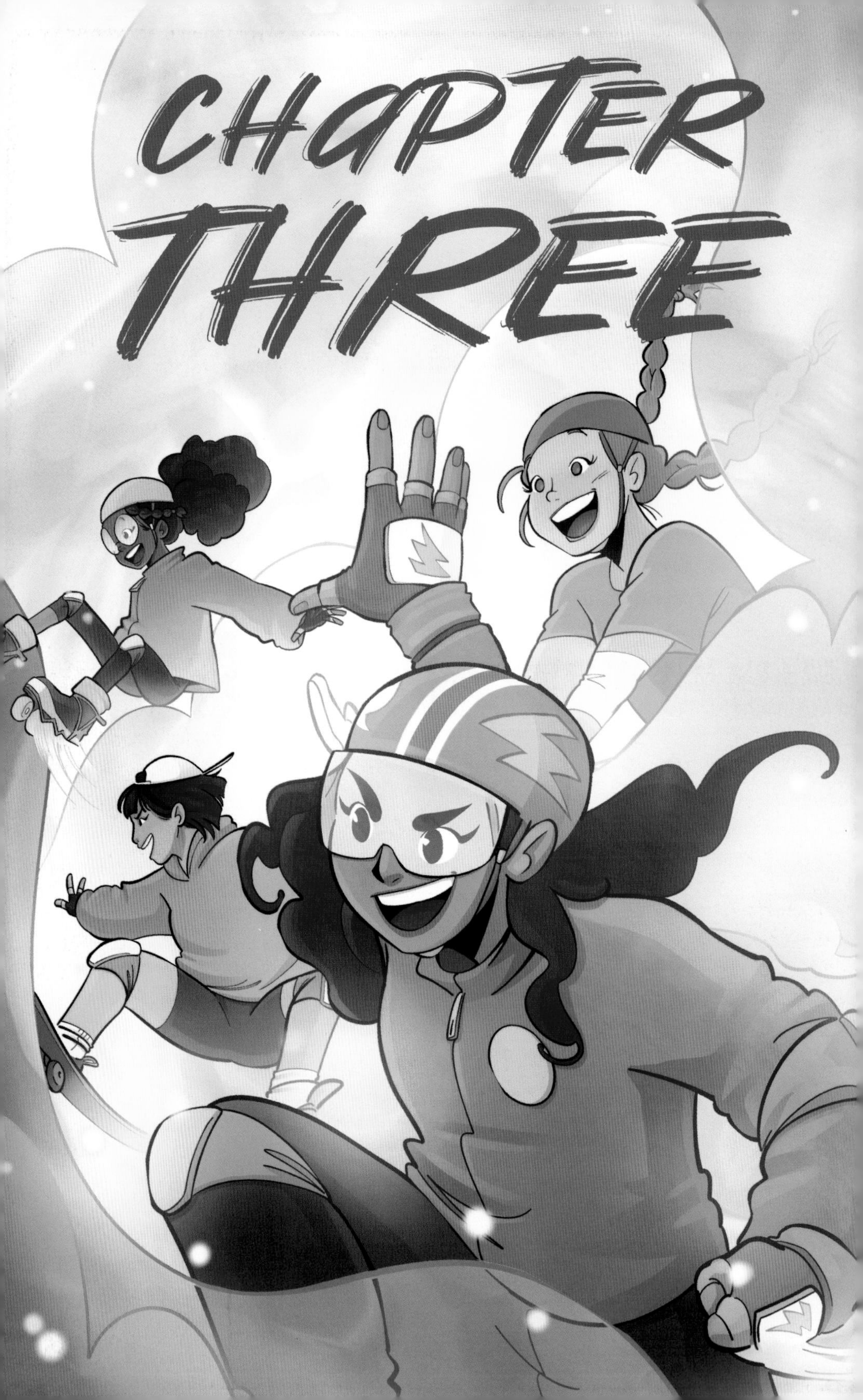
CHAPTER
THREE

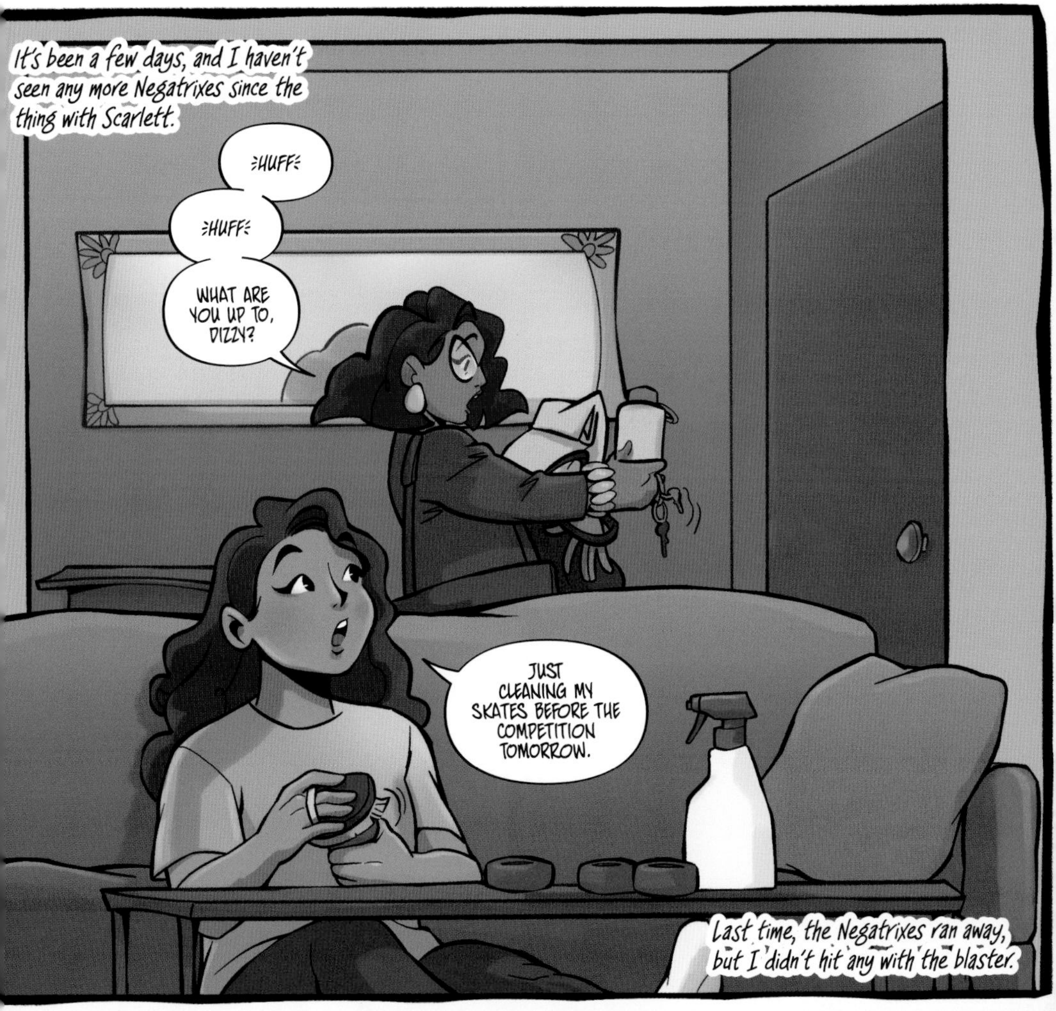
It's been a few days, and I haven't seen any more Negatrixes since the thing with Scarlett.
HUFF
HUFF
WHAT ARE YOU UP TO, DIZZY?
JUST CLEANING MY SKATES BEFORE THE COMPETITION TOMORROW.
Last time, the Negatrixes ran away, but I didn't hit any with the blaster.

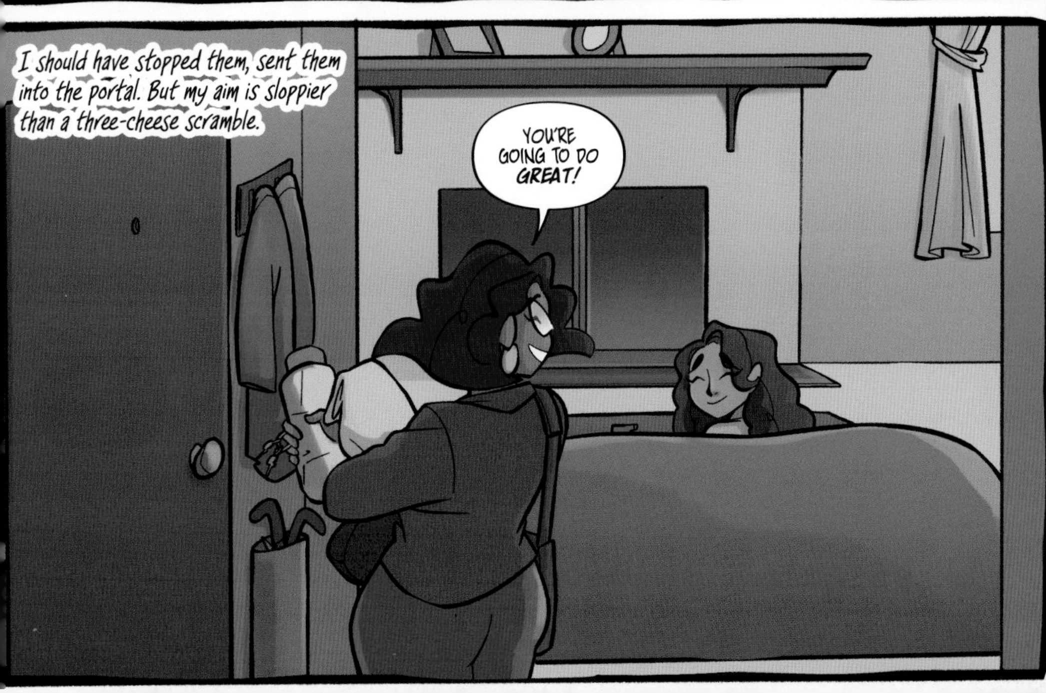
I should have stopped them, sent them into the portal. But my aim is sloppier than a three-cheese scramble.
YOU'RE GOING TO DO GREAT!

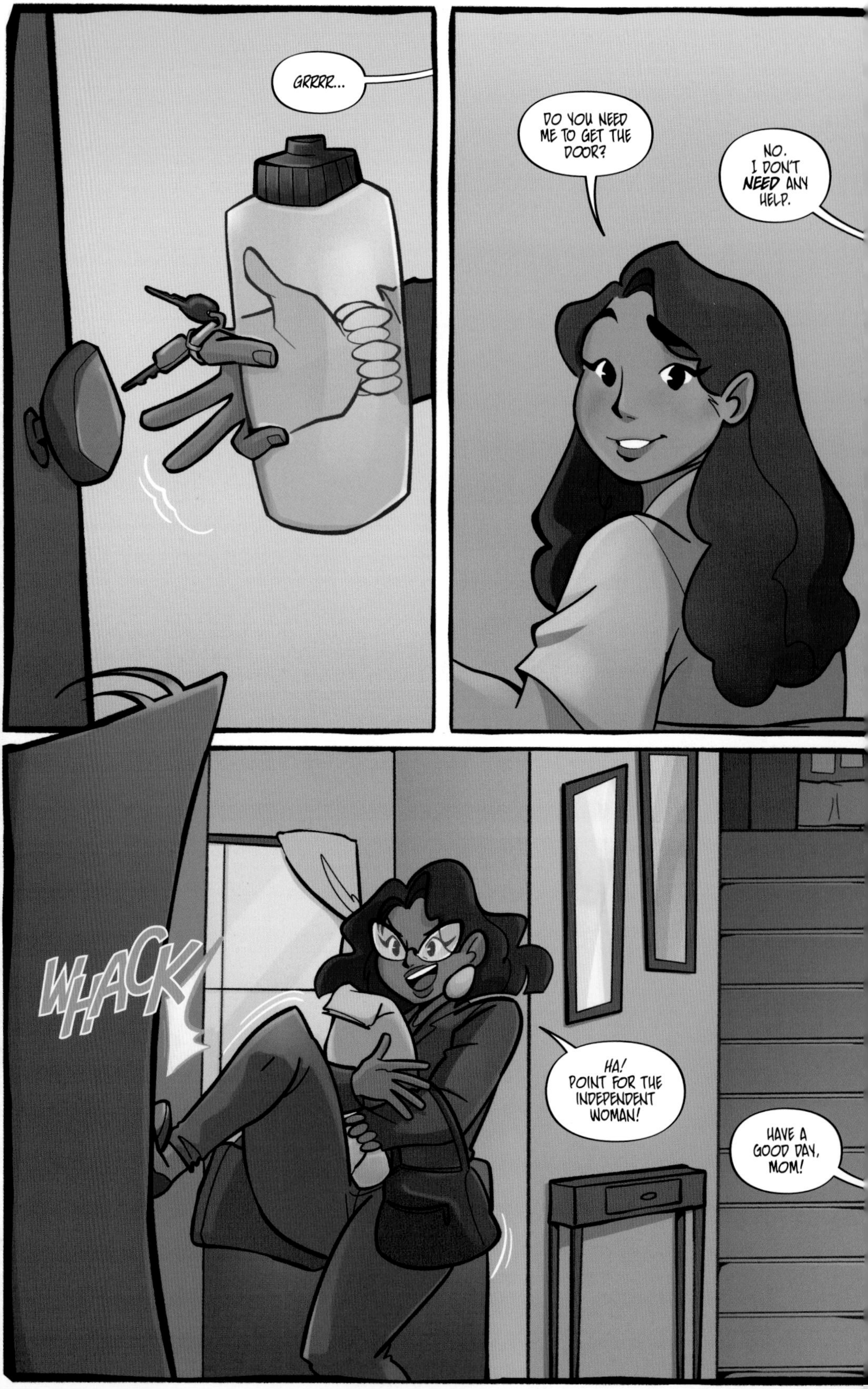
GRRRR...
DO YOU NEED ME TO GET THE DOOR?
NO. I DON'T **NEED** ANY HELP.
WHACK
HA! POINT FOR THE INDEPENDENT WOMAN!
HAVE A GOOD DAY, MOM!

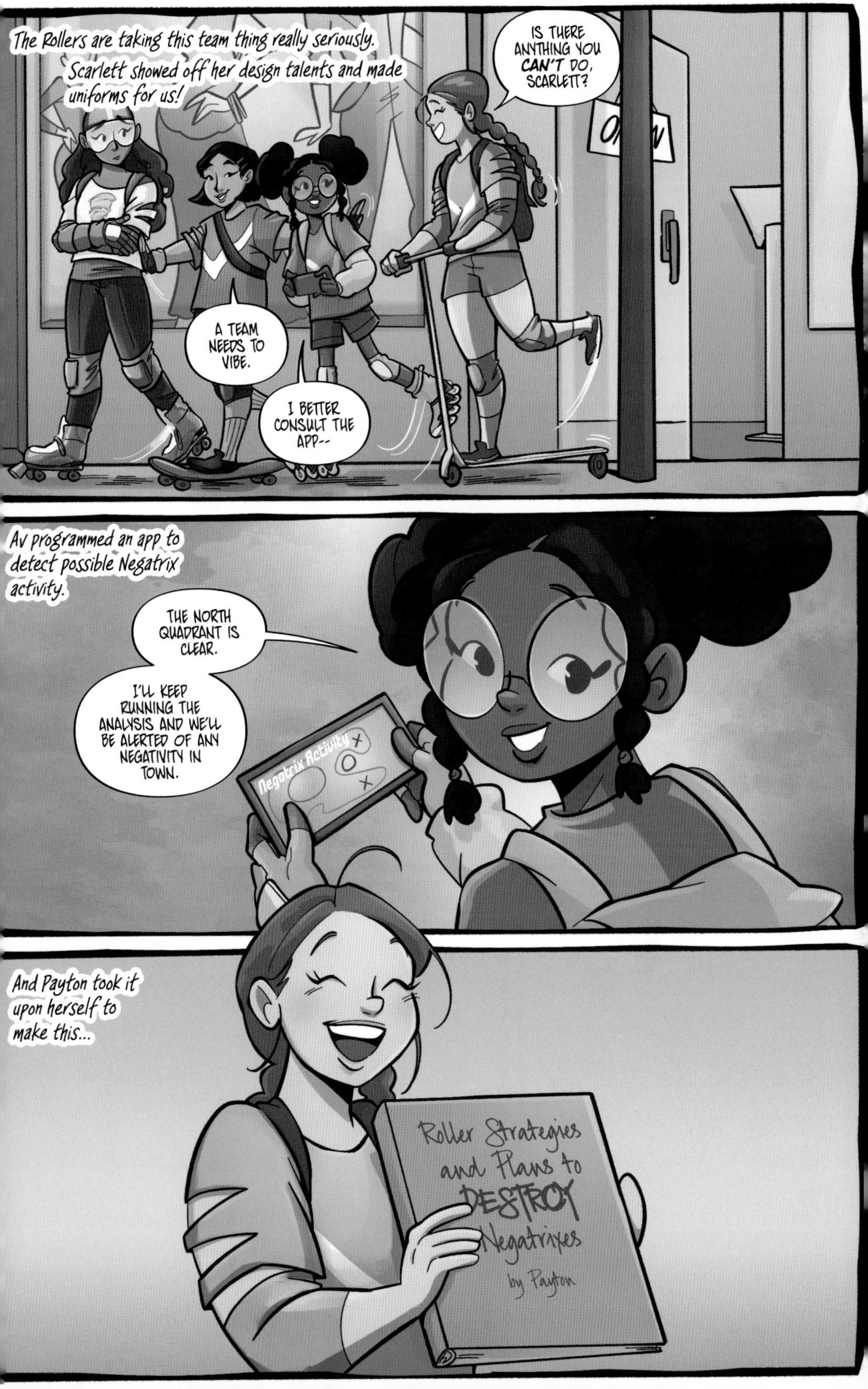
The Rollers are taking this team thing really seriously.
Scarlett showed off her design talents and made uniforms for us!
IS THERE ANYTHING YOU CAN'T DO, SCARLETT?
OPEN
A TEAM NEEDS TO VIBE.
I BETTER CONSULT THE APP--
Av programmed an app to detect possible Negatrix activity.
THE NORTH QUADRANT IS CLEAR.
I'LL KEEP RUNNING THE ANALYSIS AND WE'LL BE ALERTED OF ANY NEGATIVITY IN TOWN.
Negatrix Activity
And Payton took it upon herself to make this...
Roller Strategies and Plans to DESTROY Negatrixes
by Payton

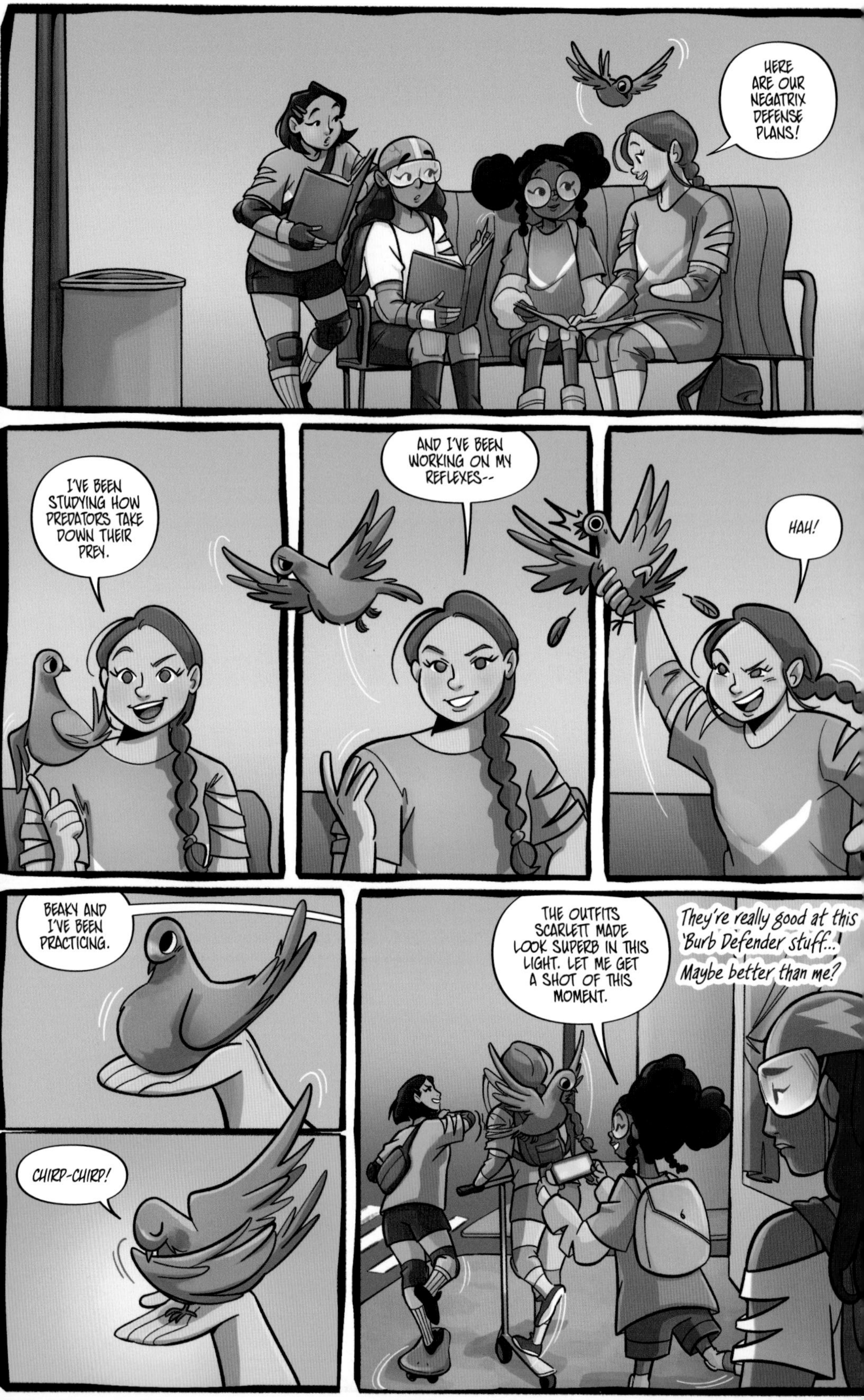
HERE ARE OUR NEGATRIX DEFENSE PLANS!
I'VE BEEN STUDYING HOW PREDATORS TAKE DOWN THEIR PREY.
AND I'VE BEEN WORKING ON MY REFLEXES--
HAH!
BEAKY AND I'VE BEEN PRACTICING.
CHIRP-CHIRP!
THE OUTFITS SCARLETT MADE LOOK SUPERB IN THIS LIGHT. LET ME GET A SHOT OF THIS MOMENT.
They're really good at this 'Burb Defender stuff...
Maybe better than me?

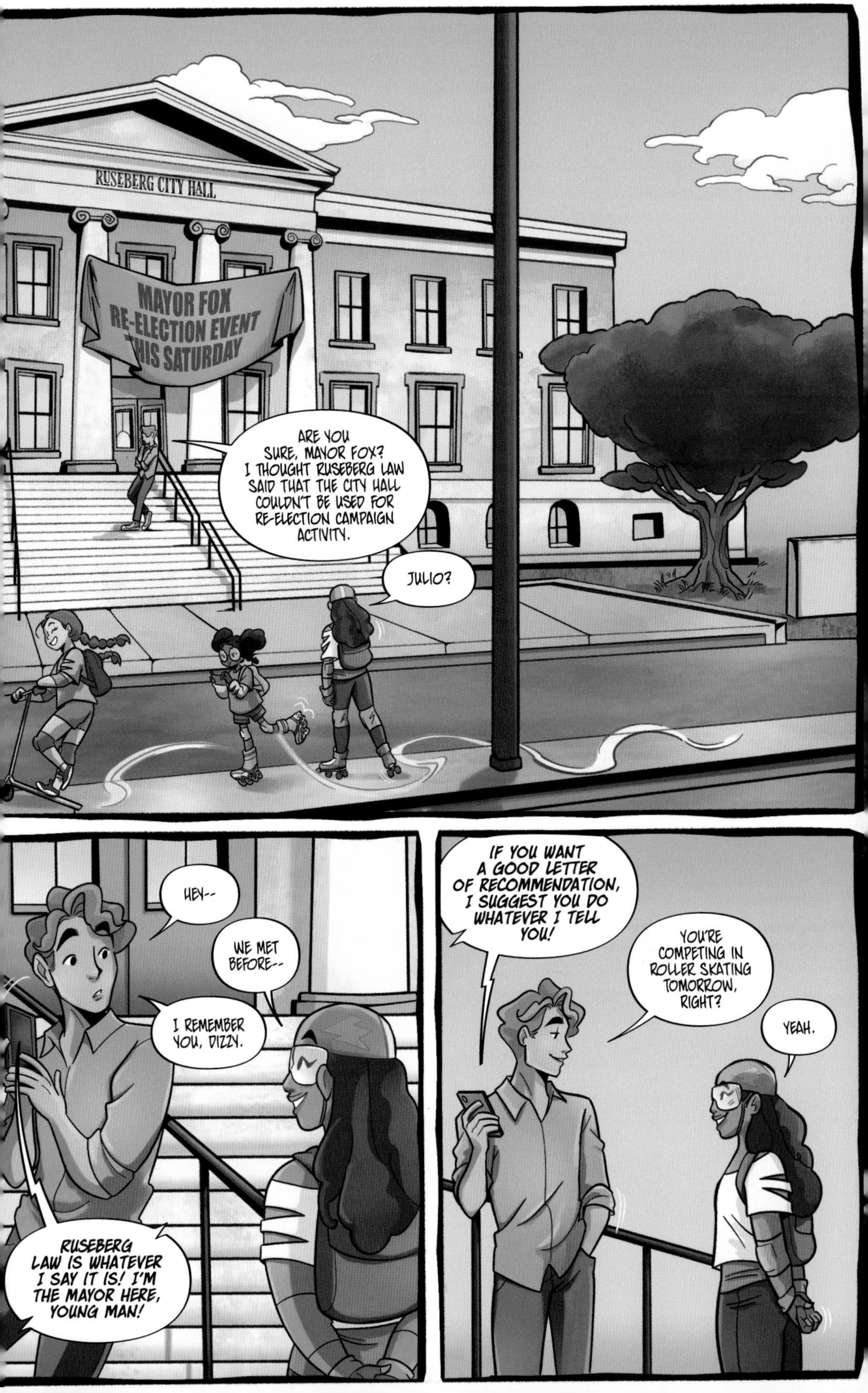
RUSEBERG CITY HALL
MAYOR FOX RE-ELECTION EVENT THIS SATURDAY
ARE YOU SURE, MAYOR FOX? I THOUGHT RUSEBERG LAW SAID THAT THE CITY HALL COULDN'T BE USED FOR RE-ELECTION CAMPAIGN ACTIVITY.
JULIO?
HEY--
WE MET BEFORE--
I REMEMBER YOU, DIZZY.
RUSEBERG LAW IS WHATEVER I SAY IT IS! I'M THE MAYOR HERE, YOUNG MAN!
IF YOU WANT A GOOD LETTER OF RECOMMENDATION, I SUGGEST YOU DO WHATEVER I TELL YOU!
YOU'RE COMPETING IN ROLLER SKATING TOMORROW, RIGHT?
YEAH.

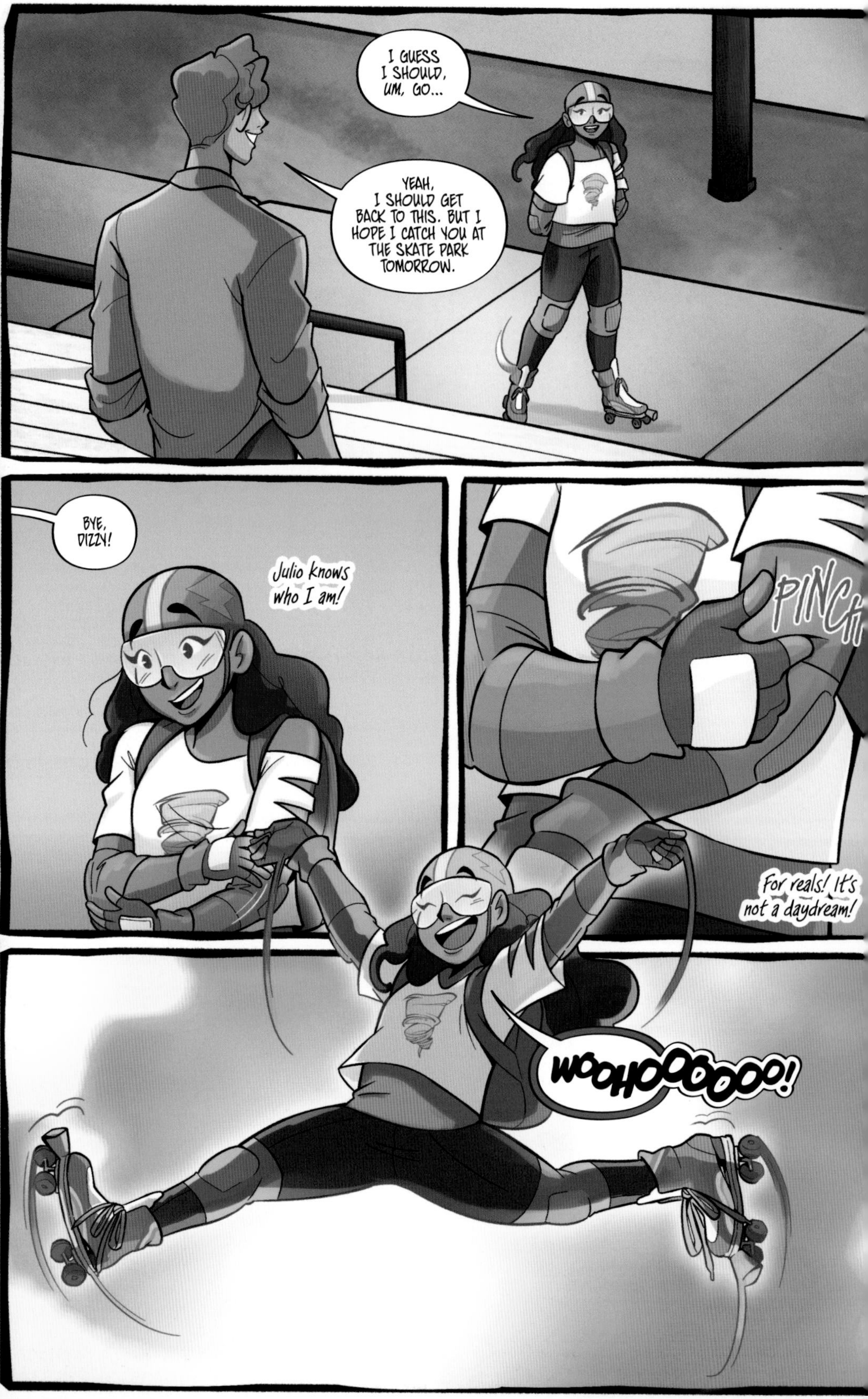
I GUESS I SHOULD, UM, GO...
YEAH, I SHOULD GET BACK TO THIS. BUT I HOPE I CATCH YOU AT THE SKATE PARK TOMORROW.
BYE, DIZZY!
Julio knows who I am!
PINCH
For reals! It's not a daydream!
WOOHOOOOOOO!

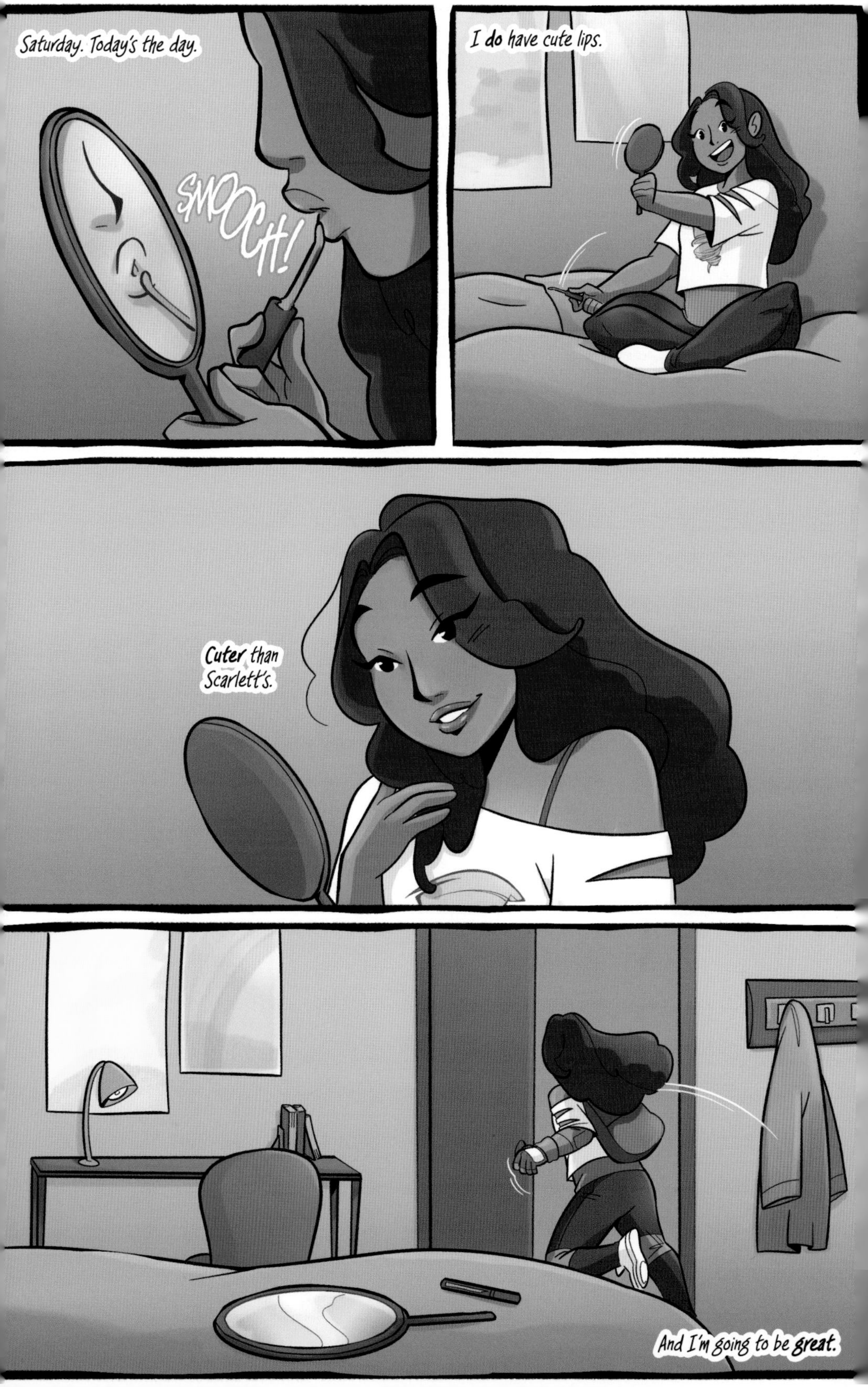
Saturday. Today's the day.
SMOOCH!
I do have cute lips.
Cuter than Scarlett's.
And I'm going to be great.

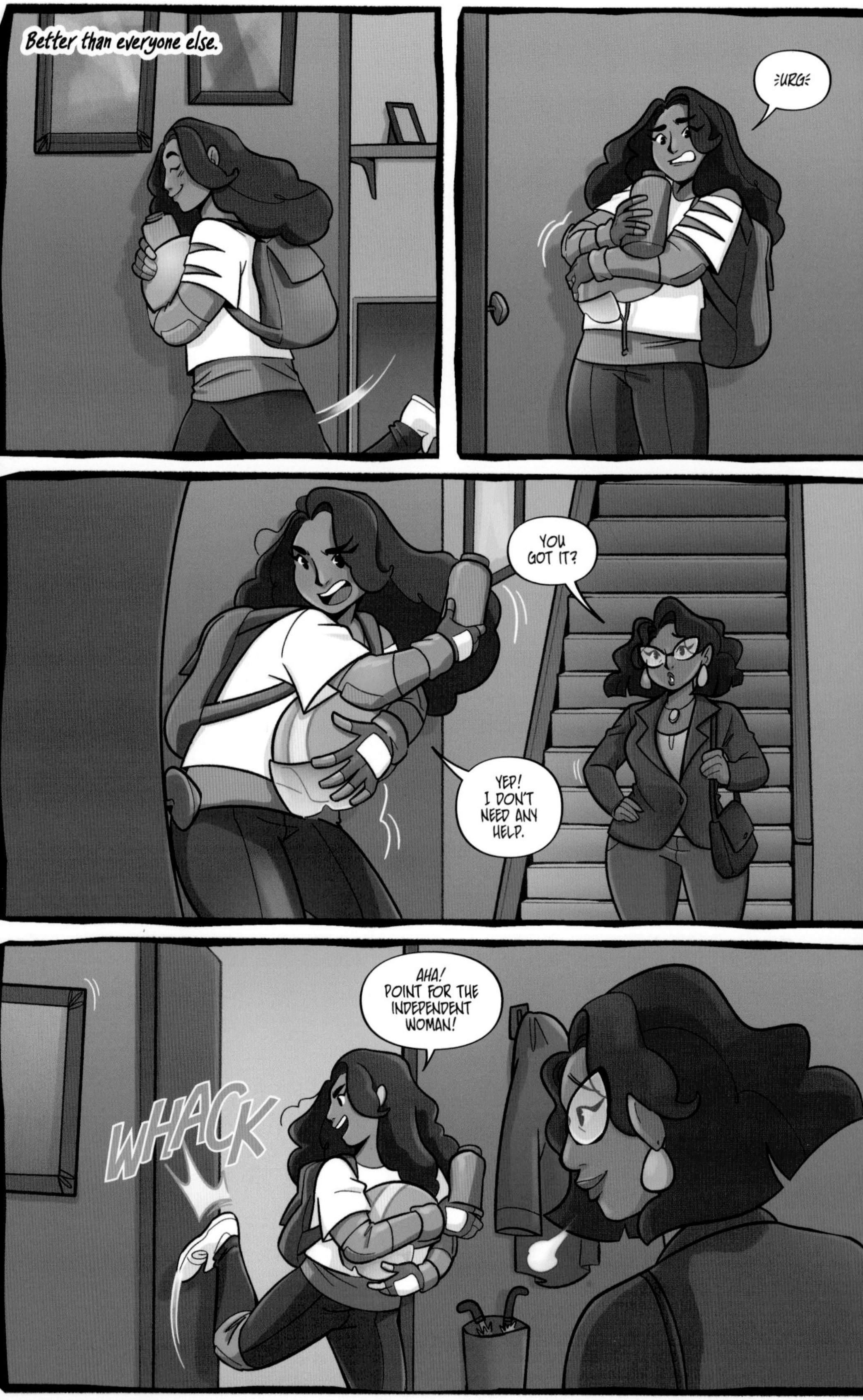
Better than everyone else.
URG
YOU GOT IT?
YEP! I DON'T NEED ANY HELP.
AHA! POINT FOR THE INDEPENDENT WOMAN!
WHACK

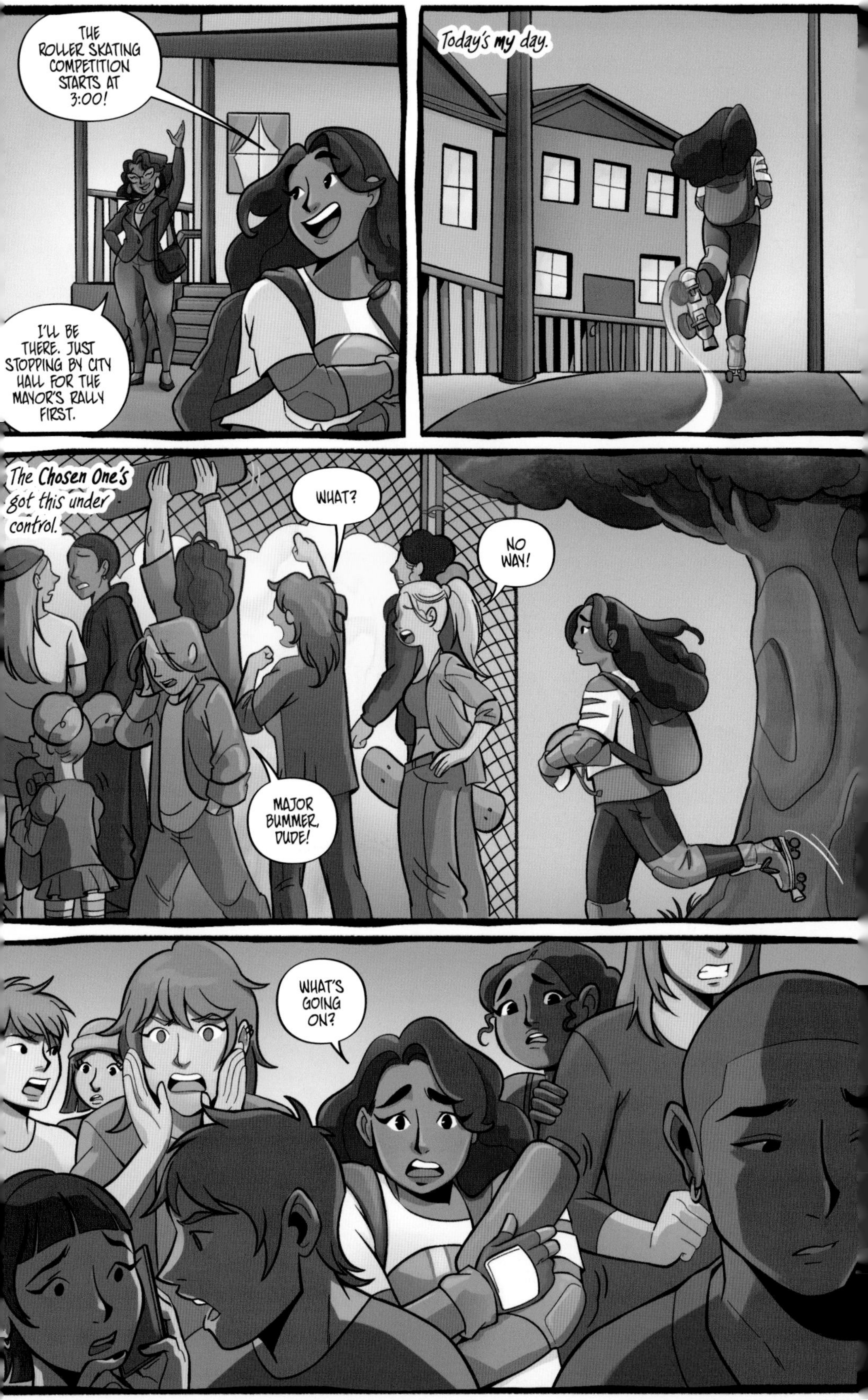

THE ROLLER SKATING COMPETITION STARTS AT 3:00!
I'LL BE THERE. JUST STOPPING BY CITY HALL FOR THE MAYOR'S RALLY FIRST.
Today's my day.
The Chosen One's got this under control.
WHAT?
NO WAY!
MAJOR BUMMER, DUDE!
WHAT'S GOING ON?

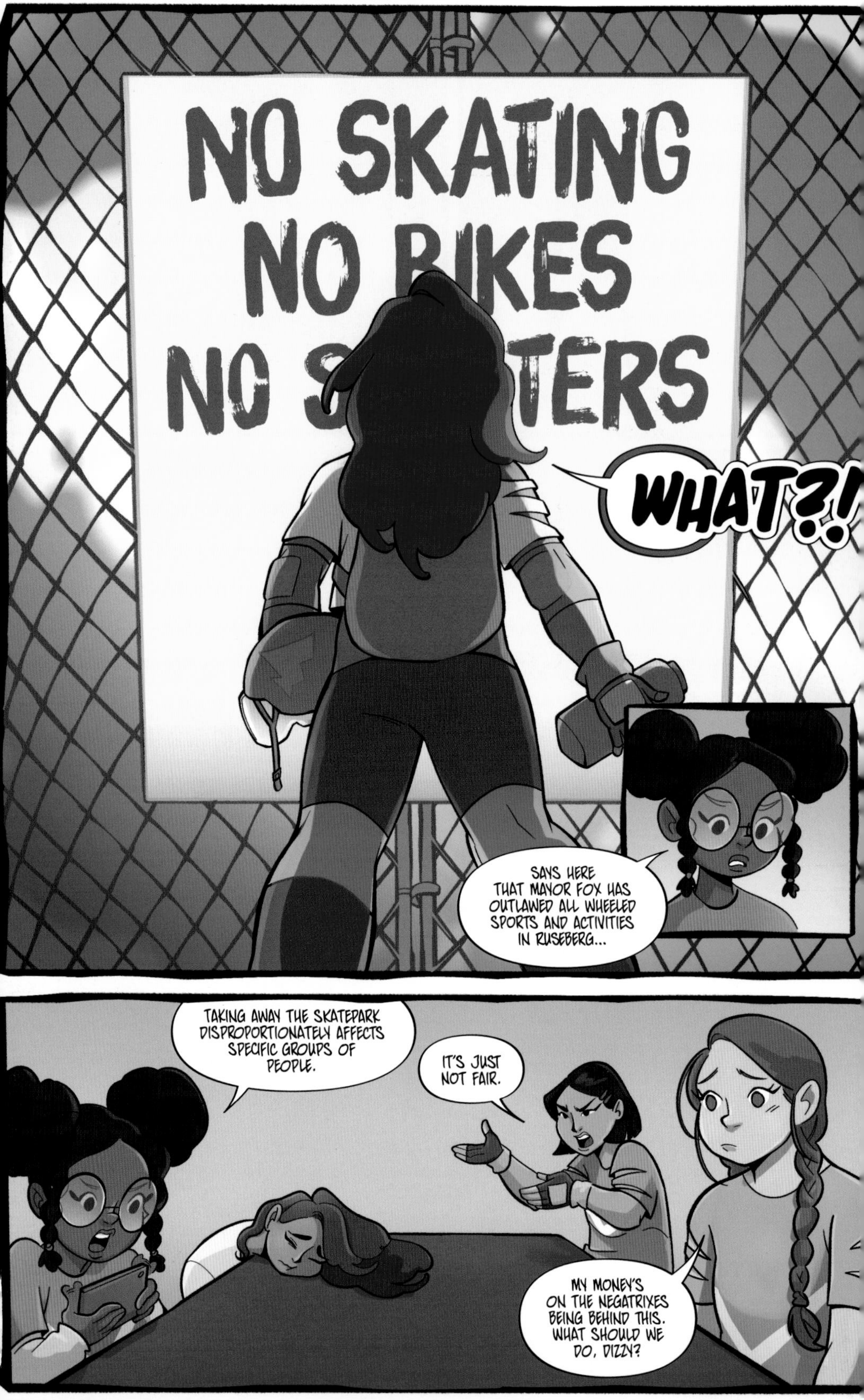
NO SKATING
NO BIKES
NO S TERS
WHAT?!
SAYS HERE THAT MAYOR FOX HAS OUTLAWED ALL WHEELED SPORTS AND ACTIVITIES IN RUSEBERG...
TAKING AWAY THE SKATEPARK DISPROPORTIONATELY AFFECTS SPECIFIC GROUPS OF PEOPLE.
IT'S JUST NOT FAIR.
MY MONEY'S ON THE NEGATRIXES BEING BEHIND THIS. WHAT SHOULD WE DO, DIZZY?

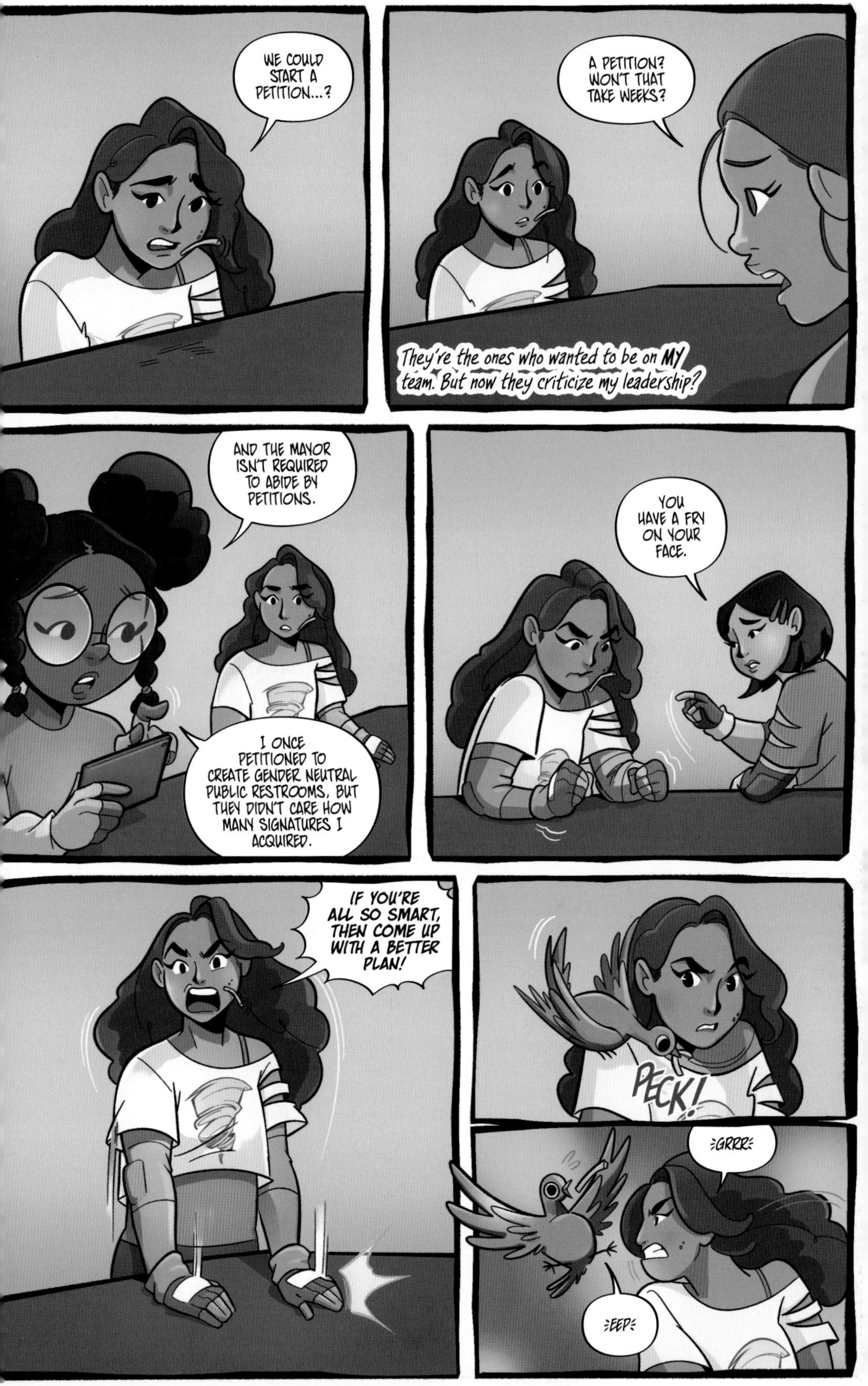
WE COULD START A PETITION...?
A PETITION? WON'T THAT TAKE WEEKS?
They're the ones who wanted to be on MY team. But now they criticize my leadership?
AND THE MAYOR ISN'T REQUIRED TO ABIDE BY PETITIONS.
I ONCE PETITIONED TO CREATE GENDER NEUTRAL PUBLIC RESTROOMS, BUT THEY DIDN'T CARE HOW MANY SIGNATURES I ACQUIRED.
YOU HAVE A FRY ON YOUR FACE.
IF YOU'RE ALL SO SMART, THEN COME UP WITH A BETTER PLAN!
PECK!
GRRR
EEP

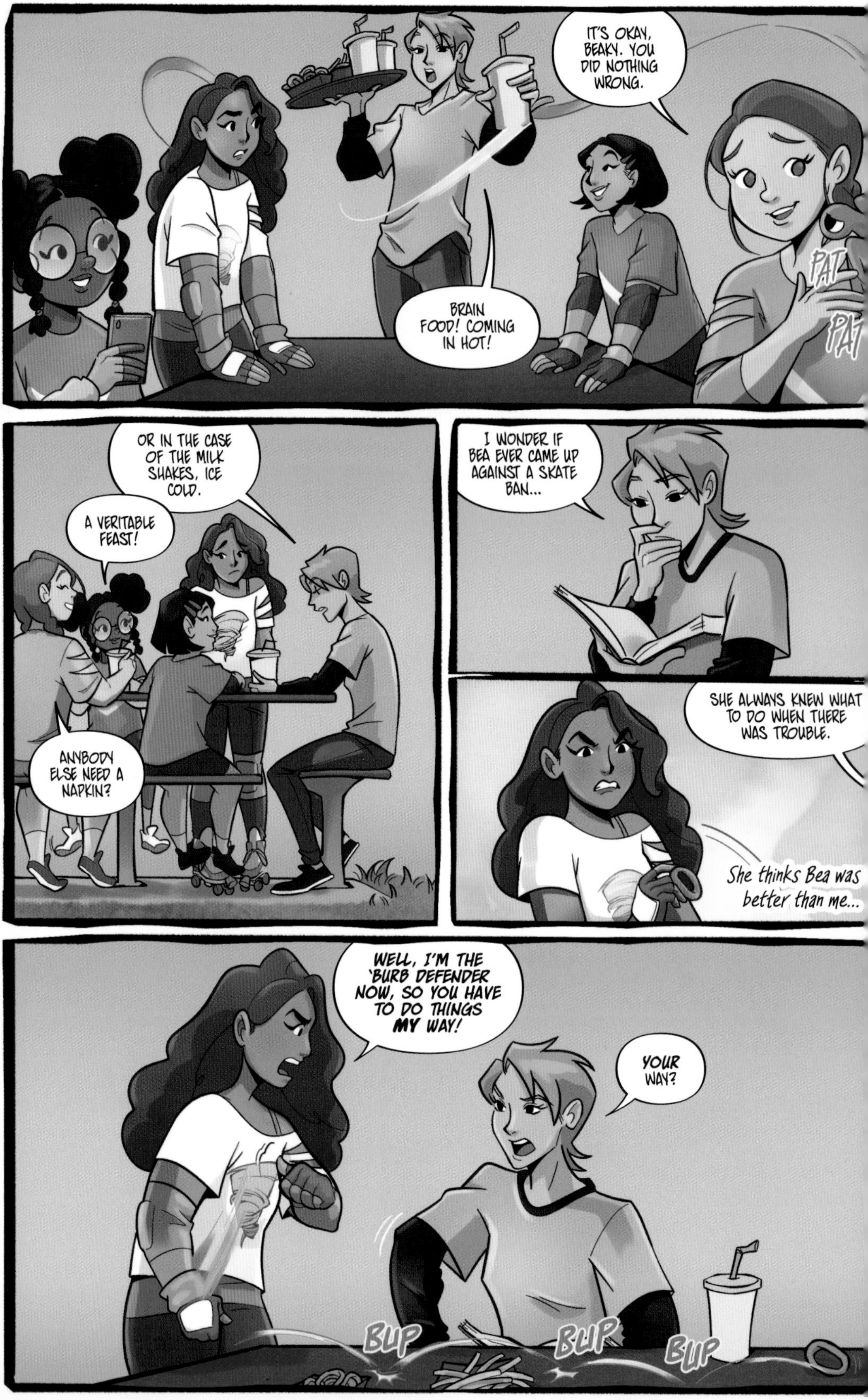
IT'S OKAY, BEAKY. YOU DID NOTHING WRONG.
PAT
PAT
BRAIN FOOD! COMING IN HOT!
OR IN THE CASE OF THE MILK SHAKES, ICE COLD.
A VERITABLE FEAST!
ANYBODY ELSE NEED A NAPKIN?
I WONDER IF BEA EVER CAME UP AGAINST A SKATE BAN...
SHE ALWAYS KNEW WHAT TO DO WHEN THERE WAS TROUBLE.
She thinks Bea was better than me...
WELL, I'M THE 'BURB DEFENDER NOW, SO YOU HAVE TO DO THINGS MY WAY!
YOUR WAY?
BLIP
BLIP
BLIP

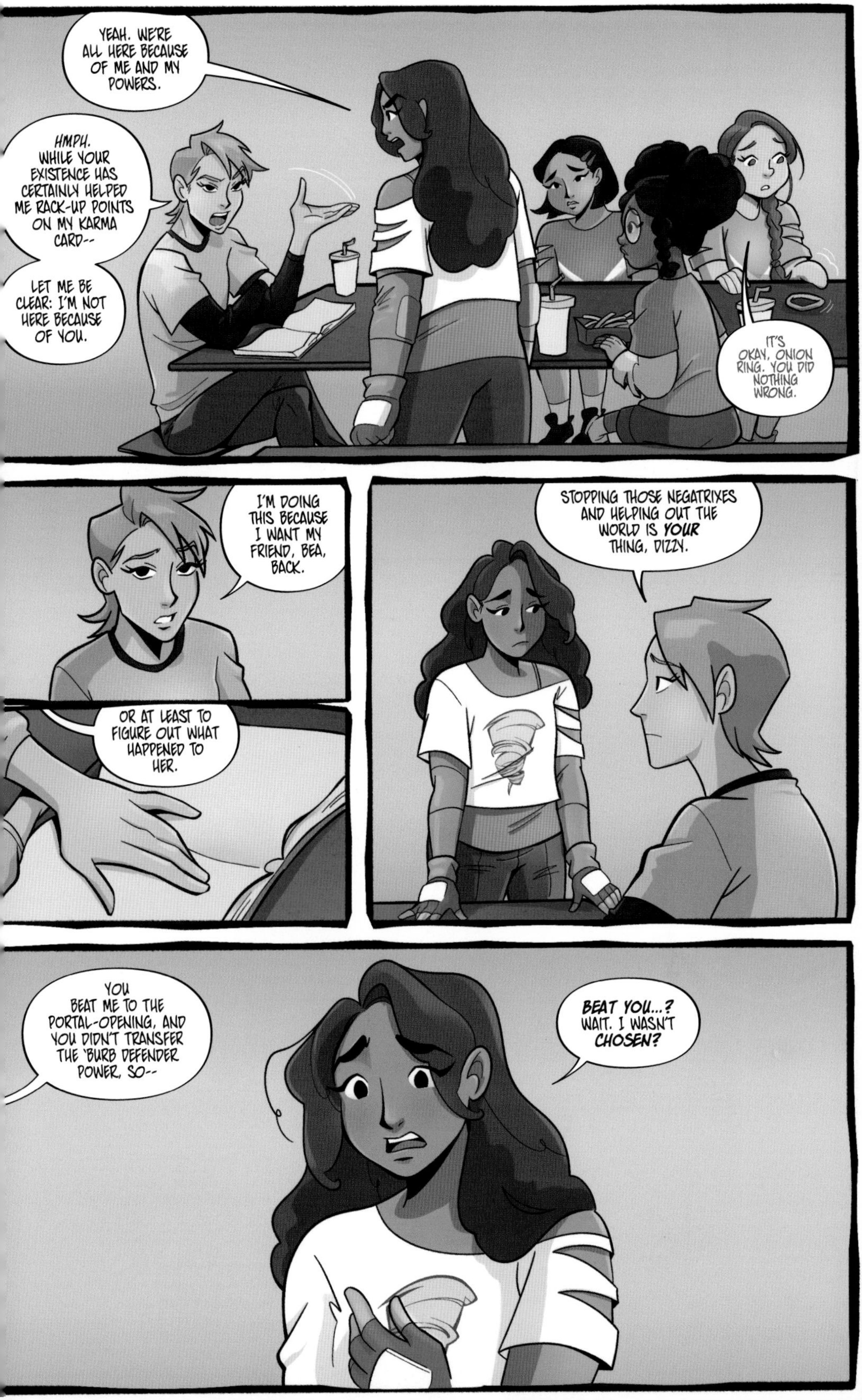
YEAH. WE'RE ALL HERE BECAUSE OF ME AND MY POWERS.
HMPH. WHILE YOUR EXISTENCE HAS CERTAINLY HELPED ME RACK-UP POINTS ON MY KARMA CARD--
LET ME BE CLEAR: I'M NOT HERE BECAUSE OF YOU.
IT'S OKAY, ONION RING. YOU DID NOTHING WRONG.
I'M DOING THIS BECAUSE I WANT MY FRIEND, BEA, BACK.
OR AT LEAST TO FIGURE OUT WHAT HAPPENED TO HER.
STOPPING THOSE NEGATRIXES AND HELPING OUT THE WORLD IS *YOUR* THING, DIZZY.
YOU BEAT ME TO THE PORTAL-OPENING, AND YOU DIDN'T TRANSFER THE 'BURB DEFENDER POWER, SO--
BEAT YOU...? WAIT. I WASN'T *CHOSEN?*

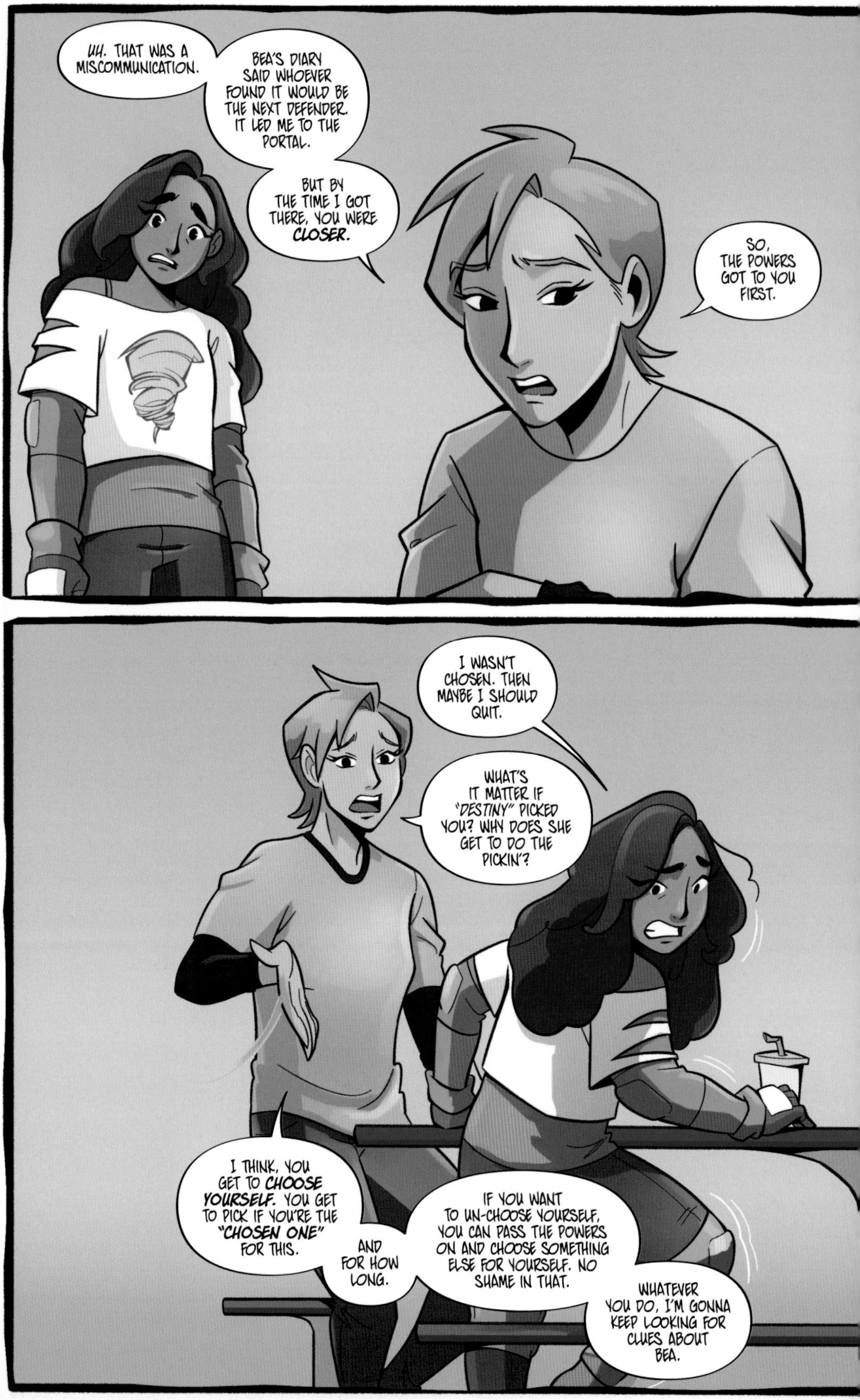
UH. THAT WAS A MISCOMMUNICATION.
BEA'S DIARY SAID WHOEVER FOUND IT WOULD BE THE NEXT DEFENDER. IT LED ME TO THE PORTAL.
BUT BY THE TIME I GOT THERE, YOU WERE **CLOSER.**
SO, THE POWERS GOT TO YOU FIRST.
I WASN'T CHOSEN. THEN MAYBE I SHOULD QUIT.
WHAT'S IT MATTER IF *"DESTINY"* PICKED YOU? WHY DOES SHE GET TO DO THE PICKIN'?
I THINK, YOU GET TO **CHOOSE YOURSELF.** YOU GET TO PICK IF YOU'RE THE **"CHOSEN ONE"** FOR THIS.
AND FOR HOW LONG.
IF YOU WANT TO UN-CHOOSE YOURSELF, YOU CAN PASS THE POWERS ON AND CHOOSE SOMETHING ELSE FOR YOURSELF. NO SHAME IN THAT.
WHATEVER YOU DO, I'M GONNA KEEP LOOKING FOR CLUES ABOUT BEA.

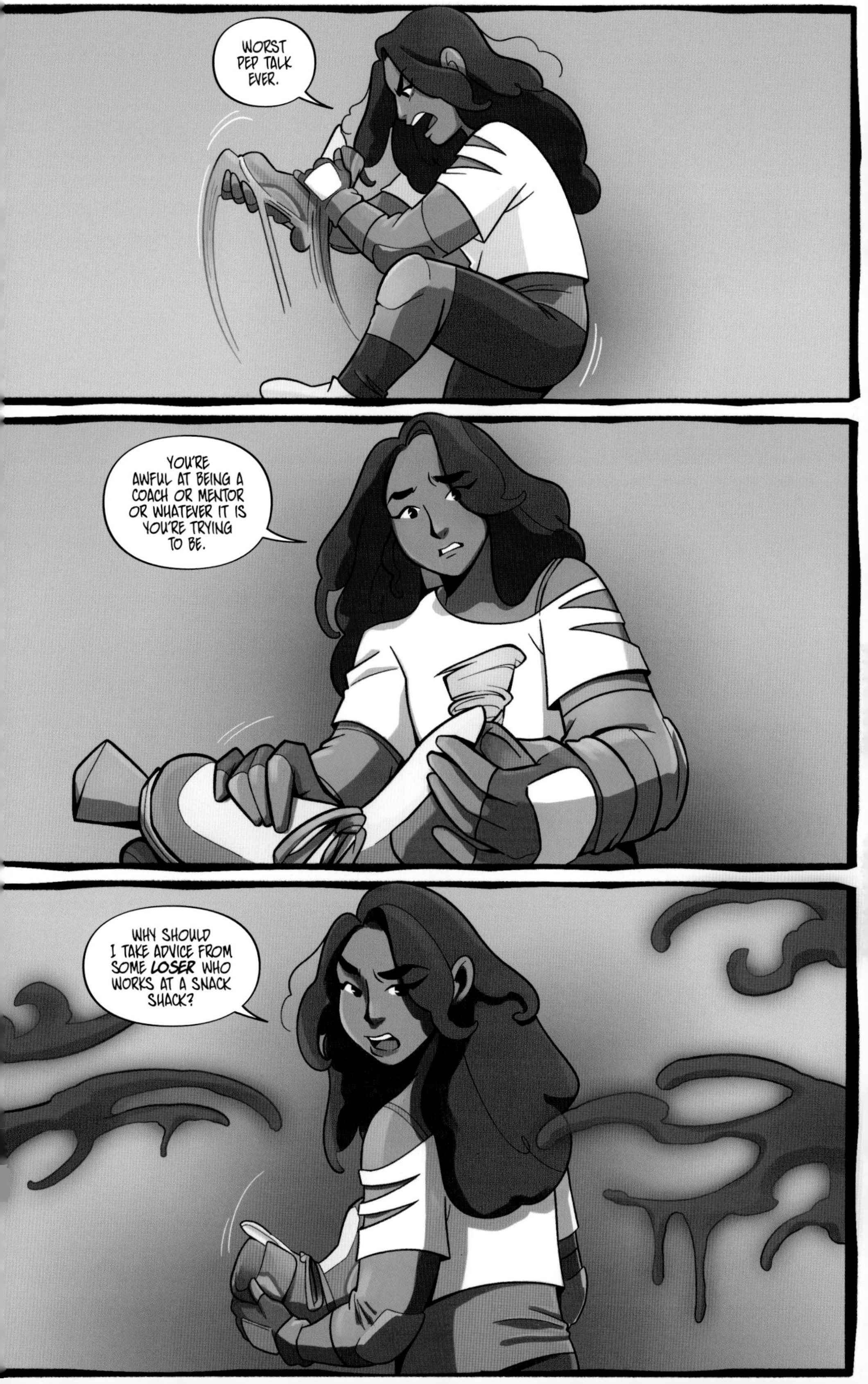

WORST PEP TALK EVER.
YOU'RE AWFUL AT BEING A COACH OR MENTOR OR WHATEVER IT IS YOU'RE TRYING TO BE.
WHY SHOULD I TAKE ADVICE FROM SOME **LOSER** WHO WORKS AT A SNACK SHACK?

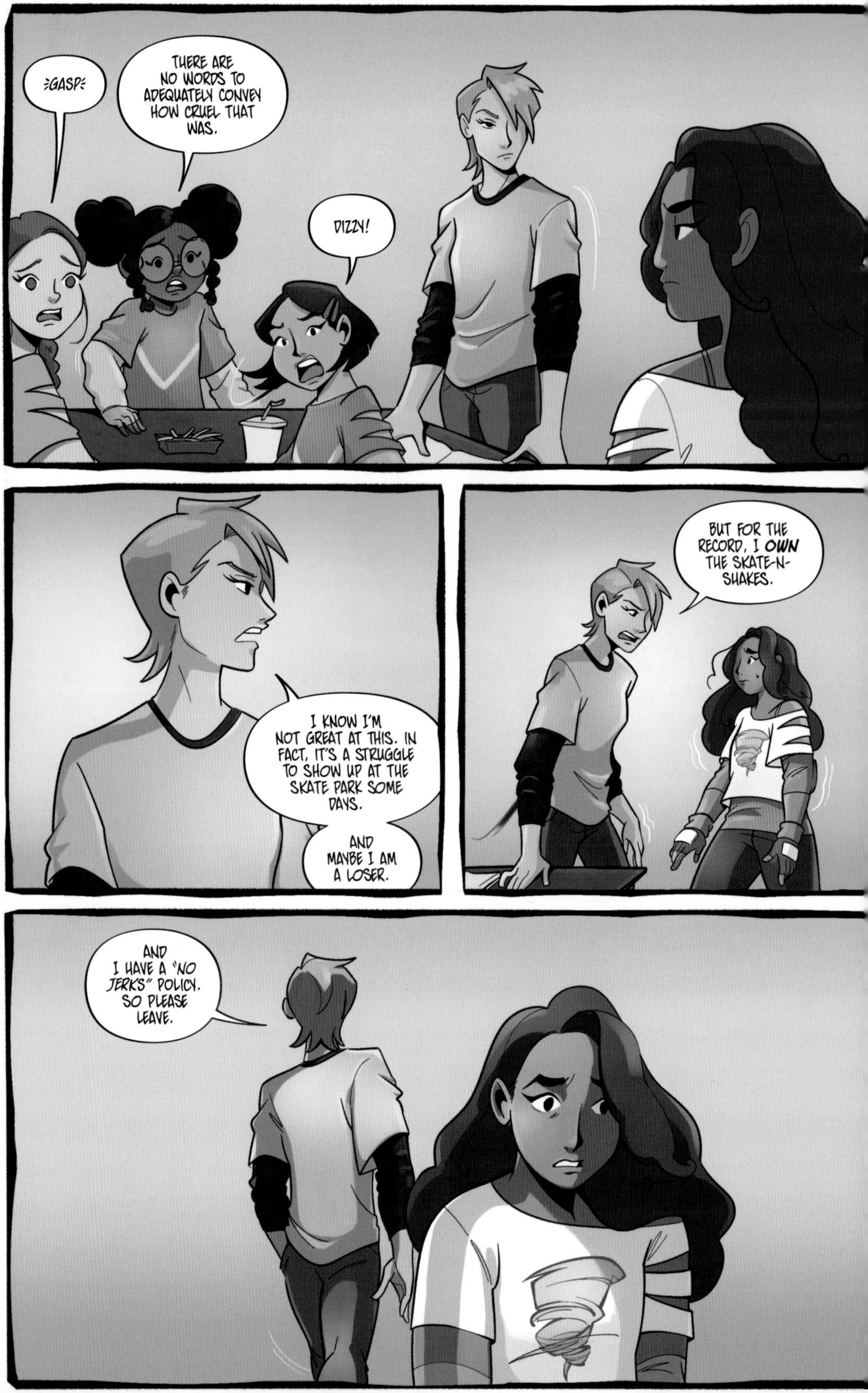

GASP
THERE ARE NO WORDS TO ADEQUATELY CONVEY HOW CRUEL THAT WAS.
DIZZY!
I KNOW I'M NOT GREAT AT THIS. IN FACT, IT'S A STRUGGLE TO SHOW UP AT THE SKATE PARK SOME DAYS.
AND MAYBE I AM A LOSER.
BUT FOR THE RECORD, I **OWN** THE SKATE-N-SHAKES.
AND I HAVE A "NO JERKS" POLICY. SO PLEASE LEAVE.

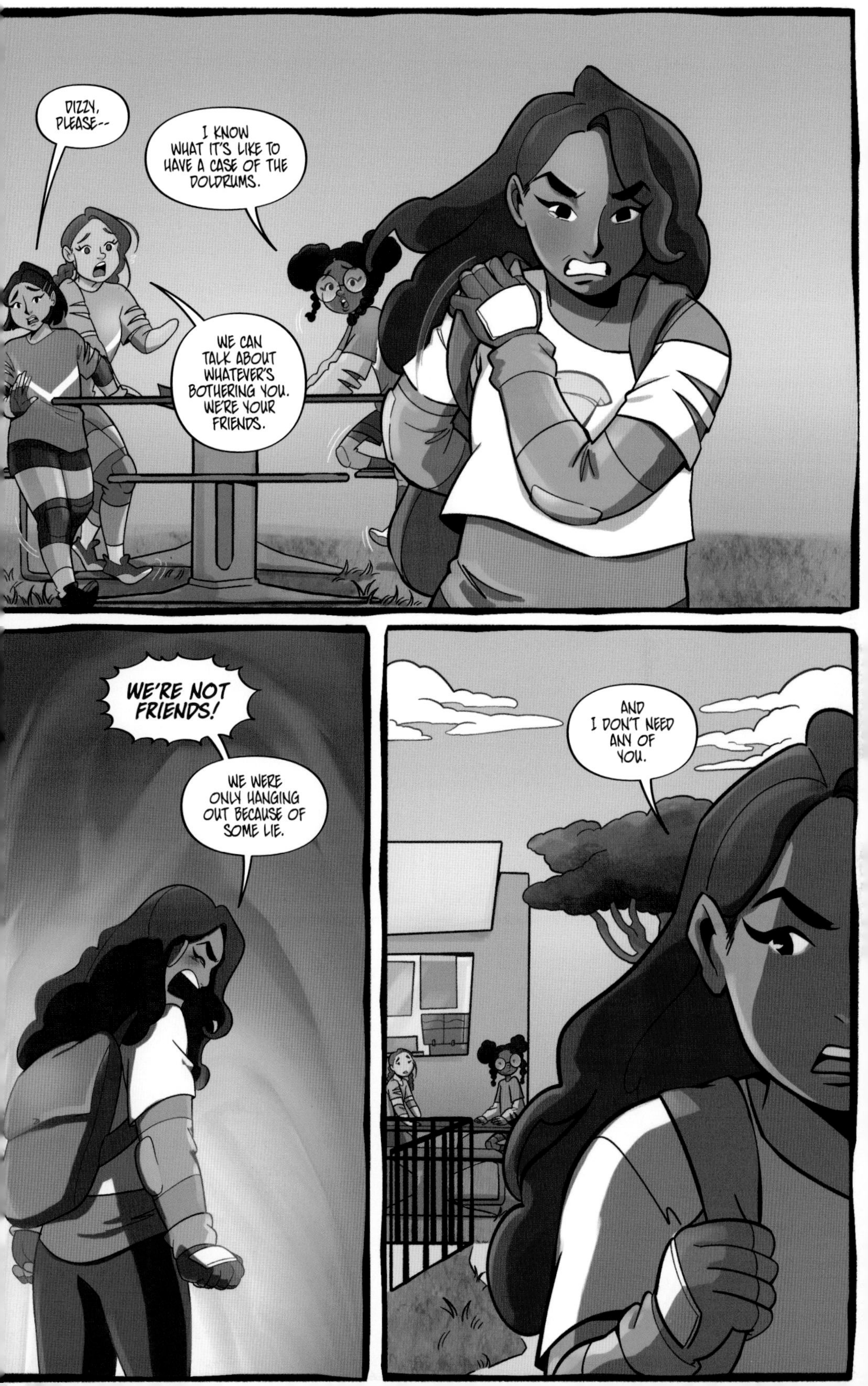
DIZZY, PLEASE--
I KNOW WHAT IT'S LIKE TO HAVE A CASE OF THE DOLDRUMS.
WE CAN TALK ABOUT WHATEVER'S BOTHERING YOU. WE'RE YOUR FRIENDS.
WE'RE NOT FRIENDS!
WE WERE ONLY HANGING OUT BECAUSE OF SOME LIE.
AND I DON'T NEED ANY OF YOU.

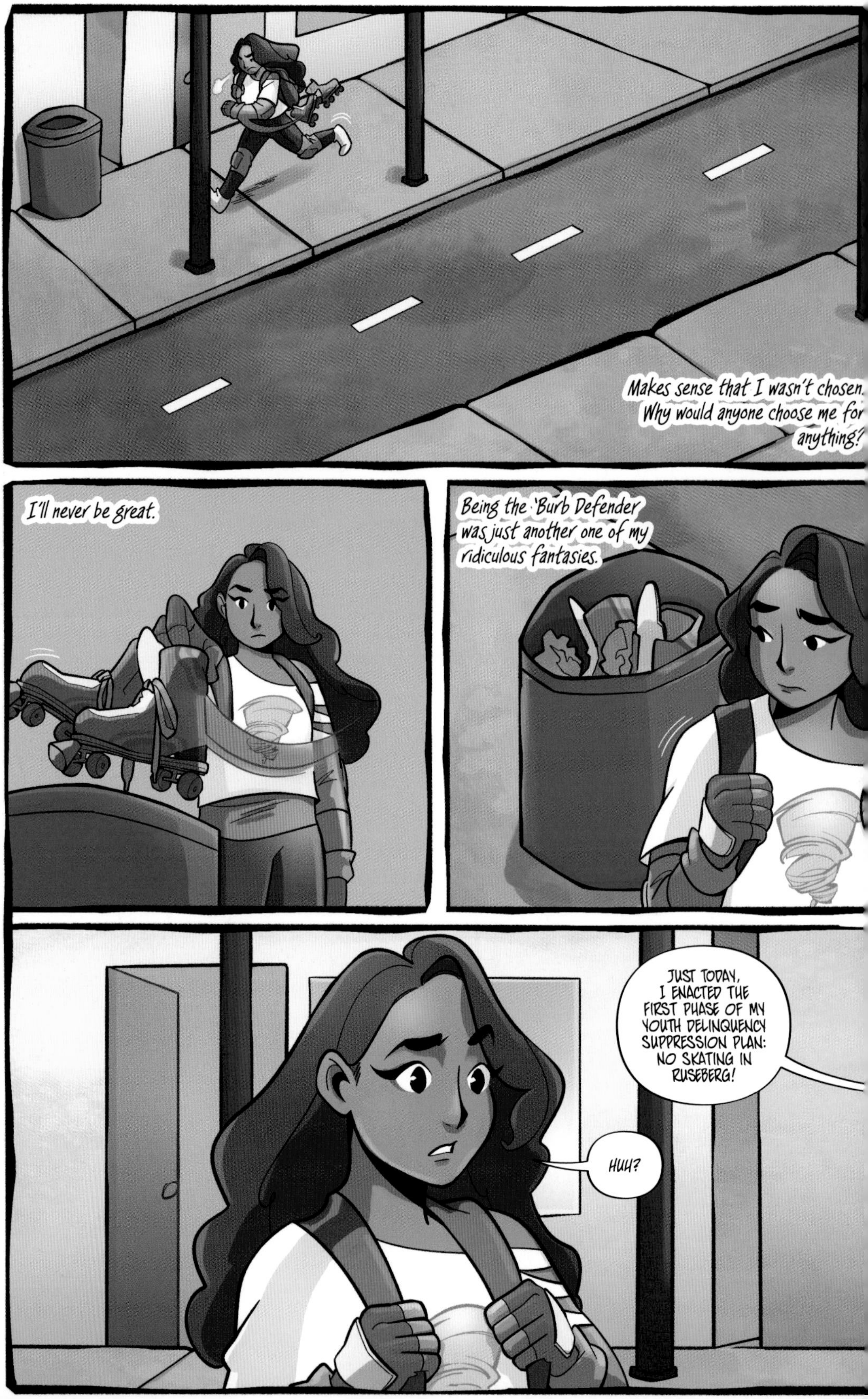
Makes sense that I wasn't chosen. Why would anyone choose me for anything?
I'll never be great.
Being the 'Burb Defender was just another one of my ridiculous fantasies.
JUST TODAY, I ENACTED THE FIRST PHASE OF MY YOUTH DELINQUENCY SUPPRESSION PLAN: NO SKATING IN RUSEBERG!
HUH?

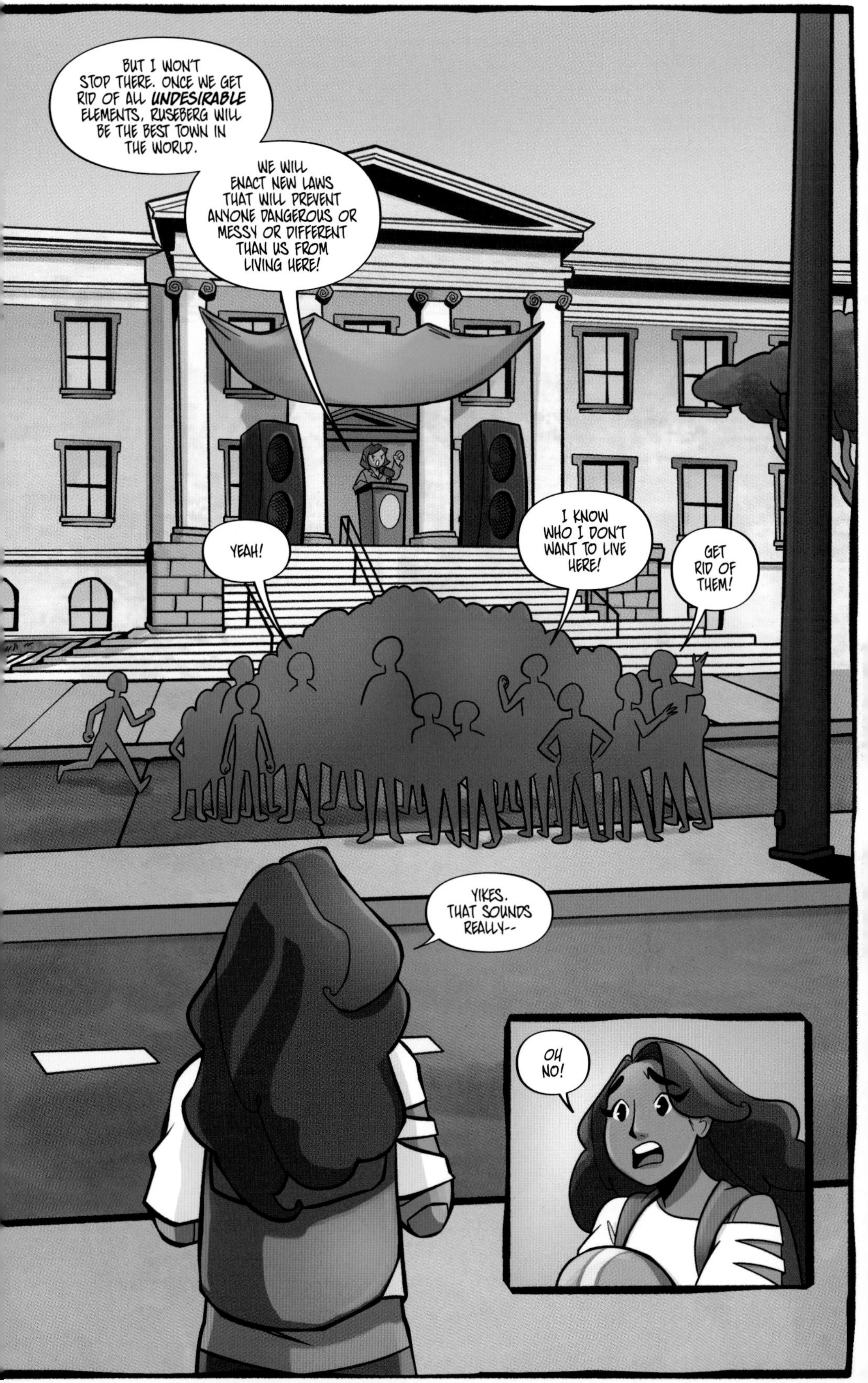
BUT I WON'T STOP THERE. ONCE WE GET RID OF ALL UNDESIRABLE ELEMENTS, RUSEBERG WILL BE THE BEST TOWN IN THE WORLD.
WE WILL ENACT NEW LAWS THAT WILL PREVENT ANYONE DANGEROUS OR MESSY OR DIFFERENT THAN US FROM LIVING HERE!
YEAH!
I KNOW WHO I DON'T WANT TO LIVE HERE!
GET RID OF THEM!
YIKES. THAT SOUNDS REALLY--
OH NO!

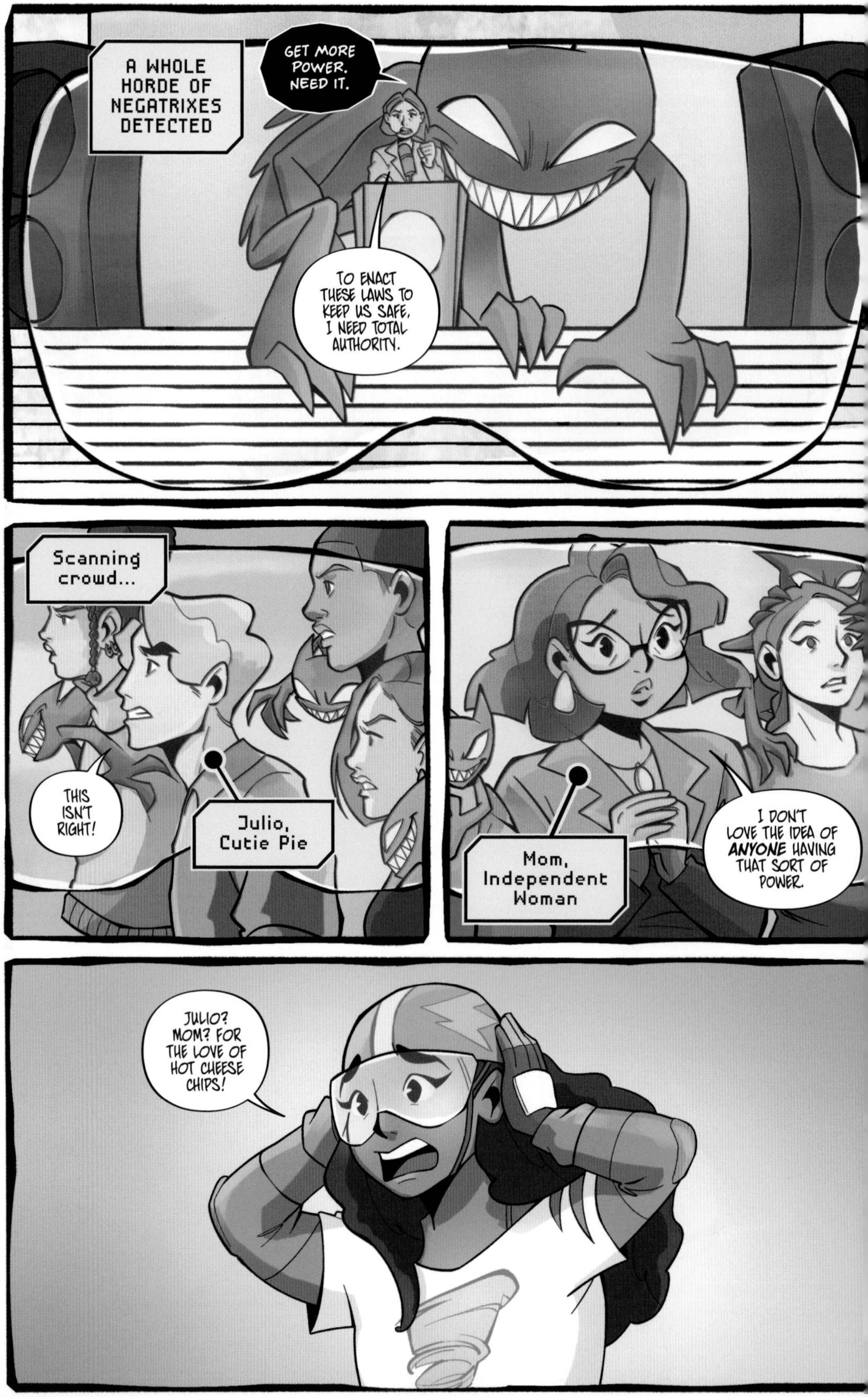
A WHOLE HORDE OF NEGATRIXES DETECTED
GET MORE POWER. NEED IT.
TO ENACT THESE LAWS TO KEEP US SAFE, I NEED TOTAL AUTHORITY.
Scanning crowd...
THIS ISN'T RIGHT!
Julio, Cutie Pie
Mom, Independent Woman
I DON'T LOVE THE IDEA OF ANYONE HAVING THAT SORT OF POWER.
JULIO? MOM? FOR THE LOVE OF HOT CHEESE CHIPS!

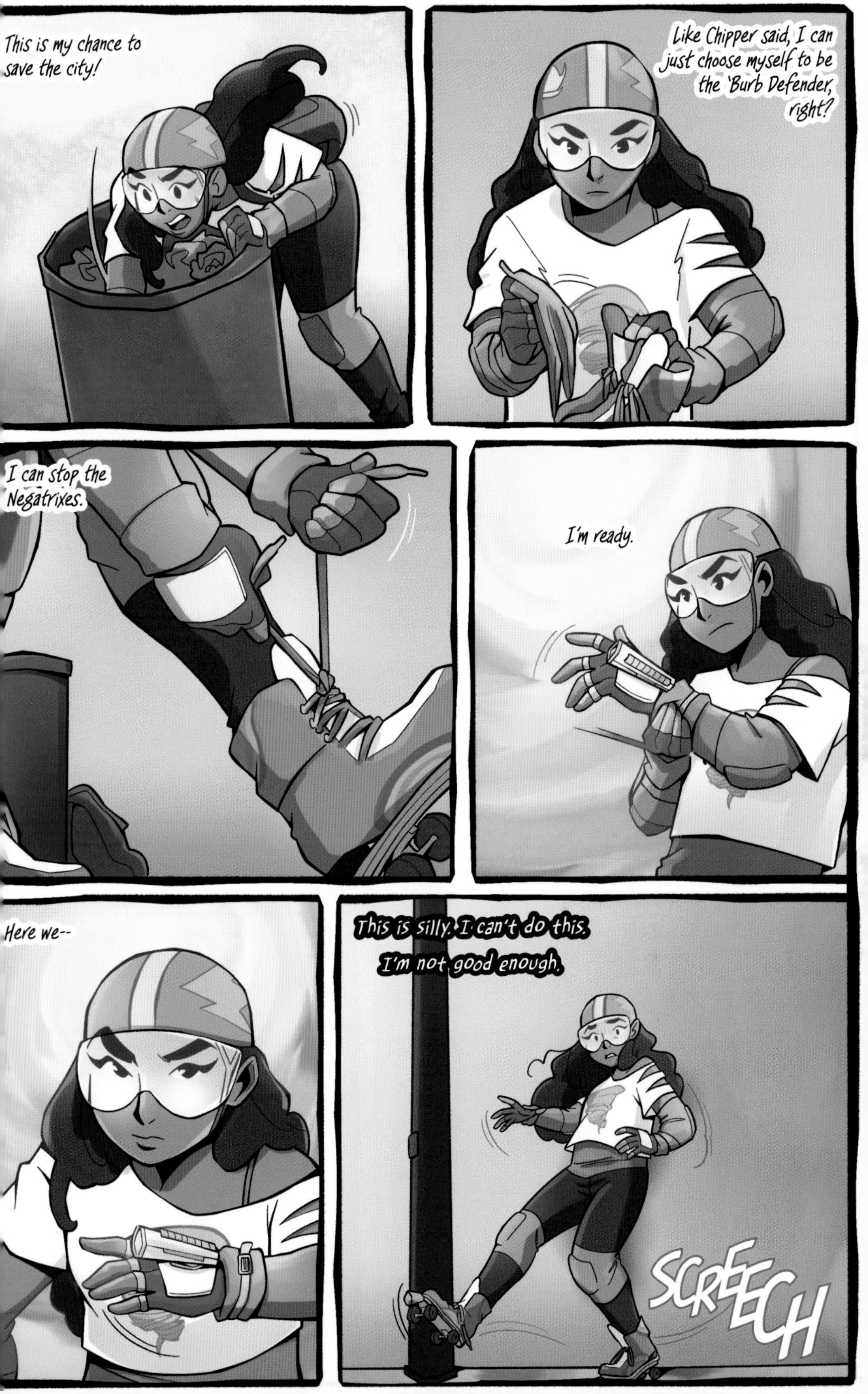
This is my chance to save the city!
Like Chipper said, I can just choose myself to be the 'Burb Defender, right?
I can stop the Negatrixes.
I'm ready.
Here we--
This is silly. I can't do this.
I'm not good enough.
SCREECH

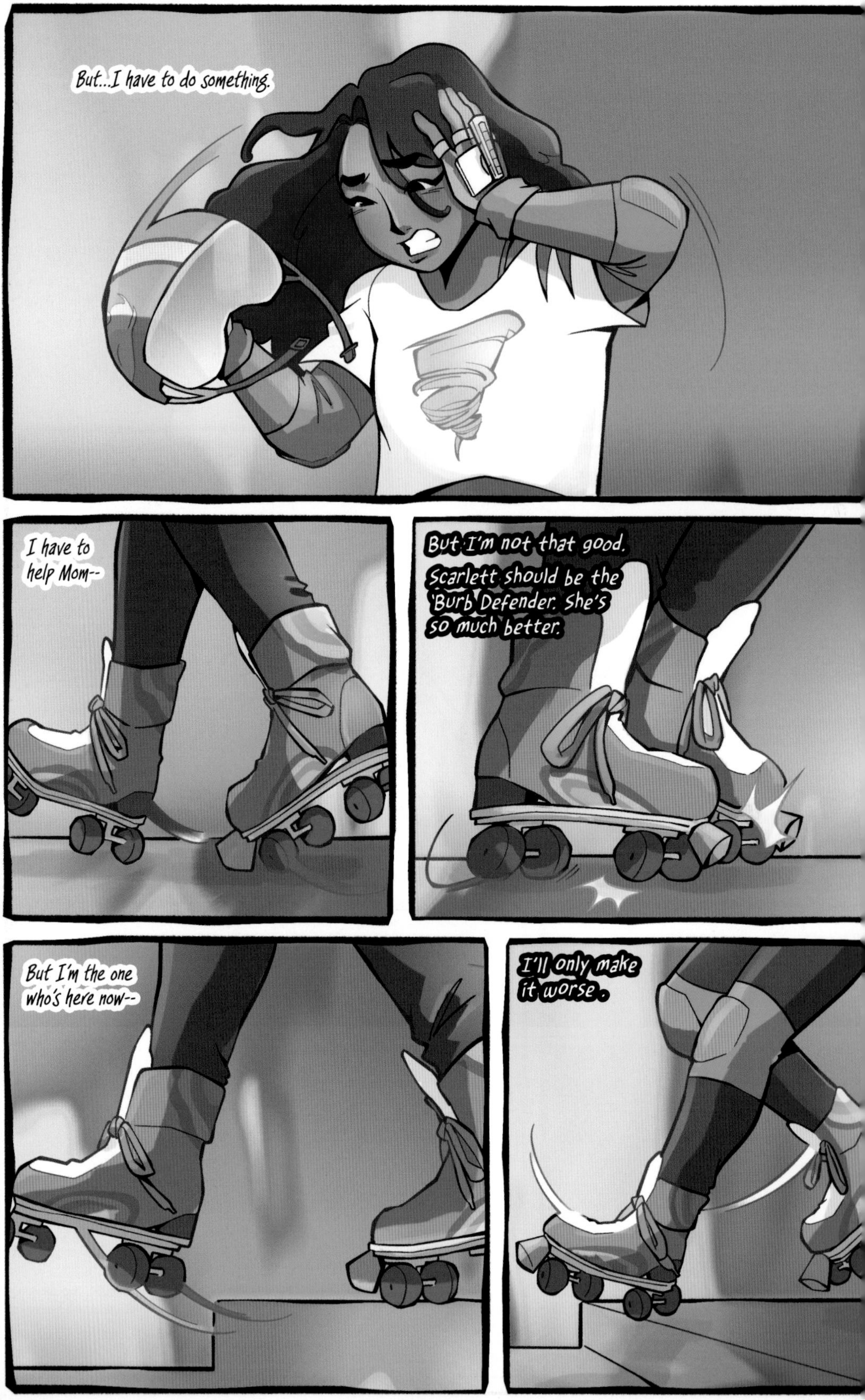
But...I have to do something.
I have to help Mom--
But I'm not that good.
Scarlett should be the 'Burb Defender. She's so much better.
But I'm the one who's here now--
I'll only make it worse.

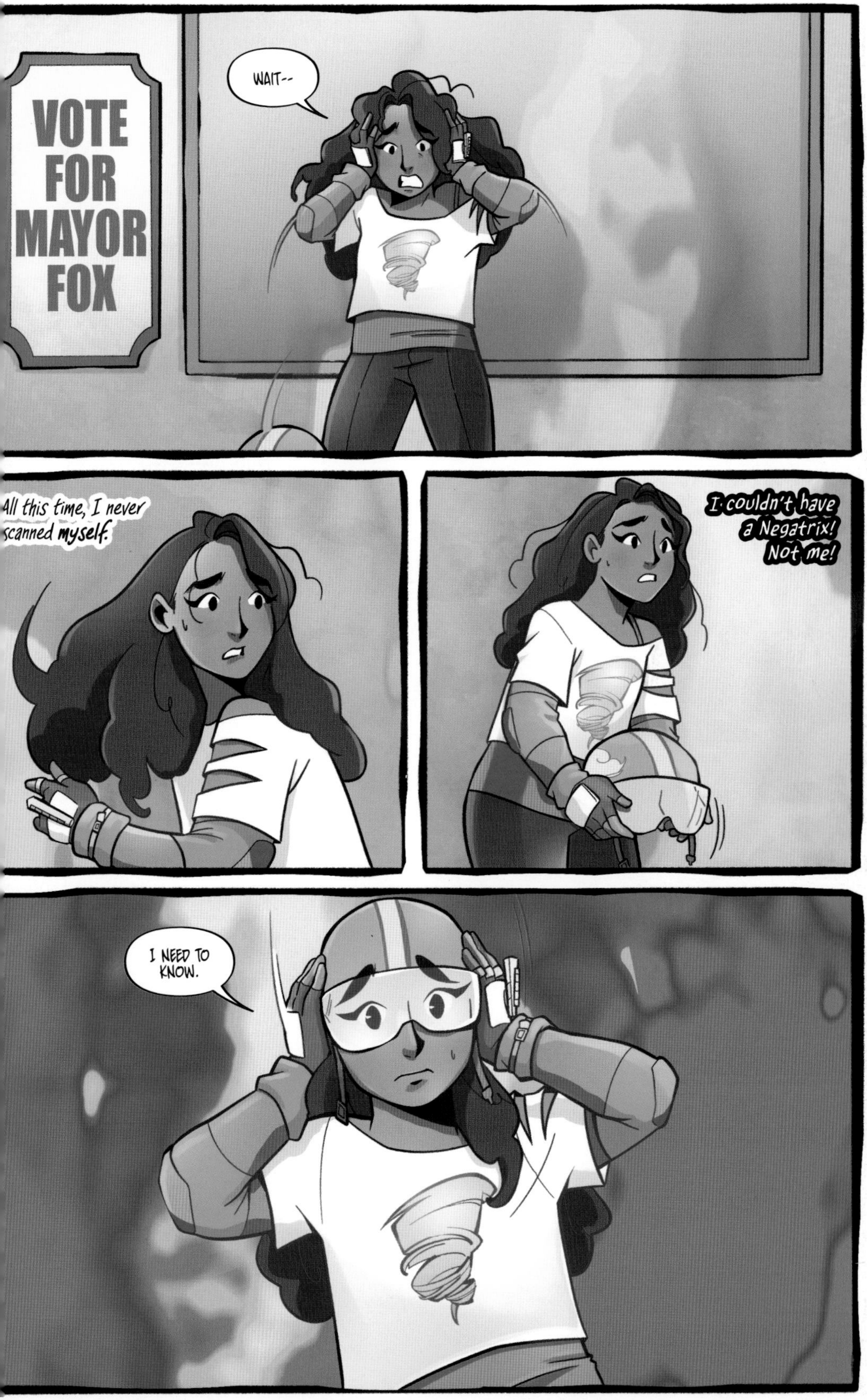
VOTE FOR MAYOR FOX
WAIT--
All this time, I never scanned myself.
I couldn't have a Negatrix! Not me!
I NEED TO KNOW.

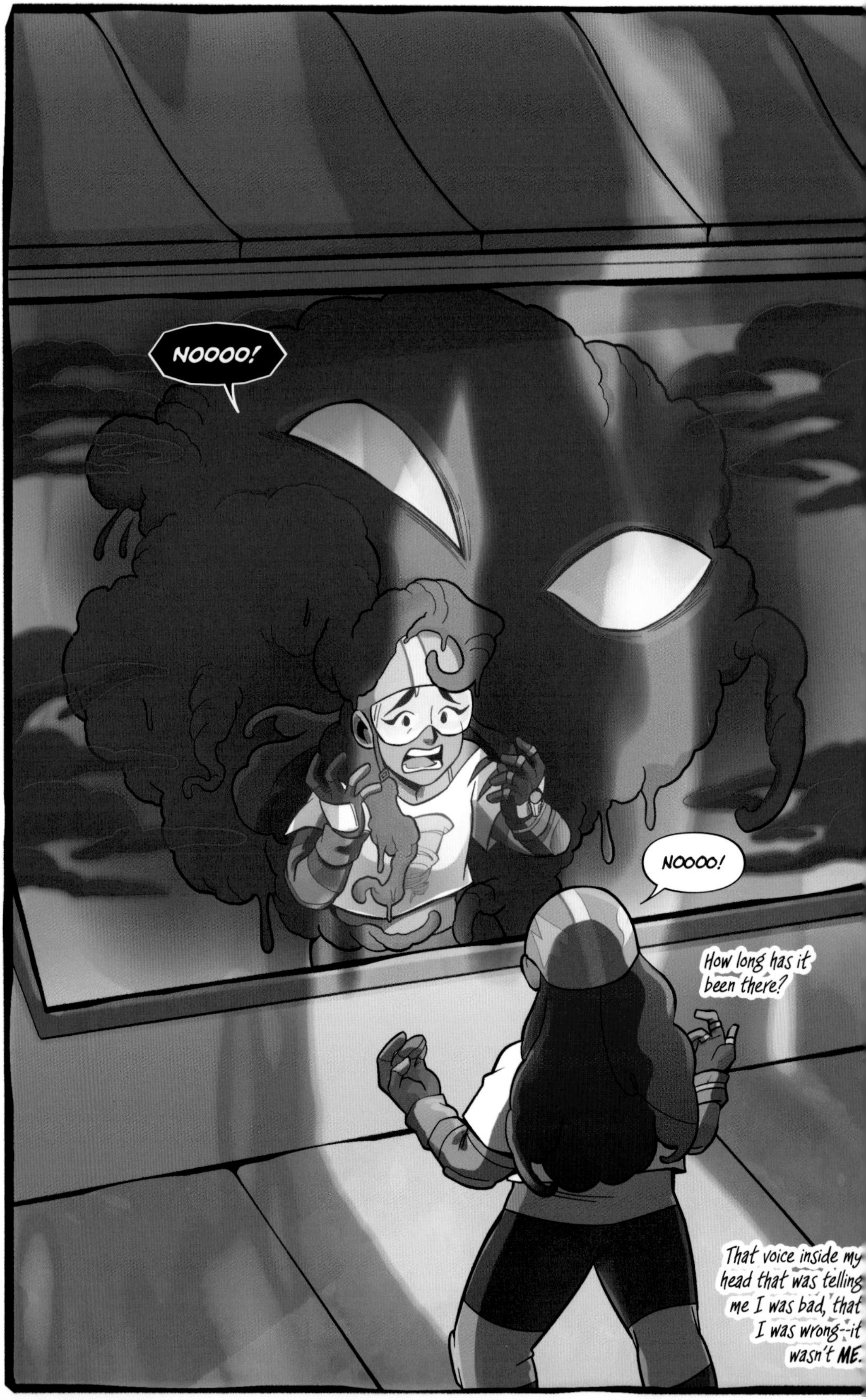
NOOOO!
NOOOO!
How long has it been there?
That voice inside my head that was telling me I was bad, that I was wrong--it wasn't **ME**.

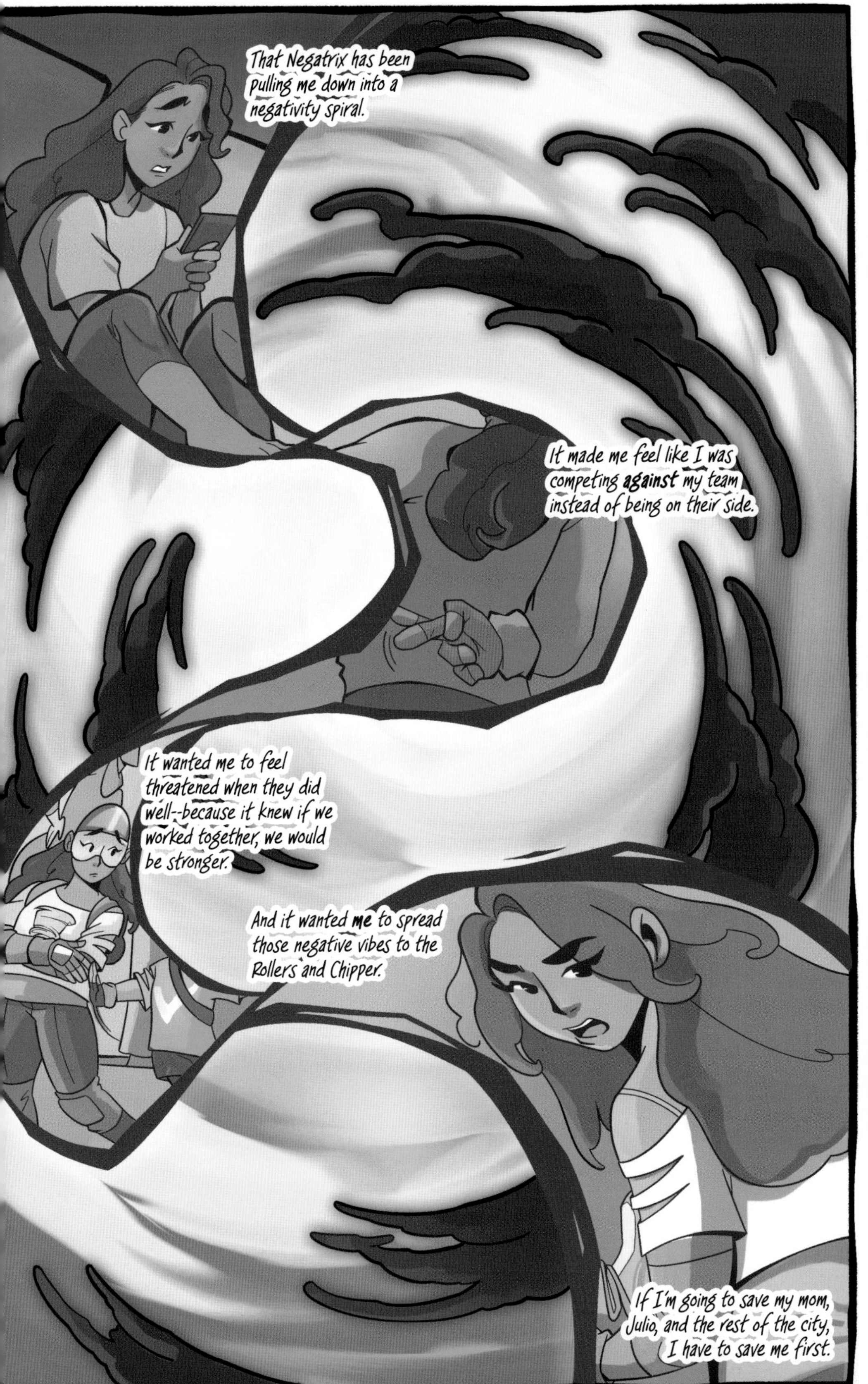
That Negatrix has been pulling me down into a negativity spiral.
It made me feel like I was competing **against** my team instead of being on their side.
It wanted me to feel threatened when they did well--because it knew if we worked together, we would be stronger.
And it wanted **me** to spread those negative vibes to the Rollers and Chipper.
If I'm going to save my mom, Julio, and the rest of the city, I have to save me first.

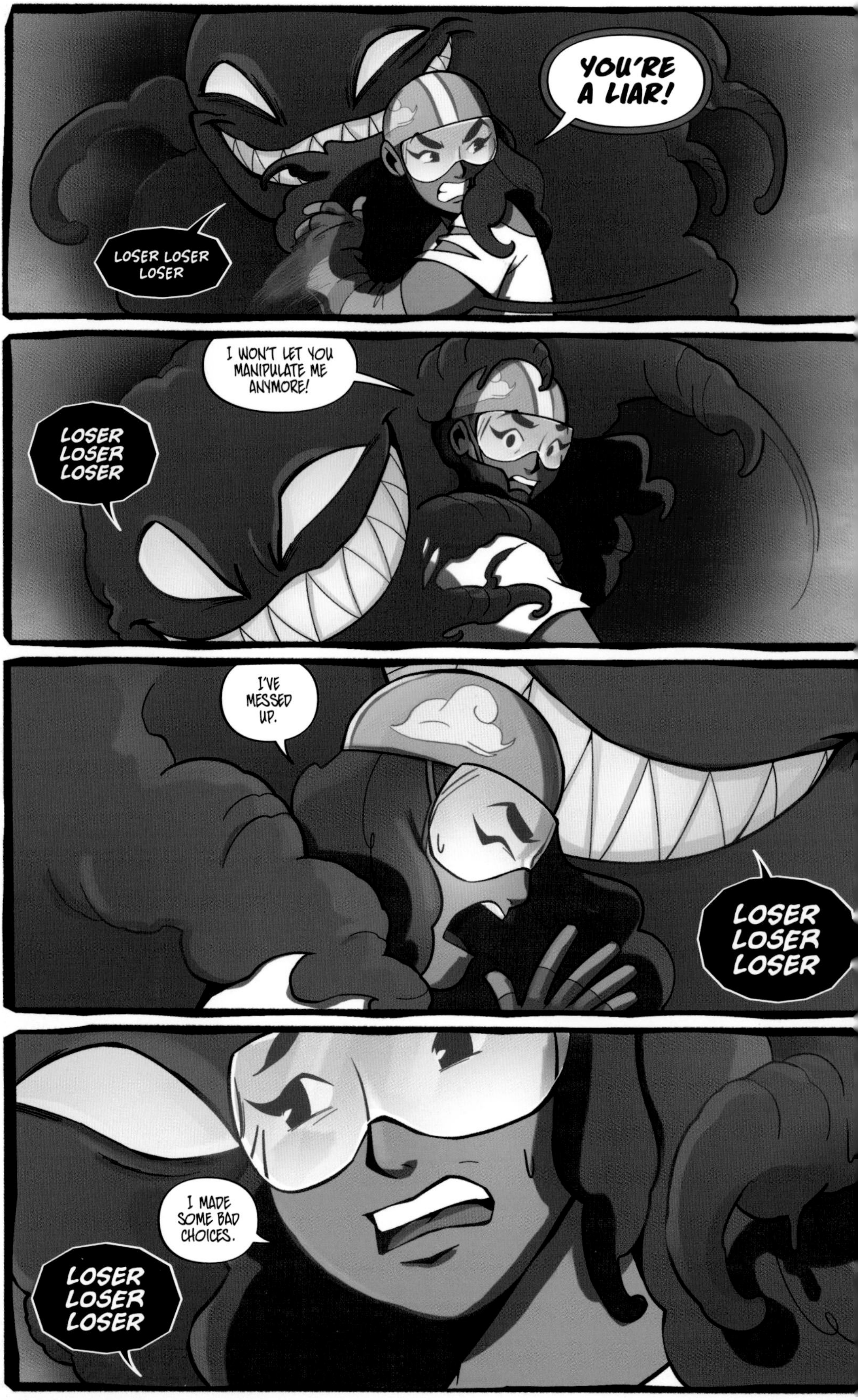
YOU'RE A LIAR!
LOSER LOSER LOSER
I WON'T LET YOU MANIPULATE ME ANYMORE!
LOSER LOSER LOSER
I'VE MESSED UP.
LOSER LOSER LOSER
I MADE SOME BAD CHOICES.
LOSER LOSER LOSER

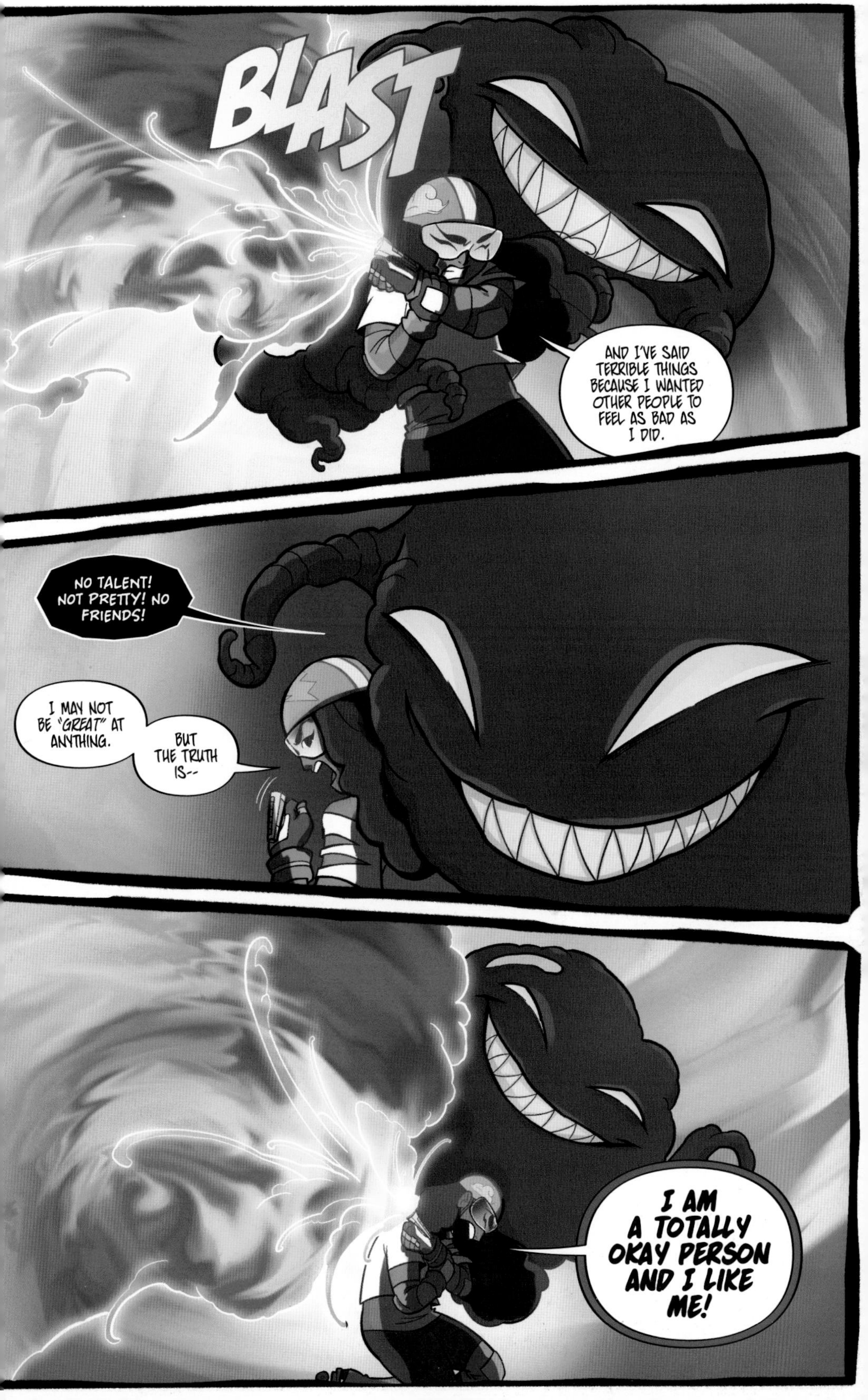
BLAST
AND I'VE SAID TERRIBLE THINGS BECAUSE I WANTED OTHER PEOPLE TO FEEL AS BAD AS I DID.
NO TALENT! NOT PRETTY! NO FRIENDS!
I MAY NOT BE "GREAT" AT ANYTHING.
BUT THE TRUTH IS--
I AM A TOTALLY OKAY PERSON AND I LIKE ME!

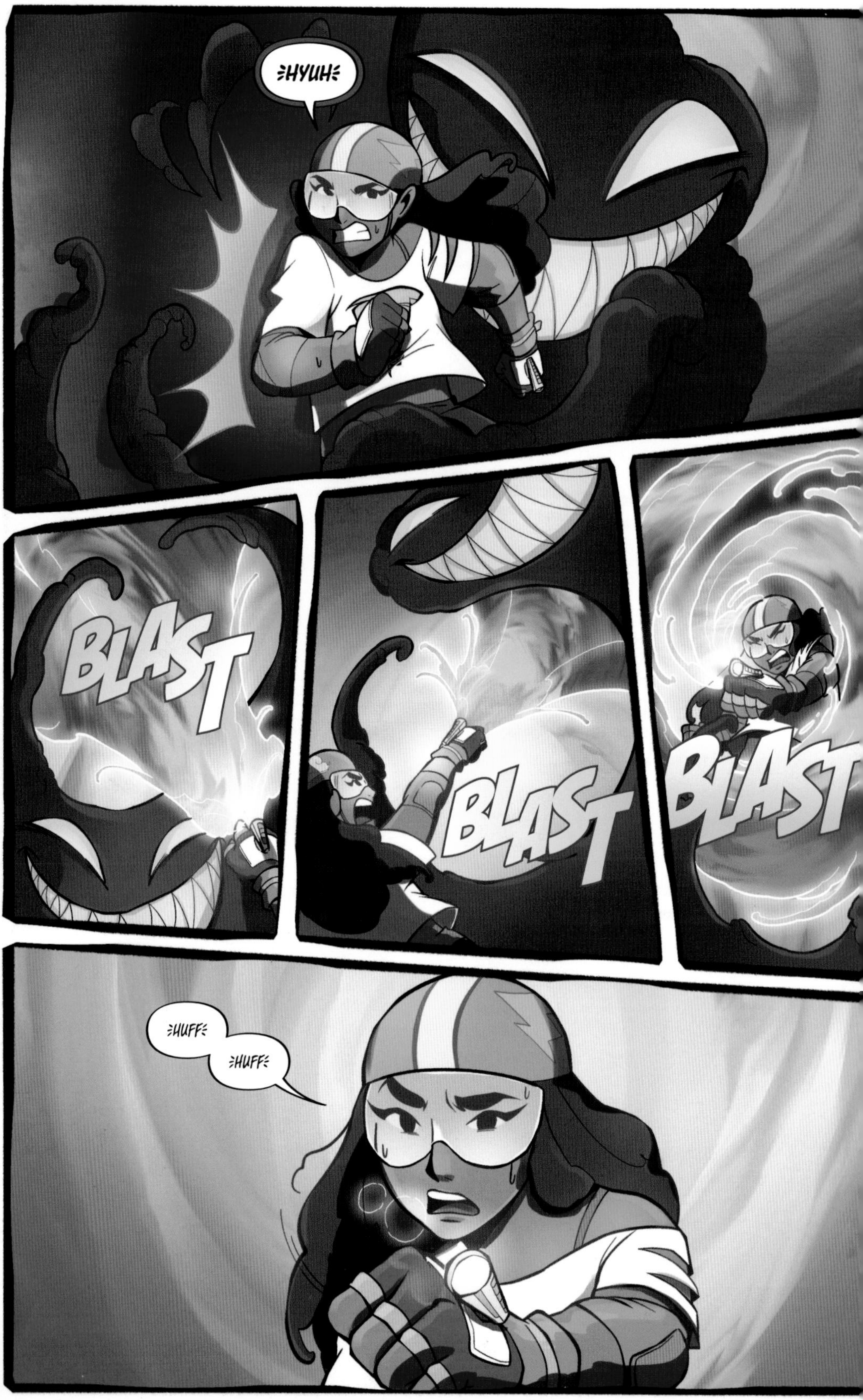
HYUH
BLAST
BLAST
BLAST
HUFF
HUFF

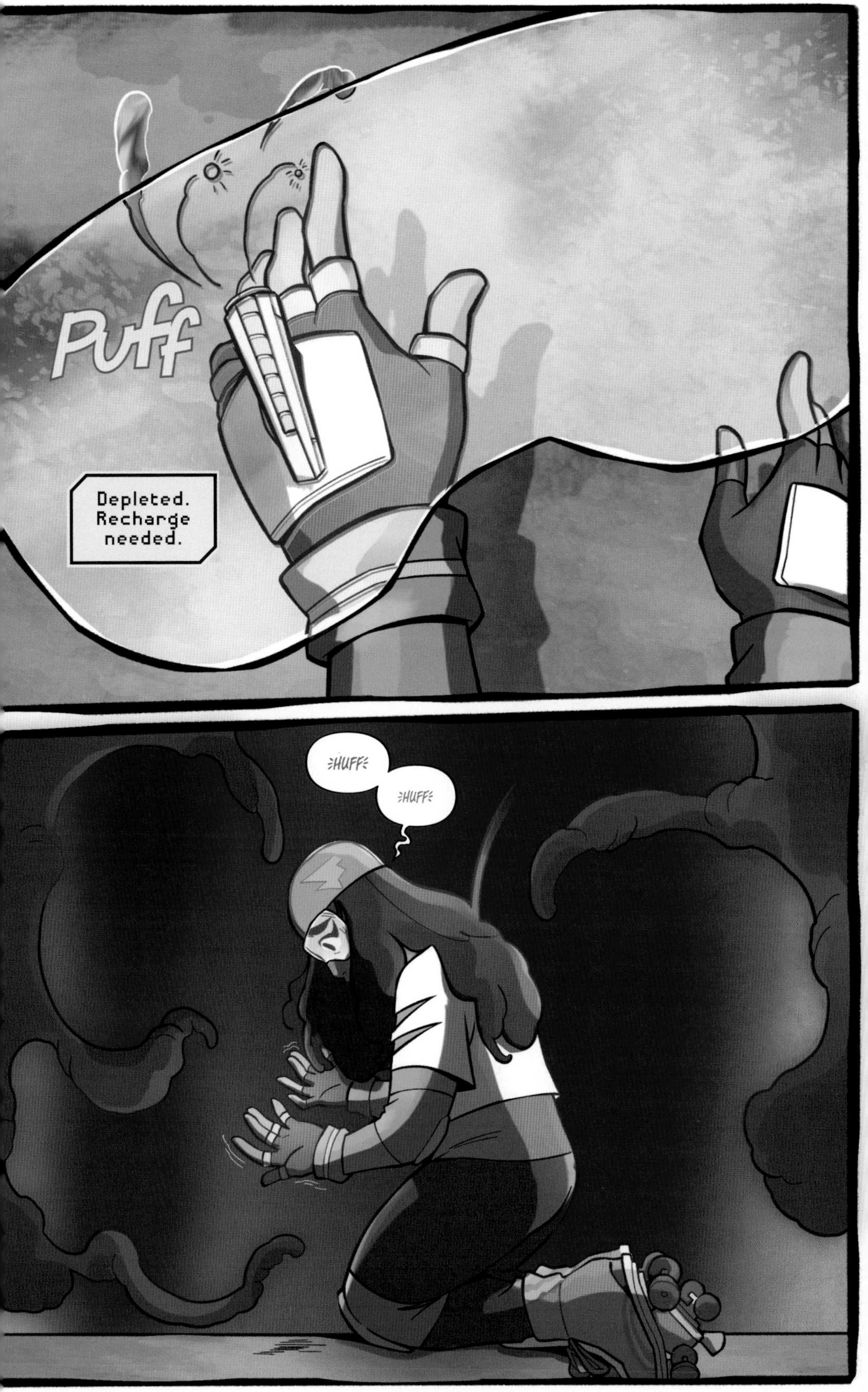
Puff
Depleted. Recharge needed.
HUFF
HUFF

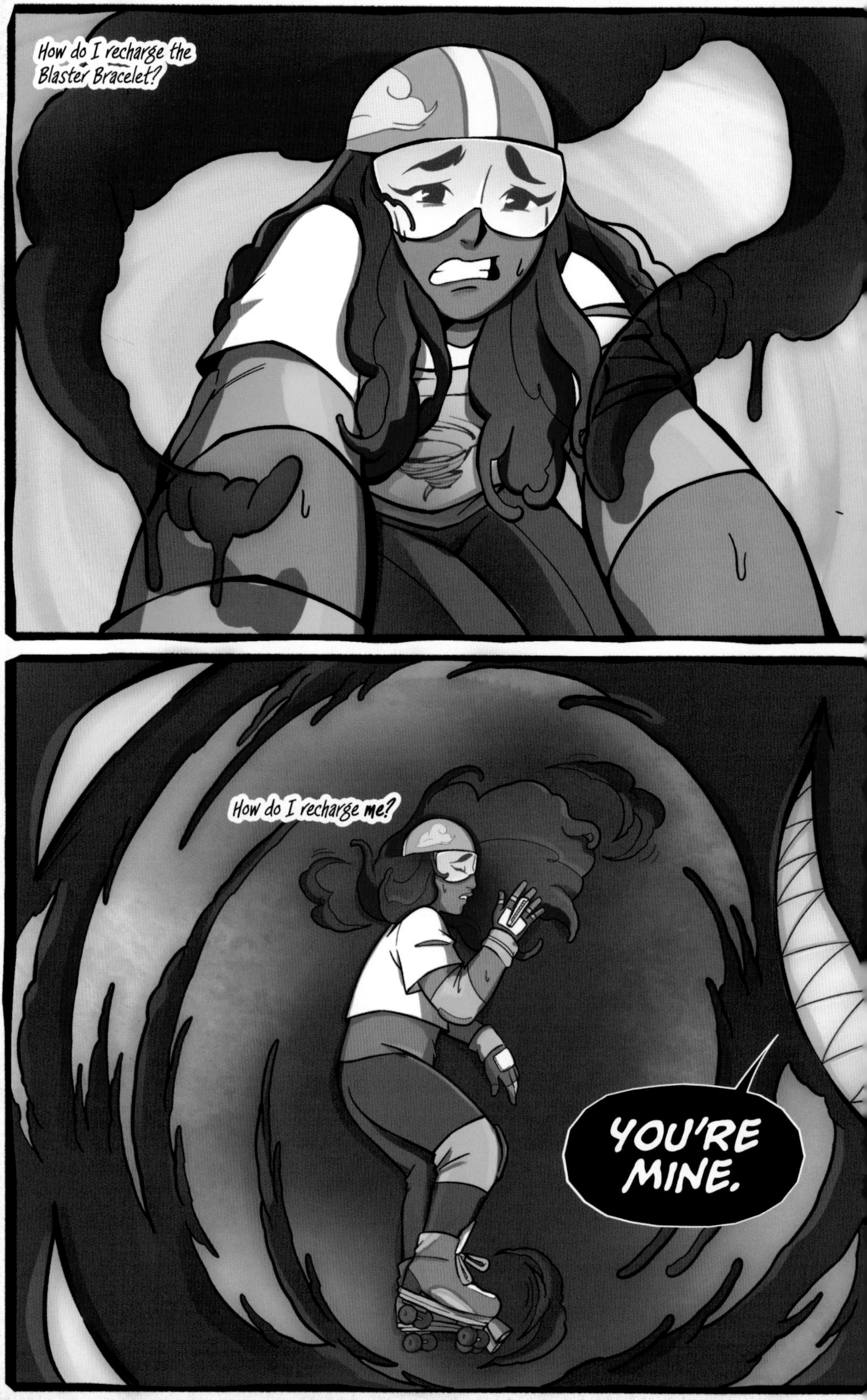
How do I recharge the Blaster Bracelet?
How do I recharge me?
YOU'RE MINE.

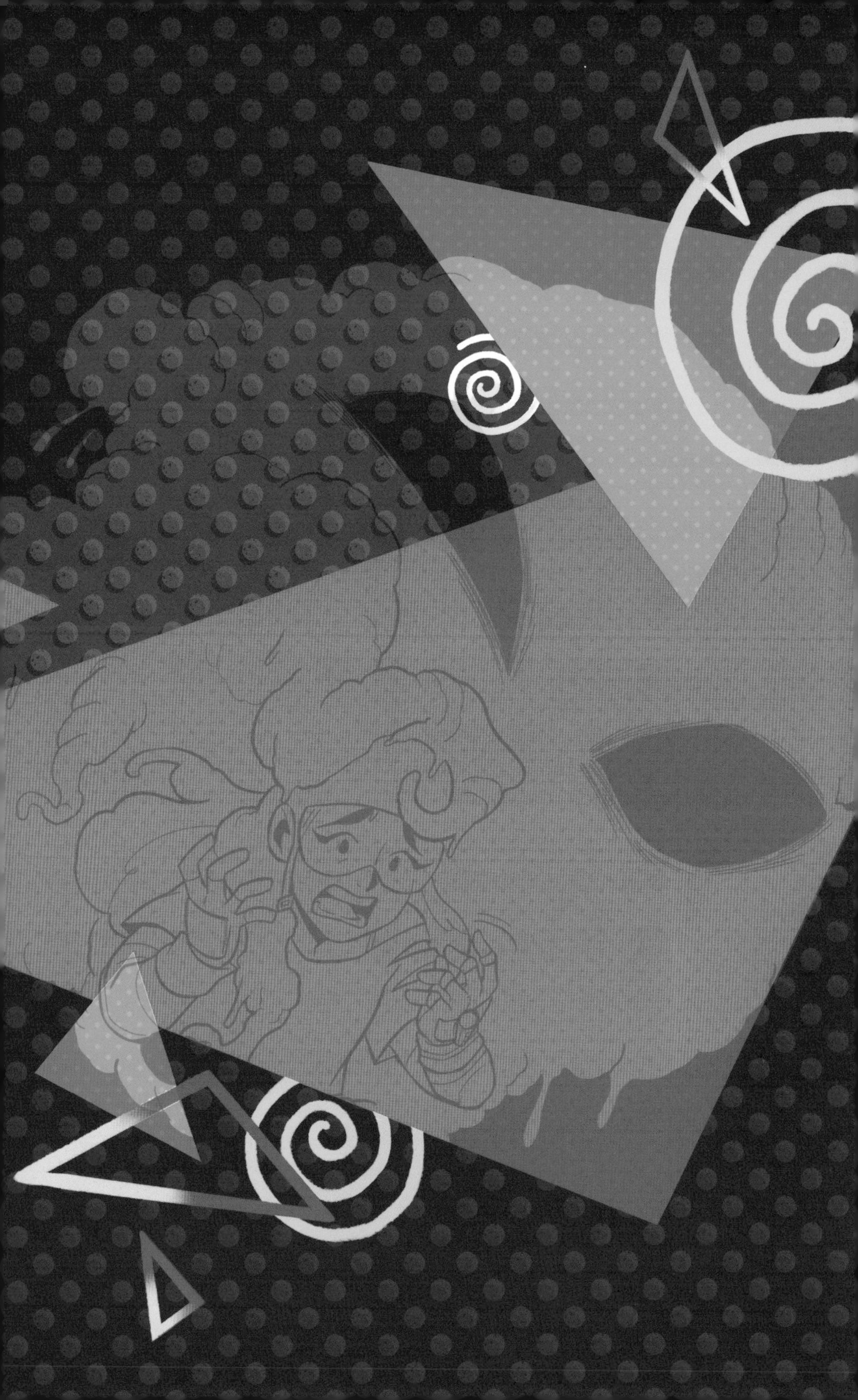

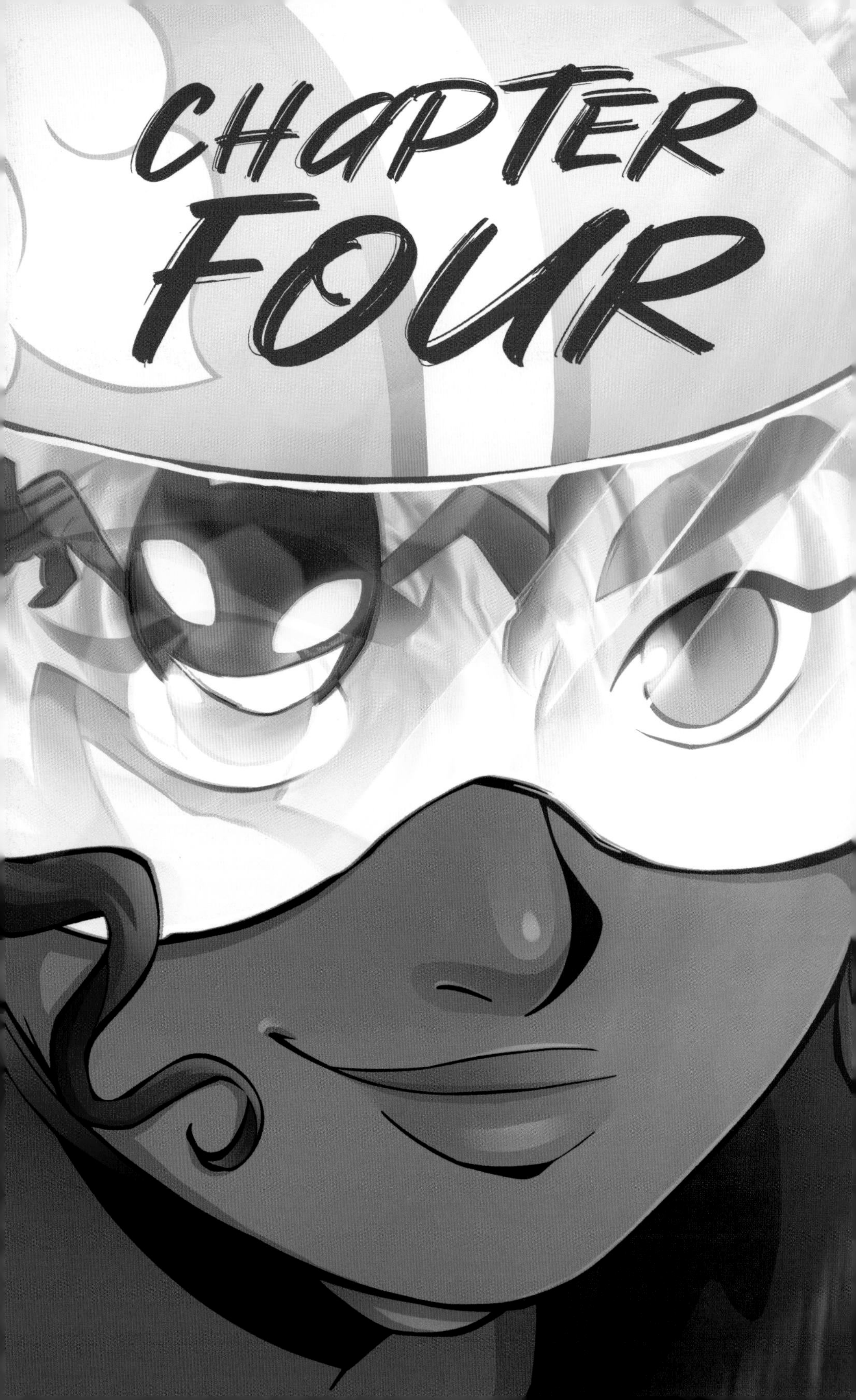
CHAPTER
FOUR

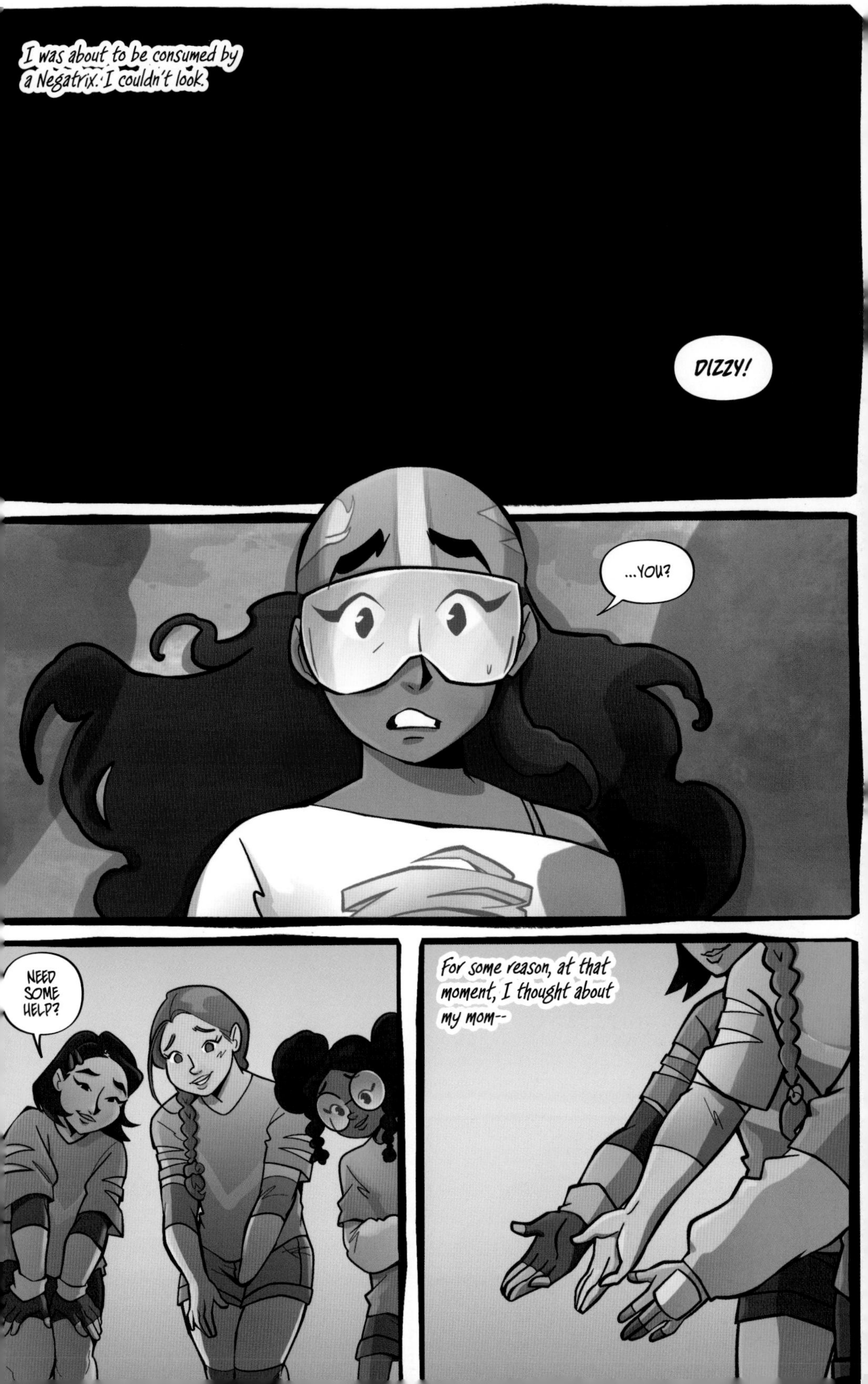
I was about to be consumed by a Negatrix. I couldn't look.
DIZZY!
...YOU?
NEED SOME HELP?
For some reason, at that moment, I thought about my mom--

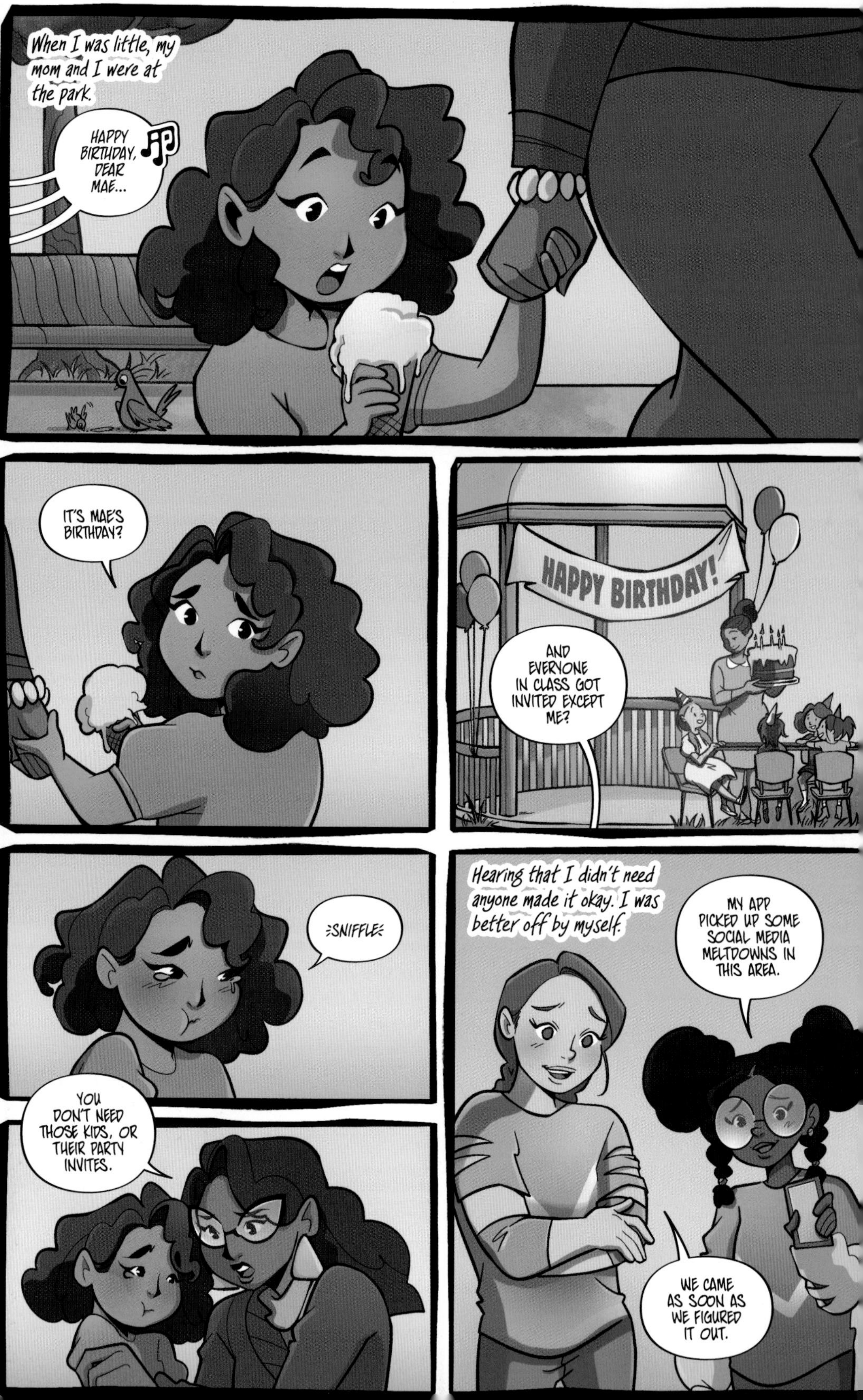
When I was little, my mom and I were at the park.
HAPPY BIRTHDAY, DEAR MAE...
IT'S MAE'S BIRTHDAY?
HAPPY BIRTHDAY!
AND EVERYONE IN CLASS GOT INVITED EXCEPT ME?
≶SNIFFLE≶
YOU DON'T NEED THOSE KIDS, OR THEIR PARTY INVITES.
Hearing that I didn't need anyone made it okay. I was better off by myself.
MY APP PICKED UP SOME SOCIAL MEDIA MELTDOWNS IN THIS AREA.
WE CAME AS SOON AS WE FIGURED IT OUT.

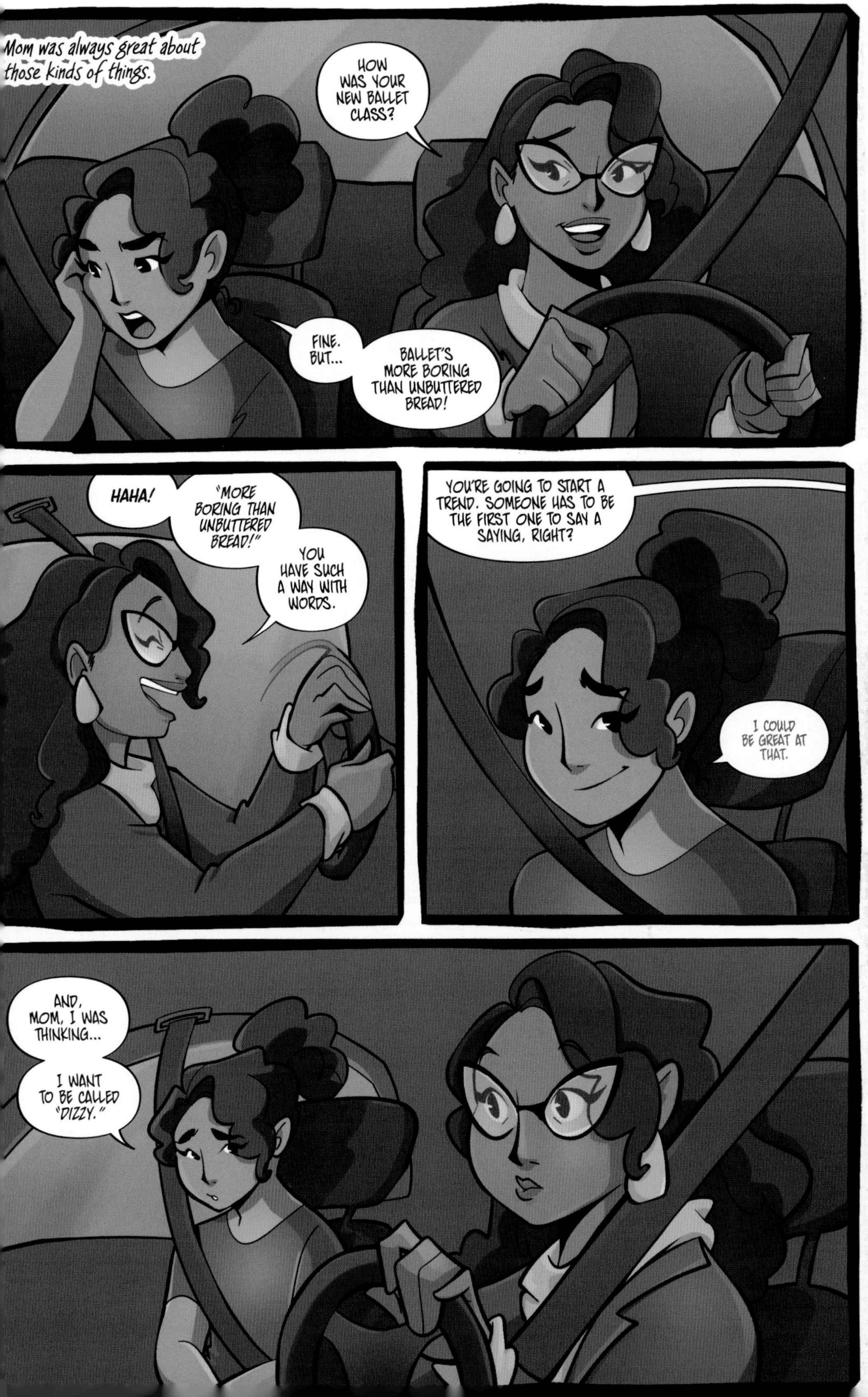
Mom was always great about those kinds of things.
HOW WAS YOUR NEW BALLET CLASS?
FINE. BUT...
BALLET'S MORE BORING THAN UNBUTTERED BREAD!
HAHA!
"MORE BORING THAN UNBUTTERED BREAD!"
YOU HAVE SUCH A WAY WITH WORDS.
YOU'RE GOING TO START A TREND. SOMEONE HAS TO BE THE FIRST ONE TO SAY A SAYING, RIGHT?
I COULD BE GREAT AT THAT.
AND, MOM, I WAS THINKING...
I WANT TO BE CALLED "DIZZY."

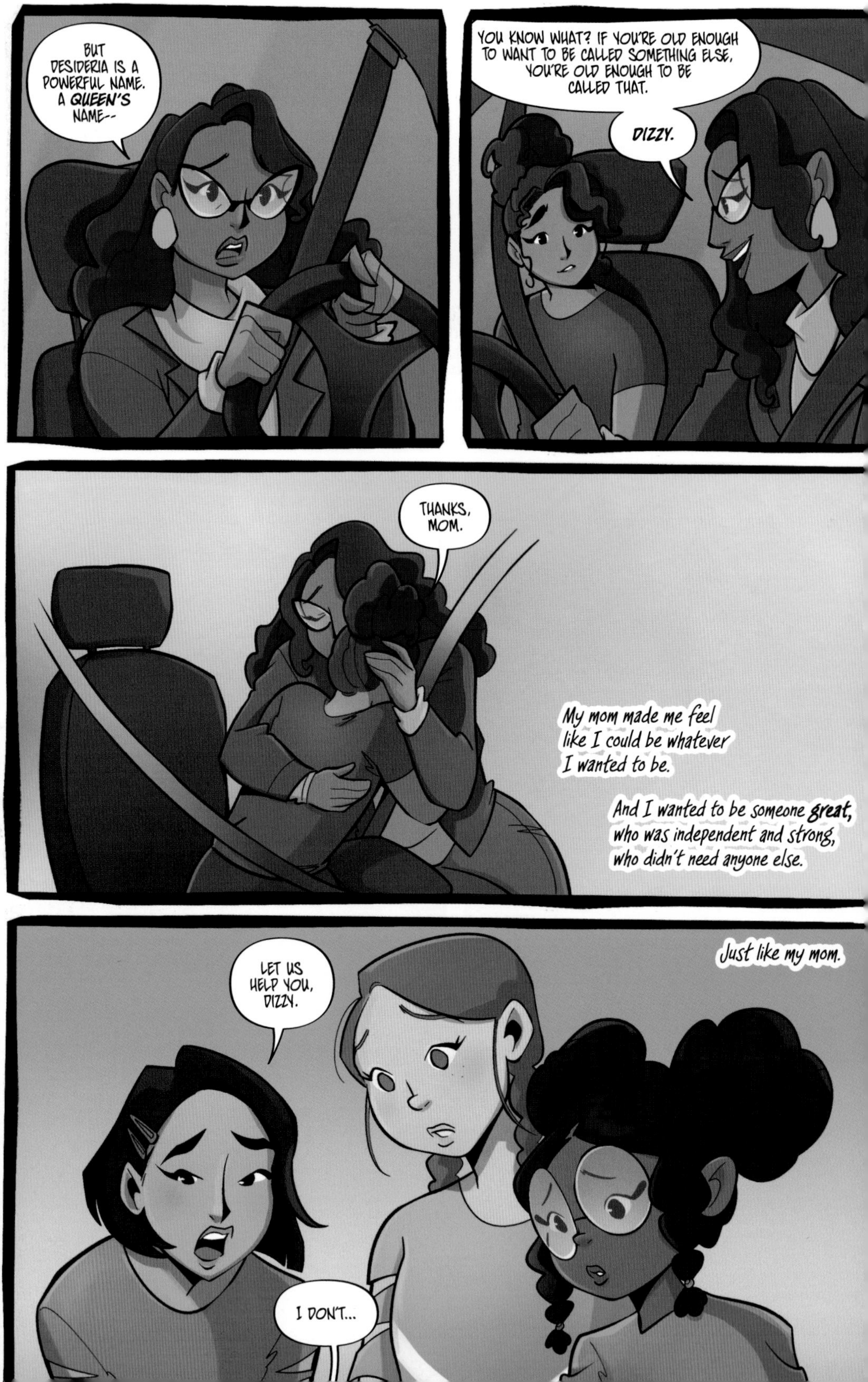
BUT DESIDERIA IS A POWERFUL NAME. A **QUEEN'S** NAME--
YOU KNOW WHAT? IF YOU'RE OLD ENOUGH TO WANT TO BE CALLED SOMETHING ELSE, YOU'RE OLD ENOUGH TO BE CALLED THAT.
DIZZY.
THANKS, MOM.
My mom made me feel like I could be whatever I wanted to be.
And I wanted to be someone **great,** who was independent and strong, who didn't need anyone else.
Just like my mom.
LET US HELP YOU, DIZZY.
I DON'T...

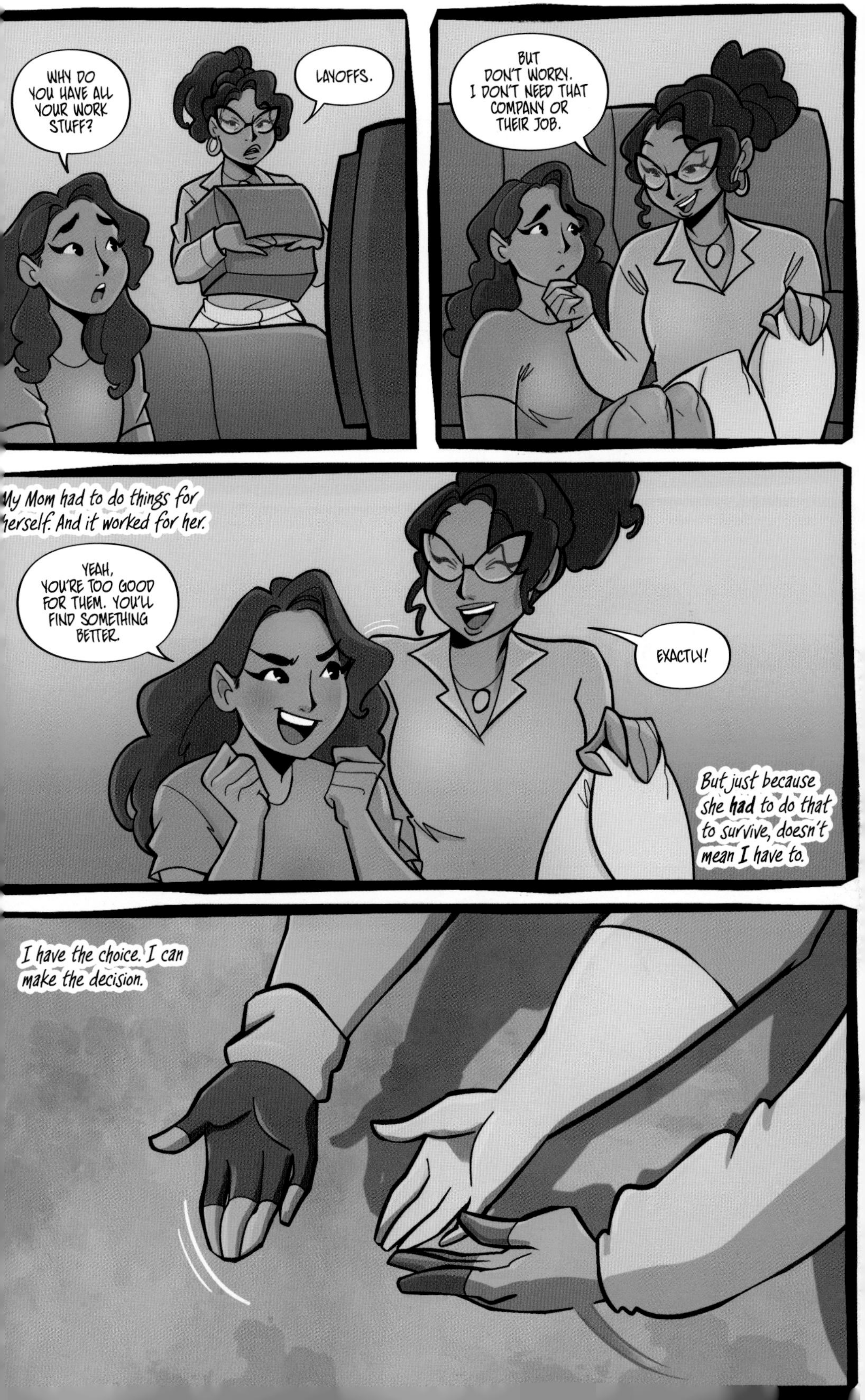
WHY DO YOU HAVE ALL YOUR WORK STUFF?
LAYOFFS.
BUT DON'T WORRY. I DON'T NEED THAT COMPANY OR THEIR JOB.
My Mom had to do things for herself. And it worked for her.
YEAH, YOU'RE TOO GOOD FOR THEM. YOU'LL FIND SOMETHING BETTER.
EXACTLY!
But just because she had to do that to survive, doesn't mean I have to.
I have the choice. I can make the decision.

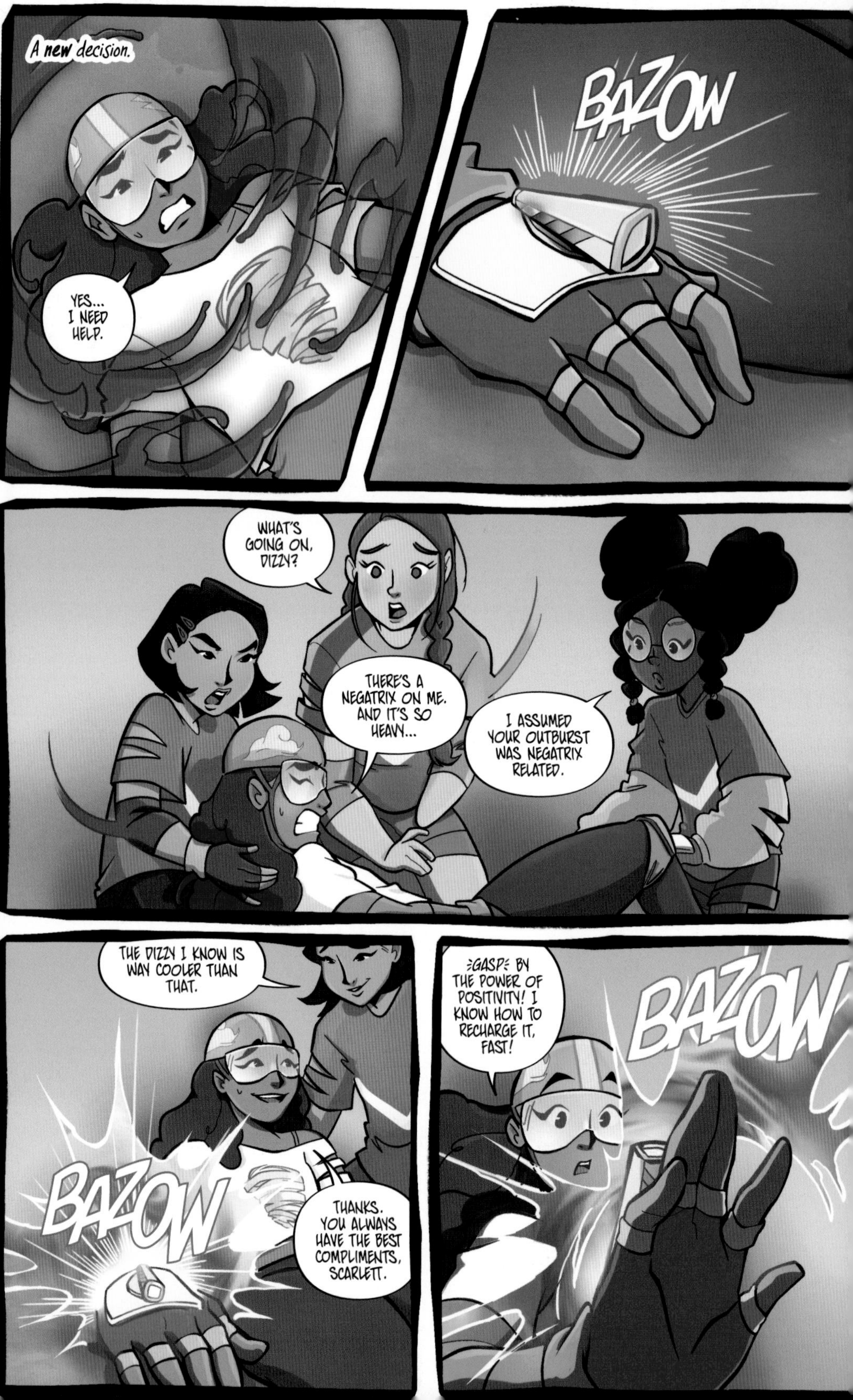
A new decision.
YES... I NEED HELP.
BAZOW
WHAT'S GOING ON, DIZZY?
THERE'S A NEGATRIX ON ME. AND IT'S SO HEAVY...
I ASSUMED YOUR OUTBURST WAS NEGATRIX RELATED.
THE DIZZY I KNOW IS WAY COOLER THAN THAT.
BAZOW
THANKS. YOU ALWAYS HAVE THE BEST COMPLIMENTS, SCARLETT.
=GASP= BY THE POWER OF POSITIVITY! I KNOW HOW TO RECHARGE IT, FAST!
BAZOW

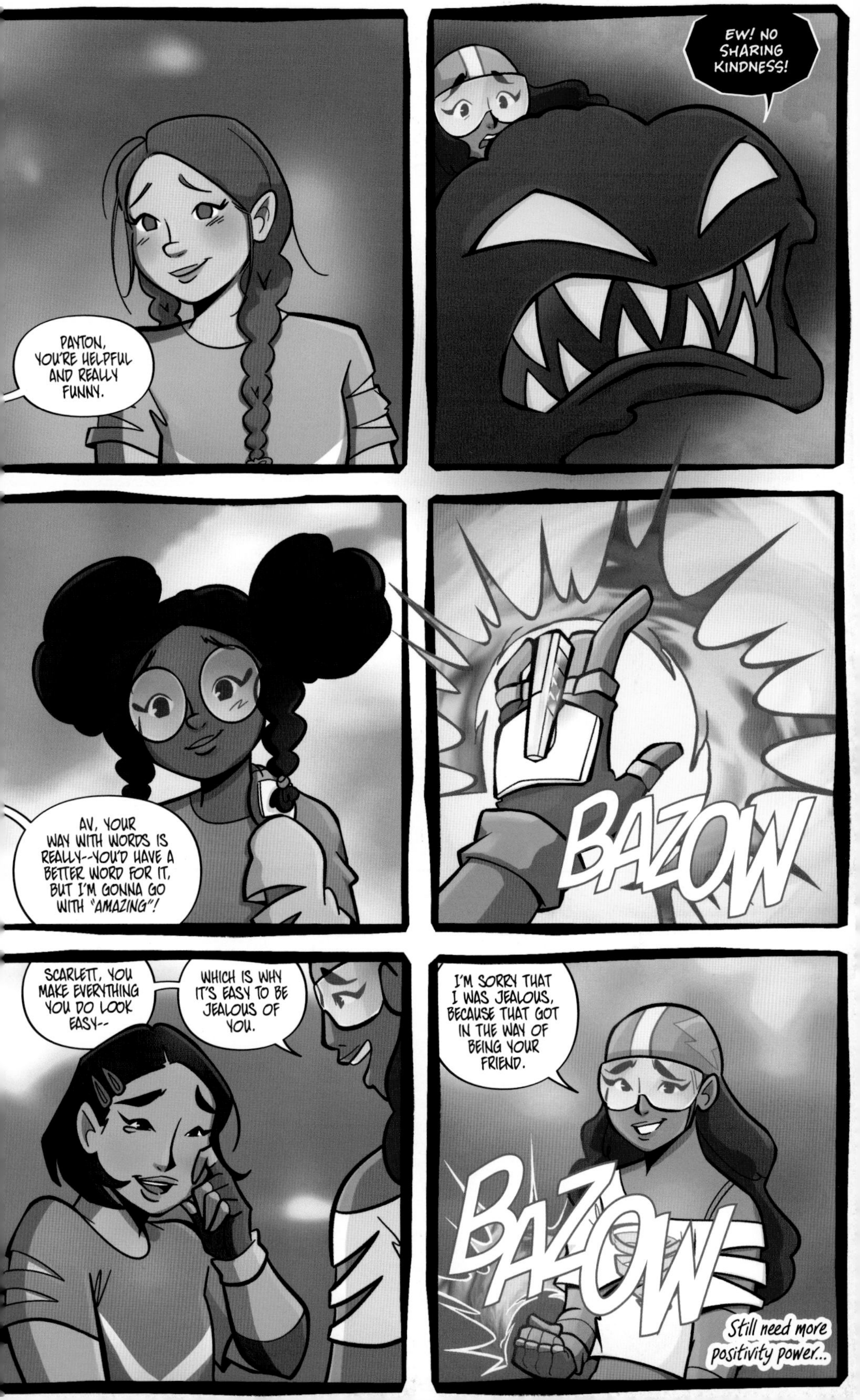
PAYTON, YOU'RE HELPFUL AND REALLY FUNNY.
EW! NO SHARING KINDNESS!
AV, YOUR WAY WITH WORDS IS REALLY--YOU'D HAVE A BETTER WORD FOR IT, BUT I'M GONNA GO WITH "AMAZING"!
BAZOW
SCARLETT, YOU MAKE EVERYTHING YOU DO LOOK EASY--
WHICH IS WHY IT'S EASY TO BE JEALOUS OF YOU.
I'M SORRY THAT I WAS JEALOUS, BECAUSE THAT GOT IN THE WAY OF BEING YOUR FRIEND.
BAZOW
Still need more positivity power...

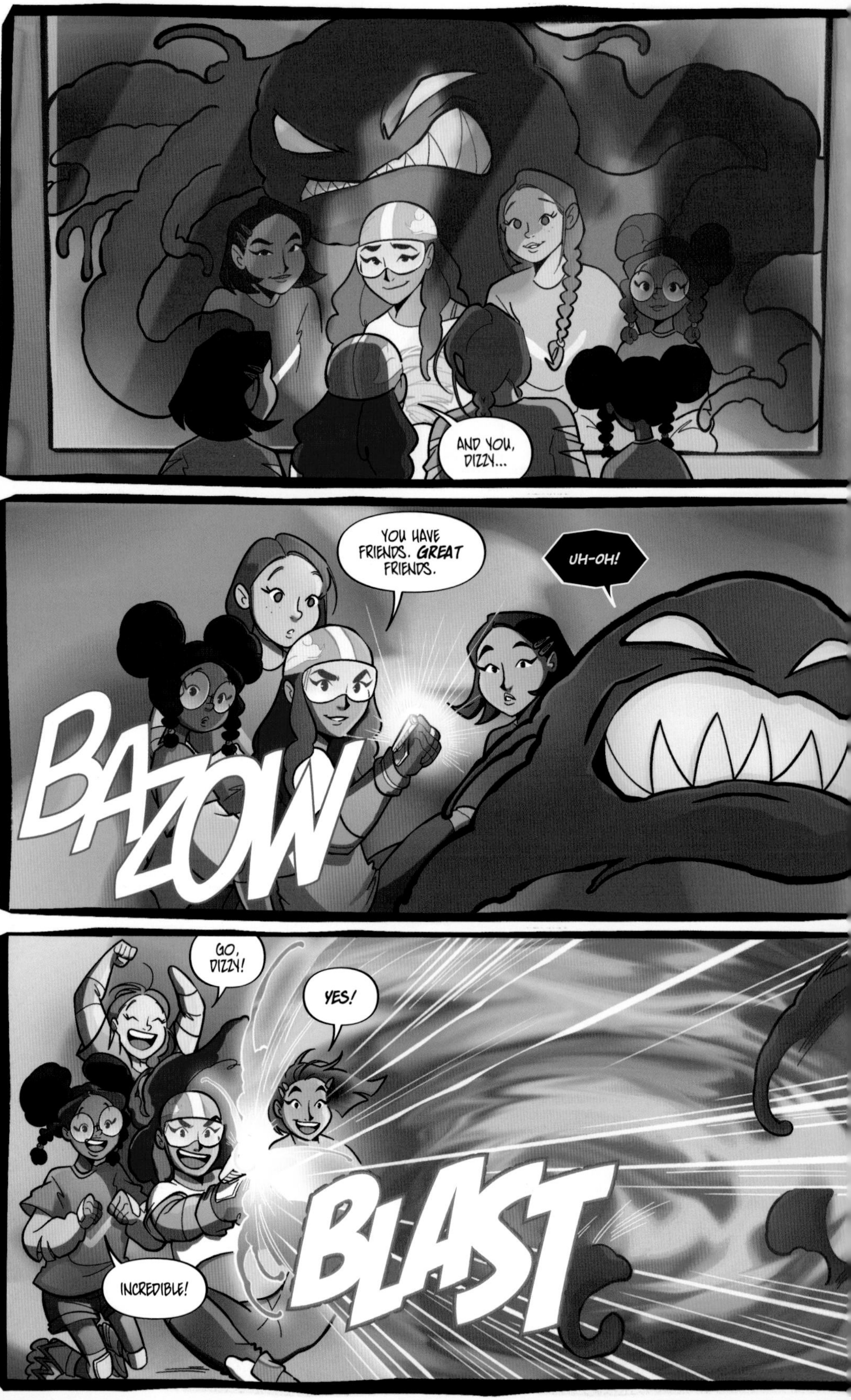
AND YOU, DIZZY...
YOU HAVE FRIENDS. GREAT FRIENDS.
UH-OH!
BAZOW
GO, DIZZY!
YES!
INCREDIBLE!
BLAST

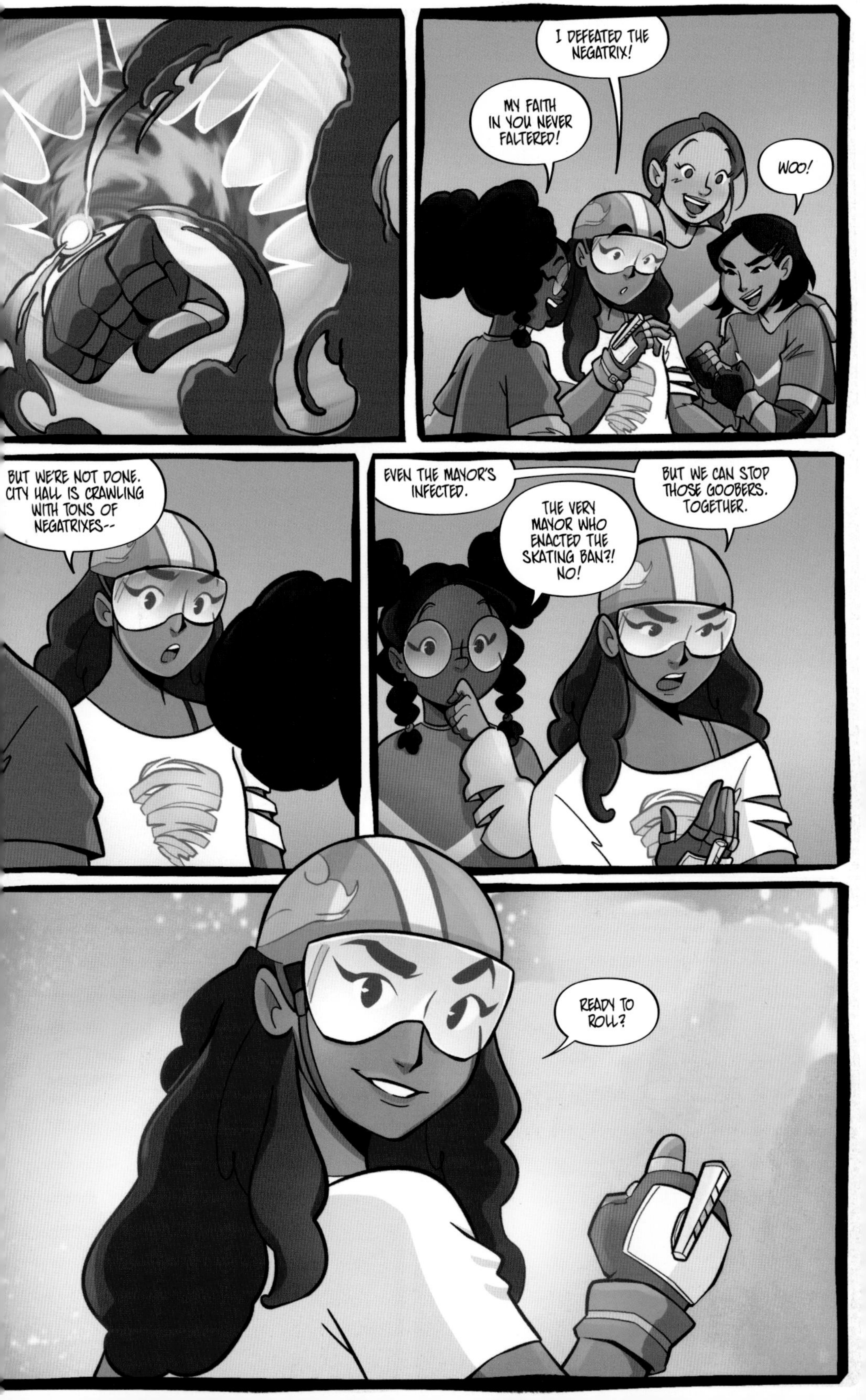
I DEFEATED THE NEGATRIX!
MY FAITH IN YOU NEVER FALTERED!
WOO!
BUT WE'RE NOT DONE. CITY HALL IS CRAWLING WITH TONS OF NEGATRIXES--
EVEN THE MAYOR'S INFECTED.
THE VERY MAYOR WHO ENACTED THE SKATING BAN?! NO!
BUT WE CAN STOP THOSE GOOBERS. TOGETHER.
READY TO ROLL?

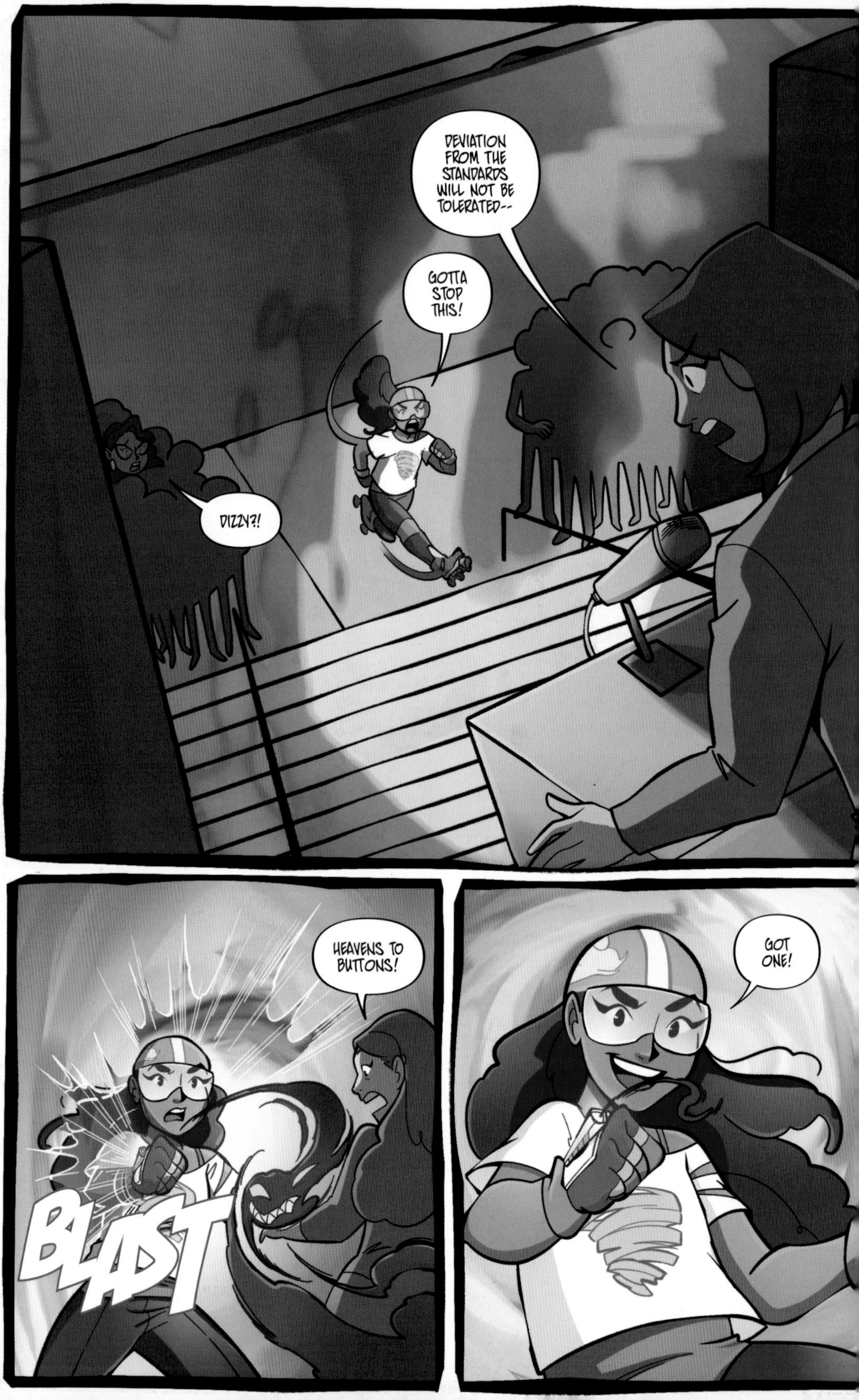
DEVIATION FROM THE STANDARDS WILL NOT BE TOLERATED--
GOTTA STOP THIS!
DIZZY?!
HEAVENS TO BUTTONS!
BLAST
GOT ONE!

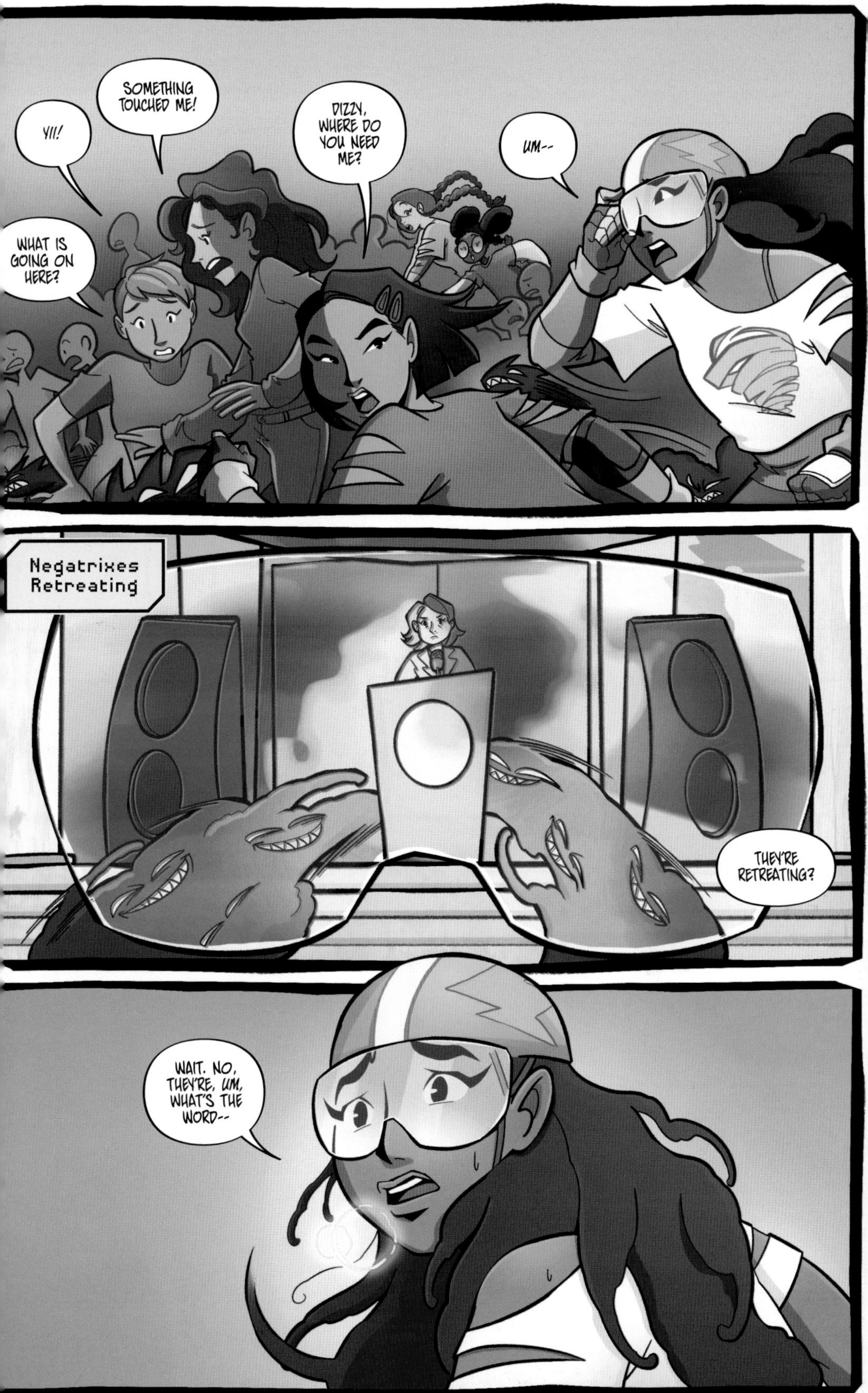

YII!
SOMETHING TOUCHED ME!
WHAT IS GOING ON HERE?
DIZZY, WHERE DO YOU NEED ME?
UM--
Negatrixes Retreating
THEY'RE RETREATING?
WAIT. NO, THEY'RE, UM, WHAT'S THE WORD--

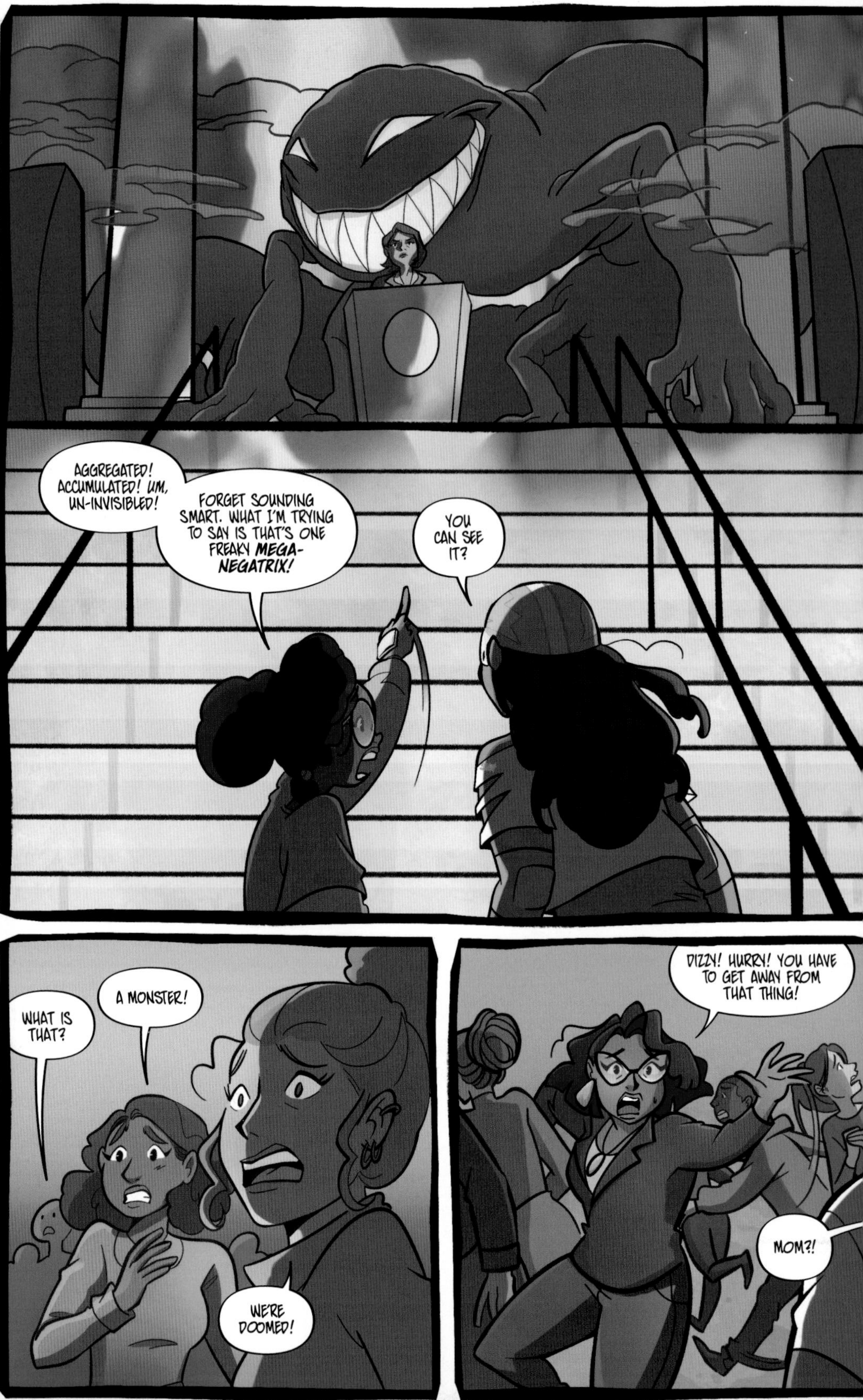
AGGREGATED! ACCUMULATED! UM, UN-INVISIBLED!
FORGET SOUNDING SMART. WHAT I'M TRYING TO SAY IS THAT'S ONE FREAKY **MEGA-NEGATRIX!**
YOU CAN SEE IT?
WHAT IS THAT?
A MONSTER!
WE'RE DOOMED!
DIZZY! HURRY! YOU HAVE TO GET AWAY FROM THAT THING!
MOM?!

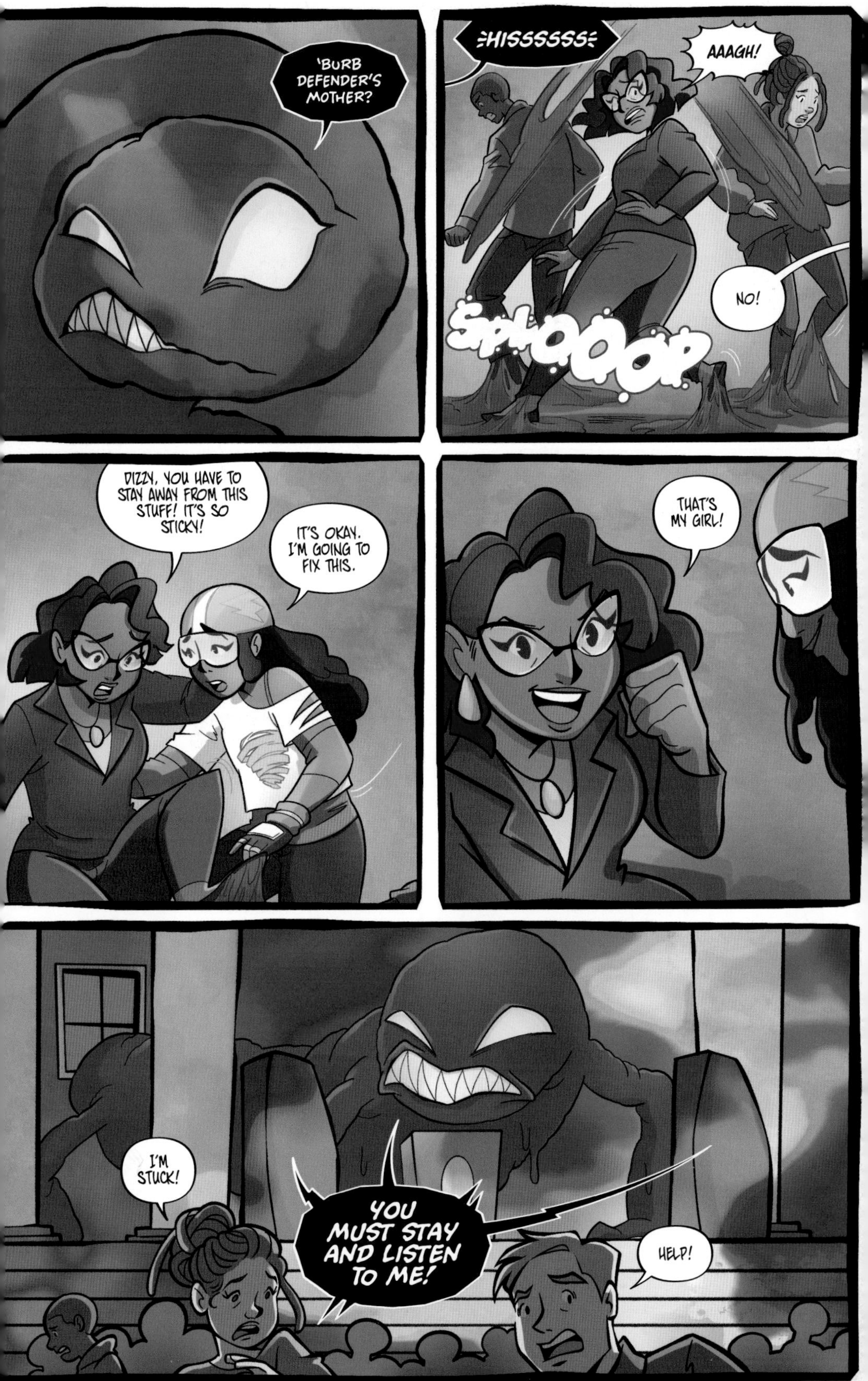
'BURB DEFENDER'S MOTHER?
HISSSSSS
AAAGH!
SPLOOOOP
NO!
DIZZY, YOU HAVE TO STAY AWAY FROM THIS STUFF! IT'S SO STICKY!
IT'S OKAY. I'M GOING TO FIX THIS.
THAT'S MY GIRL!
I'M STUCK!
YOU MUST STAY AND LISTEN TO ME!
HELP!

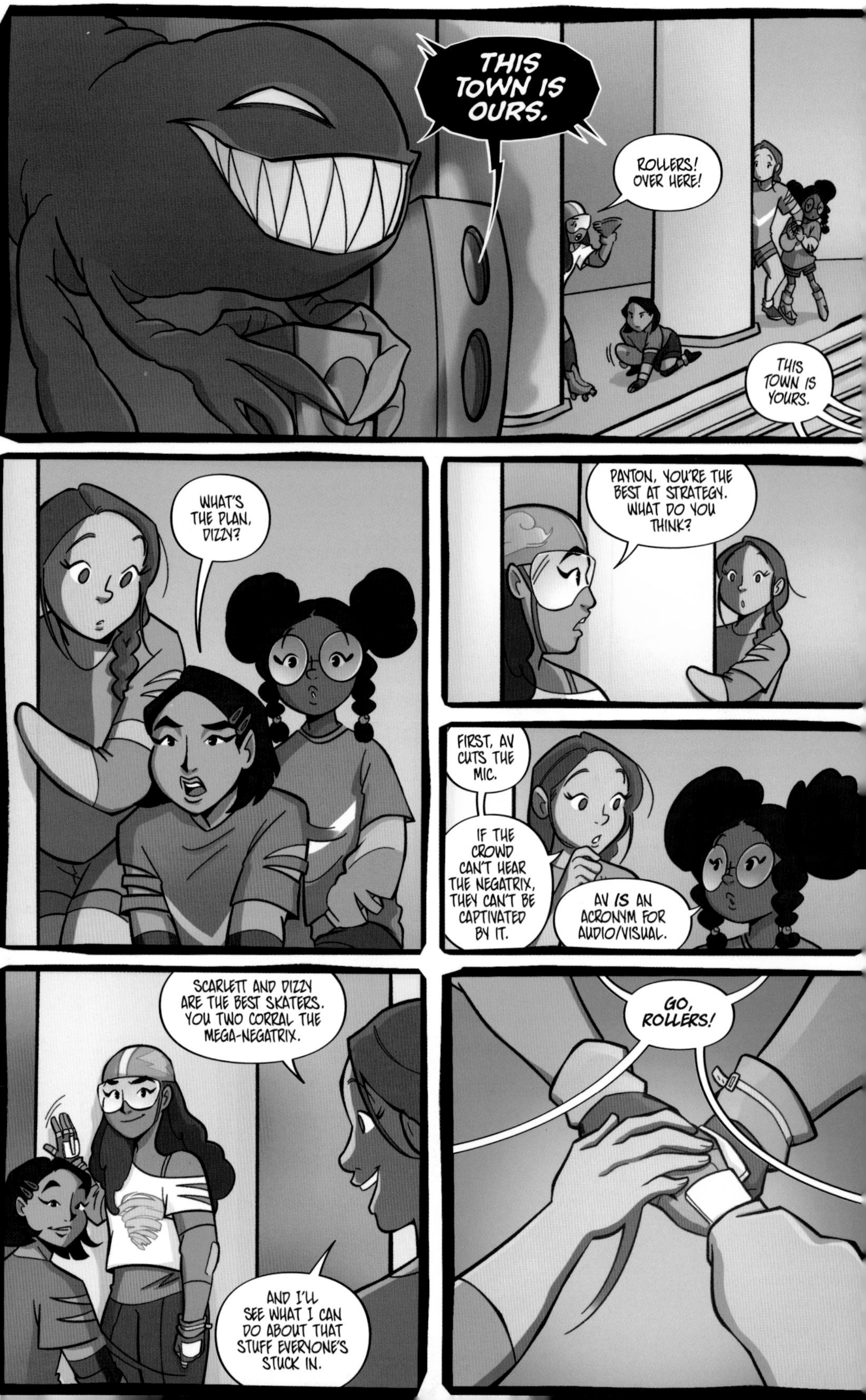
THIS TOWN IS OURS.
ROLLERS! OVER HERE!
THIS TOWN IS YOURS.
WHAT'S THE PLAN, DIZZY?
PAYTON, YOU'RE THE BEST AT STRATEGY. WHAT DO YOU THINK?
FIRST, AV CUTS THE MIC.
IF THE CROWD CAN'T HEAR THE NEGATRIX, THEY CAN'T BE CAPTIVATED BY IT.
AV *IS* AN ACRONYM FOR AUDIO/VISUAL.
SCARLETT AND DIZZY ARE THE BEST SKATERS. YOU TWO CORRAL THE MEGA-NEGATRIX.
AND I'LL SEE WHAT I CAN DO ABOUT THAT STUFF EVERYONE'S STUCK IN.
GO, ROLLERS!

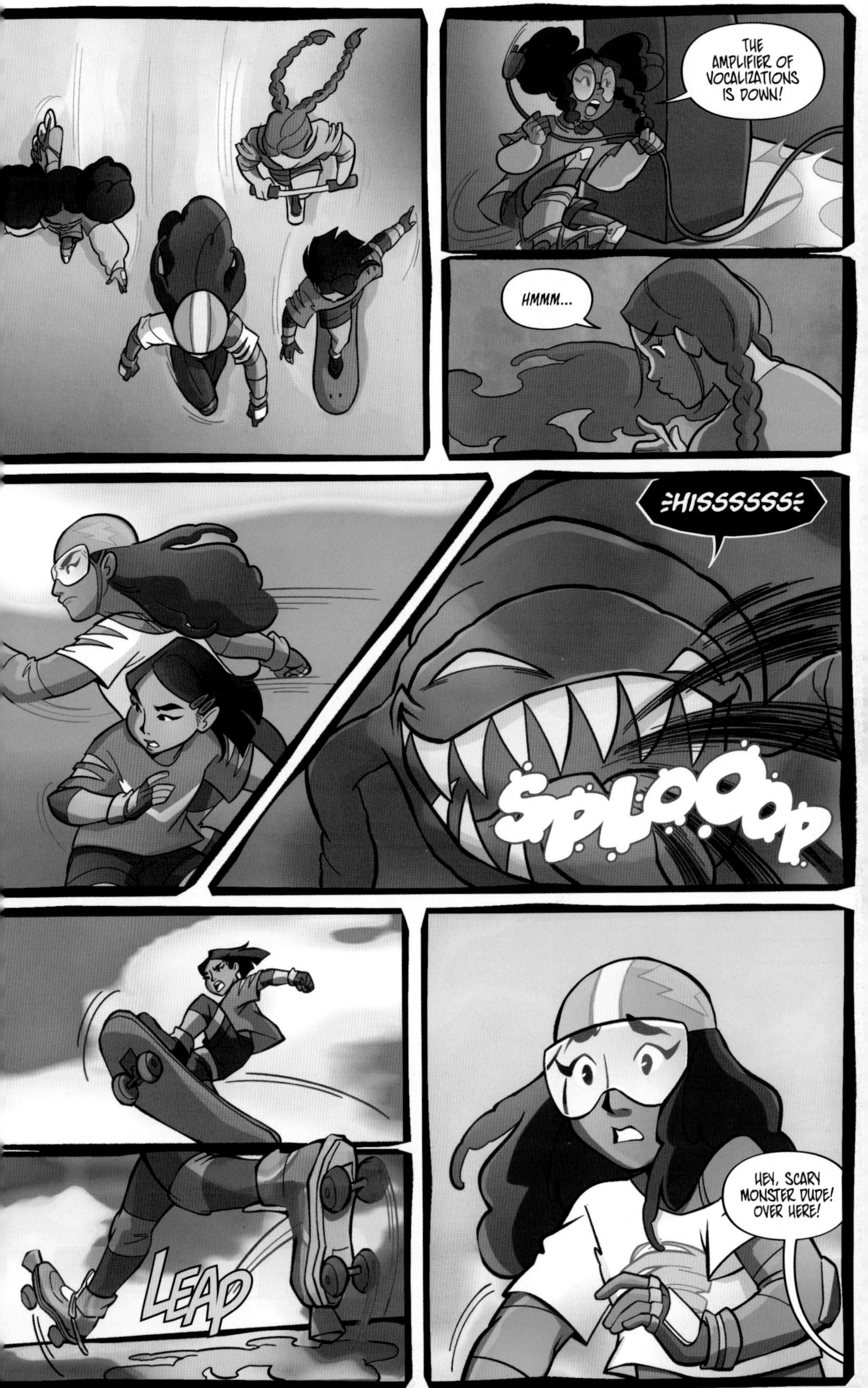
THE AMPLIFIER OF VOCALIZATIONS IS DOWN!
HMMM...
HISSSSSS
SPLOOOOP
LEAP
HEY, SCARY MONSTER DUDE! OVER HERE!

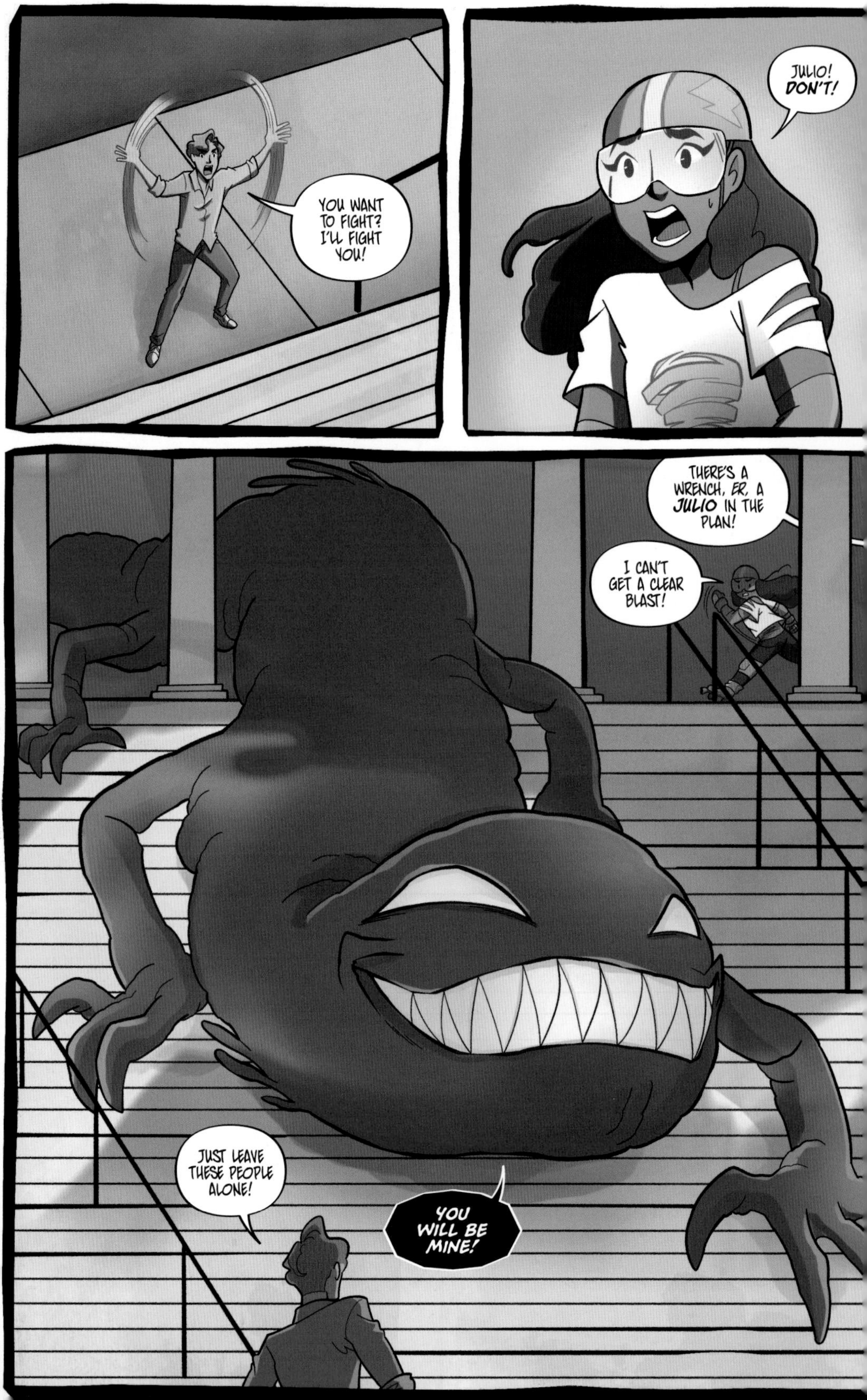
YOU WANT TO FIGHT? I'LL FIGHT YOU!
JULIO! DON'T!
THERE'S A WRENCH, ER, A JULIO IN THE PLAN!
I CAN'T GET A CLEAR BLAST!
JUST LEAVE THESE PEOPLE ALONE!
YOU WILL BE MINE!

YOU WILL BE MY NEW HOST.

UH-OH.

IT'S GOING TO TAKE OVER JULIO! DIZZY, WE HAVE TO STOP IT!

Stairs. My other arch-nemesis. Scarlett is way better at stairs.

But if I don't do it, I won't save Julio.

All these people won't chant my name.

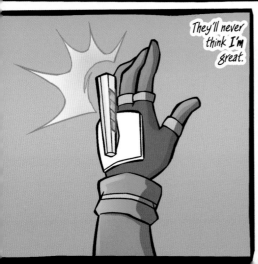

They'll never think I'm great.

SCARLETT! CATCH!

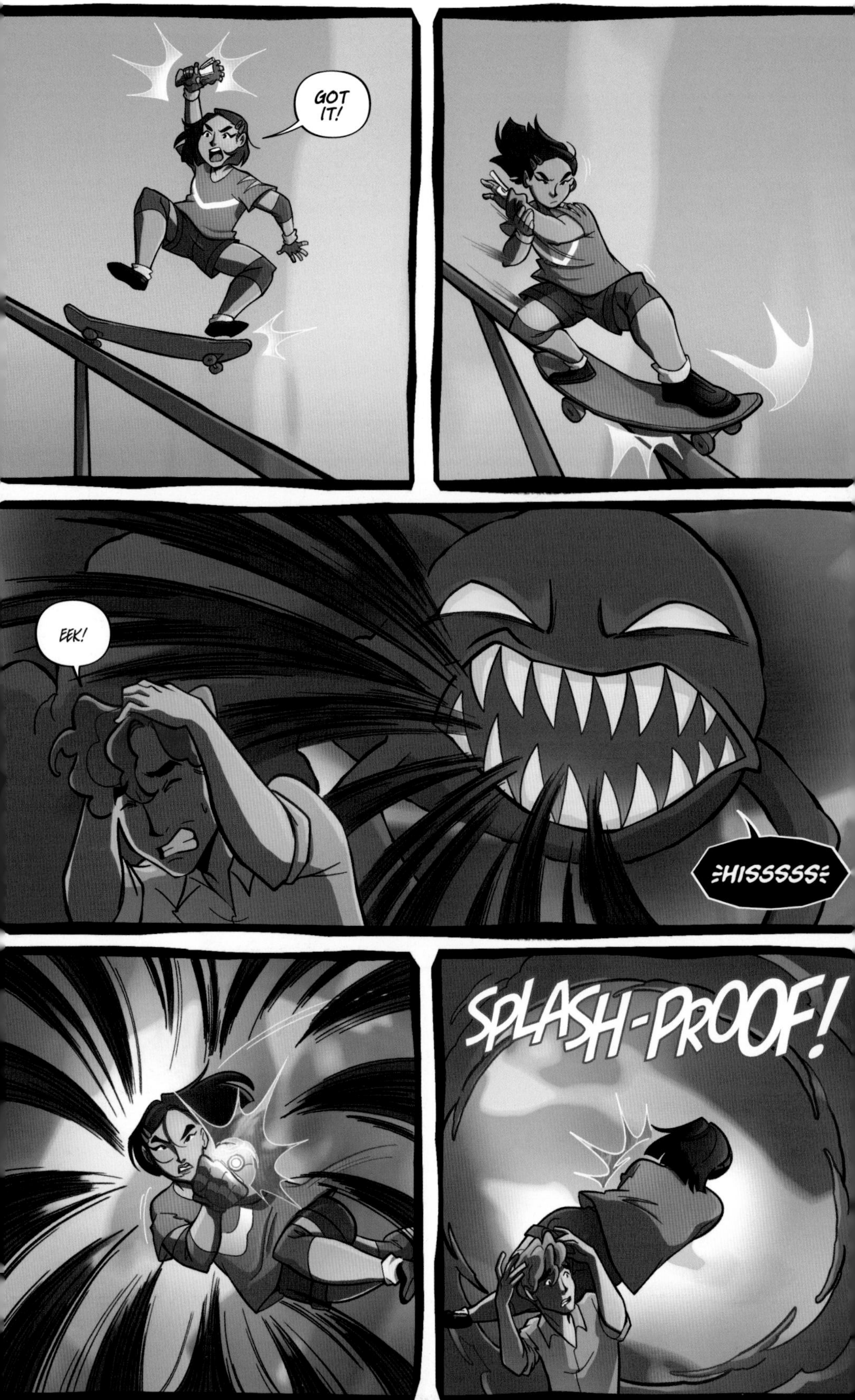
GOT IT!
EEK!
HISSSSS
SPLASH-PROOF!

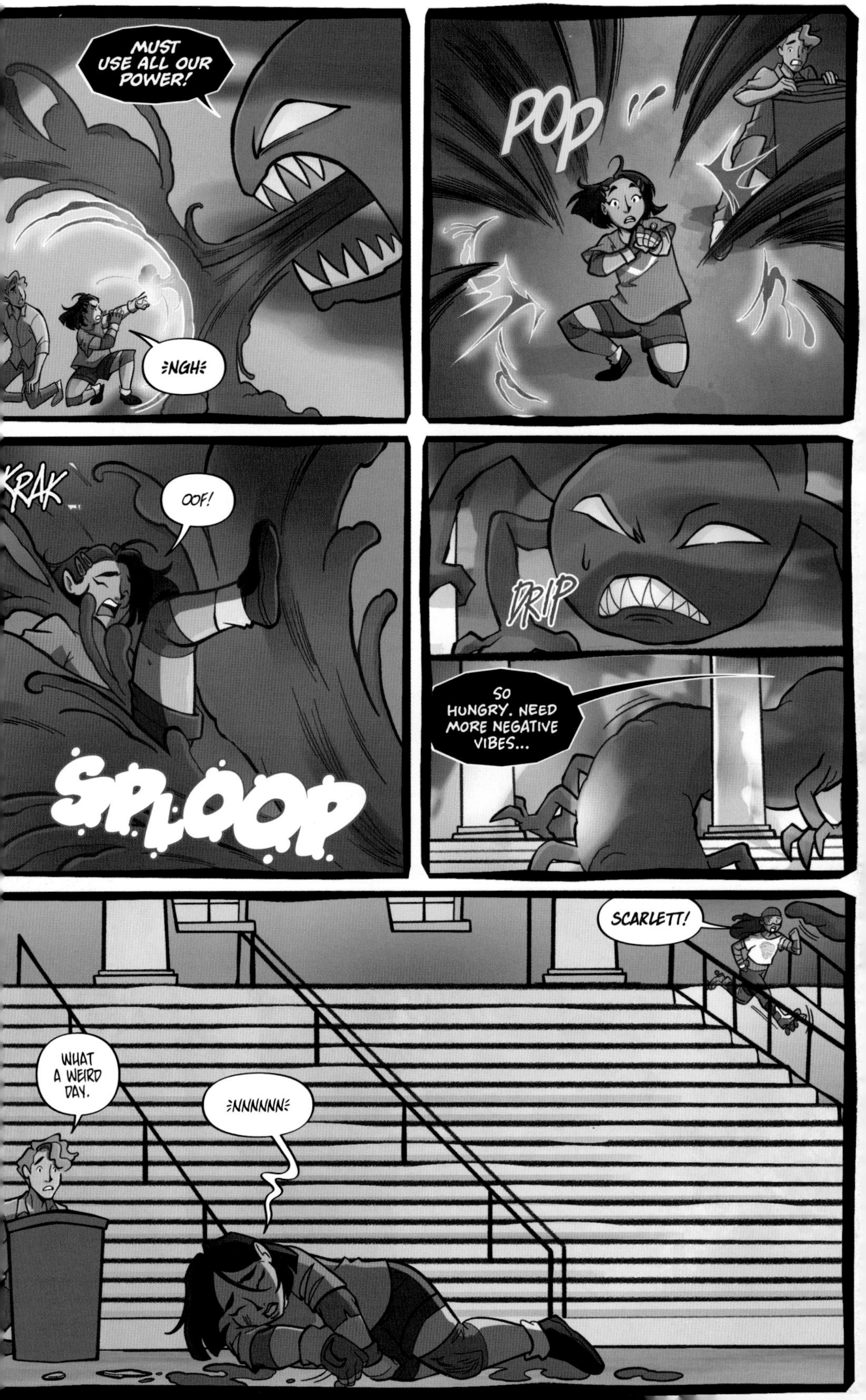
MUST USE ALL OUR POWER!
NGH
POP
KRAK
OOF!
SPLOOP
DRIP
SO HUNGRY. NEED MORE NEGATIVE VIBES...
SCARLETT!
WHAT A WEIRD DAY.
NNNNNN

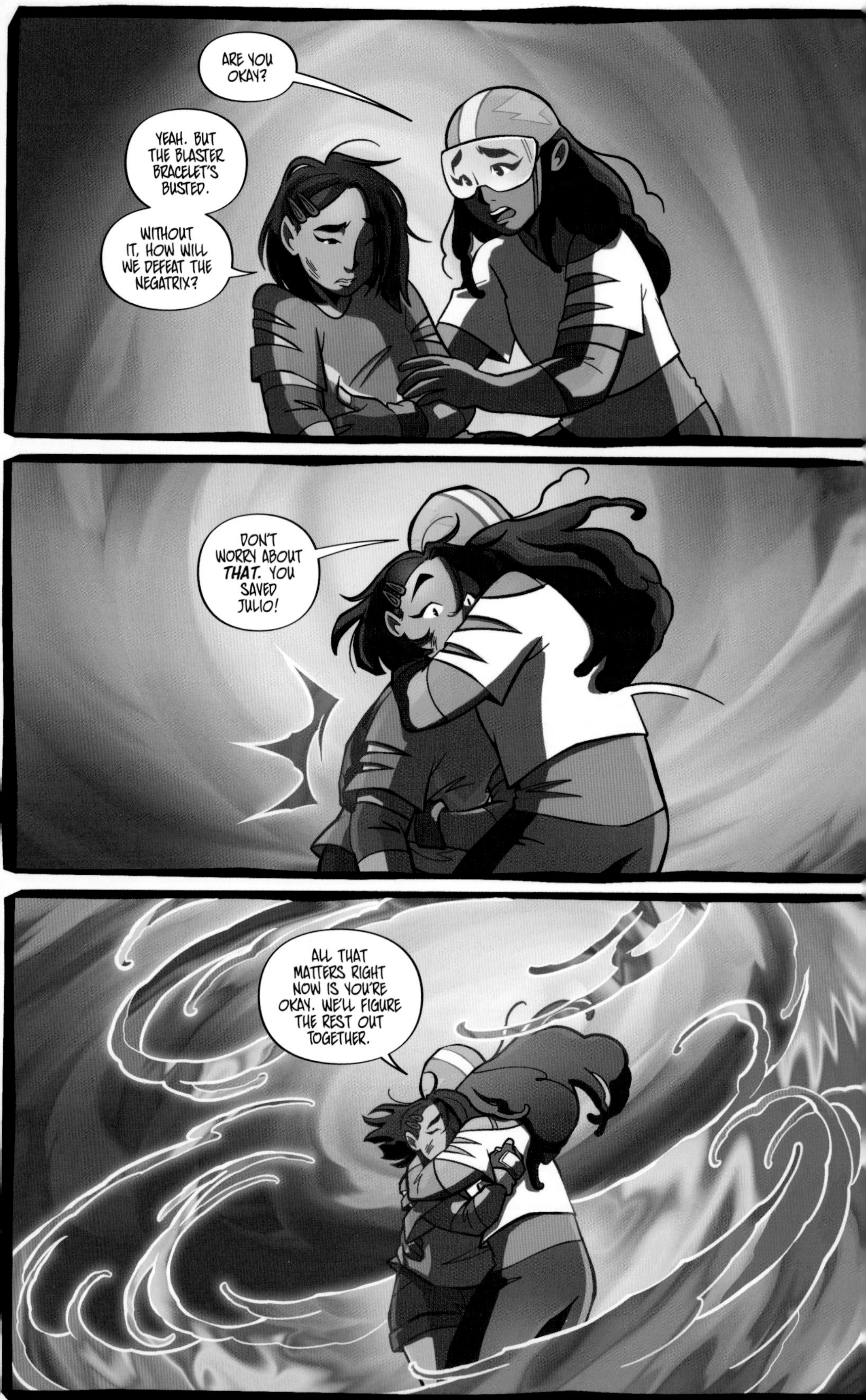
ARE YOU OKAY?
YEAH. BUT THE BLASTER BRACELET'S BUSTED.
WITHOUT IT, HOW WILL WE DEFEAT THE NEGATRIX?
DON'T WORRY ABOUT *THAT.* YOU SAVED JULIO!
ALL THAT MATTERS RIGHT NOW IS YOU'RE OKAY. WE'LL FIGURE THE REST OUT TOGETHER.

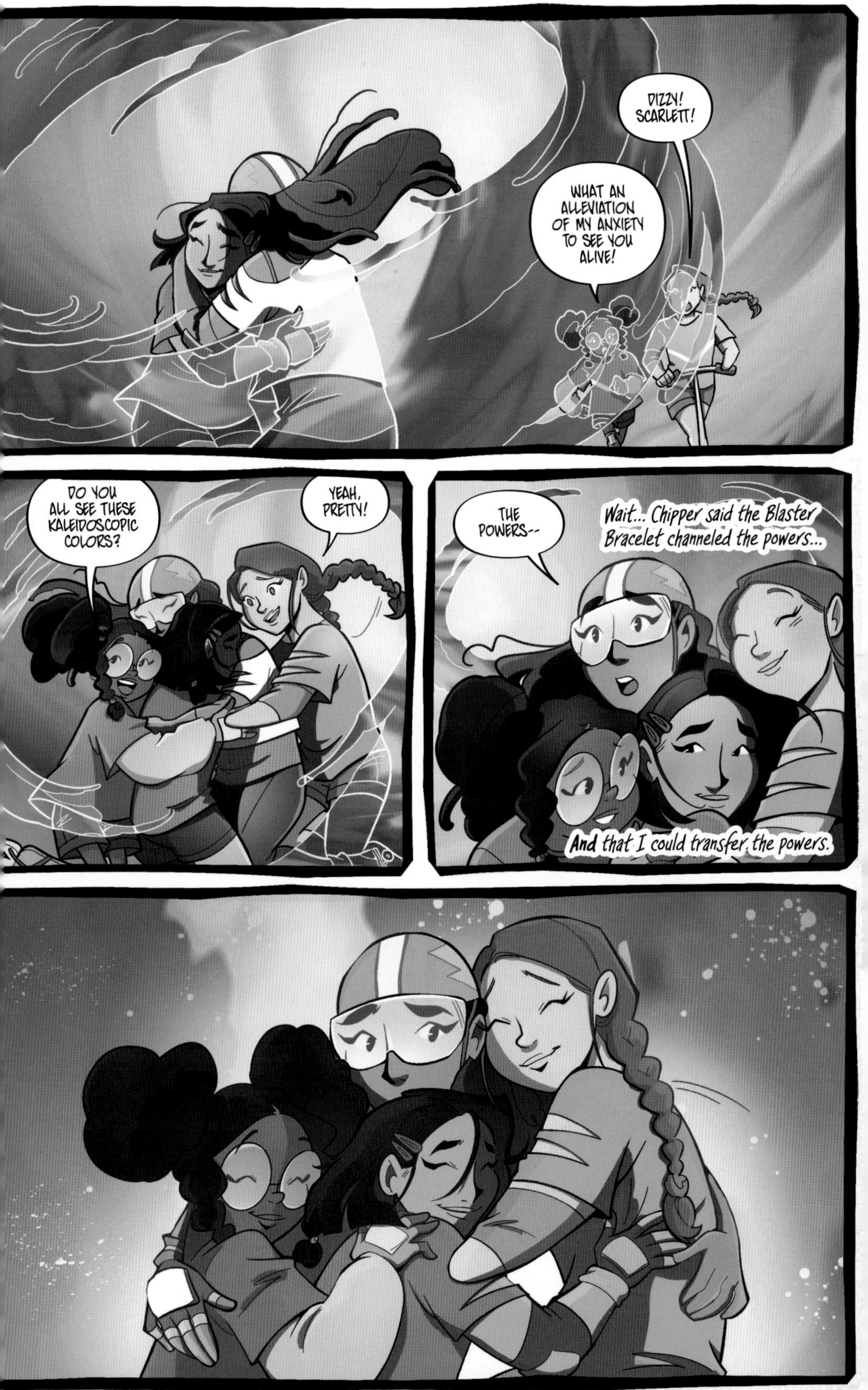
DIZZY! SCARLETT!
WHAT AN ALLEVIATION OF MY ANXIETY TO SEE YOU ALIVE!
DO YOU ALL SEE THESE KALEIDOSCOPIC COLORS?
YEAH, PRETTY!
THE POWERS--
Wait... Chipper said the Blaster Bracelet channeled the powers...
And that I could transfer the powers.

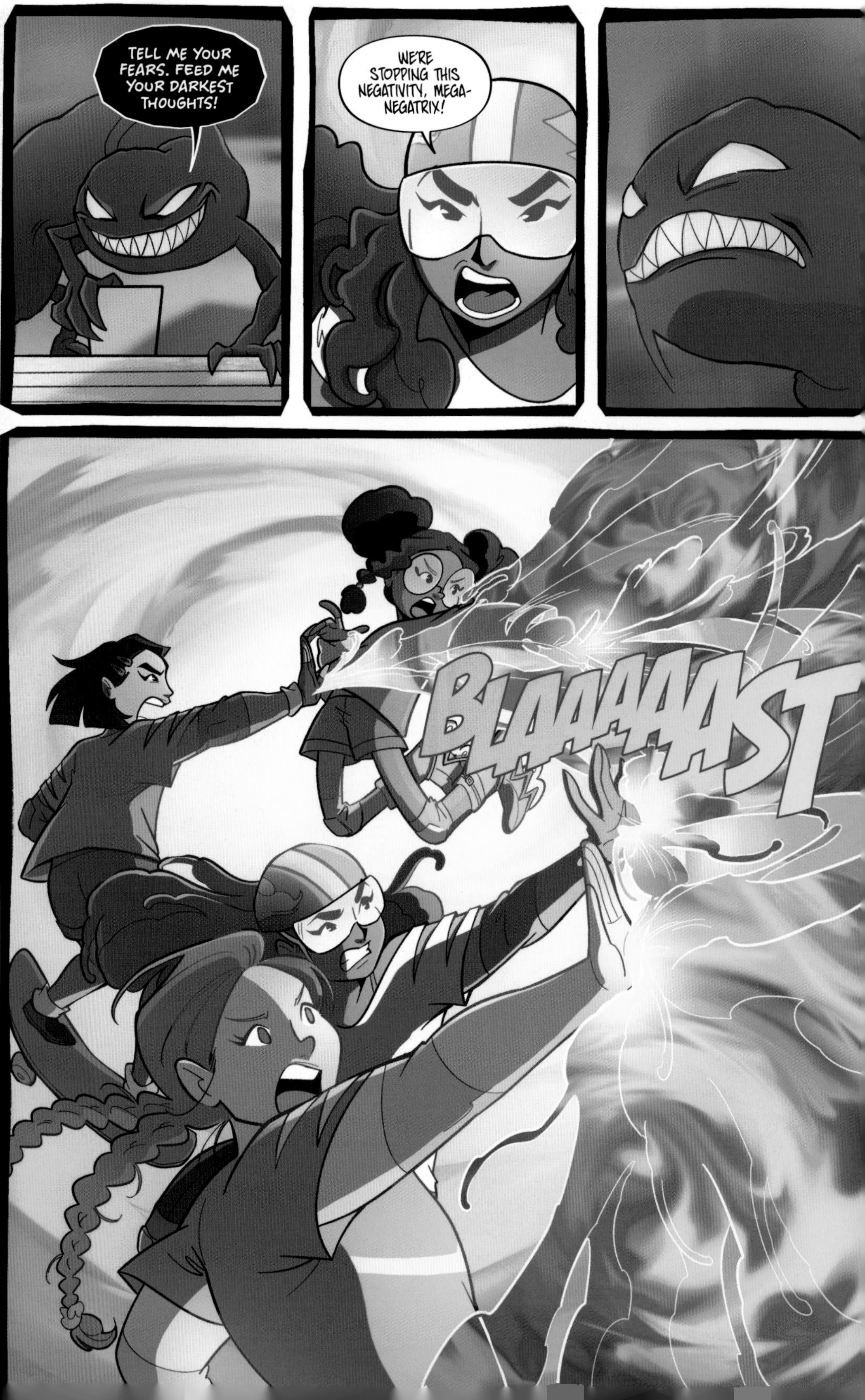
TELL ME YOUR FEARS. FEED ME YOUR DARKEST THOUGHTS!
WE'RE STOPPING THIS NEGATIVITY, MEGA-NEGATRIX!
BLAAAAAST

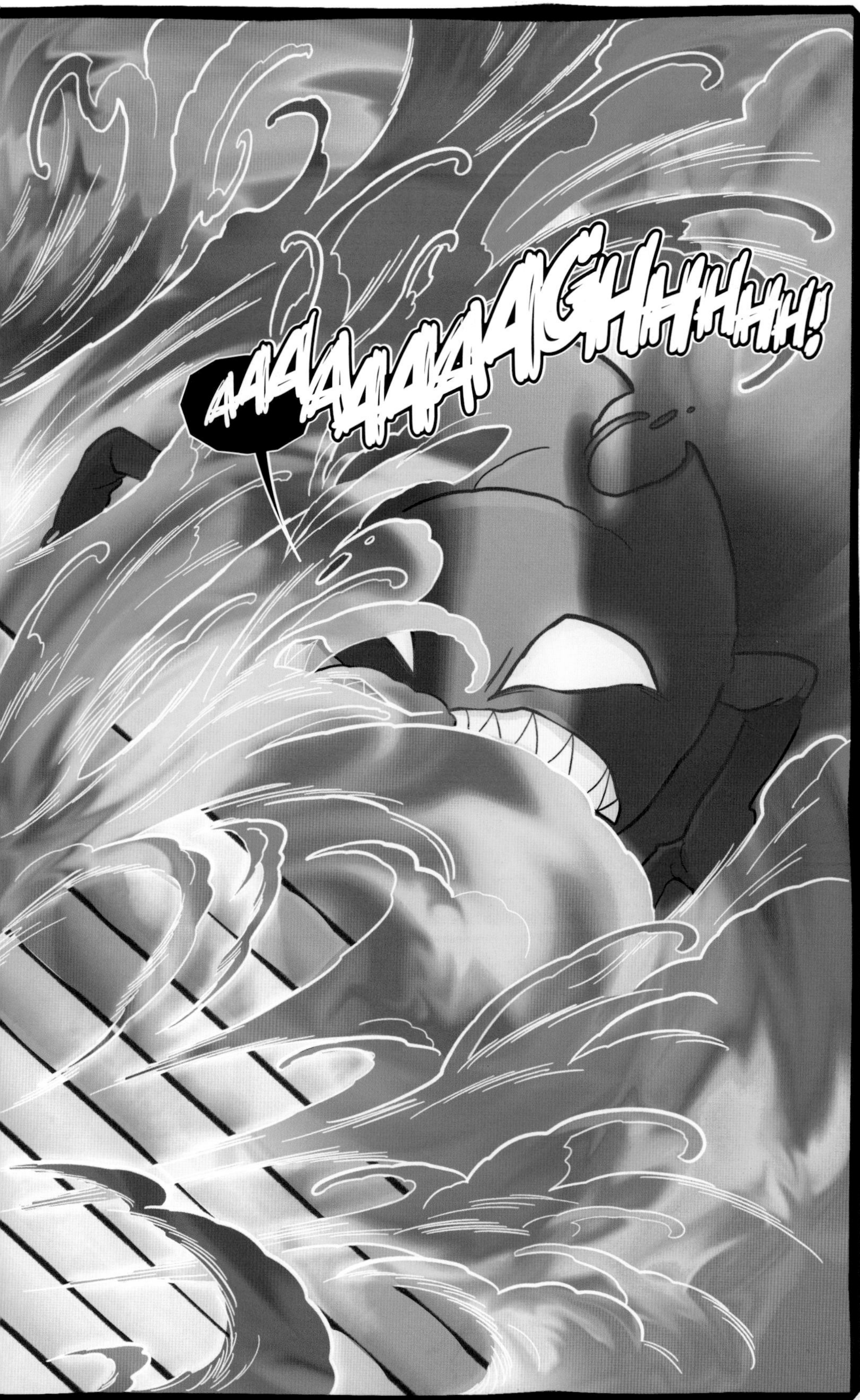
AAAAAAAAAGHHHHHH!

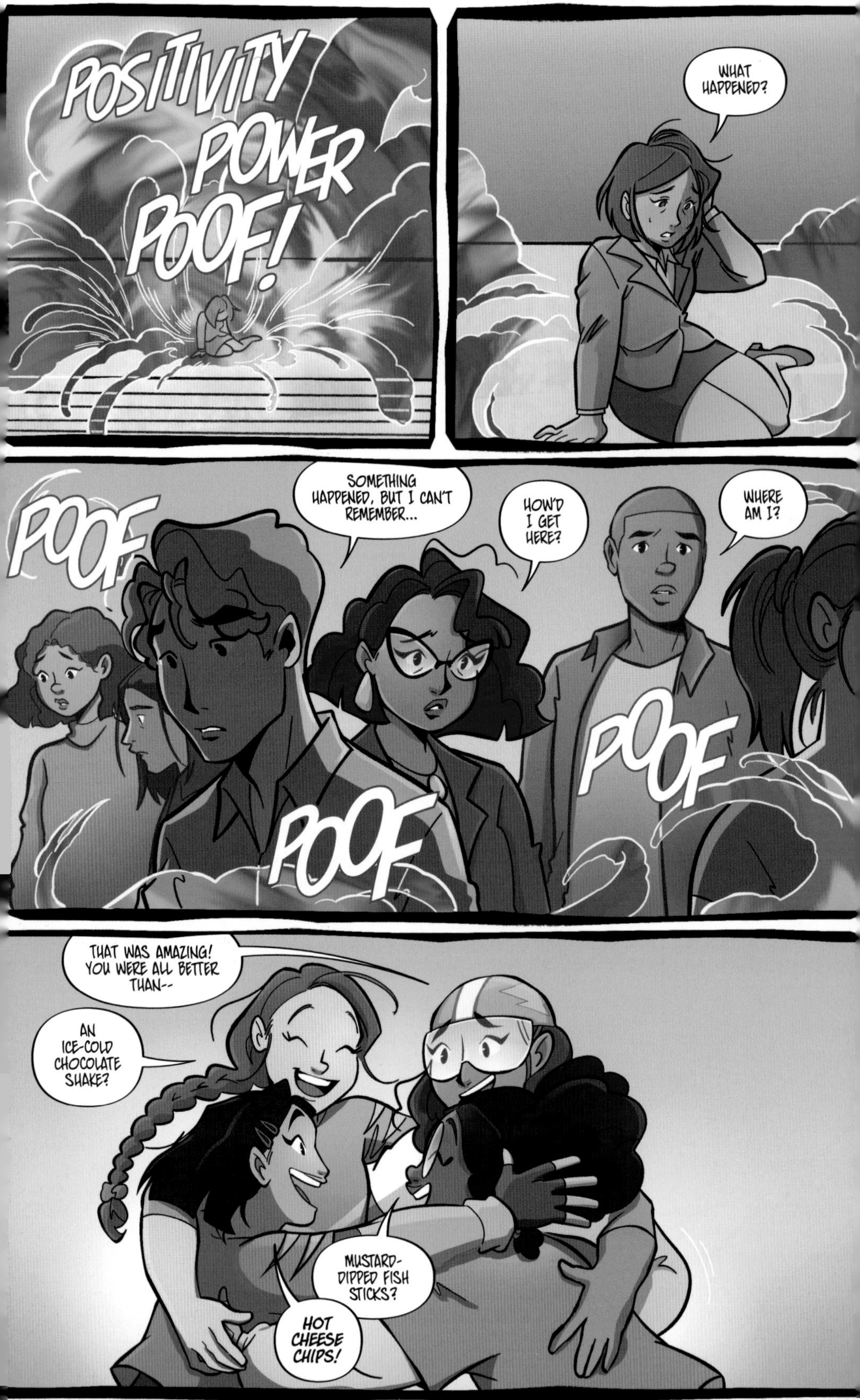
POSITIVITY POWER POOF!
WHAT HAPPENED?
POOF
SOMETHING HAPPENED, BUT I CAN'T REMEMBER...
HOW'D I GET HERE?
WHERE AM I?
POOF
POOF
THAT WAS AMAZING! YOU WERE ALL BETTER THAN--
AN ICE-COLD CHOCOLATE SHAKE?
MUSTARD-DIPPED FISH STICKS?
HOT CHEESE CHIPS!

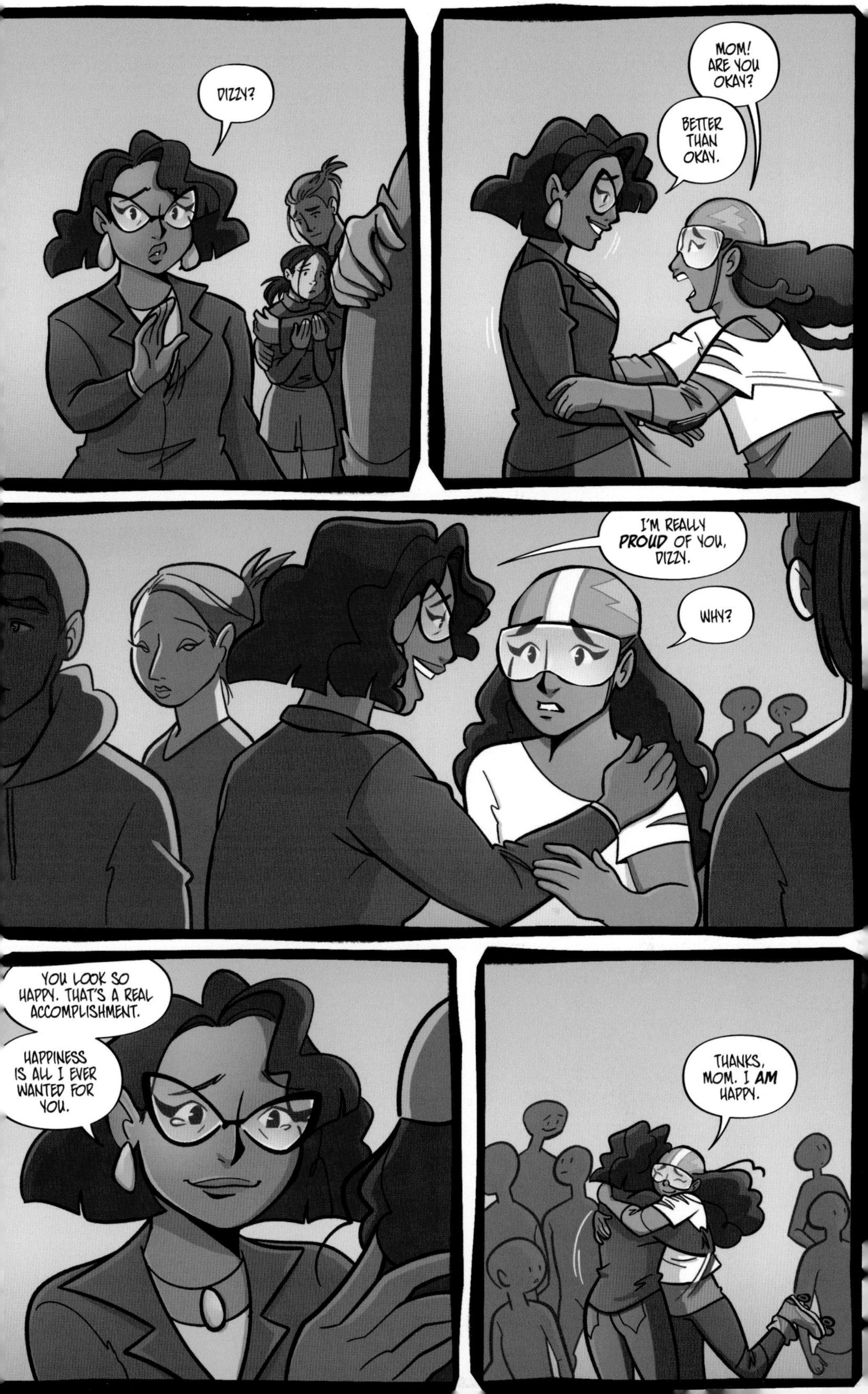
DIZZY?
MOM! ARE YOU OKAY?
BETTER THAN OKAY.
I'M REALLY **PROUD** OF YOU, DIZZY.
WHY?
YOU LOOK SO HAPPY. THAT'S A REAL ACCOMPLISHMENT.
HAPPINESS IS ALL I EVER WANTED FOR YOU.
THANKS, MOM. I **AM** HAPPY.

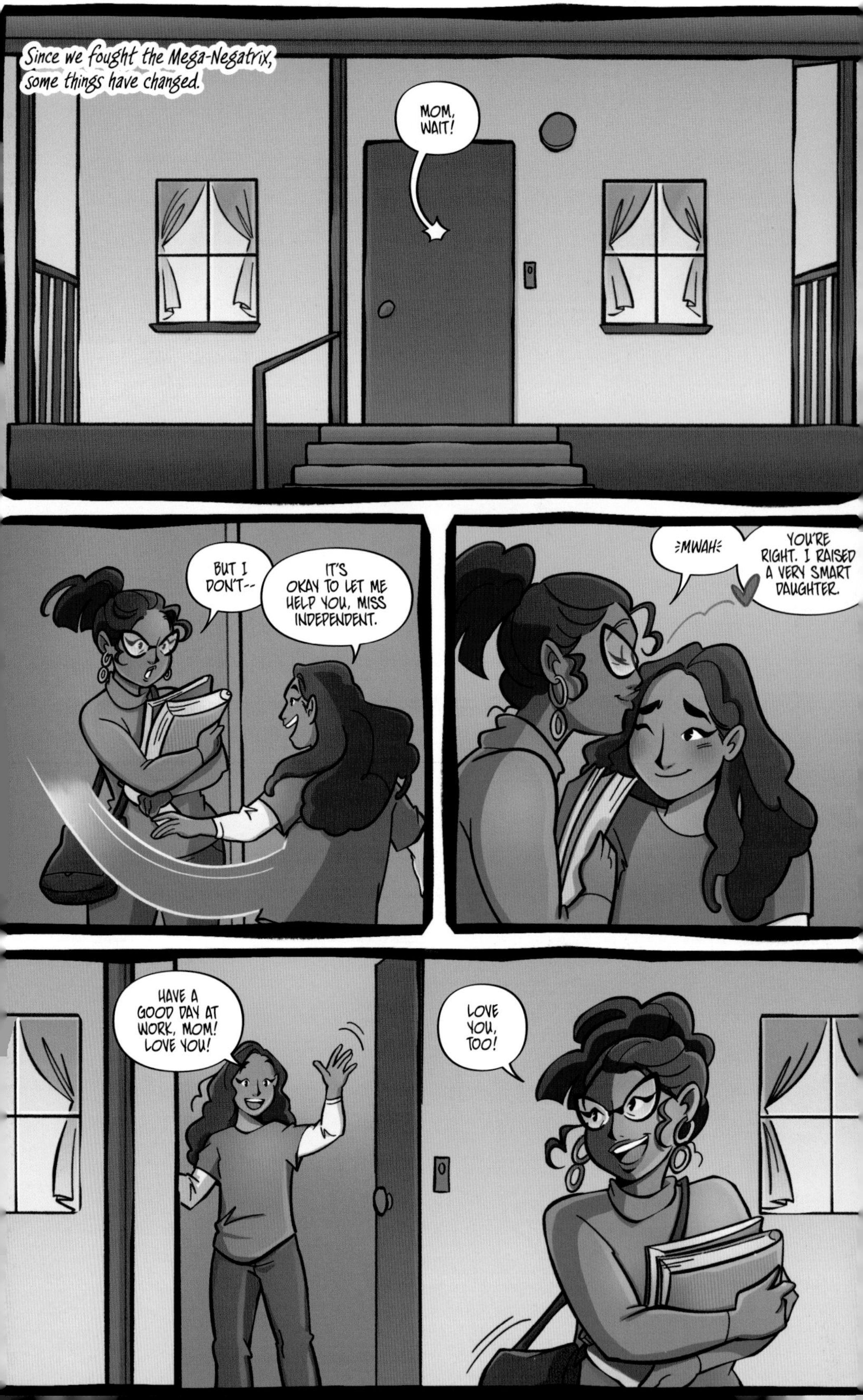

Since we fought the Mega-Negatrix, some things have changed.
MOM, WAIT!
BUT I DON'T--
IT'S OKAY TO LET ME HELP YOU, MISS INDEPENDENT.
MWAH
YOU'RE RIGHT. I RAISED A VERY SMART DAUGHTER.
HAVE A GOOD DAY AT WORK, MOM! LOVE YOU!
LOVE YOU, TOO!

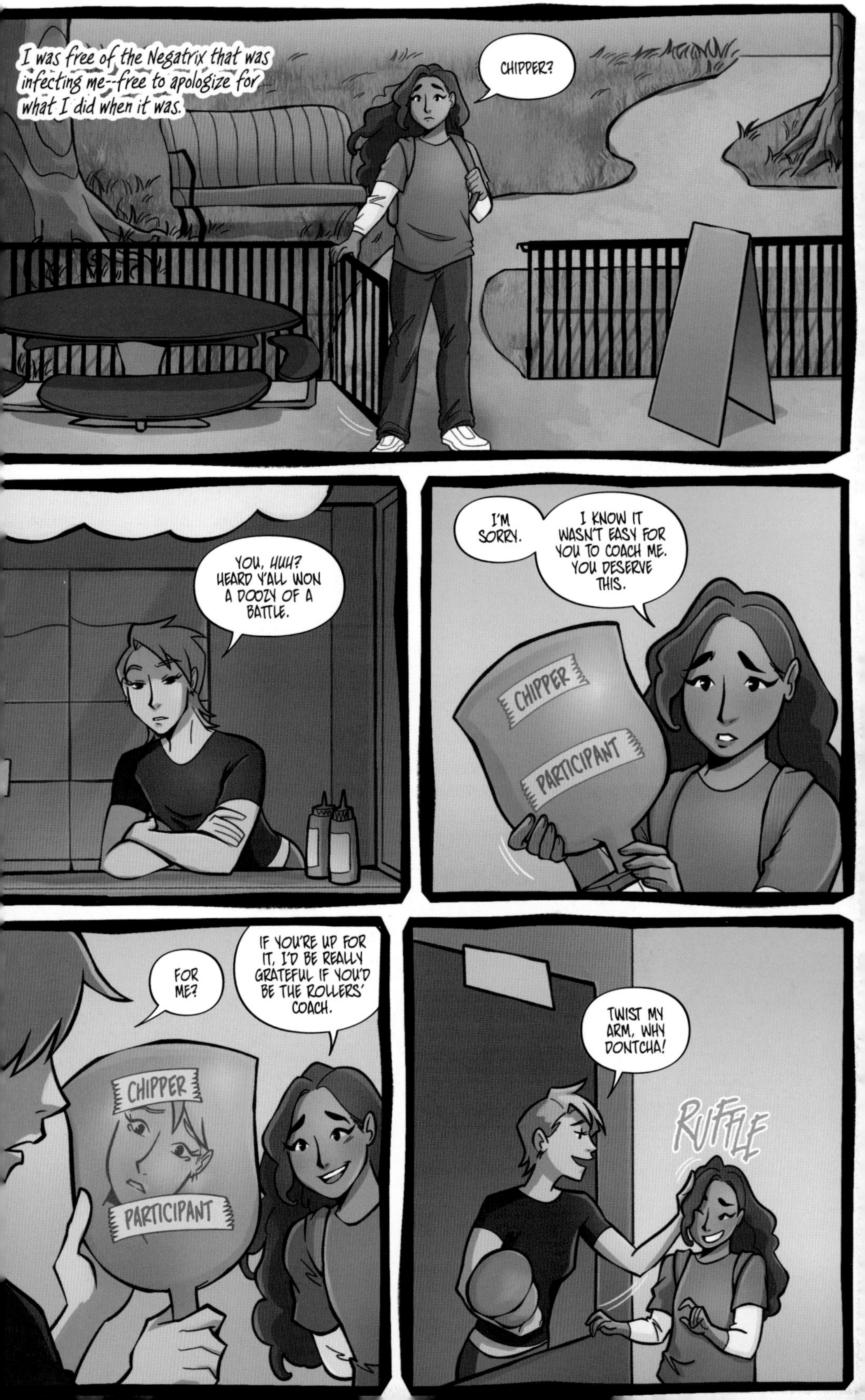
I was free of the Negatrix that was infecting me--free to apologize for what I did when it was.
CHIPPER?
YOU, HUH? HEARD Y'ALL WON A DOOZY OF A BATTLE.
I'M SORRY.
I KNOW IT WASN'T EASY FOR YOU TO COACH ME. YOU DESERVE THIS.
CHIPPER
PARTICIPANT
FOR ME?
IF YOU'RE UP FOR IT, I'D BE REALLY GRATEFUL IF YOU'D BE THE ROLLERS' COACH.
CHIPPER
PARTICIPANT
TWIST MY ARM, WHY DONTCHA!
RUFFLE

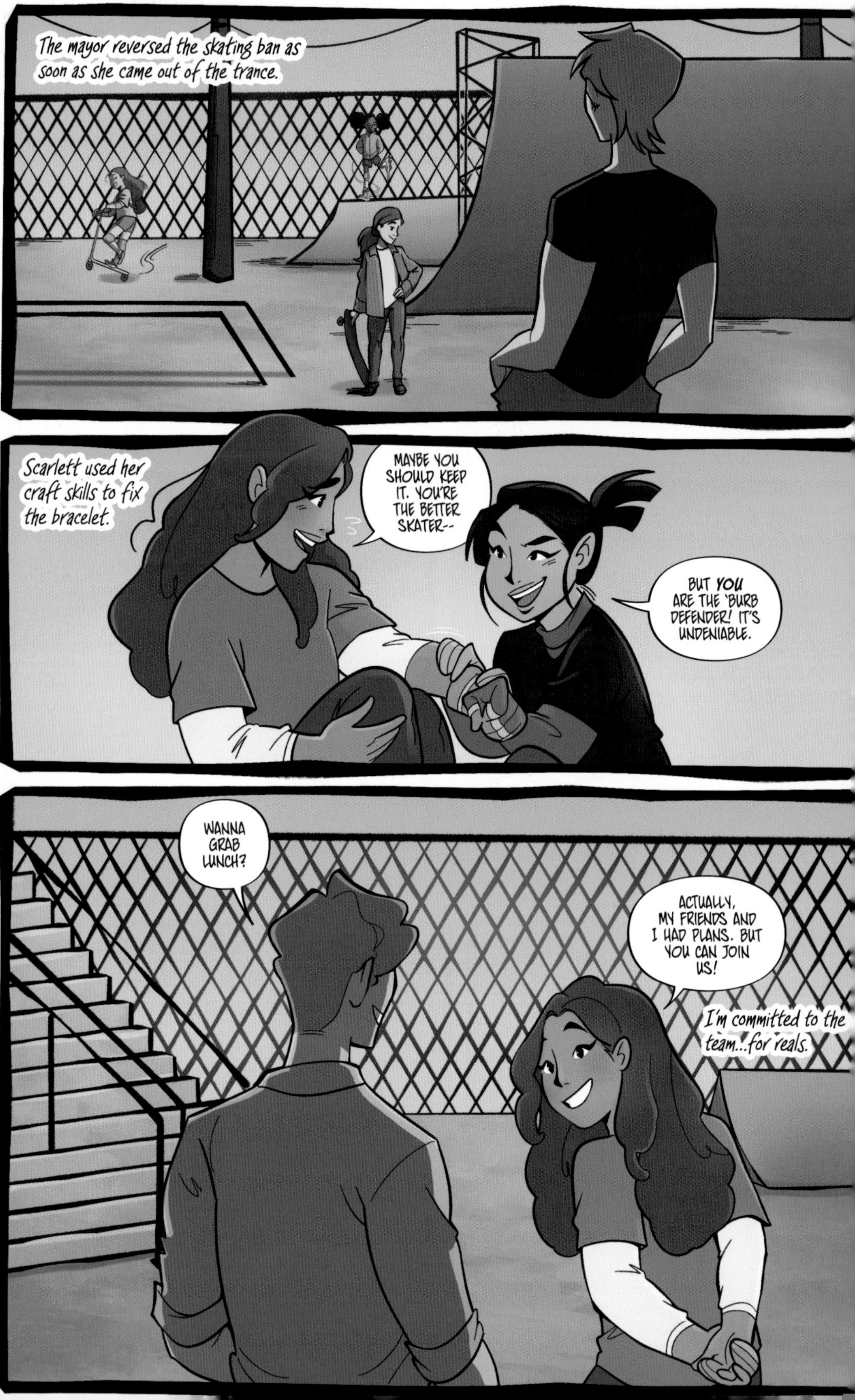
The mayor reversed the skating ban as soon as she came out of the trance.
Scarlett used her craft skills to fix the bracelet.
MAYBE YOU SHOULD KEEP IT. YOU'RE THE BETTER SKATER--
BUT YOU ARE THE 'BURB DEFENDER! IT'S UNDENIABLE.
WANNA GRAB LUNCH?
ACTUALLY, MY FRIENDS AND I HAD PLANS. BUT YOU CAN JOIN US!
I'm committed to the team...for reals.

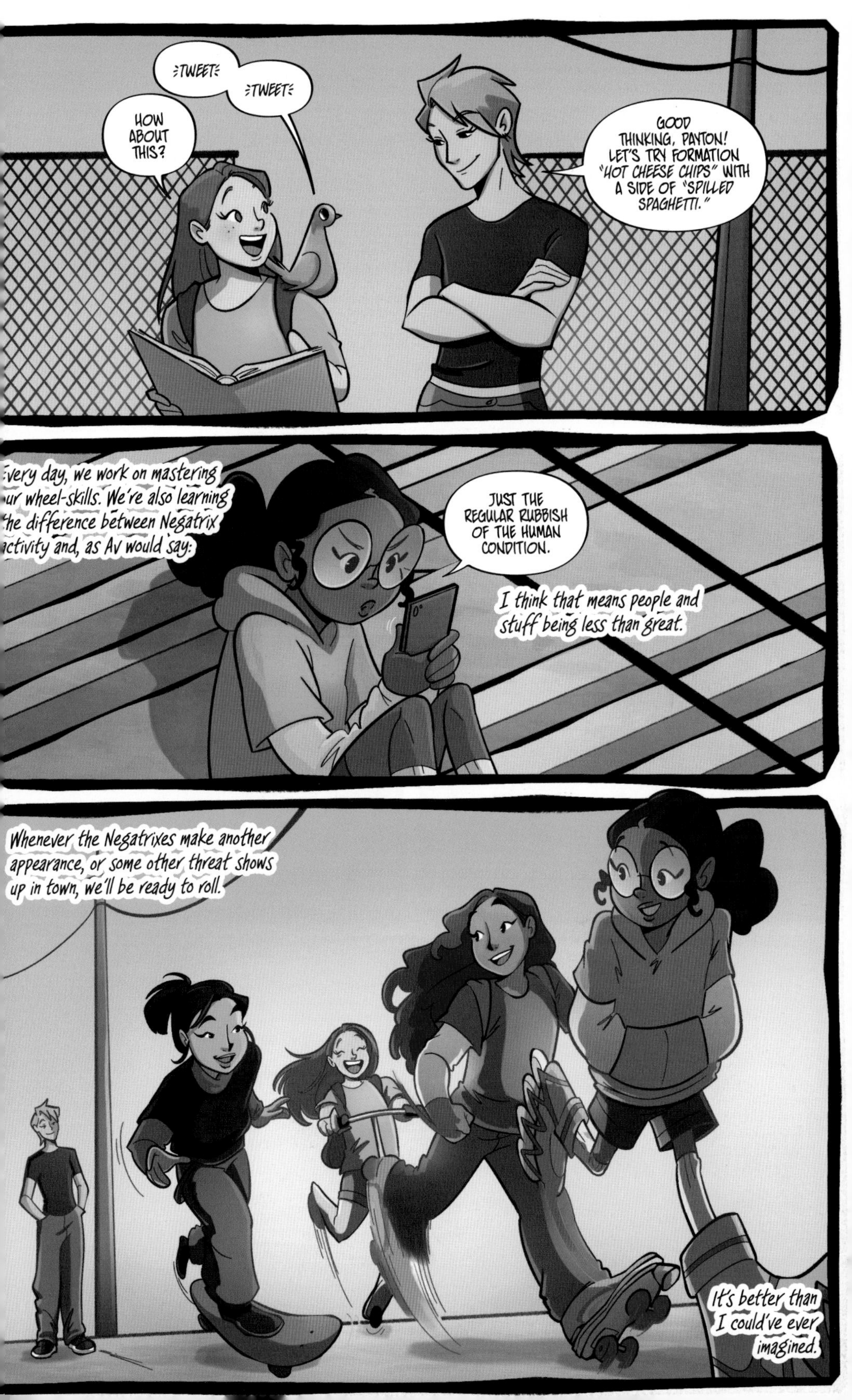
HOW ABOUT THIS?
TWEET
TWEET
GOOD THINKING, PAYTON! LET'S TRY FORMATION "HOT CHEESE CHIPS" WITH A SIDE OF "SPILLED SPAGHETTI."
very day, we work on mastering ur wheel-skills. We're also learning he difference between Negatrix ctivity and, as Av would say:
JUST THE REGULAR RUBBISH OF THE HUMAN CONDITION.
I think that means people and stuff being less than great.
Whenever the Negatrixes make another appearance, or some other threat shows up in town, we'll be ready to roll.
It's better than I could've ever imagined.

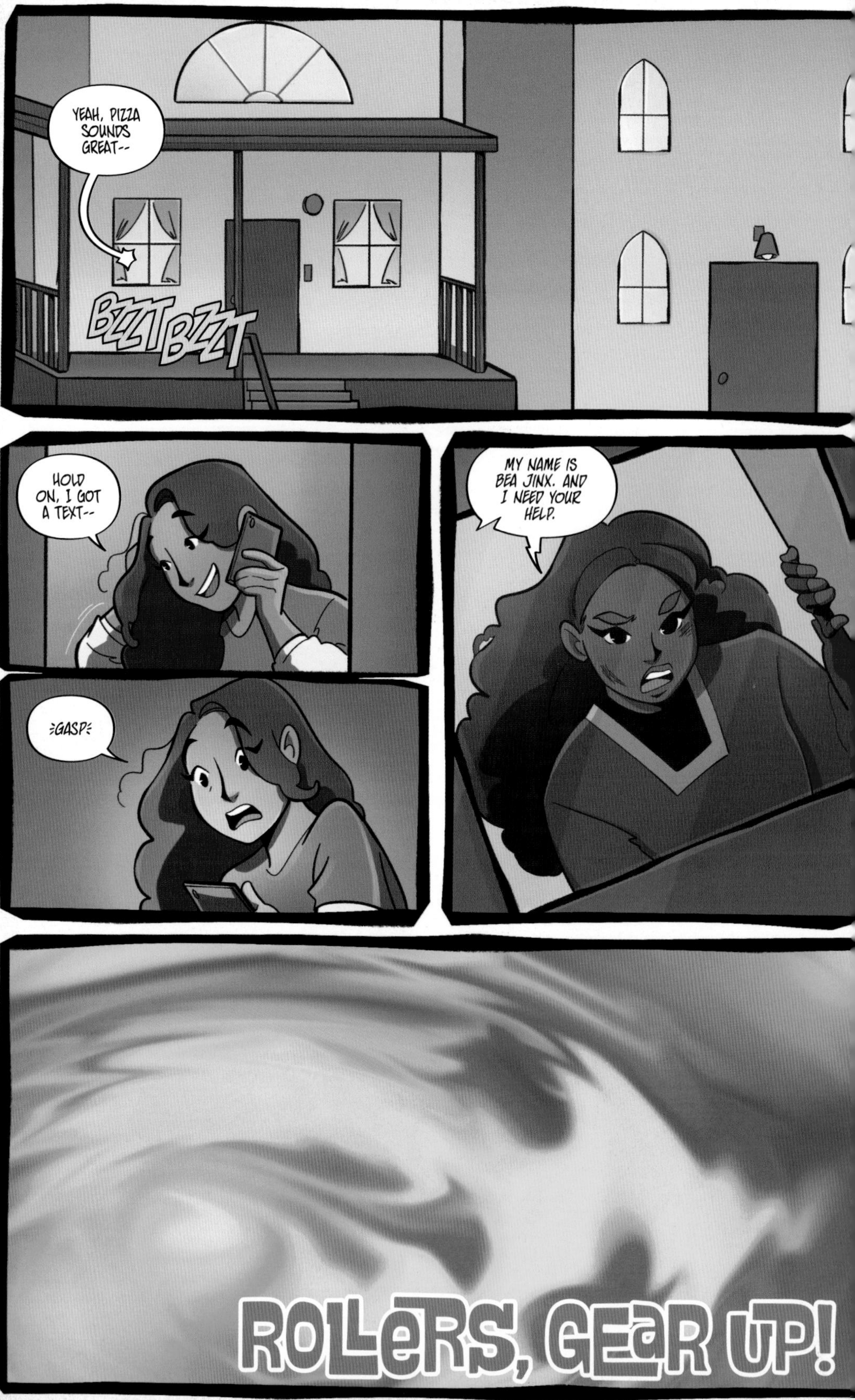
YEAH, PIZZA SOUNDS GREAT--
BZZT BZZT
HOLD ON, I GOT A TEXT--
GASP
MY NAME IS BEA JINX. AND I NEED YOUR HELP.
ROLLERS, GEAR UP!

COVER GALLERY

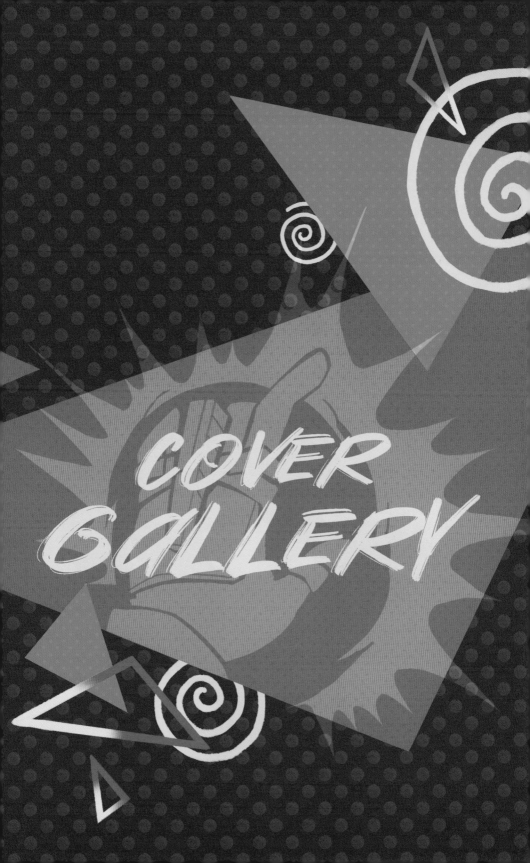

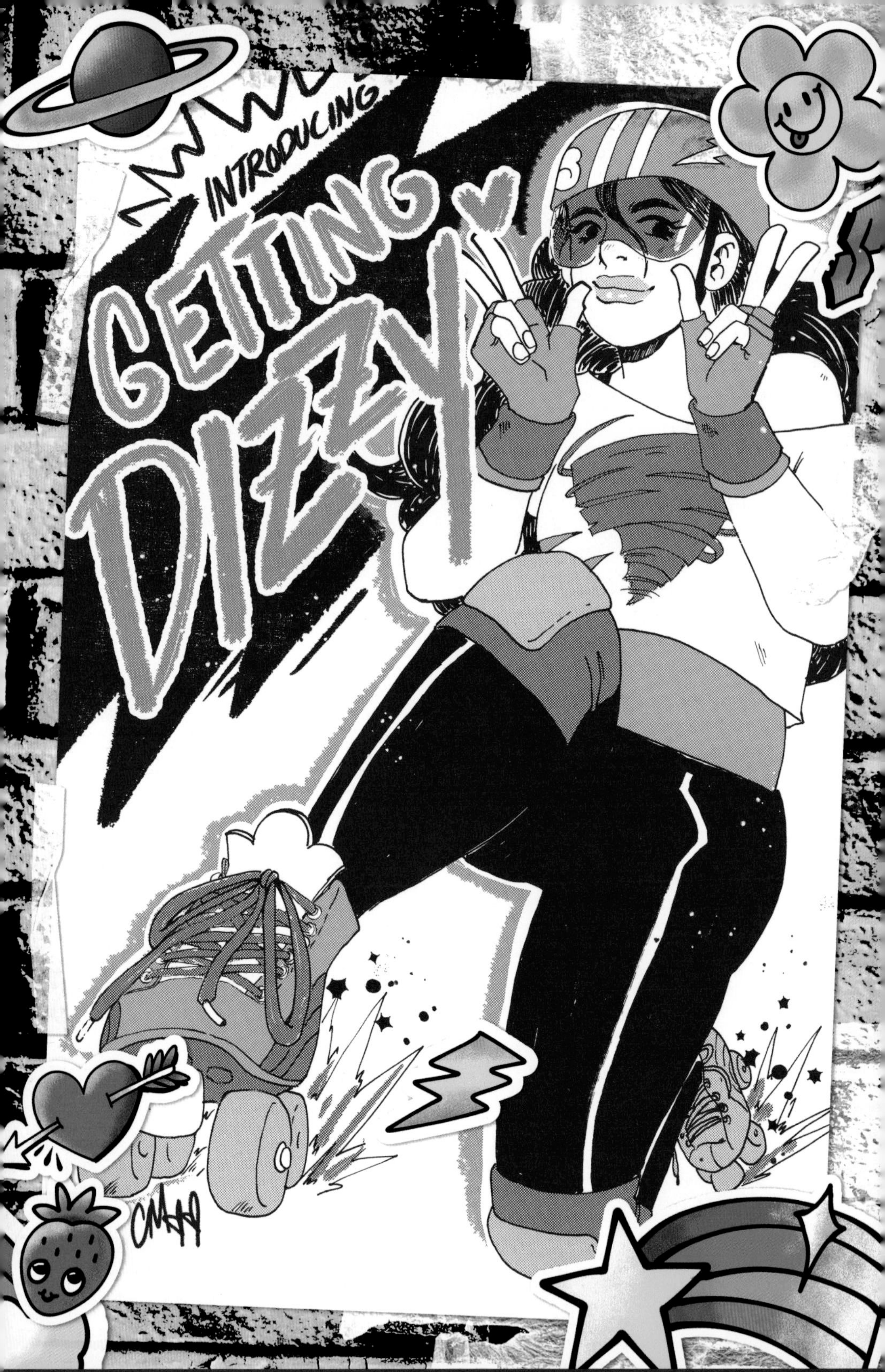
INTRODUCING
GETTING DIZZY

ISSUE #1 SKATEPARK VARIANT COVER BY **CARA McGEE**

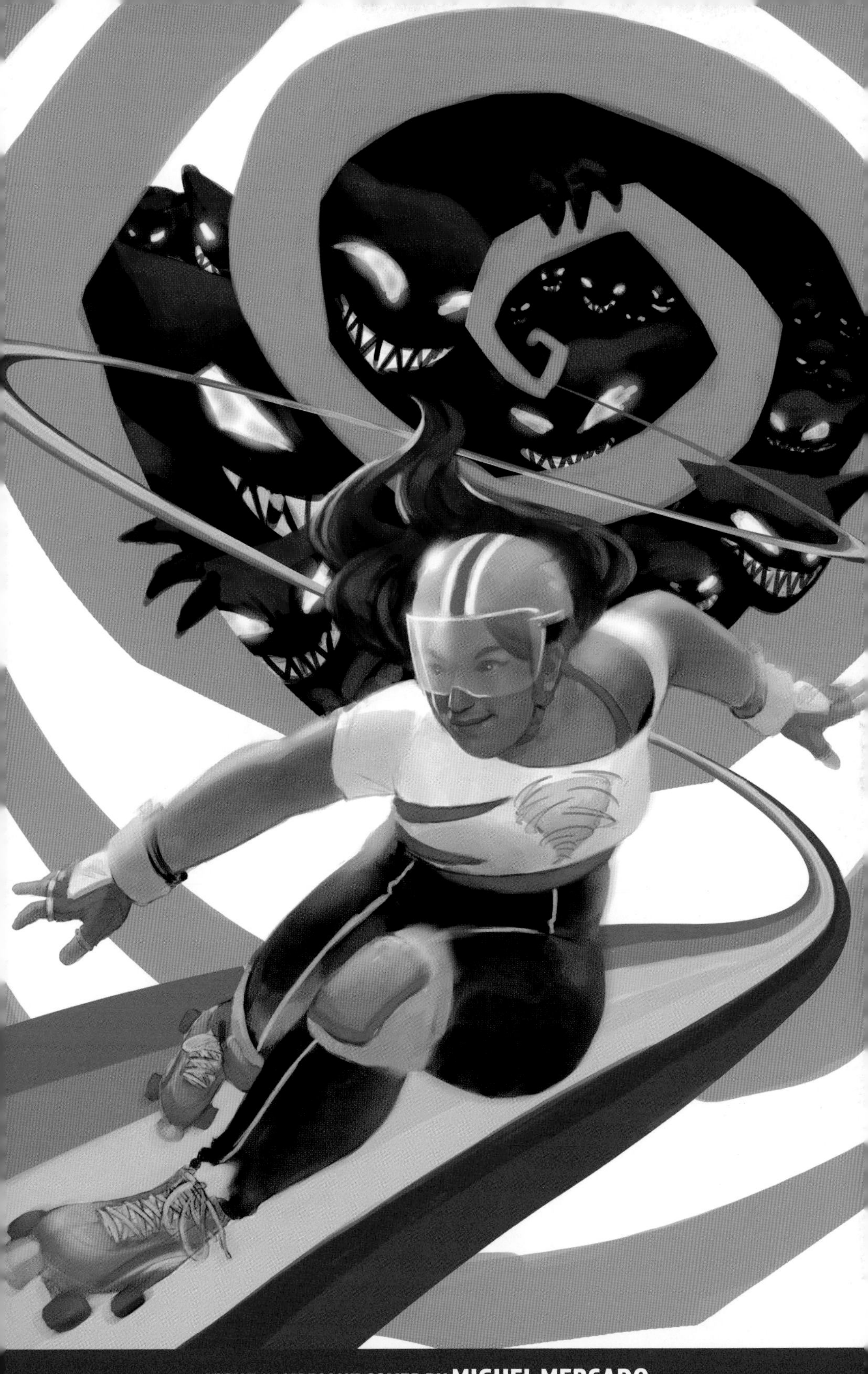

ISSUE #1 VARIANT COVER BY **MIGUEL MERCADO**

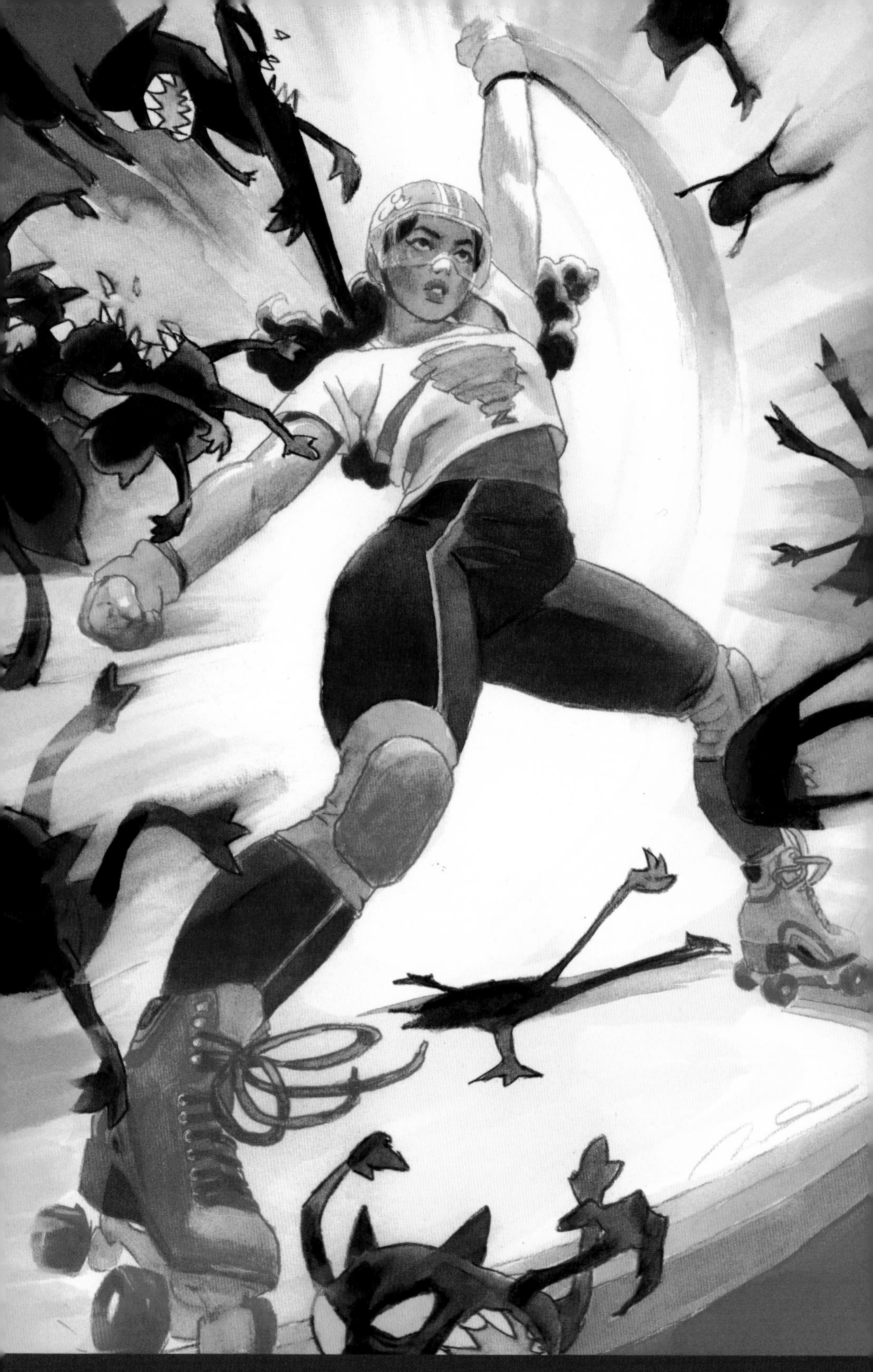

ISSUE #1 CARNIVORE COMICS EXCLUSIVE VARIANT COVER BY **GERALD PAREL**

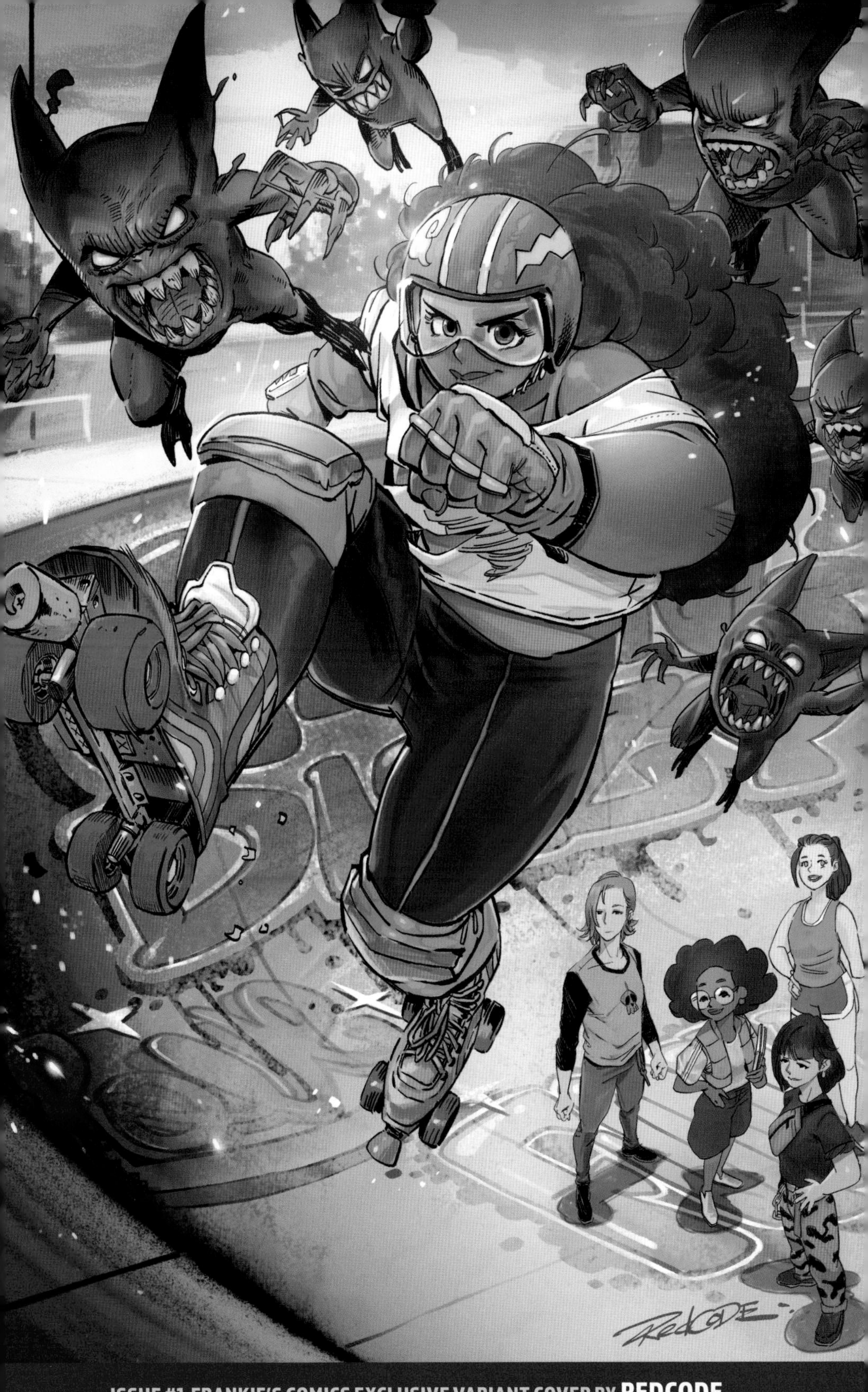
REDCODE

ISSUE #1 FRANKIE'S COMICS EXCLUSIVE VARIANT COVER BY **REDCODE**

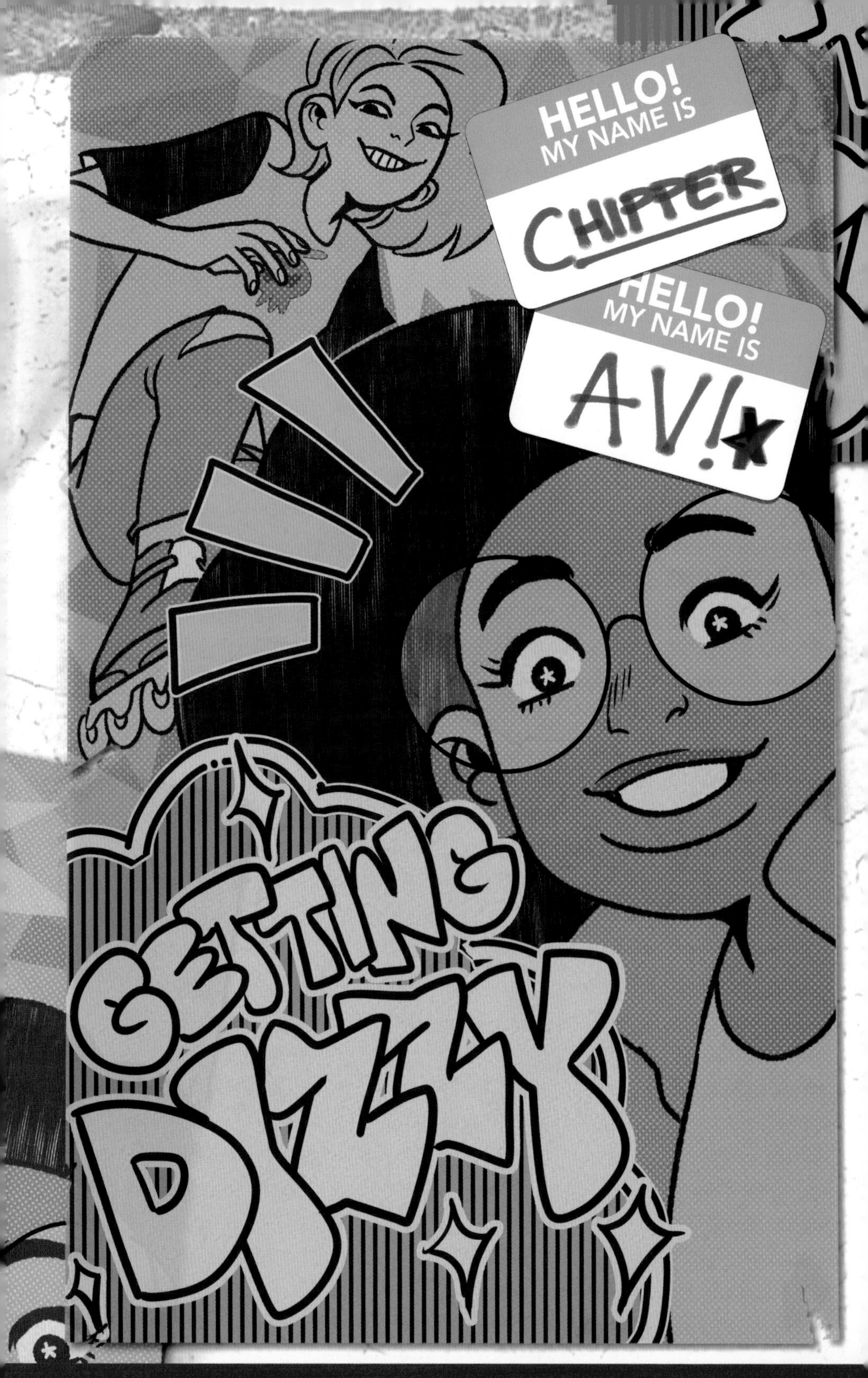
HELLO! MY NAME IS
CHIPPER
HELLO! MY NAME IS
AVI
GETTING DIZZY

ISSUE #2 SKATEPARK VARIANT COVER BY **CARA McGEE**

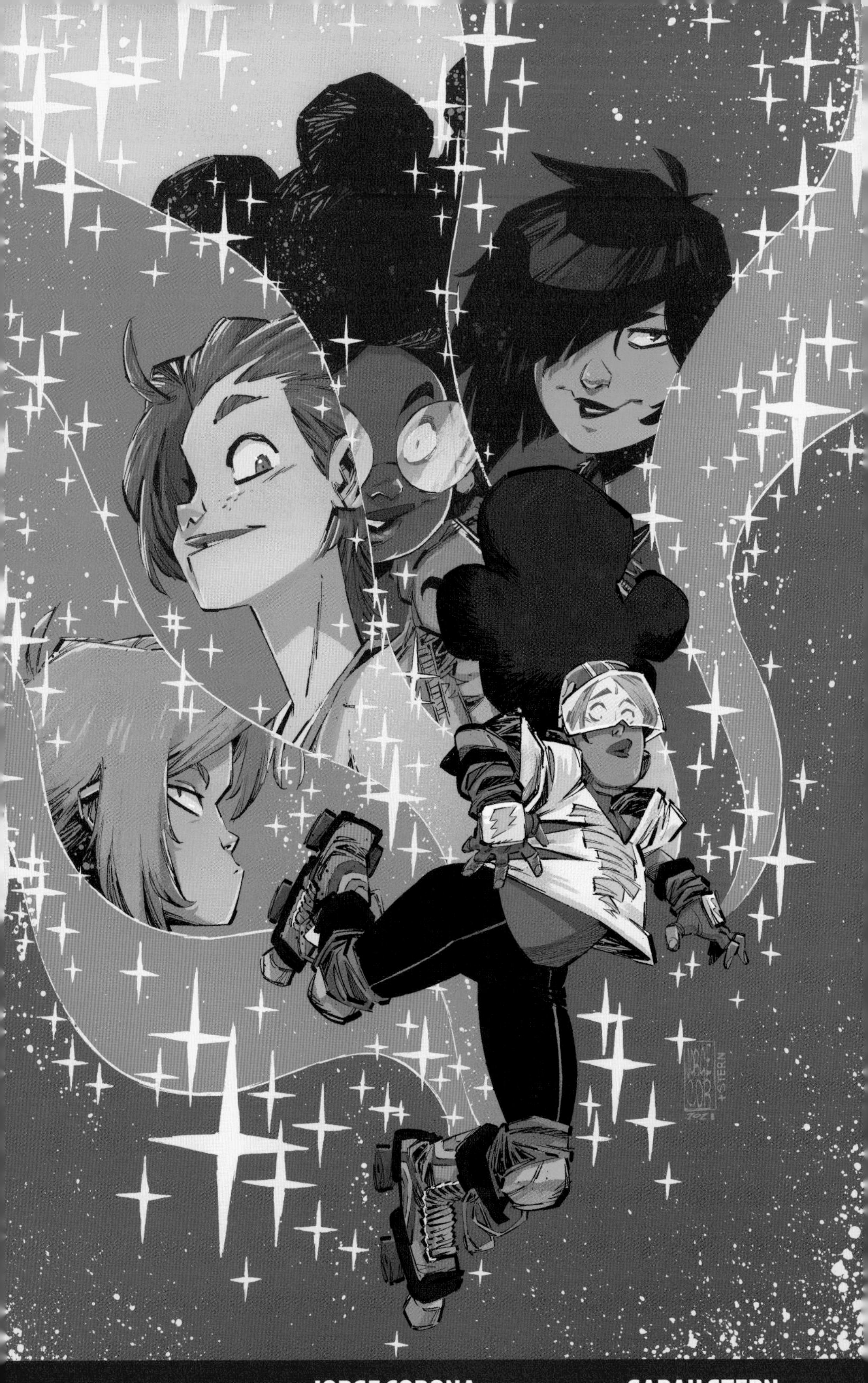

ISSUE #2 VARIANT COVER BY **JORGE CORONA** WITH COLORS BY **SARAH STERN**

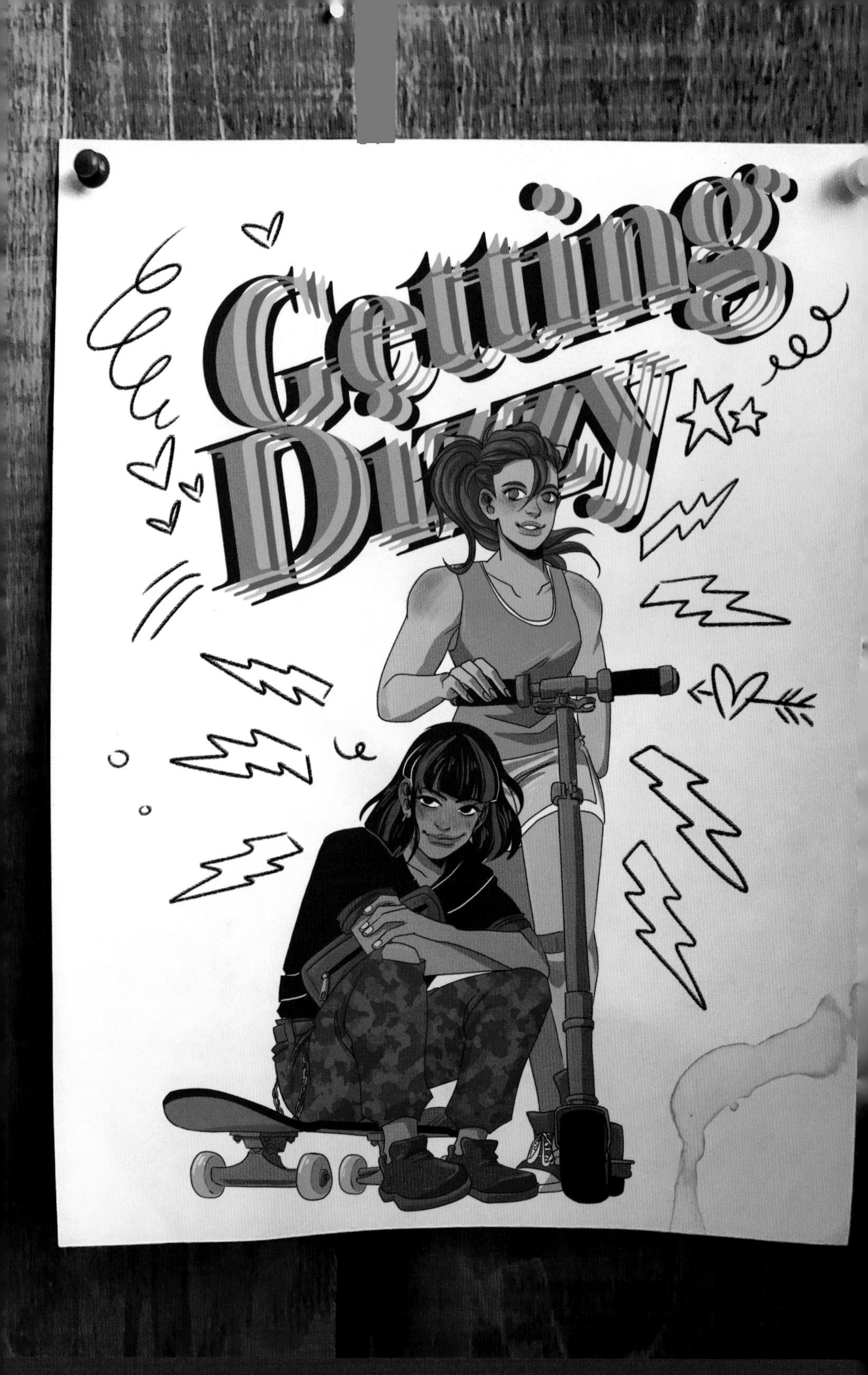

Getting
Dizzy

ISSUE #3 SKATEPARK VARIANT COVER BY **CARA McGEE**

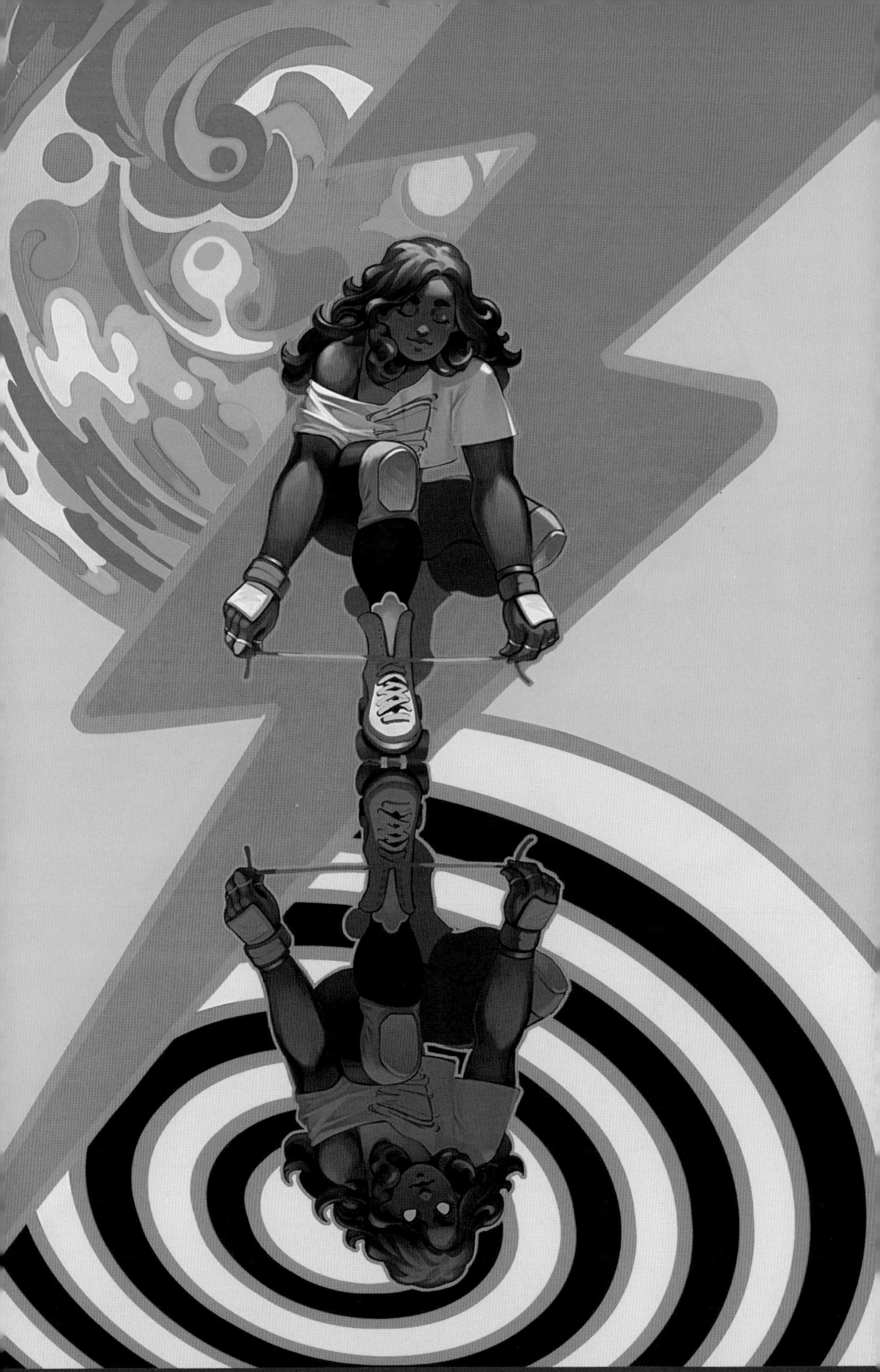

ISSUE #3 VARIANT COVER BY QISTINA KHALIDAH

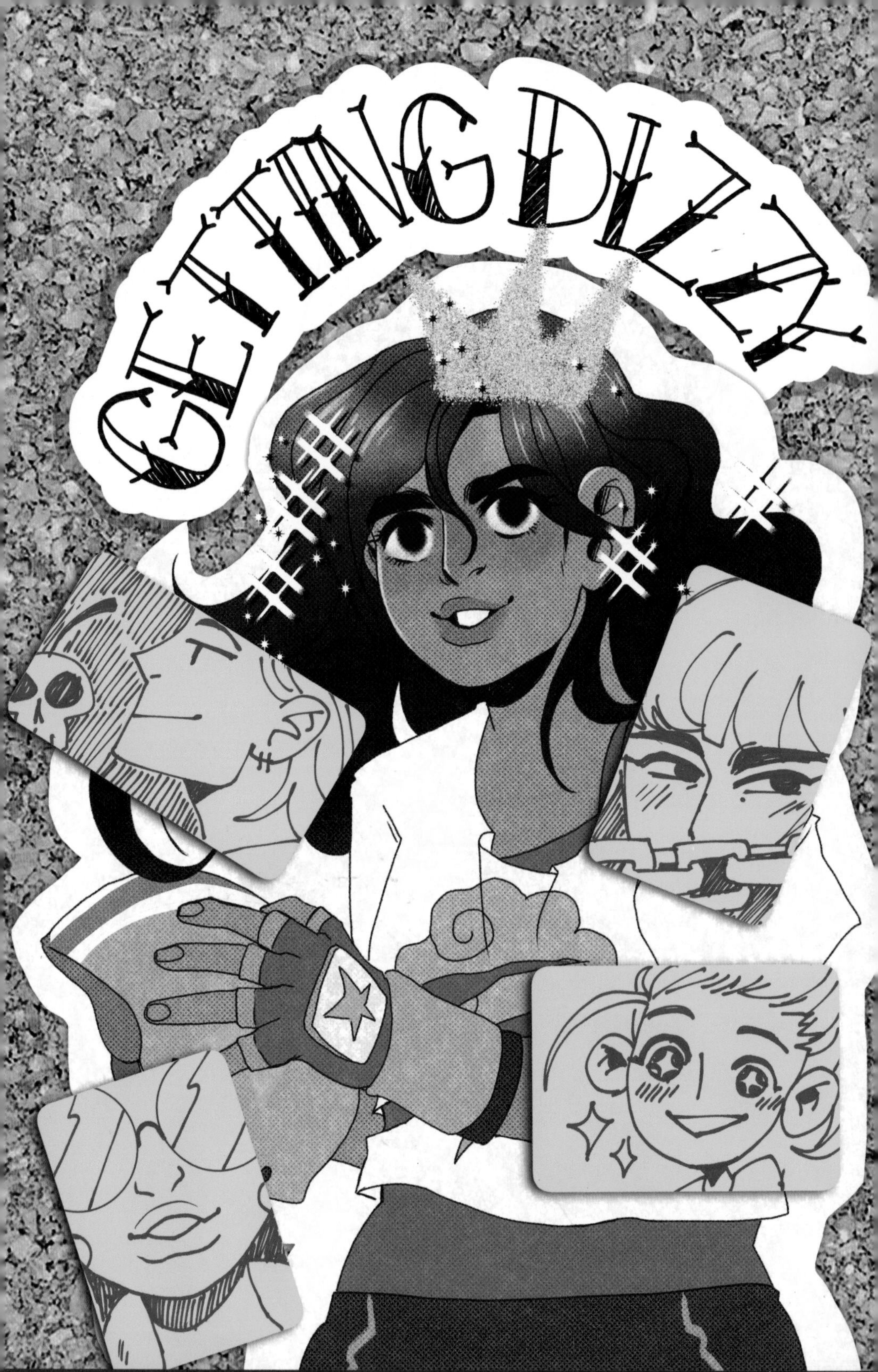
GETTING DIZZY

ISSUE #4 SKATEPARK VARIANT COVER BY **CARA McGEE**

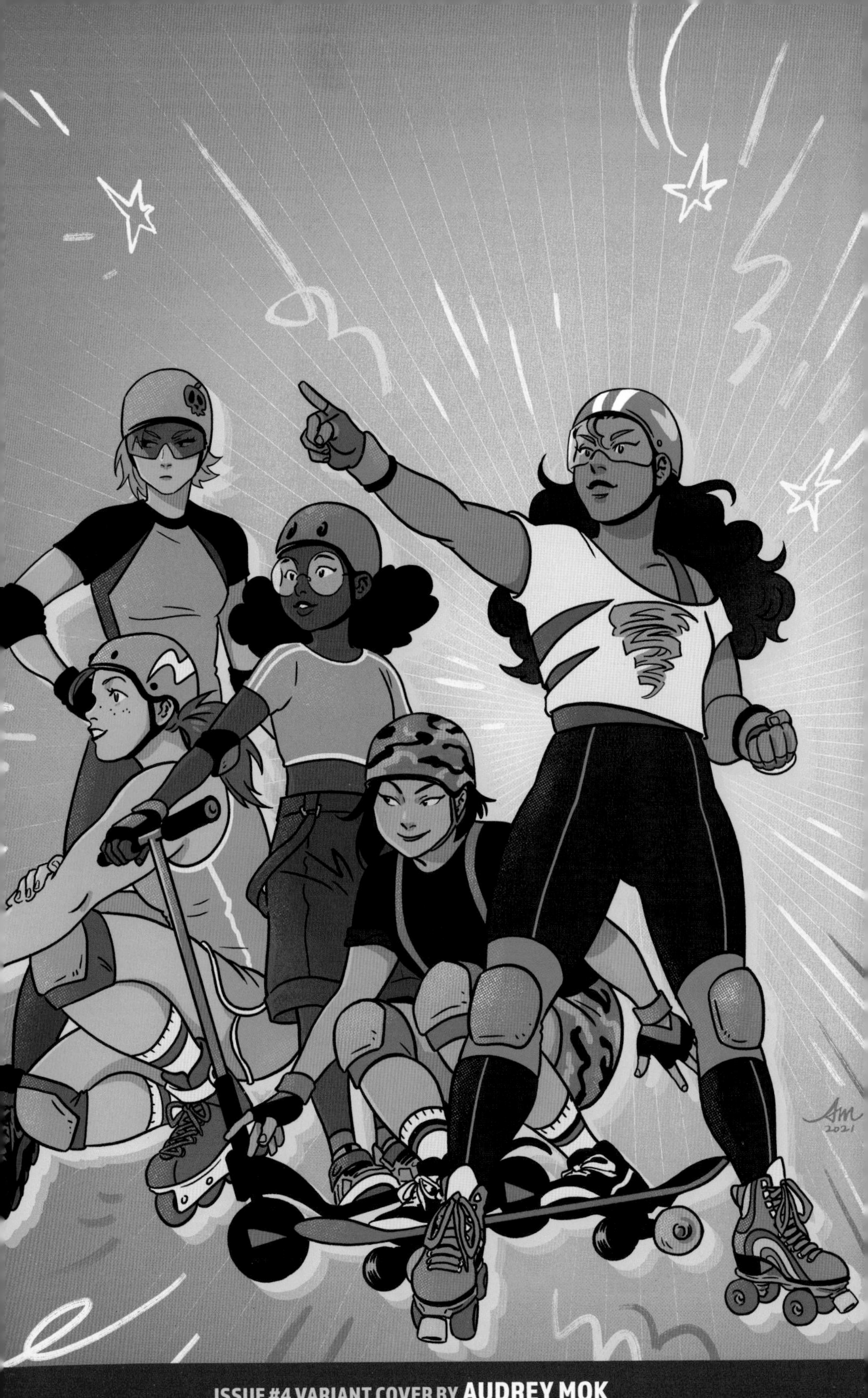
AM
2021

ISSUE #4 VARIANT COVER BY **AUDREY MOK**

DISCOVER
ALL THE HITS

STEVENSON • ELLIS • WATTERS • ALLEN
LUMBERJANES
BEWARE THE KITTEN HOLY
NEW YORK TIMES BESTSELLING SERIES

Allison + Treiman + Cogar
GIANT DAYS
VOLUME ONE

RIBON • FISH • PEER
SLAM!
VOLUME ONE

Hope Larson • Brittney Williams • Sarah Stern
GOLDIE VANCE
Volume One

THE BACKSTAGERS

TYSON HESSE'S
DIESEL
IGNITION

BOOM! BOX™

AVAILABLE AT YOUR LOCAL COMICS SHOP AND BOOKSTORE
To find a comics shop in your area, visit www.comicshoplocator.com
WWW.**BOOM-STUDIOS**.COM

Lumberjanes
Noelle Stevenson, Shannon Watters, Grace Ellis, Brooklyn Allen, and Others
Volume 1: Beware the Kitten Holy
ISBN: 978-1-60886-687-8 | $14.99 US
Volume 2: Friendship to the Max
ISBN: 978-1-60886-737-0 | $14.99 US
Volume 3: A Terrible Plan
ISBN: 978-1-60886-803-2 | $14.99 US
Volume 4: Out of Time
ISBN: 978-1-60886-860-5 | $14.99 US
Volume 5: Band Together
ISBN: 978-1-60886-919-0 | $14.99 US

Giant Days
John Allison, Lissa Treiman, Max Sarin
Volume 1
ISBN: 978-1-60886-789-9 | $9.99 US
Volume 2
ISBN: 978-1-60886-804-9 | $14.99 US
Volume 3
ISBN: 978-1-60886-851-3 | $14.99 US

Jonesy
Sam Humphries, Caitlin Rose Boyle
Volume 1
ISBN: 978-1-60886-883-4 | $9.99 US
Volume 2
ISBN: 978-1-60886-999-2 | $14.99 US

Slam!
Pamela Ribon, Veronica Fish, Brittany Peer
Volume 1
ISBN: 978-1-68415-004-5 | $14.99 US

Goldie Vance
Hope Larson, Brittney Williams
Volume 1
ISBN: 978-1-60886-898-8 | $9.99 US
Volume 2
ISBN: 978-1-60886-974-9 | $14.99 US

The Backstagers
James Tynion IV, Rian Sygh
Volume 1
ISBN: 978-1-60886-993-0 | $14.99 US

Tyson Hesse's Diesel: Ignition
Tyson Hesse
ISBN: 978-1-60886-907-7 | $14.99 US

Coady & The Creepies
Liz Prince, Amanda Kirk, Hannah Fisher
ISBN: 978-1-68415-029-8 | $14.99 US

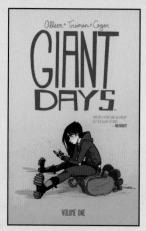